IN THE SILENCE

by

M. R. Mackenzie

What is past is not dead; it is not even past. We cut ourselves off from it; we pretend to be strangers.

– Christa Wolf

Imagine a scene in deep midwinter, as still and immaculate as a Christmas card. One of those painterly, fine art cards designed to conjure up nostalgia for a childhood half-remembered and yet not quite real. The slopes of Kelvingrove Park are coated with a dusting of freshly fallen snow, bathed in the last lingering light of the fading day. The air is calm. The park lies empty. The windows of the outer circle of houses overlooking the park emit their filtered yellow-orange glow.

A timeless scene.

A perfect scene.

Such a shame to spoil it.

You barrel headlong downhill, ploughing on as the chilled air fills your lungs, stinging them, burning them. Your heart aches and hammers so hard, you swear it's going to shatter your ribcage. You run like you've never run before. Like your life depends on it.

And behind you, they come for you. Your pursuers. The hounds to your hare. Gaining on you with each passing second. And though you're almost spent, you know they won't tire so easily.

The bottom of the slope draws near. Bare-naked trees rise up to meet you, their gnarled branches twisted painfully like the arthritic digits of an old man's hand. Beyond them, the university bell-tower looms straight and tall – two hundred and seventy-seven feet of stone, a silent witness to all that passes before it. As cold and uncaring as the air itself.

Your foot catches on a tree root, hidden beneath the snow. You go down, hands first, a blanket of white engulfing you. As you kneel there at the foot of the hill, your ragged gasps forming plumes in the air, they close in around you, pressed trousers and polished shoes forming a semi-circle. You cast around wildly in search of an escape route, but there is none. The game is up. The hare is caught.

The ranks part to let *him* through. Taller than the rest, he advances towards you, blotting out your view of the sun. He reaches down – a slender, long-fingered hand, brushing a strand of hair from your eyes, then lifting your chin, tilting your head back.

A last burst of defiance rises from some unknown depth. You stare up at him. You won't close your eyes or look away. He won't break you. He won't make you beg.

Then, from off to the side, just beyond your field of view, a balled fist connects with your head.

And the darkness swallows you whole.

1

Home

Thursday, 17 December 2009

Anna shivered and sank deeper into the collar of her coat. She'd forgotten how cold Glasgow was in December.

It was warm in the cab, almost too warm, but the memory of the bitter chill outside lingered on, as she and a dozen other commuters had stood under the awning outside Queen Street Station, all jockeying for first dibs on the next taxi to pull into the rank. It had been below zero when she had touched down at Gatwick that morning, and the snow, which had begun as her train crossed the border late in the afternoon, continued to fall thick and fast.

As they circled George Square, she peered out the window. The condensation had turned the Christmas lights outside into a hazy kaleidoscope of red, green and blue. Beyond them, she could make out the shapes of the Millennium Hotel, the City Chambers – all the landmarks that she knew by heart, no matter how long it had been since she'd last clapped eyes on them. She leaned back, shutting her travel-weary lids and soaking up the sounds around her: the tick of the meter; Elvis (Costello, not Presley) tinny on the tape deck; a patchwork of guttural voices on the cab firm's radio, their *ayes* and *naws* barely audible over the hum of the engine. Every so often, the driver would respond in a murmur so low, it was a wonder any of it was understood. But maybe that wasn't the point. Maybe they just enjoyed hearing the cadence of each other's voices, clinging to the semblance it provided of human contact as they wound their lonely ways through the city. Like far-off ships signalling one another in the night.

Her phone was vibrating against her thigh. She stirred and retrieved it from her trouser pocket. The screen identified the caller as 'RED MENACE'.

'Hey, Zoe.'

'Anna?' Zoe's voice boomed breathlessly in her ear. 'Where the hell are ye?'

'In a taxi. Just leaving the station.'

'Aw, you are *kiddin'* me. What did ye do – take the scenic route?'

'Dunno if you've noticed, Zo, but it's foul out there. Actually, it's a wonder I was able to–'

'Excuses, excuses. Just tell yer chauffeur to put his foot down, right? Let him know it's an emergency. How's am I supposed tae start this party without best pal number one?'

'Heh, yeah. I'll tell him. See you in a bit.'

She hung up and sank back into the upholstery, her eyelids drooping once again.

'Local girl, aye?'

She looked up. Her eyes met the driver's in the rear-view mirror.

'Suppose.'

'Whereabouts ye from, love? Jordanhill? Hyndland?'

The posh parts of Glasgow. The parts where people who spoke like her didn't stick out like a sore thumb. And he wasn't too far off the mark.

'Kelvindale.'

The skin around his eyes crinkled in amusement. 'Aye, figured as much. Home for the holidays, then?'

'Something like that.'

Realising he wasn't going to get anywhere with her, he made a disgruntled noise and shifted his eyes back to the road. As they passed under the shadow of the City Chambers, its beleaguered Saltire bucking and whipping in the wind, the reassuring cloak of quiet anonymity descended once again.

Just how she liked it.

***

Zoe was waiting for her next to the Wizard of Paws store on Argyle Street, her hair a flaming red beacon in the dark. As they pulled up to the kerb, her face lit up, and she broke into a run, tottering on her irresponsibly high heels.

'Hey, you! What the fuck have you done with your hair?' The hug which followed all but knocked the wind from Anna. 'God, it's one of they nights, in't it? Pure – fuckin' – Baltic. Been standin' out here for the last half-hour, practically freezin' ma nips aff. That's your fault, that is, for bein' such a slowpoke.'

'Nice to see you too. Happy birthday, slapper.'

'Aye, you too, doll, you too.' Another asphyxiating hug for good measure.

Freshly released, Anna looked Zoe up and down. 'Well. I do declare you don't look a day over twenty-eight.'

She was being facetious, but only slightly. Newly twenty-eight or not, Zoe still bore a striking resemblance to the exuberant teenager Anna had known growing up and, under the right light, could probably still pass for one. She was clearly trying to make an impression: liberally applied eyeliner, a leopard skin print parka and a sparkling mini-dress that shone and glittered every time she moved, which was to say constantly.

'Girl's gotta make an effort. You don't scrub up too bad yersel, hen. Though you're lookin' a bit peely-wally, if you don't mind ma sayin'. You really been livin' it up in the Med or did you get on the wrong plane and end up in Iceland? Mind you, I suppose it hasnae all been cocktails and sunbathin'. So do I have to call you "Doctor" now or what?'

Anna gave what she hoped passed for an easy smile. 'Still the same old Anna.'

Zoe beamed, apparently satisfied. Reaching into the inner pocket of her coat, she produced a hip flask. 'Here, get this down you. It's good for what ails ya, whatever that is.'

Anna eyed the flask dubiously. She'd never understood the appeal of drinking *before* a party. It suggested you had low expectations for the venue, or the people in whose company you were going to be spending the evening, or both. Still, when in Glasgow…She took the flask and tipped a mouthful of the foul-tasting vodka down her throat, gagging on it like a child swallowing a particularly noxious medicine after being told, *It's for your own good, darling.*

Zoe snatched the flask and swigged from it with considerably more gusto, then tilted back her head and emitted a howl of pure animalistic glee.

'Alrighty, let the festivities commence!'

***

The place Zoe had chosen for the festivities was Pulse – a trendy nightclub deep in the bowels of the West End which catered primarily towards the student crowd from the nearby university. In other words, people up to ten years younger than Zoe – or indeed Anna, who felt increasingly like she was descending into the mouth of hell as they made their way downstairs towards the steady beat emanating from the basement. As they reached the bottom, it became a full-on sensory assault – the music, an incessant, overpowering, mind-numbing beat that made her sinuses ache…the pulsating gel lights, bathing the club and the mass of gyrating bodies in a constantly alternating array of primary hues…the stuffy, artificial air, ripe with the tang of cheap deodorant and spilt liquor…

Zoe, who by now had shed her parka, grinned at Anna. 'Is this place not *mental?*'

'Mental' sounded about right, though Anna doubted they shared the same definition of the word. Still, Zoe's party, Zoe's rules.

The birthday girl craned her neck, scanning the crowd of revellers. She spotted some people she recognised and waved manically at them. 'Some pals fae work,' she explained. 'Listen, get us a coupla drinks, grab us a seat. I'll do the meet-and-greet, then we can have a proper catch-up.'

Wondering how they were going to have a proper *anything* with such an almighty racket blasting in their ears, Anna watched as Zoe strode across the floor towards her pals, yanking her dress down at the back in a futile attempt to retain a sliver of decency.

Ignoring the voice in the back of her head telling her she still had time to make good her escape, Anna negotiated her way through the throng, making for the bar, where a pair of bartenders – one female, one male – valiantly fought to keep up with a never-ending barrage of orders for tequilas, Bacardis and a slew of mixers she'd never heard of. Waiting for someone to notice her, she leant against the bar and turned to watch the revellers doing their thing. Those who weren't dancing occupied an array of tables and sofas towards the back of the room, shrouded in semi-darkness beyond the reach of the lighting fixtures. Scanning the sea of bodies, she picked out Zoe in the middle of the floor, sandwiched between two admiring men a good decade younger than herself, showing off her moves. Anna wondered whether this was part of the meet-and-greet.

No one would ever describe Zoe as conventionally attractive, but she was so open, so blasé, so comfortable in her own skin that what a detached assessment might describe as imperfections – the snub nose, the gap in her front teeth, the cornucopia of freckles covering her face and shoulders – instead became interesting quirks that complemented her character. At any rate, boys had always seemed to like her, though Anna had never been sure whether it was because they fancied her or because they saw her as one of the lads. A bit of both, probably.

'What can I get you?'

She turned to find the female bartender – a blonde beanpole wearing the regulation black T-shirt and skinny jeans sported by all the staff – eyeballing her expectantly.

'Sorry. Miles away. Um…Vodka Martini and a glass of Prosecco.'

The Vodka Martini was for Zoe, assuming her tastes in liquor were still the same – and, given that nothing else about her seemed to have changed, Anna felt reasonably comfortable in her assumption.

The woman set about preparing the drinks in the brisk, no-nonsense manner of the perpetually harangued. As she worked, she nodded past Anna's shoulder. 'Friends of yours, that lot?'

Anna chanced a glance at the dancefloor. 'Not as such.'

'Figured. No offence, but this doesn't exactly strike me as your sort of place.'

'None taken. And it's not. I'm just here for a friend. It's her birthday do and – well, I couldn't exactly say no.'

'Ah – you'll be talking about Zoe.'

'You know Zoe?'

'*Everyone* knows Zoe.'

Anna smiled. 'Right enough, yeah.'

Clutching the two glasses, she picked her way back through the crush and staked her claim on a vacant sofa far enough from the dancefloor that she might just be able to hear herself think. Zoe, she saw, was still giving it her all. She'd left her two admirers to their own devices, their appetites unsatiated, and was now bopping along to the music with a gaggle of twentysomethings, both her drink and her promise of a proper catch-up with Anna seemingly forgotten.

Oh, well. She raised her Prosecco glass. *Your good health, Anna.*

* * *

If time flies when you're enjoying yourself, the reverse is also true. Five minutes became ten, ten became twenty, and by the time a half-hour had passed, Anna was wondering why she'd ever agreed to this in the first place. Not that she begrudged Zoe a good time, but it was becoming increasingly apparent that she was very much the third wheel of this enterprise. If she'd delayed flying out by another day, she could have avoided this rigmarole altogether and treated Zoe to a night out of her own – preferably somewhere where they played music below the volume of a jet aircraft.

She sipped from her Prosecco, trying to make it last. She knew from experience that, in these situations, it was all too easy to end up drinking yourself into oblivion. In a futile attempt to make it look like she wasn't just twiddling her thumbs waiting for the earliest opportunity that she could reasonably suggest calling it a night, she alternated between swallowing tiny mouthfuls and checking her phone for messages. Not that she had any. Only a select few people had her number, and most of them were work colleagues who were well aware she was on leave.

The sound of something being plonked down on the table in front of her made her lower her phone and look up. The female bartender was standing over her. A fresh glass of Prosecco sat before her.

'But I didn't order—'

'Aye, true enough, but that one over there wouldnae take no for an answer.'

The bartender jerked a signet-ringed thumb over her shoulder. Anna craned her neck to see beyond the gyrating youths. A man stood at the bar, resting a casual elbow on the counter, a glass of his own in his hand. He was tall, chiselled, dressed in a pale designer suit clearly tailored to fit him. In a venue populated almost exclusively by T-shirts, jeans and halter-necks, he stood out like a sore thumb. Catching her looking at him, he raised his glass and tipped her a wink. She turned away with a scoff, ready to tell the bartender to take his drink back and instruct him to stick it somewhere intimate.

But there was something about that profile, about the high bridge of that nose, that gave her pause. She knew that nose. Had spent far too much time admiring it from afar during her teenage years.

She chanced another look at him. He was still standing there, still watching her, smiling mischievously.

Andrew Foley – all six foot two of him, as effortlessly cool now as he had been then. More so, in fact. The intervening years had been good to him, sculpting him into a fine figure of a man. Her heart might not have actually skipped a beat, but there was a very definite intake of breath, a light fluttering in her stomach.

Even now, as he began to make his way towards her, glass in hand, she found herself self-consciously tucking a loose strand of hair behind her ear, sitting up straight, plastering herself with the sort of smile she hoped conveyed pleasant surprise rather than the feelings of mild panic that were firing off in all directions.

The bartender raised an eyebrow. 'Take it youse two are acquainted, then? I'll leave you to it.'

Before Anna could object, she melted away, leaving her to scramble awkwardly to her feet to greet him.

'It *is* Anna, isn't it? I was sure it was. Now, of course, I'm beginning to fear I might've made a most almighty prat of myself.'

Anna shrugged airily. 'It's me.'

He laughed, took a step towards her, then remembered his glass and paused to deposit it on the table. Then came the hug – an embrace Anna's teenage self would have killed for, enveloping her in the smooth folds of his suit.

Calm down, Anna. Don't be going all wobbly-kneed and googly-eyed. Act your age.

'Well,' he said, when he broke apart, 'this is quite the surprise. I had it in my mind you'd eloped to Paris.'

'Rome. I did. I mean, I literally just got in this evening.'

'And of all the bars in all the towns in all the world…' He grimaced. 'Sorry. That sounded infinitely less corny in my head.' He gestured to the sofa. 'May I…?'

***

And so, for the next hour or so, they sat having as intimate a conversation as was possible to have over the din from the speaker system. They covered all the usual ground, including their respective post-school academic pursuits and current employment. Andrew had done well for himself: a partnership at a top accountancy firm secured on the back of a first-class honours degree from University College London. To tell the truth, Anna was a little surprised he'd chosen to settle back in Glasgow. She'd always had a sense of him being someone who was destined to go places. He must have had an offer he couldn't refuse. That, or a deep-rooted attachment to the Dear Green Place she, herself, didn't share.

As the conversation flowed, so did the wine. Andrew ordered multiple refills, which he insisted on paying for, and as time crept on, his mood grew more sombre. His old mum wasn't keeping too well, he said. She'd suffered a run of bad luck over the last few years in the form of one serious ailment after another. Having lost her own father to the Big C nearly three years ago, Anna could sympathise.

'D'you still see them much?'

'Much as I can, yeah. But you know how it is. Work, life – all that jazz has a nasty tendency to get in the way. Truth be told, I don't see them nearly as much as I'd like…or should.'

Anna tried to remember the last time she'd seen her own mother – or even spoken to her on the phone.

'Well, you've got your work cut out,' she reasoned, attempting to simultaneously banish her own situation to the back of her mind and offer Andrew a glimmer of comfort. 'Especially if you've got a family of your own now.'

Andrew looked puzzled. 'Family?'

'Well, you know – the old…'

She'd noticed his wedding ring almost straight away. In fact, her eyes had instinctively gone to his ring finger, looking for one. It hadn't come as a surprise; someone as eminently eligible has himself would undoubtedly have been snatched up post-haste. Still, it had been hard not to feel a *slight* pang of regret, if only for old times' sake.

He realised what she was getting at. A frown crossed his features. 'Oh. You know, I'd never really thought of it like that.'

'No kids, then? Well, there's still time…I mean, if that's what you both want…'

She felt slightly foolish now. She hadn't meant to pry, or to make any assumptions about his private life or ambitions for the future in that regard.

Andrew gave a somewhat strained smile in return. He fingered his ring self-consciously, then gestured to their empty glasses. 'Another fill-up?'

She could all but hear the shutters coming down.

They continued in this vein for a while longer, though the mood had taken a turn for the awkward. Anna was beginning to feel the call of nature and at length excused herself, secretly glad of the get-out. Leaving Andrew with glass in hand, she picked her way through the crowd to the ladies', where she was forced to join a line of other women while what she strongly suspected was a sexual liaison of some variety went down in one of the cubicles.

When she returned some ten minutes later, Andrew was gone. His glass sat abandoned on the table. Initially, she assumed he, too, was making use of the facilities. But as time passed and he still didn't return, she was forced to conclude that she had indeed said something to put his nose out of joint and that he'd voted with his feet.

She got up and made for the stairs. The atmosphere in the basement was decidedly stale, and she craved fresh air. As she climbed the steps, she became aware of voices above her – or rather *a* voice. Its tone was despondent, verging on maudlin, and it took her a moment to recognise it as Andrew's. She advanced up the last few steps on tiptoe and halted at the door leading out to the cloakroom, from behind which his voice was coming. She strained to make out the words, but it was easier said than done with the incessant *doof-doof-doof* emanating from the basement.

'I'm sorry. I just needed to hear your voice. I couldn't face it, you know? Couldn't face going home to *her*. She doesn't understand me, babe. Not the way you do.'

What followed was drowned out by the noise from downstairs. When she was next able to make him out properly, he was going for the conciliatory approach. 'I want to make it work – I do. It's just…I don't know. But not yet. I need time. Time to prepare her. To make her understand. Believe me, I *will* find a way for us to be together.'

Anna felt a surge of disgust. There was little doubt as to what was going on here. And now she heard a new sound – a sound so incongruous, it took her several seconds to register what it was. Andrew was *crying*. Not full-blown sobbing, but rather a quiet snivelling that could only be described as pathetic. 'All of this,' he was saying, 'all of this is a test. We'll come out of it stronger, babe, I promise you. I don't want this coming between us. I–'

There was a sudden gale of laughter beyond the door. It opened, and two silken-haired young women, wearing skirts almost as short as Zoe's, came clattering over the threshold. Anna pressed herself against the wall, partly to make way for them and partly to ensure Andrew wouldn't see her through the open door. The pair paid her not the blindest bit of attention as they tottered past in their stilettos.

As their chatter faded, Anna again strained to listen for Andrew's voice, but she heard nothing more. If he was still there beyond the door, the conversation was over. She suddenly realised just how grubby she felt. Whatever the moral rights and wrongs of what Andrew was up to, she was acutely aware she'd been eavesdropping on a man during an intensely private moment.

Feeling intensely disappointed in him and more than a little in herself, she made her way back down to the basement. She'd just reached the sofa, his half-empty glass the only sign he'd ever been there, when Zoe came bounding over, flushed from the dancefloor and positively glowing. 'Havin' fun yet? Is this place not pure amazeballs?'

Anna would have used several other words to describe the place before the one Zoe had alighted on, but right now, none of them were coming to mind. She still couldn't escape the feeling that Andrew's abrupt departure and subsequent distress were in some way a response to something she'd said – more specifically, the enquiry about family. She glanced back at the glowing exit sign above the stairs, half-hoping he'd have a change of heart and come back.

He didn't, and as time passed, their encounter became an increasingly distant memory. Zoe came and went periodically over the course of the night, checking Anna was okay and that she always had a drink in her hand. They never did get round to that catch-up she'd promised, but Anna half-welcomed the isolation, the lack of introspection and the fact that none of Zoe's extended network of friends and acquaintances deemed her to be of sufficient interest to bother her. She was fast developing a tension headache from the noise, but at least nobody was asking her to dance or trying to proposition her. So what if she cut a rather sad and lonely figure, quietly sipping her drink like the only guest at the ball without a date? *Some of us enjoy our own company,* she told herself, with enough conviction that she almost succeeded in convincing herself.

2

Please

At the actual moment of impact, he thought he'd been punched, such was the sudden and intense pressure in his lower abdomen. It wasn't until he looked down and saw the blade buried deep in his gut that he realised what had actually happened.

The lack of pain surprised him. It ought to have been excruciating, but he felt nothing more than a dull throbbing at the point of entry. It was growing in intensity, but it still didn't fit with the fact he had a knife handle sticking out of him. He should be...what, screaming? Writhing in agony? Those seemed like the natural responses. The responses he'd be expecting if the boot was on the other foot.

His attacker pulled the blade free, and the pressure subsided. A warm, wet, almost pleasant sensation began to expand from the area, soaking through the fabric of his shirt. In the silence of the still night air, he heard the pitter-patter of droplets splashing onto his shoe.

It took him a moment to realise it was blood. *His* blood.

His assailant didn't move. He – it *was* a he, wasn't it? – simply stood there, watching him, features obscured under a dark hood. Waiting.

His vision was beginning to fade. A profound light-headedness was taking hold. His knees buckled. He reached out, grasping in the figure's direction, but his fingers closed on air. He flailed with both hands, trying to steady himself, but to no avail. His legs gave way. And then he was falling, falling, falling, and the snowy carpet was rising up to meet him.

Slowly, torturously, he rolled over onto his back. The bruised night sky gazed down at him, and with it his attacker – a dark shape like a hole in the sky. The blade glinted in his hand as he drew it back, ready to finish the job.

In that instant, terror gripped him. It couldn't end now, not like this. A man shouldn't die alone, he thought. He should die loved and surrounded by friends and family. And there were so many things he still wanted to do, things he wanted to say, if only he could muster enough breath to form the words.

With considerable effort, he filled his lungs with air. 'Please,' he whispered.

He sensed, rather than saw, the figure smile.

3

Blood

They stepped out into the eerie quiet of the witching hour, Zoe swaying tipsily behind Anna. The street was empty. A light fog hung in the still, moist air. The cold cut to the bone, and they shrieked and yelled various profanities as they huddled under the neon sign above the doorway, clutching themselves in an attempt to keep warm.

At least it was no longer snowing.

They soon realised their chances of flagging down a taxi were slim to non-existent, and Zoe, evidently beginning to regret the amount of quantity with which she'd flooded her system over the last several hours, declared that she couldn't face her bed 'til she'd washed it all down with something thoroughly greasy and artery-clogging. Anna suggested the all-night café on Gibson Street. It had been a regular haunt of theirs back in the day, and its bacon butties achieved that rare symbiosis of edibility and potent hangover cure.

The thoroughfare known as the Kelvin Way is about a half-mile long, connecting Argyle Street in the south to Gibson Street in the north. During summer, when the trees on either side are in full bloom, it is a pleasant walk, providing ample opportunities to observe the various eccentricities of students and the middle classes in their natural habitat. That night, however, there wasn't another soul to be seen as Anna and Zoe tramped north, Anna dragging her travel case behind her. To their left, the university loomed beyond iron fencing at the top of a gentle slope. To their right, Kelvingrove Park was an ominous, unlit swathe of undulating, snow-clad slopes and dark clusters of trees.

As they walked, Zoe chattered endlessly, telling Anna about this school friend and that, listing who'd got hitched, who was up the duff, who was earning eighty grand and who'd vanished without a trace. Most of the seemingly endless stream of names meant little to Anna, who nodded and made noises of interest, shock or mirth as appropriate, taking comfort from the fact that, whatever the stresses of her own life, Zoe's seemed enviably uncomplicated, consisting primarily of a succession of short-term menial jobs, punctuated by meet-ups with friends and the consumption of copious quantities of alcohol.

People who didn't know Zoe well were always a bit surprised to find out she had a degree. Most took one look at her, listened to the way she spoke and decided she must have left school at sixteen after barely scraping through her Standard Grades. In actual fact, Zoe had done reasonably well at school, seeing it through to the end of sixth year and going on to do a BA in media studies at Glasgow Caledonian. They used to joke that this was a statement about the class divide between them – Anna was posh enough to get into the Sapienza and live the high life in Rome, while Zoe had to make do with Glasgow's 'other' university. It was a slightly unfair knock against a perfectly respectable institution, but Zoe loved to make out she'd been dealt a bum pack of cards in life by virtue of being born with the wrong postcode, and casting herself as a delinquent drop-out suited her narrative.

They'd met on their first day at Willow Bank Academy and immediately hit it off in spite of – or perhaps because of – their obvious differences. It was a fee-paying establishment and therefore populated almost exclusively by offspring of the well-to-do and well-heeled. Anna had ended up there because, as far as her parents were concerned, it was the done thing. Zoe, a rough-talking working-class kid from Ruchill, was there because her grandmother had scrimped and saved to send both her and her younger brother there, suffering from the tendency to lionise private education that afflicts many who have never experienced it for themselves.

Despite their differing social and economic fortunes, Anna and Zoe soon realised they had a great deal in common.

They liked the same music, laughed at the same jokes and both ranked fitting in with the crowd low on their list of priorities. They'd been inseparable all through high school, and all Anna's most cherished memories from that time involved them doing something together. Lying side by side on the hillock at the top of Ruchill Park on warm summer days, listening to music from the same CD player, one earbud each...sitting in the back of RE class trading notes on boys they fancied while their teacher wittered on about some god neither of them believed in...cannonballing starkers into the November sea on a mutual dare during a day out in Ayr, then frantically trying to locate the keys to the hut where they'd left their clothes...and of course the succession of sleepovers spent beneath the same duvet, their noses almost touching, whispering to one another into the wee hours. More than just friendship, the bond between them had been every bit as intense as that of soulmates, siblings, even lovers.

All of which made it all the more surprising that they'd failed to keep in touch once they went their separate ways. They had, of course, started off with the grandest of intentions. Bit by bit, however, communication had dried up. Phone calls were allowed to ring out and answering machine messages ended up being deleted. Emails remained unread in inboxes for longer and longer and eventually stopped being sent altogether. And deep down, Anna knew she was the one who'd been most at fault – the one who'd been so wrapped up in her burgeoning academic career, she'd allowed their friendship to wither and die.

They were about two-thirds of the way to the café when a strangled wail rent the air. They stopped dead in their tracks, Zoe clamming up mid-sentence. They looked at one another, then their surroundings, searching in vain for the source of the cry.

'What d'ye figure *that* was?' said Zoe, when no further disturbances followed. 'Some sorta animal?'

'I don't know,' said Anna, 'but I'm not sure I want to stick around to find out.'

'Where'd it come fae?'

'The park…I think.'

They both gazed out across the dark, nebulous expanse of Kelvingrove Park and to the lights in the windows of the row of houses up at the top of Woodlands Hill on its eastern edge. Their warm, reassuring glow seemed achingly distant.

'Prob'ly just a fox or somethin',' said Zoe. 'We've got 'em up in Ruchill too. Should hear the racket they make when it's mating season.' She was trying to sound upbeat, but it wasn't mating season, and there was a distinct tremor in her voice.

They pressed on, redoubling their pace. They no longer spoke, both focused squarely on reaching their destination as quickly as possible.

They were just coming to the last set of traffic lights before the end of the Kelvin Way when a figure came into view in front of them, emerging from the fog like an apparition. He wore a dark hooded top. His head was bowed low, obscuring his face. They parted to let him pass, both sensing that it was in their best interests not to get in his way. He strode through the gap between them, his shoulder colliding hard with Anna's. They turned to watch as he continued to head south, back the way they'd just come. Within moments, he was swallowed up by the fog again. His footsteps receded into nothing.

Zoe tugged Anna's sleeve. 'C'mon, let's get a move on. Too many weirdies out here the night for ma likin'.'

***

They were glad beyond measure to reach the café. And yet, even once they were safely installed in a window bay with a taxi on the way, Zoe tucking gleefully into her bacon butty, Anna's mind continued to churn. The scream might've been nothing. The figure in the hoodie might've been completely unconnected. And yet…

She looked at Zoe, HP sauce running down her chin, and decided to keep her own counsel.

After Zoe had finished eating and gone in search of the loo, Anna sat alone at the table, drumming her fingers on the surface, her misgivings about the way they'd handled what had happened out there growing by the second. *Had* anything happened out there? For her own peace of mind, if nothing else, she had to find out.

***

She entered Kelvingrove Park by its northern entrance at the foot of Gibson Street, leaving behind the streetlights and their reassuring sodium glow. She'd often walked through the park as a child, though only a handful of times after dark, and always with friends. During daylight hours, people walked their dogs in it, whiled away their lunch hours on the park benches, and in the summer months, even indulged in the odd stint of sunbathing on those rare sunny days. After dark, however, it was a different story. Even as a schoolgirl, word had reached her tender ears that it was the stomping ground of rent-boys and their clients, and over the years, it had been host to several violent attacks, muggings and sexual assaults.

Which was precisely what had made her throw caution to the wind and risk her own neck. If she opened the papers the following morning to discover some poor soul had been assaulted while she and Zoe were skipping up the Kelvin Way, nonchalantly discussing trivialities, she'd never forgive herself. She slipped a hand into her coat pocket and gripped her keys, the longest protruding between her clenched fingers like a knuckle-duster.

At first, she could barely see her own feet, but after a few moments, her eyes grew accustomed to the gloom, and she was able to make out the shapes of the snow-flocked trees and the wrought iron fencing that flanked the footpath. It was less dark in the park than it had seemed from the street. True, the clusters of trees on either side of her were as black as charcoal, but the terrain itself was readily visible, the snow a dull purplish grey.

The ground began to slope steadily downwards. Using the torch on her phone, she picked her way south, following the winding trail towards the centre of the park, where all paths converged at the Stewart Memorial Fountain. Up ahead, she could just make out the imposing shape of the monument to the Highland Light Infantry, beyond which lay the stone bridge that straddled the River Kelvin.

She was perhaps four hundred metres from the fountain when she heard it – a shrill, clear wail of anguish, coming from beyond a thicket of trees up ahead and to her left. She stopped dead. There was no doubt about it. Whoever – or whatever – had made that noise was also the source of the cry she and Zoe had heard on the Kelvin Way.

She remained stock still and listened but heard nothing more. She took a few more faltering steps, then stopped once again. What she saw caused her blood to turn to ice.

Less than fifty metres away, a shape was moving among the trees. As she watched, it emerged from the thicket and stumbled onto the footpath – a man, bent over almost double and clutching his stomach. He tottered unsteadily, turning this way and that, as if trying to work out where he was.

She drew herself up to her full height – an admittedly underwhelming five foot two – directing the beam from her phone onto him. His shirt was untucked; his belt hung loosely from his waistband, the buckle trailing behind him. It crossed her mind that she might have inadvertently broken up a transaction between a client and one of the nocturnal denizens of the park who plied their trade within its confines. She began to feel slightly foolish. In fact, she was on the verge of actually apologising when she saw it.

Blood.

Large quantities of blood, trickling from a wound in his lower abdomen, covering his groin area, his shirttails and the legs of his trousers. He was doing his best to stem the flow with one hand, but it was leaking between his fingers like water from a punctured hose.

She heard herself gasping. He must have heard her too, for he turned in her direction and looked directly at her. Light from her phone picked out the contours of his face.

Her breath caught in her throat. She knew him. Gone was the cocky smile, replaced by a contorted, painful grimace, but every other aspect of that face was instantly recognisable. The strong jawline, the high-bridged nose...

Seemingly galvanised by her appearance, he began to stagger in an uneven line towards her. She found herself reversing, shuffling backwards, the beam of her phone's torch trembling as she trained it on him.

'Please...'

It was barely a whisper, but the air was so still, Anna heard it with crystal clarity.

She couldn't move. Her legs refused to obey her brain, which was screaming, *Help him, help him, help him* over and over. He took a few more faltering steps towards her. Her phone and keys fell from her trembling hands.

He tottered, his legs giving way under him. He fell against her, clawing madly at her, clutching the hem of her coat. She recoiled instinctively, trying to push him off, but his weight bore down on her, and it was all she could do to prevent her own knees from buckling. She found herself supporting him in her arms, each ragged breath he took reverberating through her own body.

With a last effort, he lifted his head. Their eyes met, and she knew she was looking at a dead man.

And *he* knew it too.

His lips trembled. He opened his mouth, but instead of words, a thin trickle of blood oozed from the corner of his lips. He was choking. His grip on her tightened, then loosened.

Andrew Foley went limp and sank to the ground, leaving twin vertical streaks of blood on either side of her coat. He landed face-down in the unblemished snow and lay still.

4

Q&A

She found out afterwards that she'd somehow made her way back to the café, scaring the crap out of both Zoe and the proprietor when she materialised in the doorway, blank-faced and white as a sheet. At first, neither of them was able to get a word out of her. They deduced, from the state she was in, that something bad had happened – an impression that was only reinforced when Zoe noticed the blood on her coat. By the time they managed to ascertain that it wasn't hers, she'd started to come out of it and had begun talking again, though by all accounts, the words coming from her mouth were nigh on incomprehensible. Eventually, they managed to piece together enough to deduce that whatever had happened had taken place in Kelvingrove Park, and the manager took it upon himself to investigate. He returned five minutes later, looking very shaken, and said they needed to call the police right away.

The emergency services arrived in short order – and it was an arrival that would keep the denizens of the West End wagging their tongues for years to come. A veritable convoy of vehicles descended on Gibson Street, producing enough light and sound to wake the dead. By that time, Anna had come to her senses and was sitting on a stool next to an electric heater with a blanket wrapped around her. She was whisked out of the warmth of the café into the cold street, where two officers got her to confirm her name, occupation and date of birth, before bundling her into the back of a police car and leaving her to her own devices. She sat there, feeling oddly disconnected from everything that was going on. This must be what it's like to be a goldfish, she thought – confined to a glass bowl, watching the outside world as life continues without you. While she was waiting, she saw a couple more police cars and an ambulance sailing by, all flashing lights and howling sirens. When the officers returned and they finally set off some twenty minutes later, the ambulance was still stationary at the park gates.

This wasn't, she concluded, the best of signs.

***

The journey seemed to take forever, but they finally pulled into the grounds of a bland new-build brick building in the Yorkhill area. Anna was shepherded up the stone steps, past the waiting area, down a flight of stairs and into a small, stuffy room that was home to several filing cabinets and a grey-haired policeman with a paunch. He relieved her of her bloodied coat, sealed it inside an evidence bag and took her fingerprints. Standard procedure, he explained, before handing her over to a young constable with bad acne. As she turned to go, her fingers still inky, the grey-haired officer presented her with a tissue and an apologetic smile.

As she followed the constable down an interminably long and interminably narrow corridor, he kept looking back at her with what seemed like a mixture of sympathy and fascination. News of what had happened had evidently reached the station long before she had. She guessed he was new to the job. He was painfully young and had the look of a man who could still be shocked.

He ushered her into an interview room and left her there, perched on a bum-numbing plastic chair facing a large wooden table stained with coffee rings. The furnishings were modern but had already taken on the sad, dilapidated look of the overused and under-cared-for. The paint on the walls was cracked and daubed with graffiti. A message carved in biro informed her that 'THE STAFF HEAR ARE A BUNCH OF BASTERDS'. A twin tape recorder deck sat on the table in front of her, bolted to the wall. The ceiling light – one of those fluorescent affairs that gave everything a blue tinge – flickered incessantly above her.

She waited and waited, and the longer she sat there, the more convinced she became that they'd forgotten her. She wondered where Zoe was. In another, near identical room, most likely, being subjected to the same waiting game. Possibly even next door. She hoped they were treating her alright. Zoe didn't respond well to pressure and even less well to authority. She was the sort of person who would take a 'walk left' sign as an open invitation to do the exact opposite. Anna prayed she wasn't doing too much to antagonise her hosts.

She wished she had her laptop with her. It, and her papers and various other odds and ends she'd brought with her to Glasgow, were all safely tucked away in her travel case – which, unless some observant person had lifted it for her, would still be under the table at the café on Gibson Street. She hated doing nothing, and a busy work schedule meant she was always acutely aware of when she wasn't using her time productively. Since she'd got here, she could have marked – what, two essays? Three? At one point, the young officer returned with a polystyrene cup of lukewarm coffee. She asked him how long all this was likely to take, but he just shrugged and said he didn't know, sorry, and hurried out before she could ask any other awkward questions.

She turned her attention to the wall-mounted security camera, staring at her with its single unblinking eye. Were they watching her right now? Softening her up before the interrogation, hoping she'd crack and be begging to sign a full confession by the time they came for her? *Of course not. Don't be so bloody stupid, Anna.*

Still, she wondered if she was a suspect. She assumed they'd taken her fingerprints for elimination purposes, but surely they must at least be considering the possibility. *She'd* be considering it, if she was in their shoes.

She shifted in her chair, trying to get comfortable. One of the legs was shorter than the others, meaning that, no matter how she distributed her weight, she always felt off-balance. Eventually, she got up and swapped it for one on the other side of the table.

She'd just sat down again when the door abruptly clanged open behind her and two men in suits swept in. She was on her feet before they had a chance to say a word.

'Where's Zoe? Is she alright?'

'She's fine. We're just after talking to her.'

It was the older of the two who spoke, his voice gravelly but gentle. He was short and slightly pot-bellied, suffering from an aggressive onset of male pattern baldness, and had the sort of leathery, careworn face one tends to associate with people who've spent most of their lives exposed to the elements. It wasn't an unkind face, but it didn't look like the sort that did much smiling.

They sat down facing Anna. The younger detective, sporting a neatly-trimmed goatee, a long face and impeccable posture, unwrapped two cassette tapes, inserted them into the machine and pressed a button. It emitted a long, ear-splitting beep.

'Interview commencing Friday eighteenth of December 2009 at two-forty am. Present are Detective Sergeant Murray…'

'Detective Inspector Norton…'

They both looked at Anna expectantly. After a moment, she took the hint. 'Dr Anna Scavolini.'

'I'm sorry we're meeting under these circumstances,' said Norton. 'We'll try not to keep you any longer than necessary.' He took a small notebook and pencil from his breast pocket. 'Right, then. Shall we begin?'

***

And so they began. Norton did most of the talking, guiding her through the day, prompting her here and there, asking for this detail to be clarified and that point expanded upon. Occasionally, Murray would interject with a question about some seemingly irrelevant, unrelated detail, dragging her to a different point in her timeline. To keep her on her toes, probably. To see if he could make her contradict herself. It wasn't working. And, as time ticked on, it seemed to her that he was growing increasingly irritated by the precision and consistency of her answers.

Q: Which train had she caught?

A: The twelve thirty-two from Euston Platform three.

Q: When had it got into Glasgow?

A: Nineteen forty-five. More than an hour late.

Q: Which taxi firm had she used?

A: She wasn't sure. It was a licensed black cab. Did that help?

Q: What was the driver's ID number?

A: Again, she didn't know.

Q: And she'd met up with Zoe where…?

A: Argyle Street. The West End bit. Outside Wizard of Paws.

Q: And the name of the nightclub?

A: Pulse. It's a—

They knew it well.

Q: How long had they spent there?

A: Just over five hours. It was a little after one in the morning when they got out.

Q: And what had she had to drink?

A: Prosecco, mainly. Four glasses, maybe five. And a sparkling water.

So far, so humdrum. This was the easy stuff – the times, the locations, the distances. Nice, straightforward, uncontroversial questions, designed – she assumed – to put her at her ease. But throughout it all, there was the proverbial elephant in the room, that dark cloud lurking on the horizon that, bit by bit, they were inching their way towards. Until now, she'd just about hung onto her sanity by coming up with all manner of distractions to keep herself from thinking about Andrew. She'd been focusing on the trivial inconveniences – her inky fingers, the lukewarm coffee, how long she'd been kept waiting. But it was coming. Any minute now…

Norton glanced down at his notes. 'You said the victim was known to you, and that you spent some time in his company before the, er, incident.'

Anna nodded. 'It was a chance meeting. I didn't know he was going to be there.'

'How would you describe your relationship?'

She hesitated. '*Relationship* would be a bit of a misnomer. I didn't really know him all that well. I crossed paths with him a few times growing up, but that was about it. To be honest, we probably exchanged more words tonight than we ever did back in the day.'

She was playing it down a fair bit. While nothing she was saying was strictly inaccurate, she was conscious that she was omitting certain salient details – not least that she used to fancy him something rotten. Not that it was in any way relevant, she reasoned. It had been unreciprocated, and she was damned if she was going to embarrass both herself and these two men by revealing a schoolgirl crush.

'And this was the first time you'd seen him since then?'

'I've been out of the country since I was eighteen. It was the first time I'd seen *anybody* since then.'

Murray looked incredulous. 'And yet you recognised him without any difficulty after, what, ten years?'

'He was the one who recognised me. He bought me a drink. At first, I thought he was just some random idiot looking to get lucky.'

That's right, Anna. Just you leave out the bit about you going all weak at the knees. They don't need to hear that.

Murray gave a little smirk. 'That sort of thing happen to you a lot?'

Don't rise to his bait. Don't let him drag you down to his level.

She fixed him with her best steely-eyed stare. 'Oh, I don't think so. Certainly no more than any other woman who finds herself on her own in a nightclub.'

'So after he bought you a drink,' Norton cut in, 'you spent some time together talking. What about?'

Anna wrested her eyes from Murray and faced Norton. 'This and that. Family stuff, work, that sort of thing. Nothing overly important.'

'And you spent approximately how long in each other's company?'

'About an hour. I went to the loo and got back to find him gone.'

'You didn't think that strange?'

'I didn't think anything. People were coming and going all evening.'

Norton nodded, scribbling away in his book. 'And did he, at any point, say or do anything that made you think he was uneasy? Worried about something?'

'No.'

Now that's interesting, Anna. Why did you say that?

Norton glanced up from his jottings. 'You're quite sure? The smallest detail…'

'I'm sure.'

She was surprised by the force of her own conviction. Did the whole 'doing a runner' and 'crying down the phone to his mistress' business not count?

Actually, she wasn't convinced it did. The entire exchange already seemed so distant, so refracted by pulsating lights and cranium-pounding music, that she was beginning to doubt her own recollection of events. And she saw little to be gained from dredging it up now and casting aspersions on Andrew's character. Anyway, she reasoned, Norton was asking about their conversation, and the phone call hadn't been a part of that, so she wasn't exactly lying. Except by omission.

She looked Norton square in the eye. 'To be honest, it's all a bit vague. It was loud. People were coming and going. We were both drinking. Half the time, I could barely make out what he was saying.'

'And that was the last you saw of him? Until the, er, encounter in the park, that is.'

'Yes.'

Again, not strictly speaking a lie. At any rate, Norton seemed to accept it and returned to examining his notes.

'It's funny,' said Murray.

'What is?'

'You were able to tell us what time your train got in, to the minute. And yet now you're telling us you can't remember what you and he talked about…or how many glasses of Prosecco you had.'

The look of disdain he gave her as he spoke left her in no doubt as to what he was thinking. *Fuck you, prick*, she wanted to say. *I'm not some alkie staggering out of the local watering hole with no idea what day of the week it is.* Whenever she got angry, her voice invariably became markedly more Glaswegian – even the voice in her head.

But instead she kept a lid on her temper and explained, as civilly as possible, that good timekeeping was an essential part of her job, given the need to juggle preparing and delivering lectures and tutorial groups while still finding sufficient time for her own research.

'Quite so,' agreed Norton, nodding appreciatively. He looked down at his notebook and read aloud from it. 'Joint first in sociology and psychology at the *Sapienza Università di Roma*. Graduated top of your year. Doctorate in feminist criminology. Made junior lecturer at twenty-seven. Oh yes,' he nodded, catching Anna's surprised look, 'I've done my homework. Makes for quite a résumé.'

This seemed to annoy Murray even more. He shifted impatiently, moving his weight from one buttock to the other. As Anna watched him from the corner of her eye, she realised he must have chosen the chair with the shorter leg. Either that or he had something incredibly sharp lodged up his backside.

Norton examined his notes again, tapping his teeth with his pencil in a way that set Anna's own on edge. 'You attended Willow Bank Academy in Kelvindale between the years of 1993 and 1999. Correct?'

'Correct.'

'And the victim, per our preliminary enquiries, also attended Willow Bank, between the years of 1992 and 1998. A five-year overlap. I'd have thought that would mean you knew each other rather well.'

'Not really. There were over a thousand of us there at any given time. A lot of children end up there, particularly the ones with pushy parents. It's exclusive, but not *that* exclusive,' she added with a slight smile.

Ugh – why had she said that? She'd meant it as a joke, a way to thaw the ice a little, but straight away, almost before she'd finished speaking, she knew she'd misjudged things. She, as much as anyone, loathed the sense of superiority and entitlement the school had sought to instil in its progeny, but she now realised that, in the eyes of these men, she must seem like the poster child for privately-educated upper-middle-class wankery.

Seemingly satisfied, Norton turned to another page in his notebook. 'Now, this figure. The one in the hoodie going south down the Kelvin Way. What can you tell us about him?'

Anna racked her brains, trying to conjure up a mental image. 'I didn't see him for more than a few seconds. Average height and build, I think. His top and trousers were black – or maybe dark grey. It was hard to tell.'

'Male or female?'

'Male,' she replied promptly. Then, 'I mean, that would be my educated guess.'

Murray raised an eyebrow. 'Your educated guess? So you don't actually know?'

'Of course I don't *know*,' Anna shot back, imitating his supercilious tone. 'I just told you, I only saw him briefly.'

'So your use of the masculine pronoun is pure speculation on your part.'

'Well, that's the thing about the English language. Much like society, it has an inherent tendency to privilege the male.'

The corner of Murray's mouth twitched. She could tell he wasn't pleased. *Good.* Norton, meanwhile, cleared his throat and coughed into his fist. Anna got the distinct impression he was trying not to laugh.

'And do you think it's possible,' he said, after he'd regained his composure, 'that this person – male or female – could have been coming from the park when you saw them?'

Anna thought about it. There was a footpath in that general vicinity, she remembered, leading down into the park.

'It's possible. But again–' she cast a meaningful glance in Murray's direction '–that would be pure speculation on my part.'

They pressed on, finally coming to the events inside the park. Again, the same forensic questioning from Norton and the same assured, comprehensive answers from Anna. By now, she was flagging. Her head ached, and she craved sleep, but she was determined not to let it show. The last thing she wanted was for them to decide she wasn't fit for any further questioning and start the whole rigmarole over again in the morning. If they got it over and done with tonight, she could draw a line under the whole unhappy experience.

Norton made a sympathetic grimace. 'You've had a long day.'

'You could say that.'

'Me too. Maybe not quite as long as yours, but still – when I got in yesterday morning, I wasn't counting on still being here at this hour, let me tell you.'

'Sorry to be such an inconvenience.' She meant it sincerely, but it came out sounding bitter and sarcastic.

'We'll not keep you much longer. I know we're all anxious to get to our respective beds. You've somewhere to stay tonight, I take it?'

'I'm staying with Zoe. Fifty-eight Astley Street.' A thought occurred to her. 'She's not still here, is she?'

'She insisted on waiting for you.' Norton gave what Anna imagined was a rare smile. 'She must be a good friend, staying in touch all this time, offering to put you up.'

Anna found herself smiling too, in spite of herself. 'She is, yeah.'

'And that's where we'll find you, is it, if we have any further questions?'

And straight back down to earth courtesy of the ever-diplomatic DS Murray.

Anna inclined her head towards him. 'If that's where I said I'd be, that's where I'll be.' She turned to Norton. 'Can I go now?'

'Just about. Once the report's typed up, we'll get you to give it the once-over and your autograph, and then you can be on your way. You can wait here if you like, or if you'd prefer reception–'

She was already on her feet. 'I'll wait in reception. No offence, but I need some air.'

Norton eased himself out of his seat. 'None taken. DS Murray will see you out.'

Anna would far rather have seen her own way out than spend another minute in the company of DS Murray, but she managed to refrain from saying so. She turned to go.

'One last thing.'

Norton's voice stopped her in her tracks.

'You've been exceedingly cooperative in answering all our questions. Before you go, I'd like to give you the opportunity to ask *us* anything that's on your mind.'

Anna hesitated. Loath though she was to prolong this any longer than necessary, there was one question that, in spite of her best efforts not to think about it, had been gnawing away at her ever since she'd come to in the café. She knew it would continue to do so if she didn't get a definite answer.

'Just one thing. Is he dead?'

Norton rested his knuckles on the table. He looked at her, jaw set, studying her intently and wordlessly. It was as if he was gauging her resolve, trying to work out whether she was strong enough to hear the truth.

'Yes,' he said at last. 'He is. I know that probably isn't what you wanted to hear, but it is what it is.'

Anna said nothing. She'd known it was coming, but she'd still expected it to hit her like a sledgehammer when he actually said it. And yet, there was nothing there. Just a strange sense of…well, not so much indifference as a gnawing emptiness. And even now they were watching her, the two detectives. Judging her response, or lack thereof. Wondering just what sort of person feels nothing when they've been told that an old acquaintance with whom they've just spent the evening drinking and reminiscing is dead.

And well they might, for she was wondering exactly the same thing.

5

Old Times

Another ride in the back of a car, listening to indistinct chatter on the radio. Anna stared listlessly out of the window, watching as the affluent West End with its bohemian affectations gave way to stark, post-industrial Maryhill. She recognised the locations passing before her eyes, but none of them seemed entirely real. She was glad of the uncharacteristic silence coming from the seat opposite – she doubted she'd have been able to muster much in the way of a response if Zoe decided to strike up a conversation.

The old Callahan family home was in a residential area near Ruchill Park in the north of the city. The semi-detached houses were uniformly small, narrow and council-owned – a far cry from Anna's own upbringing in her parents' sprawling three-storey villa in Kelvindale. Their police driver pulled up to the kerb, asked them if they needed anything and took their non-response as confirmation that his services would not be further required. Anna stood watching as the car pulled away, her capacity for independent thought and action in woefully short supply.

Zoe finally spoke. 'Fuckin' hell, Anna.'

'Yeah.'

'I mean, Jesus H. Christ.'

'I know.'

She shivered and clutched herself. The police had kept her coat as evidence, and the flimsy fine-knit pullover she was wearing offered little protection against the elements.

Zoe came to her senses. 'Sorry. Here's me just standin' here giein' it laldy while you're busy turnin' intae an ice lolly.'

They headed up the garden path, Zoe dragging Anna's travel case. She'd retrieved it from the café and jealously guarded it throughout their internment at the police station. She'd just succeeded in locating her key when the door flew open, seemingly of its own accord. Warm light flooded the street.

'Jesus fuck, Victor!' Zoe shrieked, glaring at the figure standing in the doorway. 'You tryin' to gie us both a coronary?'

Victor shrugged sullenly, something between an apology and a *fuck you too*. It was only when he leaned out of the house and peered past Zoe that he noticed Anna standing behind her.

She raised a hand in half-hearted greeting. 'Hey, Victor.'

He swallowed heavily, his eyes like saucers. 'H…hi.'

Zoe and Victor – like two peas in a pod in so many ways, but in so many others like chalk and cheese. They'd been born just under two years apart, Zoe first and then Victor following in her wake – a pattern which had been maintained ever since. Where Zoe exuded self-confidence and a healthy lack of regard for what others thought of her, Victor had always just seemed plain uncomfortable in his own skin – a lanky six feet with oversized pink ears that jutted out from under a shock of ginger curls. He stared at them blankly, as if unsure of the correct protocol in situations like these – which only served to further incur his sister's wrath.

'Fucksake!' she hissed, still loud enough for Anna to hear. 'You think she wants to stand out here all night with you gawpin' at her? Aye, it's Anna. Aye, she's had the night fae hell. Shift!'

Muttering a barely inaudible apology – or perhaps an attempt at a retort – Victor shuffled aside and let them in.

Victor and Zoe's paternal grandmother had brought the pair of them up single-handedly after their parents were killed in a car accident when they were four and six years old, respectively. A redoubtable figure, she'd never once complained about the lot she'd been dealt, and though she'd passed away herself a couple of years ago, her presence could still be felt in every corner of the little house, from its utilitarian but comfortable furnishings to the faint smell of cinnamon that still seemed to pervade the air. Anna was bowled over by how instantly familiar every nook and cranny seemed. As a teenager, she'd probably spent as much time here as in her own home, and she still knew it like the back of her hand.

Like stepping into the past.

They climbed the narrow staircase, Victor lugging Anna's case as he brought up the rear. Zoe's bedroom was at the end of the first-floor landing, past the bathroom, past Victor's room, past their granny's old room – now being used as a box-room for, as Zoe explained, *all the old shite we couldnae part wi'*. Victor set the case down on Zoe's bed and completed his impression of a porter by backing off and standing by the door, waiting to be dismissed.

Anna felt Zoe's hand in the small of her back and her lips close to her ear. 'You want me to call your mum?'

Anna shook her head. Truth be told, the absolute last thing she wanted was for her mother to get wind of this from her hideaway in Saint-Tropez. All she'd do was make a scene and probably, as was her habit, infer that Anna had somehow brought it on herself.

Zoe turned to go. 'Back in five. Why don't you get settled?' She made for the door, grabbing Victor by the arm and hauling him after her.

Alone at last, Anna took stock of her surroundings. Like the rest of the house, Zoe's room was a veritable nineties time capsule, the walls adorned with posters of the bands the pair of them used to listen to back in the day – the Cranberries, Camera Obscura, others whose names she couldn't remember.

She turned to the dresser by the window. The frame of the large circular mirror was adorned with photos – a mixture of dog-eared polaroids and digital print-outs. Zoe and Victor's late parents were there, and their granny, and the two Callahan siblings themselves, as children and later as teenagers. As Anna moved closer to the dresser, she realised that she herself appeared in several, mostly with Zoe – the pair of them crammed into a photo booth, pulling silly faces; Zoe pouting at the camera, making a moustache with a strand of her own hair, Anna doubled up in hysterics by her side; a tipsy Zoe with her arms around a bemused-looking Anna, planting a kiss on her cheek...

Her eyes strayed to her reflection in the mirror. The contrast between it and the surrounding snapshots of her younger self was unnerving. The sunken eyes, the pallid skin, accentuated by her raven-black hair...What had happened to the carefree teenager in the pictures with the sparkling eyes and wide grin? Where did she go?

Kneeling beside the bed, she opened her case and began to take out the things she needed – toiletries, pyjamas, her medication, a change of clothes for the following day. She contemplated unpacking the rest of her things but decided against it. No sense making herself *too* much at home.

She was brushing her teeth at the sink in the narrow bathroom, the backs of her legs pressing against the side of the bath just like in the old days, when she became aware of voices downstairs. Raised voices. Angry voices. She couldn't make out the individual words, but the accuser was clearly Victor. Zoe's voice was shrill and defensive in comparison, but she was giving as good as she got, getting louder with each stream of invective, drowning out Victor's responses.

Curiosity getting the better of her, Anna crept into the landing, toothbrush still in her mouth, and leaned over the bannister, trying to make out what was being said. A moment later, the living room door flew open. Zoe stormed out into the hallway, turned and yelled, 'Aye, away back tae yer cave, dickwad!' The door slammed in her face. For a moment, Zoe stood there, fists clenched, seething at it, then turned towards the stairs.

Anna hurried back into the bathroom. She rinsed and spat, then bolted down the corridor to the bedroom, Zoe's mutinous footsteps clumping up the steps behind her. She dived under the covers and was sitting innocently checking her phone when Zoe breezed in, nonchalant as you like.

'Alright, doll?'

Anna nodded.

Zoe beamed. 'Grand.' She kicked off her boots and headed over to the dresser. There, she tied back her hair and set about removing her makeup, humming a ditty as she went about her business. Anna watched with growing amusement as she peeled off her lash extensions and began dabbing under her eyes with a wipe.

'Listen, I know things didnae get off tae the best start, but it's all uphill from here. I've got a whole action plan for us – loads and loads of proper girly activities just for the two of us. Course, we dinnae have to stick to the itinerary. We can do whatever you want. I mean, if you wanna just sit around in your pants and eat chocolate ice cream–'

'Zoe!'

Zoe turned to face her. 'What?'

She still had eyeshadow on one side of her face, making one eye appear vastly bigger than the other. The effect served to make her look a little mad.

'Just…don't ever change, okay?'

Zoe frowned, then shrugged to herself, accepting this as a reasonable request. 'Aye, alright, then.'

She turned back to the mirror. Anna watched as she removed the last vestiges of makeup, then unzipped her party dress, let it fall to the floor and kicked it to one side. She changed into a baggy, oversized T-shirt with 'Wanna see my cock?' emblazoned on it underneath a picture of a rooster, then jumped into bed and rolled over to face Anna, smiling at her with her big beaming eyes.

'Just like old times, huh?'

Anna smiled back – a weary, wistful smile. 'Listen, Zo, I really appreciate you letting me crash. You didn't have to.'

'Och, away!' Zoe batted her arm. 'You think I'm gonnae let you fritter away your hard-earned moolah stayin' in some poncy hotel? You know there's always room here for you.'

'I know. What I mean is, I realise I haven't exactly been forthcoming when it comes to keeping the channels of communication open–'

'It's fine. You've been all busy what with your fancy degree and that, and I…well, eh…dunno where I was goin' wi' that.'

Anna decided to take her at her word. If Zoe said it was fine, then chances were it probably was.

'Listen,' she said, changing tack, 'is Victor really pissed off about something?'

Zoe looked uneasy. 'How d'you mean?'

'It's just, I heard the two of you going hammer and tongs. Is he not happy about me staying here?'

Zoe made a rueful face. 'Aw, it's no about you, doll. Well, it sorta is, but mostly it's about me.'

Anna propped herself up on her elbow, giving Zoe a quizzical look.

'It's…well, it's about what happened. The whole "you and the deid body" bit. He thinks it's my fault.'

'How's he work *that* one out?'

'Oh, you know – if I hadnae kept us out 'til all hours, if I'd've brought you straight home after 'stead of takin' us for bacon butties, if I hadnae gone for a slash and left you on your lonesome… Honestly, it's like I'm your personal minder or somethin'.'

'Did you tell him that, contrary to popular belief, I am actually accountable for my own actions?'

Zoe made an emphatic face. 'Big time.'

'Hence the whole door-slamming incident,' said Anna.

'Aye. The boy's got a lot of pent-up frustration in him. S'all 'cause he's no gettin' any action, 'cept of the one-handed variety.'

'And you know this how?'

'Come on – who in their right mind would want to shag a ginger?'

'Been near a mirror lately, Zo?'

'Aye, but I've got my winning personality tae compensate for my unfortunate birth defect.'

This made about as much sense to Anna as anything else that night, and she accepted it with a philosophical nod.

'Anyway, s'no like he's got any rope tae swing fae. He's the one who couldnae be arsed comin' to his own sister's birthday bash, the antisocial wee shite.' Zoe fell silent for a moment, sitting with her arms folded, stewing at the injustice of it all. Then, as abruptly as a snap of the fingers, the cloud lifted and her good mood returned. 'So are you for turnin' in? I dunno about you, but ma heid's pure buzzin'.'

Anna looked at her watch. It was after four, and yet, knackered as she was, she knew trying to sleep now would be futile. The cogs of her mind were still turning and would continue to unless she found a way to distract herself from recent events. She had a whole bunch of questions she wanted to ask Zoe, but she knew now wasn't the time. It would only wind them both up even further.

'Put the light out,' she suggested, 'and we can talk for a bit.'

'Right you are, pal.'

***

For a while, they lay facing one another in the dark, talking about nothing of any great merit – what music they were both listening to, what films they'd seen recently. In many respects it was, as Zoe had said, just like old times – or rather a slightly perverse parody of them, both of them considerably older and yet still sharing the same bed in the same room in the same house, as if an entire decade and more hadn't gone by since they'd last done this. It put Anna in mind of a recurring dream she had in which her adult self was inexplicably back at school, going to the same classes, with the same teachers and classmates. In those dreams, she was the only one who'd aged. All the others were still their teenage selves, trapped in a time warp from which only she seemed to have escaped.

Their exchanges became more sporadic. Anna could tell from Zoe's increasingly fuzzy responses that she was drifting off. After a while, she stopped responding altogether, and shortly afterwards began to snore gently, her warm breath blowing a gentle breeze on Anna's cheek.

Anna lay there in the dark, staring up at the ceiling, her mind churning ceaselessly despite her best efforts to empty it. She kept coming back to Andrew – to his wide, petrified eyes as he lay dying in her arms. There was a void inside her, waiting to be filled by some sort of quantifiable emotion. Was it a delayed response, she wondered? Was it suddenly going to hit her like a bolt out of the blue? Or was she genuinely indifferent to it all? Did their past acquaintance really count for so little?

And what of the phone conversation she'd overheard? Had she made the right call in not divulging it? What if the lover she'd heard him pleading with had been the last person he'd spoken to before…?

Eventually, she drifted into an uneasy state of semi-consciousness, her more lucid moments mingling with her dreams until she could no longer be certain where one ended and the other began.

6

Renfield

Friday, 18 December

Renfield woke to the sound of a door banging, followed by a distant voice yelling a stream of invective. Groaning, he reached for the alarm clock atop the bedside table, angling it towards him. 7:45. Morning. Not that you could tell this time of the year, with the sun not deigning to show its face 'til long after most of the world was already out and about. Still, 7:45 was as good a time to greet the day as any. He wasn't due on shift until noon, but if he didn't get up, he'd just lie there ruminating on matters beyond his control.

He swung his legs over the side of the bed and headed for the bathroom, instinctively dipping his head to avoid hitting the doorframe. He was six foot four and all lean muscle, his pokey flat built with someone of considerably smaller stature in mind. He showered and urinated, then put on his work uniform – trainers, T-shirt, jogging bottoms and fleece with 'Anytime Fitness Gym' embossed on the breast. Not exactly Selfridges, but then the gym wasn't exactly the Harbour Club. And besides, nobody looked at him twice in a getup like this. Which was how he wanted it.

He headed through to the kitchen and turned on the tap at the sink. It made a grinding sound and half-heartedly coughed up a few spurts of water. Pipes must be frozen again. As it sputtered and whined, he held a pint glass under it and waited for it to do its thing, while with his free hand, he wiped condensation from the window and peered out at the grey dawn. His flat overlooked the Necropolis – a bleak sight at the best of times, made all the more depressing by the fact it was currently languishing in the grip of deepest, darkest midwinter. Barely visible in the pale half-light were the uneven rows of tombstones – monuments, odes to long-forgotten men and women whose names he'd never know. One day, he knew, he, too, would join them in the frozen earth.

He always got like this at this time of year – maudlin, introspective, memories of the past slowly eating away at his innards. It didn't show on the outside – he worked hard at cultivating a gruff, unapproachable exterior all year round – but in that last week or so before Christmas, the façade always became that bit harder to maintain. He wondered if it was like this for the others, or if they, somehow, had managed to bury their guilt and move on. If indeed they'd felt any guilt to begin with, of which he was doubtful.

He stirred. The water was maintaining a steady flow now; his glass was brimming over. He turned off the tap and gulped the contents down, not stopping until it was all gone. And yet, it did nothing to quell the dull sense of foreboding that was growing in his belly.

7

The Morning After

Several miles north and a few hours later, Anna dragged herself upright, screwing up her eyes against the crepuscular rays filtering through the curtains. At first, she couldn't work out where she was or how she'd got there. Then, as her eyes adjusted, the familiar sights from so many bygone sleepovers came into focus and the events of the previous night came flooding back. She squinted at the hands of her watch. Quarter to eleven. She couldn't have slept long, given that it had been after four when they'd turned out the light and God knows how much later when she'd finally been able to settle. *Settle* being particularly inapt in this case, since what little sleep she'd got had been disturbed and fitful. On the other side of the bed, Zoe was sleeping the sleep of the innocent, face-down and snoring like a rhinoceros.

Anna crawled out of bed and shuffled towards the door, rubbing her crusty eyes. Zoe continued to sleep on, blissfully unaware that the bedcovers had been dragged astray and her T-shirt had ridden up to her waist, leaving her bare arse winking in the sunlight. Anna hesitated for a moment, then stole back over and covered her up, restoring her…well, with Zoe, 'modesty' probably wasn't the right word.

She took her medication box through to the bathroom, where she shook out two oval pink and white pills and downed them with water, before heading downstairs in her pyjamas. There was nobody else about. She went for a rummage in the kitchen, then took her Rice Krispies through to the living room and sat nestled in the threadbare settee, watching the weather forecast. A heavy snow front was making its way down from the north and was expected to hit the Central Belt by Sunday. Residents were being urged to keep an eye out for vulnerable neighbours and not plan any unnecessary journeys.

Once she'd finished eating, she found Zoe's battered laptop tucked under the sofa, its lid covered in stickers promoting a variety of bands and causes of varying degrees of worthiness. She connected it to the phoneline and spent a quarter-hour or so taking care of various pieces of pressing and not-so-pressing business, then directed the browser to the Alitalia website and searched for flights to Rome.

I'm only looking, she told herself. Just satisfying idle curiosity. I'm not actively planning a getaway.

Oh really, Anna? Is that why you've got your passport open in front of you? Or did you just bring it out to admire it?

Truthfully, she'd been mulling over the idea of cutting her stay short since last night. She'd always known coming back would be difficult, though she'd been anticipating the stirring up of some bad memories, not the brutal death of an old acquaintance before her very eyes. But escape was still a possibility. Her case was upstairs, not yet unpacked, and she had her passport and an open return rail ticket back to Gatwick. She could walk out the door right now and leave literally nothing behind.

Except Zoe.

Zoe, whose idea it had been for her to come in the first place. Who was the one who'd spent ages talking her into it, *to get away from it all, doll.*

She couldn't do that to her. No way.

She leaned back and stretched. She was stiff and sore all over, and her head felt like it was swimming in thick fog. She needed to get out of the house for a bit to clear her mind, give herself a chance to think.

She stole back upstairs and, taking care not to disturb the slumbering Zoe, got changed into her running gear. The thin Lycra wasn't exactly designed for the sort of temperatures that awaited her outside, but that wouldn't matter once the blood was pumping in her veins. She did some limbering up exercises in the hallway, then let herself out, locking the door and posting the key through the letterbox.

Running was one of the few extracurricular activities she'd taken seriously as a teenager. Willow Bank placed great emphasis on athletic prowess – 'A healthy mind and a healthy body', as the prospectus so tritely put it – and it was made clear to all students that they were expected to 'voluntarily' enrol in at least one organised sporting activity. While many of the other girls chose netball or hockey, she'd taken up the more individualistic pursuit of track running, where the emphasis was on singular achievement rather than being a team player. That way, if she fucked up, she had nobody to blame but herself. She'd been pretty good at it, as she was at most things she applied herself to, and landed a spot in the West Scotland Athletics Championships in 1998. She hadn't won anything, but the same week the medals were doled out, she'd got straight A's in her Highers, which she considered a more than acceptable consolation prize.

Pacing herself, she headed south from Ruchill, following the canal as it wound its way down into Kelvindale. Though she'd set out without a firm destination, by the time she reached Maryhill Road, she had only one place in mind.

***

She entered Kelvingrove Park through the same gate she'd used the previous night. This time, however, she took a left turn, following a path that wound uphill. The ground climbed steeply before her. Away to her right, she could see the university bell-tower rising up, its spire disappearing into low-lying cloud. She continued along the path as it hugged the contours of the hill, running parallel to the semicircle of townhouses overlooking the park. She could scarcely reconcile how the place looked in the crisp light of day with the events that had occurred just a few short hours ago, and it wasn't until she came within sight of the spot where Andrew had died and saw the police tape fluttering in the wind that reality hit home.

She slowed to a standstill and watched from her vantage point as three technicians, their white overalls all but blending into the snow, performed a forensic examination of the crime scene. There had been no further snowfall since the body had been removed, the indentation left behind visible even from a distance. The surrounding area was tinged pink where blood had seeped into the snow.

At the top of the hill, a solitary crow took flight, soaring off into the grey sky with an angry shriek. Anna turned and looked up towards the houses. On the footpath running around the outer perimeter of the park stood a big, burly man in a cagoule, his bushy unkempt hair blowing in the breeze. Like her, he was watching the techs, though as she continued to stare up at him, his gaze shifted from the crime scene to her.

She quickly averted her eyes and moved on. She couldn't put her finger on why, but something about the man's presence made her feel decidedly uncomfortable.

**

It was just after midday when she made it back to Astley Street, worn out from what had turned out to be a far more intensive run than she'd anticipated. To avoid the park on her way back, she'd taken a somewhat circuitous route, adding an extra mile and a half to her journey. Flushed and sweaty, she was dreaming about the hot shower and change of clothes awaiting her when she spotted a grey Volvo parked outside the Callahan house. Straight away, she saw this as a bad omen. Her fears were confirmed when she drew level with the house and caught sight of the two detectives who'd interviewed her the previous night standing at the living room window, talking to a flustered-looking Zoe.

Anna stopped. She couldn't face this. Not again. Not so soon. She considered doing an about-turn and high-tailing it back the way she'd come, but at that moment, Murray glanced in her direction and spotted her. He motioned to Norton, who turned and did a passable job of pretending not to see her.

Anna gritted her teeth and stomped up the path. She'd no sooner let herself in than Zoe appeared in the hallway, shutting the living room door behind her and hurrying to head her off. The expression on her face was ominous.

'How long have they been here?'

''Bout twenty minutes. Christ, it's like pullin' teeth tryin' tae keep they pricks entertained.'

'What do they want?'

'You. Beyond that? Fuck knows.'

'Tell them—'

At that moment, the living room door opened, and Norton poked his head out. 'Dr Scavolini! I thought it was your voice. If you could give us just a few moments of your time.'

'I'm just in from a run.' Anna motioned to the stairs, hoping he'd take the hint and at least allow her to freshen up.

'I can see that. We won't take up any more of your time than necessary.' He gestured for her to join him. 'Please.'

Sitting in her sweat-soaked Lycra being grilled by these two men was, to put it mildly, not top of the list of things she wanted to do that day, but she saw little alternative but to do as she was told. She gave Zoe a look signifying *pray for me*, then followed Norton into the living room.

Norton shut the door and indicated for Anna to take a seat. She acquiesced, eyeing the two men warily. They already had a substantial height advantage over her, and the fact they remained on their feet while she slowly sunk into the folds of the settee only served to reinforce the power imbalance.

'I trust you're well rested,' said Norton pleasantly.

'About as well as can be expected.' *Ugh – too standoffish.* She gazed up at the detectives with an expression she hoped communicated a willingness to help. 'What do you want?'

'What we want, Ms Scavolini,' said Murray, 'is your cooperation.'

Norton took out his notebook and pencil, licked his finger and started to leaf through the pages, as if he needed to be reminded of why they were here. He found what he was looking for, gave a silent, epiphanic *ah!* and looked up from the page to Anna. She was left with the sense that he was gilding the lily somewhat.

'You said last night that you came upon the victim a little after one-thirty.'

'Yes.'

'And that you and he had parted company at Pulse at around ten.'

'That's right.'

'It's just that I'm struggling a little with the timeframe. That would mean a gap of around three and a half hours between him leaving the nightclub and turning up dead a mere half-mile away. We're having difficulty accounting for his movements in the interim.'

'I can only account for my own movements,' said Anna, 'and as far as I'm concerned, I've already done that.'

'You couldn't have got the time wrong? Perhaps you were together longer than you think. We all know what it's like when the wine starts to flow.'

This was a more subtle variation on what Murray had insinuated the previous night. 'I was clock-watching most of the evening. I know what time he left. Look, there are loads of pubs and clubs in the area. He could have gone on to any one of them. Maybe some lowlife spotted him at the bar, figured him for an easy target, followed him, tried to mug him…?'

'I suggest leaving the detective work to the detectives, Ms Scavolini,' said Murray, in the sort of high-handed, patronising tone that made her want to throttle him.

'I've told you everything I know,' she said, deliberately directing her reply to Norton.

'Alright.' Norton scribbled something in his notebook and turned to another page. He paused, pupils dancing back and forth as he skimmed whatever was written there. 'There is one other matter I'd like to return to. We're trying to create as accurate a timeline as possible of yesterday's events. You told us last night you heard a sound that might have been a scream as you were making your way up the Kelvin Way.'

Anna nodded.

'And it was approximately how soon after this that you had your encounter with the man – or woman – in the hoodie?'

She replayed the incident in her mind. 'Only a couple of minutes. Maybe three.' She could see where this was going. 'You're wondering if there was enough of a gap between the two events for the killer to have stabbed Andrew and legged it to the Kelvin Way.'

'It had crossed my mind,' Norton admitted. 'Though that would assume that the scream, if indeed it was a scream, coincided with the actual moment of the attack – which isn't necessarily the case. As I recall, you heard another such scream some time later, once you'd entered the park.'

'Can I ask *you* a question? Do you think the figure in the hoodie was the killer?'

Until now, she'd been operating under the assumption that she'd seen the killer fleeing the scene prior to her entering the park. But if she hadn't, if the hooded figure had merely been an innocent passer-by, then it meant that, while Andrew was bleeding to death in her arms, the person responsible could have been a whole lot closer to her than she'd ever imagined. The thought made her queasy.

'It's not really about what we think,' said Norton levelly. 'It's about the possibility. At any rate, we'd very much like to trace this figure. We'll be releasing the victim's identity later today, to coincide with the evening news. We're hoping someone will come forward.'

But he didn't, to Anna's ears, sound overly hopeful. It must be exasperating, operating in the dark like this, relying on half-remembered snippets of information.

'It's a shame you can't ask the deceased about his movements,' she said, trying to inject a little levity into the proceedings. *Christ, 'the deceased'.* Already she was using their words, relegating Andrew to the status of an abstraction, a thing.

Norton gave the slightest of smiles. 'Hmm, yes. If only. More than anything else, I'd dearly love to get inside his head.' He looked at Anna imploringly. 'Are you certain there was nothing to suggest he was anxious about something? His leaving without a word doesn't sit well with me. Is it possible, for instance, that he could have seen someone there and been spooked by them?'

'Aren't we straying into the territory of speculation again?' She glanced in Murray's direction. Murray said nothing.

She thought again about Andrew's phone call. Once more, the opportunity was there for her to bring it up. Norton had clearly come here in the hope that she would divulge something she hadn't the previous night – some new information to help move their investigation in the right direction. If she tossed them some red meat, so to speak, it might encourage them to leave and let her get on with her day. Though, on the other hand, it might just make things worse. They'd want to know why she hadn't mentioned it last night.

And why hadn't she? Was she protecting Andrew, she wondered, or herself? Was this about avoiding casting a dead man in a less than favourable light, or was it about keeping her own nose clean? From the start, she'd been doing everything she could to distance herself from him and, by proxy, the life she'd left behind a decade ago. It wasn't about anything so trivial as being embarrassed by the fact she used to fancy a good-looking older boy, or not wanting people to know she'd overheard him snivelling in the cloakroom to an illicit lover. It was about keeping the past in the past and avoiding becoming a part of this developing narrative. The alternative – allowing herself to be sucked back in wholesale – risked ripping open wounds that had taken years to heal.

She looked Norton square in the eye. 'I'd like to help you, I really would. But I've told you absolutely everything I can think of.'

Norton considered this for a moment, then gave a shrug of acceptance. 'Fair enough. But if anything else should come to mind, you'll get in touch?'

'Of course,' she said, fervently hoping this was the last time she'd have dealings with either man.

'In that case, we shan't trouble you further.'

He turned to go, beckoning to Murray. Murray glanced in Anna's direction – a look that could have frozen meat – but dutifully followed his boss.

That's right. Just keep walking – out of that door and out of my life.

As he passed the coffee table, Norton came to a halt. He glanced down at Zoe's laptop, lying on the surface, lid closed. As Anna watched, he took out his pencil, hooked the rubber end under the lid and raised it. The screen came to life. The Alitalia website was still open, showing the list of flights to Rome.

'Planning on going somewhere?' he inquired, with almost casual indifference.

'Keeping my options open.'

'Always a wise move.' He gestured to her passport, lying on the table next to the laptop. 'I, ah, take it that's up to date?'

'Of course.'

'Can I see it?'

So casual, so offhand. Without even thinking, Anna reached for it and handed it over. Norton studied the front cover. Flicked through to her mugshot and particulars. Tilted his head. Held it up to the light. Turned it every which way as if looking for signs of forgery. Then, almost before Anna realised what was happening, he'd slipped it into his breast pocket.

She was on her feet in a flash. 'Hey! What d'you think–'

'For safekeeping.'

'But you can't...'

Norton turned to face her, seemingly oblivious to her umbrage. 'Dr Scavolini,' he said, in a tone that was calm but also very firm, 'you are a material witness to an extremely serious crime, and I'm not yet convinced you've told me everything you know – whether you realise it or not. This morning, I sought authorisation to compel you to remain at our disposal until our enquiries reach a satisfactory conclusion. That means any premature flights to Rome are, for the time being, out of the question.'

Anna stared at Norton, mouth agape, fists clenched with impotent rage.

'Don't worry,' Norton continued, as he turned and made for the door once more. 'You'll get it back in due course. In the meantime…well, we know where to find you, don't we?'

He strode out, Murray trotting behind him like a loyal and now unmistakably satisfied canine companion.

Anna followed them to the hallway. They brushed past Zoe – who was doing a spectacularly poor job of pretending she hadn't been standing outside the living room with her ear to the door the whole time – opened the front door and made off down the garden path.

It had been Norton's plan all along, no doubt. He'd have scoped out the laptop and passport the moment he arrived and known full well she'd been entertaining notions of eloping. He'd been toying with her all this time, the bastard. And now she was trapped, as surely as if he'd thrown her in a cell and locked the door. She cursed her own sloppiness in leaving both items lying around for him to find.

Zoe shook her head in disbelief. 'Fuckin' cheeky wee shites! What were they after?'

'My passport,' Anna spluttered. 'They took my bloody passport.'

8

Grounded

Anna drew the polyester curtain shut and turned the tap on full. The showerhead spluttered into life and ejected a deluge of icy water which knocked the breath from her. She stood, fists clenched, braving the assault as the temperature gradually increased. Before long, it was piping hot, and yet still, she endured. With a near-scalding torrent cascading over her, the sound of its hammering on the tub floor drowning out everything else, she began to pound the tiled wall in front of her with her hands – half-heartedly at first, but rising in both velocity and intensity until she was going at it like a mad thing, a primal scream building to a crescendo.

Half an hour later, she emerged, feeling suitably refreshed and a good deal calmer. The immediate rage had subsided. So, too, had the shock of Andrew's death. Already, she had sufficient distance from last night's events to be able to regard them with a certain detachment. It was clear the police had precious little to go on, and Norton's questioning had had more than a hint of desperation about it. He'd practically encouraged her to postulate a motive.

Of course, the most obvious explanation, and the one she'd presented to Norton, was that Andrew's murder was nothing more elaborate than a mugging gone wrong, with no premeditated thought involved. But what if there was more to it than that? What if he'd been deliberately targeted, and not simply because whoever knifed him had taken one look at the cut of his suit and concluded he was rich pickings? What if his infidelity and the murder were connected? An act of vengeance by a jilted partner, perhaps? It sounded far-fetched, but then so did finding a man bleeding to death in Kelvingrove Park.

She knew this was going to gnaw away at her until she came up with some answers. Her therapist would no doubt have said she was driven by a desire for closure, or to impose order on a disordered world. She didn't believe in the former and had long ago concluded the latter was unachievable. She just knew she had to do *something* or go stir crazy.

Telling herself she wasn't getting sucked into anything, just making some casual enquiries, she retrieved her own laptop from her case, hooked it up to the phoneline, navigated to Google, typed 'Gavin Price' into the box and hit Enter. The first of several hundred pages of results loaded. She refined the search to 'Gavin Price Glasgow' and was rewarded with what she was looking for – a link to a profile on the university website.

Gavin was Andrew's cousin and, unlike Andrew, could be described as more than a passing acquaintance. Growing up, he'd lived a few houses down from Anna, and they'd spent a fair bit of time in each other's company as children before largely going their separate ways as teenagers. He was a year younger than her, and at that tender young age, even a year felt like a massive gulf, as if generations lay between them rather than mere months. Anna remembered him as a friendly but slightly frustrating boy – clever and bookish like her, but with a certain tendency to act the clown, playing down his intelligence, as if it was something to apologise for.

Like his older cousin, to whom he bore more than a passing resemblance, he'd grown into a handsome specimen, judging by his profile picture. Gone were the glasses and braces he'd sported as a boy, his blond curls tamed into a close crop. In fact, were it not for the familiar sight of a small mole just above his upper lip, Anna could have been forgiven for thinking she had the wrong Gavin Price. He'd studied corporate law at Glasgow, according to his profile, landing a teaching post in the university's Law and Social Sciences department. She'd had no contact with him since leaving school, and she couldn't predict how he'd respond to a call out of the blue on this of all days. But she felt she had to see him. To offer her condolences, yes, but it was about more than that. She also wanted to see if she could fill in some of the blanks about Andrew.

As she made her way downstairs, a filthy cackle wafted up from the living room. 'Haw, you've got a filthy mind, you! Aye, there's bits of *you* I wouldnae mind givin' a wee nibble…How? What bits were *you* thinkin' about?'

Anna stepped into the doorway to find Zoe lounging on the settee, twirling a lock of hair around her pinkie, her phone clasped to her ear. Catching sight of Anna, a look crossed her face reminiscent of a child caught with her hand in the cookie jar.

'Anyways,' she said hastily, 'catch yese later.' She closed the lid of her phone and sat up, scooting over to make room.

Anna took a seat next to her. 'Didn't mean to interrupt anything.'

'Nah, ye didnae. Just sittin' here contemplatin' life's great mysteries. So what's the goss? You public enemy numero uno or what?'

Anna smiled. 'More of the "or what". Cops are playing their cards close to their chests. But I don't think they like me much. Especially that Murray.'

Zoe scowled. 'He's a prick. Whole time they were interviewin' me, he was sat there, pure giein' me the evil eye, like I'd shat in his ice cream sundae. And what's with the goatee? Ye've got tae wonder 'bout a man who goes out his way to look like he's got someone's pubes stuck to his chin.'

Anna, tickled pink by the mental image, stifled a laugh.

Zoe beamed. 'Good tae see you wi' a smile on yer face again, hen. Anyhoo, they must know it wasnae you. They've got forensics and whatnot. They'll be able to work out you were with me when it happened.'

'Maybe. It's not an exact science. More like an educated guess. I'm pretty sure extremes of hot and cold make it difficult to nail down an exact time of death.'

Zoe's eyes widened theatrically. 'So what you're sayin' is you might've snuck out and plunged the dagger in while I was shakin' ma booty on the dancefloor?' She caught Anna's look and winced. 'Too soon?'

'Little bit.'

'That why they took your passport? 'Cause they think it was you?'

Anna shook her head. 'No.' Then, with more conviction, '*No.* They just…don't want me leaving just yet.'

'Well, that's okay, isn't it? 'Cause you're not leavin'.'

'No, I'm not.' *Not yet, anyway.* 'But it's the principle of the thing, isn't it? It's a bit like being grounded. You might not have been planning on going out, but you sure as hell resent that choice being taken away from you.'

Zoe reflected on this comparison. 'Aye, right enough,' she said, not sounding overly convinced.

They fell into silence. Anna still didn't have any burning desire to discuss what had happened, but she knew from bitter experience that Zoe could be like a dog with a bone. If she thought someone was holding out on her, she'd keep needling and needling them until they cracked. Anna was more than capable of keeping her own counsel, but all the same, she didn't feel she could hold out on Zoe indefinitely.

'So what did they ask you last night?' she said, glancing at her sidelong. 'The police, I mean.'

Zoe screwed up her nose. 'God, a whole buncha things. Wheres and whens, mostly. No that I was able tae help them much there. *Way* too blootered tae remember any specifics. And they asked me about you. How long ye'd been away, how ye'd spent the evenin', stuff like that.'

'And what about the…the victim? Did they tell you anything about him?' She studied Zoe's face carefully as she spoke, wondering just how much she'd managed to overhear of her little chat with Norton and Murray earlier.

'No a peep. I asked who he was, but they said they werenae allowed to say. Pretty daft, really – I mean, it'll be all over the fish-wrappers by teatime anyway, right?'

Anna kept her eyes on Zoe, watching for any sign she might not be telling the truth. She couldn't detect any, which was pretty conclusive. Deception wasn't one of Zoe's strong suits.

She hesitated before speaking. 'It was Andrew Foley.'

No response. Zoe just gazed back at her, her expression blank. Then, recognition dawned. All that was missing was the cartoon lightbulb above her head.

'Andrew Foley? Like, Andrew Foley who was at school wi' us? *Him?*' She sat back, open-mouthed. 'Whoa! Christ on a bike, what were the odds?'

Anna gave a potted summary of the evening's events, though, as with the police, she left out the phone call. 'So you had no idea? I was wondering if maybe you'd invited him.'

Zoe frowned, considering. 'No *exactly*, but I s'pose there was the Facebook invite: "Zoe's B-day. Pulse, eight 'til late. Come one, come all." He could've seen that, I guess, like if he was friends wi' someone I'm friends wi'. But then, I cannae think why he'd've bothered. He wasnae really part of our circle. Heh, never even came up and introduced hisself.' This latter point seemed to irk her the most. 'Still–' she raised her eyebrows dramatically '–small world, eh?'

Anna smiled tightly. Despite her best efforts to contain herself, Zoe clearly found the whole affair rather thrilling. Having been the one who'd borne witness to Andrew exsanguinating before her very eyes, it was an enthusiasm Anna couldn't bring herself to share. It had been easier last night, when they'd both still been shocked into monosyllables.

Zoe sat up straight and decisive. 'Right, so what's the plan, Stan? I thought mibby we could go off on a wee jaunt. There's loads of stuff ye'll no have seen. The Lighthouse, the IMAX, the ice-rink at Silverburn…anythin' take yer fancy?' She grinned expectantly at Anna, as if they hadn't just been talking about a dead man.

Anna didn't relish the thought of pricking Zoe's balloon. But nor did she relish the thought of spending the afternoon following her on a whistle-stop tour of Glasgow's consumerist temples with so many unanswered questions still rattling around inside her head.

'Actually, I thought I might go and see Gavin Price.'

Zoe frowned. 'Gavin Price? As in specky Gavin wi' the curly hair and the mole on his lip? He was—'

'Andrew's cousin, yeah. I reckon I ought to show my face. You know, pay my respects.'

'You any idea where to find him? Is he even still *in* Glasgow?'

'I, uh, looked him up earlier.' She suddenly felt vaguely stalkerish. 'He teaches at the uni.'

'Oo-ooo!' Zoe cooed, rising up on her haunches and ogling Anna as if she'd just confessed to committing an act of public indecency. 'Check you, havin' a crafty Googling session. Hope ye remembered to wipe yer browser history after.'

Anna rolled her eyes and batted Zoe's arm. 'Oh, get to France! Just 'cause that's all you use your computer for. Anyway,' she added, a touch haughtily, 'I just think it'd be appropriate for me to put in an appearance, that's all.'

'Aye, fair enough.' Zoe gave her a smug, knowing look. 'Just don't go doin' anythin' I wouldnae.'

Anna got to her feet, trying hard not to smile at Zoe's infectious buoyancy. She couldn't resist firing a parting shot, and giving her something to keep her filthy mind occupied for the rest of the day.

'Well,' she said primly, 'knowing you, that leaves me a hell of a lot of leeway.'

Zoe gave Anna a look of mock-severity. 'Are you suggesting I'm defined purely by my philandering ways and penchant for levity?'

'Well…'

Zoe picked up a cushion and hurled it in Anna's direction. Anna ducked it and fled the room, Zoe's guffaws ringing behind her.

9

Gavin and Andrew

Gavin sounded surprised when Anna rang him on the number listed on the university website. Surprised and more than a little distracted – which she supposed stood to reason. In fact, given what had happened, she was somewhat taken aback to find him at work. Still, she reasoned, Andrew was a cousin, not a sibling or a parent, and life, as the saying went, stood still for no man. In any event, he'd remembered who she was with minimal prompting and agreed to meet her.

A little before the appointed hour, she made her way up the steep hill towards the Neo-Gothic façade of the university. It was the last day of term, and the campus buzzed with activity as students said their goodbyes and emerged from the library with armfuls of books they'd no intention of reading over the Christmas break. At the entrance to the Gilbert Scott Building, where she and Gavin had arranged to meet, a crowd of Chinese tourists armed with cameras stood in a semi-circle, facing an overly-animated tour guide who was addressing them in loud, vaguely patronising tones. As Anna approached, the group moved off, revealing a sign pinned to a sandwich board by the entrance:

THREE PER CENT:
HOW WE FAIL VICTIMS OF SEXUAL VIOLENCE
Dr Mark Westmore
Department of Law and Social Sciences
5 pm – Bute Hall

The speaker's name meant nothing to her, though the subject matter piqued her interest. If she was still around at five o'clock, she'd see if he had anything worthwhile to say.

Gavin arrived fashionably late and fashionably attired, pinstripe trousers visible beneath his overcoat. He was obviously trying to impress someone, though Anna didn't care to guess whether that someone was her or his employers. It wasn't his clothes, though, that struck her the most. She'd been unprepared for just how much he resembled his cousin in the flesh. She wasn't sure if this was something that had occurred as he'd got older or if she'd simply never noticed it before, but now she found herself taking in those same chiselled features and high-bridged nose, and for a moment, it was like the dead had come back to life.

They headed to the Lemon Tree, a little café in one of the lanes near the university, chose a small table near the window and gave their orders to a bouncy waitress who had 'cash-strapped student' written all over her. Gavin helped Anna out of her coat and hung it on the back of her chair before taking his own seat.

'I got the phone call first thing this morning,' he said, volunteering the information apropos of nothing. 'You don't expect…well, it's not exactly the sort of news you can anticipate, is it?'

'Have you been in touch with the rest of the family?'

Gavin nodded. 'It was his dad who phoned me. They're in bits, as you can imagine. His mum's taken to her bed. She doesn't keep well at the best of times, but this has just about finished her.'

No mention of a wife, she noted, though one clearly existed. She nodded morosely. 'Tough times.'

'Yeah.'

They fell silent. Anna felt decidedly uneasy, unsure what sort of tone she should be striking. She'd have been on surer footing if he'd just burst into tears or something.

'I've got to confess,' Gavin said, once the waitress had been and gone with their order, 'yours was probably the last voice I'd expected to hear again. So you're back, then? Properly back, I mean?'

'More of a flying visit, really. I did plan on staying through Christmas, but…well, it depends.'

'On what?'

'On how things pan out, I suppose.'

'You got somewhere to stay?'

'Why, you offering to put me up?'

Gavin laughed awkwardly. 'Well, to be honest, I'd be a little concerned people might talk.'

Anna winced. It had come out sounding way more flirtatious than she'd intended. *A pox on Zoe and her innuendos.* She felt her cheeks reddening. 'Oh God, no, I didn't mean…'

Gavin smiled, flashing a row of large, regular upper teeth. 'I'm just yanking your chain! Sorry. I just meant, are you in a hotel or a guesthouse or…'

'I'm staying with Zoe,' she said, decidedly relieved, the glow in her cheeks receding. 'I don't know if you remember her. Same year as me, went on to do media at Cali…'

'Red hair? Bolshie? Pair of you pretty much joined at the hip? Yeah, I remember her.' He smiled almost wistfully. 'Bit of a character, wasn't she? It's nice you've both stayed in touch all these years.'

'So what about you?' she said, not wanting to correct him. 'Are you still in contact with any of the old gang?'

He made a dismissive gesture. 'You know how it is. When you're that age, you think the relationships you form will last forever. But then you get older, you go your separate ways…After a while, you realise just how little you actually had in common with any of these people.'

They sat in silence for a while, sipping their respective drinks. The little bell above the door tinkled. Anna glanced over her shoulder to see a couple of lanky studenty types entering, conversing earnestly. The intrusion jolted her out of her reverie, reminding her that she hadn't just come here to while away the hours drinking espressos. She turned to face Gavin with renewed purpose.

'If you don't mind me asking, how much were you actually told about the murder?'

Gavin looked up sharply, no doubt wondering about the sudden change in topic – or indeed why she was asking about this at all. 'Not much. Why?'

She chose her next words carefully. 'What I mean is, were you told anything about the circumstances?'

'I only know what his dad told me,' he said, rather tetchily, 'and I doubt the police will have been in a hurry to furnish him with all the gory details. That's what they do in these situations, isn't it? Tell you it was all over quickly and suchlike.'

'I suppose.'

'How did you come to get wind of this, anyway? I was told they hadn't made his identity public yet.'

Anna found herself with a sudden, overwhelming urge to lie. *Don't get sucked into this. Come up with some story. You don't have to make yourself a part of this narrative.* But she couldn't. Like a scab you know you ought to leave alone to heal, she was compelled to pick at it. To dig deeper. To uncover what lay beneath.

'I was the one who found him.'

He shook his head and laughed. 'Yeah, right.'

She said nothing, and in the silence that followed, the reality slowly dawned on him.

'You…you're actually serious?'

She nodded.

Gavin opened his mouth, thought better of what he was going to say and closed it again.

Anna offered an anaemic smile. 'Yeah. Kind of my reaction too.'

'But that's…God, are you alright?' It was the strongest emotional response he'd shown to anything so far. He reached across the table to touch her hand, then changed his mind and gripped the handle of his cup instead. 'How was he…I mean, what sort of state was he in?'

She thought about telling him the truth and swiftly decided against leaving him with that image. 'I'd rather not…'

'Of course, of course.' He nodded vigorously. 'I won't make you relive it. But…*how?* What did the two of you come to be doing in Kelvingrove Park in the middle of the night?'

She told him, more or less. She left out the mysterious phone call, but she included everything up to the point of actually finding him – their chance meeting, the distant scream, the mysterious figure in the hoodie, her decision to head into the park to investigate.

'I'm sorry,' she said. 'Really I am. I know the two of you were…'

'We weren't close,' said Gavin, his voice husky. 'Not really. Not lately, anyway. I mean, maybe once upon a time…But he was just a cousin. Not even much of a cousin – a second cousin, really. How close are you to your second cousins?'

'Point taken. But still, if one of them…you know…I think I'd still be…'

'I'm fine, Anna,' he said firmly. 'Don't worry about me.' He fell silent and went back to toying with his now empty cup.

'So you hadn't been in touch with him lately?'

'Not really. We spoke by phone a couple of weeks ago. He rang to see if I wanted to get together at some point during the holidays.'

'And did you?'

'Actually, I kind of blew him off. Said I was working all through Christmas. To be honest, I just couldn't be arsed making small talk with someone I barely knew anymore.' He laughed humourlessly. 'Guess that's not something I'll have to worry about now.'

She wondered whether this glibness was a coping mechanism – a way of saying *Look how unaffected I am by all this.* Society dictated that, in situations like these, men were meant to be all stoic and stiff-upper-lipped. Strong for the womenfolk. She wanted to tell him it was okay – that he didn't need to put on a front, pretending to be unaffected by what had happened. But then, perhaps he might be telling the truth. Perhaps they really *had* lost touch. And given that her contact with her own mother amounted to a handful of strained phone calls a year, she could hardly criticise someone else for being similarly estranged from a considerably more distant relation.

'And how did he seem? He didn't sound…odd, or anything? You know – worried, apprehensive? Like maybe–'

'Like maybe he thought someone was going to knife him in cold blood?' There was a sneering note in Gavin's voice that she found profoundly ugly. 'No, can't say that thought ever entered my head while we were chatting.'

She offered him a conciliatory smile. 'Sorry. Tell me about the good times instead. When did you last see him? How was he then?'

The frown left Gavin's face, replaced by a look of mild confusion. 'That's the thing – we hadn't crossed paths in years. Not since the wedding.'

'Oh?' She tried to sound surprised. 'He was married?'

Gavin smiled. 'I know what you mean. I never figured him for the settling down type either. He actually asked me to be best man, if you can believe it. Had to bullshit my way through the entire speech. Just picture it – me getting up in front of a sea of fat old aunties in their glad rags, solemnly declaring him to be a model of Catholic sobriety. I reckon they genuinely thought he was still an innocent wee laddie on his wedding night, bless 'em.'

He chuckled at the memory. Anna made herself join in, though she didn't see what was supposed to be so funny.

'And his wife…?'

'*Juliet.*' Gavin raised an eyebrow, pronouncing the name in a caricatured Morningside accent. 'She was a cut above and no mistake. Born into money – *serious* money. Not quite landed gentry, but you took one look at her and knew she'd never have to work a day in her life, even without hoodwinking some poor schmuck into providing for her. Her rellies all boycotted the wedding. Didn't think our Andrew was good enough for their *dahling* Jules. Well, either that, or she never bothered to tell them–'

'And this Juliet,' said Anna, getting in before Gavin had a chance to go off on an extended reminiscence, 'where would I find her?'

Gavin looked puzzled. 'Why?'

'Pay my respects?' It was the same line she'd used on Zoe, and it sounded even less plausible now. Surely it was time to admit, at least to herself, that this whole enterprise was a fishing expedition?

Gavin gave her a quizzical look. 'You hardly knew him.'

'I know, but I was the last one to see him alive. I kind of owe it to her.'

'She won't thank you for it. Believe me.'

Anna continued to stare at him expectantly, and at length, he relented. 'Fine. Thirty-seven Kirriemuir Road, Bearsden. You can't miss it. It's the one with two conservatories. But don't say I didn't warn you.'

She was on her feet almost before he'd finished speaking.

He looked up in surprise. 'You're going now?'

She stopped in her tracks, one arm in, one arm out of her coat. 'Yeah. I figured, while it's still daylight. Why, are you wanting to come?'

She hoped he'd say no. It would be easier to ask the questions she wanted to without him there.

He shook his head. 'Nah, an audience with the Duchess isn't exactly my idea of hijinks, 'specially not at a time like this. Besides–' he scraped back his own chair '–I've a million and one things to take care of. You know how it is, this time of year.'

'Tell me about it. The life of an academic, eh? Who'd have it?'

'Ah, you know you love it.' He smiled at her.

Remembering her manners, she smiled back. 'It was nice seeing you again. I'm sorry we didn't keep in touch…and I'm sorry about Andrew.'

He pulled on his overcoat. 'Hey, while you're in town, if you're ever in the mood for another coffee, or a meal, or…'

'We'll see. Bye, Gavin.'

He flashed a tepid wink. 'TTFN.'

10

Shame

Renfield clocked in at the gym at midday and spent the first couple of hours of his shift going about his business in his usual fashion – head down, responding to his colleagues' attempts to include him in their conversations with monosyllabic grunts.

He'd been working at the Anytime Fitness Gym for the past six months as a leisure assistant, which in effect translated as 'general dogsbody'. Unblocking the toilets, taking out the trash, being dispatched to stop loitering youths scaring off the punters. If there was a job nobody else fancied doing, Renfield was your man. It was hardly a calling, but then beggars couldn't be choosers. He'd been a lot of things in the years since he'd left school – bouncer, hospital orderly, refuse collector. This one had its downsides, but at least his co-workers were largely content to leave him to his own devices.

Mop and bucket in hand, he was on his way back from cleaning up a spillage when he noticed some of his colleagues clustered around the reception desk. There was gaunt-faced Liam with the stringy hair, and fat Kev who manned the desk. Pool attendant Johnny was there too, one hand resting on the back of Kev's chair. As Renfield approached, Kev's voice met his ears.

'Y'know, strictly speakin' youse are responsible for your ain keys. We gie you they wristbands for a reason.'

'I already *told* you, it slipped off.' A teenage girl's voice – high, lilting, plaintive. 'It's not *our* fault you make them so loose.'

As Renfield continued his approach, the girl in question came into view. Two girls, in fact, both wearing two-piece bathing suits and dripping water onto the carpet. One – the source of the voice, he assumed – was leaning on the counter, all fluttering eyelashes and pouting lips, while her friend stood a little way back, hand on hip, wearing a sheepish, simpering smile. Renfield judged them to be around sixteen or seventeen, but these days, it was so difficult to tell.

Johnny tut-tutted solemnly. 'These things've got adjustable straps. One size fits all, yeah? If a wee kiddie can keep hold of his, how come youse can't?'

The girl leaning on the desk sighed, blowing a strand of caramel hair out of her eyes. 'Aw, c'mon, mister, give us a break. You must have a master set somewhere.'

Johnny shook his head grandly. 'Oh, I dunno, that sounds highly irregular. How do we know you're who you say you are? You might be chancin' yer arm, giein' us this sob story when what you really want is for us to unlock some poor sap's locker so's you can make off wi' his credit cards.'

'Ah, c'mon, Johnny.' Liam now, stepping effortlessly into the role of Mr Reasonable. 'To be sure, they don't look like a coupla master crims to me.' He flashed the girls a conspiratorial wink. They giggled obediently.

Renfield never failed to be amazed at the brazenness of teenagers – especially the girls. These two were wearing so little, they might as well be naked, and were clearly all too aware they were being leered at by this trio of sad, lecherous older men. And yet they seemed to revel in it, batting their eyes and fanning their bosoms on cue. Was this normal to them? Did they think it was just how things were? The one doing the talking was by far the more precocious of the two, the twin triangles of her bikini top barely covering her generous breasts, a navel piercing glinting in her flat stomach.

Johnny stroked his chin, looking the pair of them up and down, taking his time. 'Well, looks can be deceivin'...'

'Look, mister.' The one with the piercing furrowed her brow as she gazed up at him. 'Our *clothes* are in that locker. You don't want us to go walking around like this all day, do you?'

'Oh, we certainly cannae have *that*,' said Johnny, while Liam and Kev, barely able to control themselves, nudged one another and tittered. 'Well, alright, girls, seein' as how it's me and I'm a trustin' sort. But mind, the slightest inkling youse've been less than honest with me and I'll be personally marchin' youse up to Mr Macdonald's office to explain yourselves. Thisaway.'

The two girls trotted after him, the damp fabric that clung to their backsides leaving little to the imagination.

'Bye, girls!' said Kev with a cheery wave. 'Come and see us again sometime.'

The departing pair glanced briefly over their shoulders before disappearing from view in another fit of giggles.

With a shake of his head, Renfield melted away.

***

An hour or so later, he headed through to the staff canteen to grab a bite. He wasn't especially hungry, but it was a long shift, and if he didn't force something down now, it would be ten at night before he got another opportunity.

The canteen was a long, low-ceilinged and badly-lit affair squirrelled away in the basement, hidden from the prying eyes of the public. Employees of various designations sat clustered in little groups around Formica tables. In the far corner, a TV chattered away, the mid-afternoon news studiously ignored by all and sundry.

As Renfield made his way over to the rickety machine that dispensed barely-edible sandwiches, he heard a shout.

'Haw, big man!'

He turned to see Kev beckoning to him. He was sitting with Liam and two other men Renfield recognised from the admin side.

'Care tae join us?'

Renfield could think of few things that he cared to do less, but all the other tables were occupied. And you got a more peaceful life if you just went along with things. He fed his coins into the machine, collected his egg and cress sandwich and headed over.

As he sat down, Kev turned to the two office drones, continuing what was clearly an ongoing story.

'Aye, so anyways, I'm sittin' there, mindin' my ain, when up come these two absolute stunners, barely a stitch on, just on the right side of legal, and they're like "Mister, we've lost our key." Well, youse can imagine what like *we* were – right?' He turned to Liam for confirmation.

'Aye, I wiz strugglin' tae keep ma eyes fae poppin' out, me. And then, they wiz stugglin' tae keep a whole lot mair than that fae poppin' out, amirite?'

As Kev and Liam high fived, Renfield, unable to help himself, let out a snort of disgust.

Liam turned to him with a scowl. 'You got a problem, Renfield? Bit too racy for you?'

'No.' Renfield kept his eyes on the table. 'There's just…no need for it, that's all.'

'Aw, hark at him!' said one of the admin guys. 'Thinks he's above it all. Nothin' wrang wi' eyein' up the local talent. And if'n they've got a problem wi' it – well, they shouldnae be dressin' that way in the first place, should they?'

'Aye, lighten the fuck up, Renfield,' said Liam. 'You're nae better'n us, pal, so don't sit there sneerin' at us. Think I didnae see ye skulkin' back there wi' yer bucket 'n' spade?'

A large, stupid smile spread across Kev's large, stupid features. 'Aye, aye, he was 'n' aw. Couldnae keep his eyes tae hisself, could ye, big man?' He flashed a conspiratorial wink.

'Shut it,' said Renfield.

But the others were in full flow now, each egging the other on to greater heights of vulgarity.

'Haw, look! He's goin' red.'

'Aye, so he is. Here, know what I'm thinkin', Kev? I'm thinkin' there he is, lurkin' there wi' a massive stawner, slippin' a crafty hand into they baggy togs o' his–'

Renfield swung around to face them, ready to give them both barrels. But the words never reached his mouth. His eyes fell on the TV, visible beyond the heads of the two jokers. The newsreader occupied one half of the screen. The other was given over to a blown-up picture of a face out of the past – a chiselled face, with a high-bridged nose. The fabric of his pricey suit created a shimmering pattern on the oversaturated screen.

Renfield's chair hit the floor as he lurched to his feet. He moved towards the TV, cutting a swathe through those in his path. He had to get closer, to hear what the newsreader was saying.

But then, the text at the bottom of the screen was pretty unequivocal:

KELVINGROVE PARK MURDER

'...described as a brutal and unprovoked attack. Police are urging anyone who was in the area in the early hours of the morning to come forward with any information.' Pause. 'Sport now, and Aberdeen beat–'

The broadcast continued, but Renfield had heard all that was of interest to him. He stood facing the screen, staring at the newsreader, who, now he'd dispensed with the serious news and moved onto the fluff, had replaced his expression of grave solemnity with the sort of grin that invited a punch.

Someone was calling Renfield's name. He turned to see his four fellow diners gawping at him. Liam's lips were moving. He was saying something to him. Something about *a current affairs devotee* and *sharin' what's so good wi' the rest of us*. Renfield didn't bother trying to work out what he was jabbering on about. It wasn't important. None of it was. This place, these people – none of it mattered.

He began to move, pace quickening as he made for the exit.

'Renfield!'

'Where you goin', man?'

'Fuck's the matter wi' him?'

He broke into a run, a dozen pairs of eyes burning into his back as he fled down the corridor, their mocking laughter ringing in his ears. He didn't care. He was consumed by one thought and one thought only.

Rosco.

He had to see Rosco.

Had to warn him what was coming their way.

11

Juliet

Anna stood at the foot of the driveway, gazing up at the sprawling detached villa beyond a generous, well-tended garden. Bearsden was an affluent suburb on the outskirts of the city and home to some of the largest and priciest houses in Greater Glasgow. This one, a white Tudor-style affair, was massive even by local standards. Even the toffs must think the owners were toffs.

She approached the house, the crunching of her shoes on gravel unbearably loud in the still air. A small bolt-on vestibule at the front of the building served as a sort of gatehouse. She stepped inside and rang the bell. A melodic chime echoed in the hallway beyond. After a few moments, she saw movement in the form of a shimmering haze behind the frosted glass door.

The woman who opened it was young, in her early twenties at most, blonde and puffy-lipped. She wore a pleated skirt, thigh-high boots and a knit polo-neck – one of those figure-hugging affairs that makes your boobs look massive. Her hooded eyes regarded Anna suspiciously as she hung on the door.

'Hello,' Anna began, 'is–'

'Who is it?' a sharp voice called from somewhere in the house.

'It's some woman,' the girl called back, eyes not leaving Anna.

'What does she want?'

Anna leaned past the maid or au pair or whatever she was. 'Mrs Foley? Can I speak to you? It's…it's about your husband.'

Initially, there was no response. The girl closed the door to little more than a crack, blocking Anna's view of the cavernous interior. She heard slow, deliberate footsteps in the hallway. 'It's alright, Kelly-Marie,' said the sharp voice. 'I'll handle this.'

The door opened fully to reveal a woman in her early thirties, with sharp cheekbones and fine, mousy hair. She wore a silk dressing gown, which she clutched about herself defensively, as if she expected a gust of wind to blow it open at any minute. She was extremely thin, which only made the baby bump she sported all the more conspicuous.

'Mrs Foley?'

The question was unnecessary. No one could mistake this woman, with her air of regal superiority, for anyone other than the lady of the house.

'Do I know you?' Juliet's voice was sharp, cut-glass – and yes, had a vague hint of Morningside about it.

'We haven't met, no. My name's Anna Scavolini. I'm–'

Juliet sighed with weary resignation, eyes raised towards the ceiling. 'Let's just get this over with, shall we?' She turned to Kelly-Marie, who was standing in the shadow of the door, eyes on the floor. 'You'd better make some tea, I suppose. You *can* make tea, can't you?'

Kelly-Marie departed, head still low.

As Anna stepped over the threshold, she thought she caught a whiff of something sweet, like sherry. She chanced a glance at her host. Was it her imagination or was Juliet swaying slightly, as if her centre of gravity wasn't quite where she'd expected to find it?

She wasn't, was she? Surely not in her condition?

Juliet led Anna to an airy living room overlooking the expansive back garden, then flopped down on a sofa without offering her guest a seat. Taking the initiative, Anna perched gingerly on a high-backed scallop chair. The two women regarded each other across the glass-topped table between them, the antipathy coming from Juliet's side so strongly, Anna could practically smell it.

In the resentful silence that ensued, she sized up the room. The place was ornate and lavishly decorated to a fault but, in contrast to Zoe and Victor's modest-but-homely semi, about as welcoming as a showroom house. She found it hard to imagine anyone actually living here, let alone kicking off their shoes for an evening in front of the telly. There were no photographs of the family – just a grim-looking oil painting above the fireplace showing a bucolic landscape circa the 1800s, with a farmer guiding his ox-drawn plough across a field.

'Oh, do you like it?' Juliet sounded surprised. 'It's a Hamish Stanley. An original. Acquired in an auction last year. The cost would have bankrupted *most* people.' She gave a small, self-satisfied laugh.

Anna managed to make herself smile. 'It's very nice.'

'No it's not. It's ghastly. *He* chose it. But then, he always did have questionable taste.'

There was an insult buried in there somewhere, but Anna had neither the patience nor the inclination to unpick it.

'I'm sorry to just show up like this. You know, while you're still grieving.'

Juliet gave a thin, patient smile. 'Of course you are, my dear. Everybody's sorry. You should have seen it earlier. Queue a mile long at the door. All the great unwashed lining up to tell me what a thoroughly *marvellous* fellow my late husband was. How his passing left a cataclysmic void in the natural order.' Her features twisted into a scowl. 'Pissants.'

Anna began to wonder whether Juliet was quite sane.

'Your husband, I…he…'

Juliet cocked her head to one side, fixing Anna with a sidelong look that could have curdled milk. 'You were one of his *friends*.'

The way she stressed 'friends' left no doubt as to what she was implying.

'Oh, don't worry. I knew about them all. The Maggies, the Donnas, the Alexandras, the Kirsteens – the good-time girls with their soft curves and easy smiles. But in the end, he always came back, like a loyal dog…or a bad penny. And I always forgave him his trespasses.'

'I–'

Before Anna could get a word in edgeways, however, Juliet was on her feet, neck craned towards the door. 'Are you making us tea,

Kelly-Marie, or a sodding seven-course dinner?' She turned back to Anna with a roll of her eyes, settling on the sofa once more. 'I suppose it happened at a party.'

'I'm sorry?'

'Andrew met most of his *friends* at parties – several of whom have already made contact to discuss the capital to which they mistakenly believe they're entitled.'

'Mrs Foley, your husband and I weren't–'

'Oh, Juliet is fine.' She waved her hand dismissively. 'After all, from a certain perspective, you're practically family. Though I'm afraid you've left it rather late in the day, my dear. If it was first come first served, you'd be fresh out of luck. And, if you'll permit so bold an observation, you're not his usual type.'

'And what type is that?'

'Blonde. Blue-eyed. Narrow waists and big tits. Cheap, tawdry little sluts. Oh, speak of the devil.'

Anna looked up as Kelly-Marie arrived, bearing a tray loaded with china crockery and an elaborate-looking French press. Juliet watched disdainfully as she placed it on the table and poured tea into two matching china cups.

'Yes, I'm afraid he wasn't a subtle man, my husband. Tended to go for women of a more meretricious variety.' Juliet glanced up at Kelly-Marie. 'You know that word – meretricious? Means tacky and worthless, like a piece of cheap tat you find in a gift shop.'

Kelly-Marie looked at Juliet as if she'd just been slapped – which, metaphorically speaking, probably wasn't far wrong. 'Can I go now?' she said stiffly.

Juliet sighed loudly. 'You can jump in the nearest bog for all I care. Yes, go. Go for a walk or a smoke, or whatever it is you people do. Go on, shoo!'

For a moment, Kelly-Marie hesitated, a pained look on her face, torn between obeying her mistress and something else – something Anna couldn't quite place. Then the moment passed, and she scuttled out of the room, casting a final apprehensive look over her shoulder as she went.

Juliet shook her head. 'He chose *her* too, incidentally. Brought her into the house so I'd have someone to keep me company while he was away on his long trips, or so he claimed. In reality, we both know what she was selected for.'

She picked up one of the cups and sipped from it, her puckered lips scarcely touching the china. Anna took some to be polite, though she was increasingly coming to wonder why she should bother with any pretence of civility amid such an atmosphere of open contempt. Mind you, Providence appeared to be on her side. She'd come here hoping for an insight into married life with the Foleys, and she was getting it, in spades.

Juliet cast a baleful eye in her direction. 'You don't say much, do you? What's the matter? Cat got your tongue?'

Anna said nothing. She couldn't decide whether her feelings towards Juliet amounted to disgust or pity. Both seemed equally valid at present.

'So then, when did you and he become acquainted? Inquiring minds want to know.'

'We were at school together.'

'As far back as that? I'm impressed. His liaisons didn't normally last more than a week or two.'

'We didn't exactly keep in touch.'

'Then I can't imagine what it is you think you can lay claim to. I'm afraid a sticky fumble in the back seat of daddy's car at sixteen doesn't entitle you to so much as a brass penny.'

'I wasn't fucking him, okay?'

She wouldn't normally have used language like that in front of a complete stranger, but she'd reached the end of her tether with Juliet's steady outpouring of passive-aggressive bile, and calling a spade a spade seemed the most expedient way of putting an end to all this fake civility.

'Then why are you sitting in my living room, drinking my tea?' A brief pause, then, more hesitantly, 'Why *did* you come here?'

She was becoming increasingly agitated, Anna noticed – drumming her fingers on the arm of the sofa, her brows knitting together as she pondered something.

'They told me it was a woman who found him. A foreign name. Anne something, I think, or was it Anna? Anna…'

'Scavolini,' said Anna quietly.

Juliet's eyes met Anna's. Her expression morphed into one of mortification as realisation hit home.

'Christ, what you must think of us.'

Before Anna had a chance to say what she was thinking, Juliet was on her feet, smoothing down her dressing gown, rearranging the cushions on the sofa.

'You've caught me at a bad time, I'm afraid. Normally, I'm washed and dressed by this time of day. Last night's news took the wind out of me, you understand.' She was talking quickly, *very* quickly. 'Plus I've had a string of well-wishers on the telephone since first light, and there are so many things that need taken care of, and–' She came to an abrupt halt and turned to face Anna, clutching a cushion against her swollen stomach. 'I suppose I should be thanking you, really.'

It clearly took her considerable effort to say it.

'I'm not sure I've done anything to warrant it.'

'Well, what does one normally say in these situations, then? Anyway, you…oh, I don't know, you gave him succour in his final moments on earth, or however it goes.'

The guilt hit Anna right between the shoulder-blades. A part of her wanted to lie, to leave Juliet with the impression of it having been a beautiful moment, with her cradling Andrew in her arms and whispering reassurances to him as he slipped away peacefully. But she suspected her host would see straight through it. Now was the time for the direct approach.

'Juliet, before Andrew was killed, we met in a nightclub in the West End. He didn't stay long, but I happened to overhear him on the phone to someone. I, er, I think he was talking to a lover.'

Juliet's expression remained impassive. 'What did he say?'

'It was hard to make much of it out. A bunch of stuff about him wanting to make it work between them, how he was going to find a way for them to be together.' She hesitated, wondering if she'd already divulged too much. 'I'm telling you because I think there's a good chance this woman, whoever she is, was the last person to speak to him. I wondered if you had any idea who she might be.'

Slowly, deliberately, Juliet lowered herself back onto the sofa. 'They were all more or less interchangeable, so no, I'm afraid I have no idea who his flavour of the month happened to be. But I'm not convinced it makes much difference whether she was a Susan or a Betsy-May or a bloody Cassiopeia.' A sudden thought. 'You haven't told Laurel and Hardy, have you?'

'Who?'

'Oh, you must have met them. That great clot Norton and that supercilious prat Murray.'

Anna gave a silent 'O' of understanding.

Juliet grimaced. She was back on surer footing now, hiding behind that familiar cloak of sarcasm. 'Ghastly, aren't they? Glasgow's finest, or so I'm told. I'm not sure which of them is worse. So have you?'

Anna shook her head.

'I'd be grateful if it were to remain that way. I know how the tabloids work. They do so love their dead saints. Right now, as they prepare to go to press, they'll be dedicating whole paragraphs to what a tragic state of affairs this is, but the slightest whiff of sexual impropriety and they'll no doubt conclude he had it coming.'

Anna nodded. The desire for privacy, for the whole world not to know your business, was something she understood. She knew her next question was going to be the most delicate of all, but after coming this far, after getting far more out of Juliet than she'd ever expected, she knew she'd only regret it if she didn't ask.

'I know how this is going to sound, but are you aware of anyone with a potential motive for wanting to, er, to...'

'To what, dear? Don't let's be coy. You're asking if I can think of anyone who would have wanted to do him in.'

Anna gave a small nod that was somewhere between sheepish and apologetic. 'I thought, perhaps, an aggrieved lover, or–'

Juliet laughed and shook her head. 'Well, no one could ever accuse you of possessing an overabundance of tact.' The smile faded from her lips. 'Perhaps you've misunderstood me. My husband's faults were legion, but he was nonetheless my husband. What you're suggesting is not only absurd, it's incendiary.'

Too late, Anna realised Juliet thought she was accusing *her* of Andrew's murder. It had come out all wrong. She opened her mouth, ready to protest, but it was too late. Juliet was on her feet now, tilted slightly to one side as if correcting a non-existent imbalance.

'I'd like you to leave now. I don't feel much like entertaining anymore.'

There seemed little point in protesting. Anna had well and truly put her foot in it, and in any event, she sensed she had as much chance of penetrating Juliet's tin-plate exterior as of getting a straight answer from a New Labour spin doctor. She allowed herself to be escorted to the door, Juliet watching her every step of the way, as if she didn't trust her not to make off with the family silver. In the vestibule, Anna retrieved her coat from the stand.

'There's to be a memorial service tomorrow,' Juliet suddenly announced. 'His parents arranged it. They won't release the body yet, so…' She trailed off. She was trying very hard not to look Anna in the eye.

'I hope it goes well.'

'None of my lot will be there. Daddy never approved of my marrying a Pape.' Juliet sniffed ruefully. 'Nothing quite beats watching grown men fighting over who's got the biggest Jesus, eh?'

Anna gave a flicker of a smile. From an early age, she'd carved a different path from that of her parents, consciously rejecting their values, their politics and, perhaps most scandalously of all, their Judaism. Once it had become clear her newfound atheism wasn't 'a phase', religion became a strictly taboo topic in the Scavolini household.

As she turned to go, Juliet reached out and grabbed her wrist, holding her in a claw-like grip. Anna swung around and tried to pull away, thinking for one brief, irrational moment that Juliet was going to attack her.

'Ten o'clock,' she said, looking at Anna with intense eyes. 'St Lucian's on Claremont Road.'

For a moment, Juliet looked both incredibly helpless and incredibly lonely – as desperate for human contact as the next person. For reasons Anna couldn't pinpoint, the thought that such vulnerability could exist behind that hard shell unnerved her beyond measure.

'I'll see what I can do,' she said, avoiding Juliet's eye and knowing full well that there was no way on earth she was going to do any such thing. She extracted herself from Juliet's grip and hurried out into the encroaching twilight.

***

At the end of the driveway, she found Kelly-Marie leaning against the gatepost, nursing a cigarette. She was wearing a duffel coat with the hood up and put Anna in mind of a pupil sneaking an illicit fag behind the school bike sheds.

'You survived, then? Never mind – her bark's worse than her bite.'

'You shouldn't let her treat you like that.'

It sounded hopelessly feeble, but she felt compelled to say *something* about the behaviour she'd witnessed back at the house.

Kelly-Marie's features contorted into an ugly sneer. 'Didn't notice you leaping to my defence. But then, if I had a quid for every stiff-neck who looked the other way...' She raised her cigarette to her lips and took a long, hard draw.

'You should get out of there.'

The words were out of Anna's mouth before she was even conscious of uttering them. She shut her mouth, embarrassed, as Kelly-Marie looked up sharply.

'You mean do a runner?' She seemed to regard the very idea as outrageous. 'I can't just leave her.'

'Why not? She's not going to show you any gratitude for sticking around.'

Kelly-Marie lowered her cigarette and gave Anna a long, hard stare. 'She's *vulnerable*.'

'You mean the drinking?'

The girl shut her mouth and stared at Anna obstinately. Without blinking, she lifted her cigarette to her lips and took a defiant drag.

Seeing that she wasn't going to get any further with her, Anna turned to go. As she stepped out into the street, she heard Kelly-Marie's voice behind her.

'It was me.'

Anna turned to face her. 'Excuse me?'

'I heard you earlier, talking to her ladyship. Asking about who he was ringing the other night, saying he wanted to find a way to be together. Well, it was me.'

Anna said nothing. She tried to picture the dynamic between them – Andrew, Juliet, Kelly-Marie. What must it be like, all three of them living together under the same roof?

'He was forever saying stuff like that,' the girl went on. 'How we were meant to be together, how he was going to get a divorce and the pair of us were going to run off together to Barcelona or Barbados or wherever.' She gave a small, sad smile. 'Course, I never really believed it…but it's nice to dream, right?'

'I guess,' Anna said, thinking Kelly-Marie needed to get herself a fresh set of aspirations.

'You knew him from before, right?'

'I knew him. Why?'

Kelly-Marie hesitated for a moment, a look of uncertainty in her eyes. Then, moving closer to Anna, she leaned in, dropping her voice to a whisper. 'When we were…y'know, doing it…he liked to call me "Jenny". Any idea what that was all about?'

'I haven't a clue,' Anna managed to say.

She wondered how many more revelations were going to emerge from the twisting annals of this family. One thing was for sure – she had no desire to find out. No desire to dig any further into this poisonous household. Right now, she wanted to turn around, walk away and never come back, and never hear the name 'Andrew Foley' again as long as she lived. She turned on her heels and hurried off into the gloom.

Had she had the presence of mind to take one last look back at the house, she might have seen Juliet watching her from the kitchen window. She stared out, still for a moment, then picked up the phone and began to dial.

12

Three Per Cent

The taxi dropped Anna off at the university a little after five-thirty. She bolted across the concourse and into the main building, scrambled up the stone staircase and stepped out into the open-air expanse of the West Quadrangle. The bell-tower loomed above her, lit up in golden-red against the night sky.

She hurried through the cloisters, footsteps on the stone floor echoing around the high arches. As she climbed the stairs leading to the stately Bute Hall, she could hear a man's voice intoning above her – his words, distorted by an echo, unintelligible. She reached the top of the stairs and heaved open the heavy oak-panelled door, wincing as the hinges groaned in protestation.

She needn't have worried – the audience inside was too engrossed to even notice. The backs of two hundred heads greeted her, the rows of seats divided by a narrow aisle. At the front, dwarfed by his ecclesiastical surroundings, was Dr Westmore. He stood in the middle of a podium, foregoing either notes or the lectern parked off to one side.

He was a slight man, no more than five foot six, in his early thirties and dressed down for the occasion, his pullover and plimsolls at odds with the grandeur of the venue. His sole concession to academic cliché was a pair of wire-rimmed half-glasses perched precariously on the end of his beak-like nose.

'We've discussed some of the common myths relating to sexual violence,' he said, 'and I suspect I have a fair idea what most of you are thinking. *Oh, but we're not like that. Educated, sophisticated people like us couldn't possibly hold such backwards views.* And perhaps you're right. Perhaps the two hundred or so people in this room do indeed buck the trend. Perhaps you're all uniquely enlightened.'

His accent was flat and neutral, belonging neither to one place nor another. There was the merest hint of Glaswegian in there, as well as something else Anna couldn't place. Unable to find an empty seat, she slipped into the shadows beneath the rear balcony and remained standing.

'But I'd hazard a guess that's not the case. Odds are that at least a minority of you – and indeed most likely more than that – hold precisely these views, however subconsciously. And in any event, to assume it's all okay because you personally know better constitutes a profoundly dangerous state of complacency. It's for that reason that I now want to show you just how pervasive these attitudes actually are.

'At the beginning of this talk, I promised a dramatic reading, for which I shall be calling on the services of a volunteer who kindly offered to provide me with some assistance. Carol?'

A narrow-shouldered woman rose from her seat in the front row and joined Westmore on the platform. She wore a pair of small thick-rimmed glasses and had her hair in a messy blonde bob that had nonetheless probably required considerable effort to achieve that particular look. Anna judged her to be just on the wrong side of thirty – perhaps an adult learner or a postgrad whose PhD had run on longer than expected. She had a feeling she'd seen her before, but she couldn't think where.

Westmore stooped to pick up a couple of sheaves of A4 from the podium floor. Keeping one for himself, he handed the other to Carol, who stepped behind the hitherto unused lectern – the veritable witness in the dock.

'The setting is the High Court of Justiciary in Glasgow. I know this doesn't look much like a courtroom, but I'm relying on you to use your imaginations. It's a warm summer's day – again, imagination – and you, the jury, have been selected to try a man accused of rape. His advocate, Mr Cyril Meacher QC – that's me – has called his client's alleged victim to the stand.' He gestured to Carol. 'She has a name, of course, but in the interests of protecting the innocent, we'll refer to her only as "Ms Smith".'

For a moment, he was silent, his head bowed as if in prayer. The whole room was deathly still. 'Tell me, Ms Smith,' he said finally, turning to face the lectern, 'what was your relationship with my client?'

The change in his voice was palpable. Where previously his tone had been unassuming, almost conversational, it now became high-handed and arrogant, like that of a man utterly convinced of his own moral and intellectual superiority. It took Anna a moment to realise this was all part of the performance. She focused on Carol, who was doing a creditable 'bunny in headlights' impression.

'I…what do you mean?'

Westmore harrumphed impatiently. 'It's a straightforward enough question, Ms Smith. What was your relationship?'

Carol's eyes darted briefly to the script. 'We…we went out once or twice.'

'Once or twice? Be specific, please, Ms Smith.'

Carol lifted her head, meeting Westmore's eyes defiantly. 'Alright, then. Twice.'

'Twice.' Westmore rolled the word around in his mouth, as if sampling its taste. 'You went out together twice. Three times in total, if we include the night of the incident which you allege took place. And what did you make of him – my client – during your first encounter?'

'What did I…?'

'Yes. What were your overall impressions of him? Any shared hobbies or interests? Did he, in the parlance of the common man, give good craic? He must have had *some* redeeming qualities, otherwise I fail to see why you would consent to seeing him again on not one but two subsequent occasions.'

'I…I thought he was a good laugh,' Carol muttered.

'So you liked him.' Westmore shrugged as if to suggest it was okay, that nobody was going to judge her for that. 'And, by the same token, he presumably liked you, wouldn't you say?'

'I don't know.'

'Oh, I imagine he must have. Otherwise, he wouldn't have accepted the invitation back to your flat after the second date, would he?' He looked up from the page, eyes locking onto hers. 'That *is* what happened, isn't it, Ms Smith?'

'Yes.' Her reply was barely audible.

A broad, satisfied smile spread across Westmore's features. 'And what happened next, after you got there?'

'We…we had coffee. We talked some more. Listened to music. We…'

'You took him into your bedroom and had sexual intercourse with him, did you not?'

The witness shut her eyes in resignation and nodded.

Westmore turned to the motley array of students, university staff and members of the public seated before him. His posture became less aggressive, his tone reverting to its earlier non-confrontational mode. 'At this point, an objection is raised by the advocate representing the prosecution, arguing that the witness's previous sexual history with the accused has no bearing on the case. This is upheld by the judge.'

He turned back to Carol, a faux-conciliatory look on his face as he shifted back into character. 'I apologise. This line of questioning is sometimes a little…shall we say, indelicate? It can be embarrassing, having your affairs dragged into the public eye.'

'I'm not embarrassed,' said the woman quietly.

'No.' Westmore stroked his bristly chin with the back of his thumb. 'No, I suppose not. Would it be fair to say, Ms Smith, that you are what's known in the trade as a good time girl?'

'Sorry?'

'Do you enjoy the company of men, Ms Smith?' He enunciated each word carefully, as if addressing someone hard of hearing or whose first language wasn't English.

'I…'

'The evidence would suggest you do, given how little time you wasted in seducing my client.' Westmore shook his head and gave a whistle of admiration. 'Second date, eh? He probably couldn't believe his luck.'

And so it went on. Another objection was raised, for all the good it did. Westmore, or rather Meacher, was on a roll now, subjecting the witness to a succession of obsessively detailed questions as to the specifics of her sexual relations with the accused, including a digression into what sort of underwear she'd been wearing on the night of the assault. None of this was new or particularly surprising to Anna. She'd read enough courtroom transcripts, and spoken to enough victims, to be all too familiar with this line of questioning.

At length, Westmore called a halt to the proceedings. 'I fancy,' he told the audience, 'that you've seen enough to understand the point I'm trying to make. A round of applause for my wonderful assistant Carol, in the role of Ms Smith.'

The applause was scattered and muted, the audience clearly torn between acknowledging Carol's contribution and demonstrating their disdain for what they'd just witnessed. In the awkward silence that followed, Carol stepped down from the podium and resumed her seat.

Westmore faced the audience, hands clasped behind his back. 'You can see what's going on, of course. The references to the previous consensual sexual encounters, to her choice of underwear...The implied air quotes around 'incident' are a particularly effective touch. In short, in the mind of the esteemed Cyril Meacher QC, if a woman wears a thong and enjoys an active sex life, her consent can be taken as a given.

'Now, I know what you're thinking – the advocate is a creep of the first order, and no sane person would give any credence to this crude, cynical attempt at character assassination.' He looked up, as if checking to see if everyone was still with him. They were. 'And yet that's just what happened. Of a jury of seven women and eight men, only three believed the accused was guilty. In spite of the wealth of evidence against him, he walked free.'

An intake of breath here, a mutter of consternation there. Anna sensed a ripple of genteel outrage spreading through the hall.

Westmore waited until the hubbub died down before continuing. 'I wish it were possible to label this outcome a fluke, to blame it on the perfect storm of an atypically unscrupulous defence and an atypically unenlightened jury. Regrettably, however, scenarios like the one you've just witnessed are the norm, not the exception.

'The fundamental principle of trial by jury is that the accused is judged by a representative cross-section of society. What, then, does the prevalence of acquittals in cases like these tell us about that society? It tells us that, even when presented with incontrovertible evidence to the contrary, a majority of the population – men *and* women – still choose to believe the victim is lying.

'Is it any surprise, therefore, that so few victims report their attackers? Who, in their right mind, would submit themselves to such a debasing ordeal, particularly when they know all too well that the chances of a successful conviction are remote?' He scanned the faces before him, and it seemed to Anna that his eyes lingered on her for longer than anyone else in the room.

'I promised earlier that I wouldn't attempt to confound you with statistics, but these are simply too staggering to pass up. Even if you take nothing else away from this lecture, I ask that you remember these numbers, because they are a millstone hanging around the neck of this supposedly civilised society to which we all belong.

'In this country, Scotland, during the period of 2006 to 2007, nine hundred and twenty-two sexual assaults were reported to the police. Of these, a mere sixty-five proceeded to trial. Of the sixty-five victims who had their day in court, twenty-seven saw their attacker sent down. Twenty-seven out of nine hundred and twenty-two. Would anyone care to take a stab at telling me what proportion of those assaults originally reported resulted in a conviction?'

Dead silence. If anyone had worked it out, they weren't broadcasting it.

Westmore was silent for a moment, and once again Anna, who had already done the calculation in her head, felt his eyes lingering on her face.

'I'll tell you. It's *less than three per cent*. The lowest rate of conviction for a quarter of a century.

'Which brings us to the nub of this paper, and why I subtitled it "How we fail victims of sexual violence". Because it's not merely the judicial system that fails these women. It's us. All of us. The rate of conviction for sexual assault is, by a significant margin, the lowest among all offences against the person, borne out of society's adherence to the same pernicious myths about rape and its victims that have blighted us since time immemorial. And until we eliminate those prejudices, we will continue to be the country with the lowest rate of conviction for rape in Europe – a miserable three per cent.'

He gave the slightest of bows and stepped back.

This time, the applause into which the entire room erupted was anything but half-hearted. Chairs were scraped back as the audience got to its collective feet to give Westmore a standing ovation. As she joined in, Anna was dimly aware of a blur of blonde hair sweeping past her as a solitary figure beat a hasty exit.

It wasn't until afterwards that she realised it had been Carol.

***

The lecture was followed by a Q&A session, during which Westmore answered every question put to him eloquently and with good grace. Anna had a few of her own that she would have liked to pose, but given the seemingly never-ending sea of raised hands, she opted instead to keep a low profile and give those who'd actually turned up for the whole thing a shot. She stuck around afterwards for the wine reception and found herself wandering through the throng, glass in hand, feeling that familiar sense of alienation she always experienced in public gatherings like these.

Everyone seemed to have broken off into their own little cliques, leaving no room for an outsider like herself.

She was surveying the buffet table when she felt a hand on her back.

'Either I made a bigger impression on you than I thought, or you just can't keep away from this place.'

She turned to find Gavin standing next to her, grinning broadly.

'I could say the same of you. I wouldn't've pegged this sort of thing as your cup of tea.'

'It's not – not really, anyway. More like a favour to a friend. The man of the hour, in fact.' Gavin affected a mock-whisper. 'He was worried he wouldn't be able to draw a big enough crowd.'

Anna looked at the teeming masses. 'No danger of that.'

'I'll let you in on a secret. I had to bribe most of them.' He took a grape from the fruit bowl and popped it in his mouth.

Anna eyed him curiously, trying to figure out what his game was. He'd seemed unusually resigned about the small matter of his cousin's death earlier, but now he was like a different person again. Mischievous and decidedly silly, like a schoolboy trying overly hard to impress a pretty girl. Grief did strange things to people, she knew, but there had to be more to it than that. He seemed almost manic.

'Gavin,' she said cautiously, 'are you drunk?'

'Mm. I heartily recommended it. Cures a multitude of ailments.' He deftly grabbed a flute of wine from a passing tray. 'You manage to get hold of Juliet?'

'I did, but I don't think she liked me very much.'

'Told you.' Gavin swallowed a mouthful, knocking it back like water. 'Tends not to hold others in high regard, does our Jules. What did you talk about?'

'Nothing much.' Anna had no desire to dwell on Juliet, Andrew or their dysfunctional marriage for any longer than necessary. 'So do you know Dr Westmore well?'

Gavin scoffed. 'His *students* call him Dr Westmore. Yeah, me and Mark are like this.' He curled one forefinger around the other in imitation of links in a chain. 'First bumped shoulders as undergrads in the early noughties. Course, he had to show me up by going on to do the PhD while I contented myself with a master's – but don't let's hold that against him. We share an office these days, now they've merged Law and Social Sciences. Fancy a one-on-one? Contrary to outward appearances, he's actually quite personable.'

Anna, still acutely conscious of her late arrival, opened her mouth to object, but Gavin paid no heed. He stood on tiptoe to scan the crowd. Spotting the man in question, he raised a hand and hailed him. Westmore, speaking to a couple of distinguished-looking older men at the other end of the hall, turned and gave a smile and nod of recognition. He excused himself and made his way over.

'What's this, Price? You boring the ears off this poor woman with your far-fetched flights of fancy?'

'You're one to talk, Marky-boy. Not so very long ago, you were sending an entire room to sleep with yours.'

'So *that's* where the snoring in the back row was coming from.'

They both laughed. Anna watched in bemusement, with the distinct impression that she'd just been party to a joke which had gone over her head.

Mark turned to her, acknowledging her with a nod and a smile. 'Hello.'

'Anna's an old friend from school,' Gavin explained. 'Came all the way from sunny Rome to hear you pontificate, more fool her.'

Anna considered setting him straight, but decided against it.

Gavin laid a hand on each of their shoulders. 'I'll leave you kids to get acquainted.' And then, before Anna could object, he was off, disappearing into the crowd.

She turned to Mark and rolled her eyes. 'He always like this?'

'You should see him when he hasn't had his medication.'

She caught his eye, saw the twinkle in it and found herself smiling. Normally jokes like this at the expense of mental health set her teeth on edge, but she couldn't help herself. He seemed charming and affable, with the sort of perpetual air of self-deprecation she tended to find attractive in a man, and unlike Gavin, she didn't get the sense that he was trying too hard.

'Listen,' she said, 'I didn't ask him to drag you over here. I'm sure there are a million and one people who want to bend your ear.'

'Nonsense. Between you and me, I was glad of an excuse to escape. I noticed you earlier, actually – standing over there, all on your lonesome. Reckoned you could do with some company.'

Anna gazed into her empty glass, avoiding his eye. 'Hadn't realised I'd made myself look *that* conspicuous.'

'Of course, whenever I spend an inordinate amount of time admiring the buffet spread at one of these things, it's because the conversation leaves something to be desired.'

'Oh no!' she insisted, horrified. 'I was just–'

A sly smile spread across Westmore's lips. 'I'm kidding. Relax. Though I wouldn't blame you. Frightful bores, this lot. Mark Westmore, by the way.'

She accepted his handshake. 'I know. I mean – Anna Scavolini.'

'A pleasure. I…' He frowned. 'Wait a sec. Scavolini? I think I might've come across something of yours. That paper on the pathologising of female offenders in legal discourse?'

'You've read it?' She couldn't help but sound surprised. It had been her first published work, derived from her undergraduate research and printed in a little-known Italian journal.

'Well, in translation, admittedly. Astute, persuasive and refreshingly free of waffle. I must confess, though, I'd never've pegged you as a Weegie.'

Anna smiled again. 'Yeah, they still haven't found an acceptable way of rendering the glottal stop in the written word.'

'Mm. A tricky conundrum. So tell me, what's a Glaswegian expat doing back in the mother country?'

'Well–'

But before she could get round to figuring out how she was going to answer that question, a portly middle-aged man strode over and clapped his arm across Mark's shoulders. 'So this is where you've been skulking!' he boomed genially, ignoring Anna completely. 'Listen, old son, there's a chap from Trinity you absolutely must have words with.'

'I'm having words with someone *now*,' said Mark sharply.

The man gave Mark a wounded look. 'Please yourself,' he sniffed, and headed off, mustering all the grace of a deflated soufflé.

Mark turned to Anna and winced. 'My head of department. I should probably humour him. This whole thing wouldn't have happened without some serious string-pulling on his part. Plus, he's buying me dinner.'

Anna made an understanding face. 'Oh, well, if he's buying you *dinner*…'

'The curse of being made to jump through continuous hoops to secure funding. I'm sure you can sympathise. Well, Anna Scavolini, it was fleeting but most agreeable. I hope we run into each other again.'

She watched until he was swallowed up by the crowd, then turned back to the buffet table, once again feeling decidedly like an outcast. In the brief time they'd spent together, Mark had succeeded in putting her at her ease, but now he was gone, and Gavin – the only other person she knew here – had disappeared too, leaving her once again feeling awkward and self-conscious. She could make an effort and inveigle herself into one of the various little groups dotted throughout the hall, but that sort of networking was a skill she'd never quite perfected, much less enjoyed.

She'd just decided she was going to give it another five minutes tops, then slip out the back way, when she felt a hand on her shoulder. She turned to find Mark facing her, a wicked glint in his eye.

'I've been thinking…I've had just about all I can stand of this lot, and the prospect of spending the rest of the evening schmoozing with the doyens of the faculty over poppadoms and spiced onions doesn't exactly fill me with joy either. How would you feel about skipping dinner with me?'

As a rule, Anna was as far from impulsive as it was possible to get. She liked her routines, and she weighed up every decision carefully, assessing the positives and negatives before committing to any course of action. And she certainly wasn't in the habit of running off with men she'd only just met.

But tonight was different. Perhaps it was because she was still smarting from her treatment earlier by Norton and felt like doing something seditious. Or, more likely, because the idea of spending more time in the company of this intriguing, amusing and – *admit it, Anna* – rakishly handsome man held considerable appeal. For whatever reason, his suggestion stirred some latent rebellious streak within her – and that very fact surprised her as much as it thrilled her.

She only hesitated for a moment before accepting.

13

A Good Life

Shortly after eight pm, a Renault Scénic pulled into the driveway of a modest semi in one of the more desirable suburbs of the Southside. Across the street, Renfield watched as the man he knew as Rosco got out of the driver's seat and thrust open the sliding rear door. Two small girls in matching outfits hopped out and ran to the other side of the car where their mother, a stocky woman with wavy hair, scooped one into her arms and took the other by the hand.

Renfield's eyes remained on Rosco as he locked the car and retrieved his house keys. He was bigger than Renfield remembered – a sedentary lifestyle and a lack of wanting for anything had filled him out, making him look older than his twenty-seven years.

Renfield crossed the road and strode up the driveway. 'Rosco!'

Rosco and the rest of his family stopped in their tracks and turned to face Renfield. The woman drew the girls closer, while Rosco's eyes narrowed to suspicious slits. It occurred to Renfield that he must look wild and desperate, standing there in his hoodie and trackie bottoms in the perishing night.

'Ross,' said the woman apprehensively, 'who's this?'

'It's alright, Shonagh,' said Rosco quietly. 'Take the girls inside.'

Shonagh, distrustful eyes still on Renfield, didn't move.

'Now, Shonagh!'

With considerable reluctance, Shonagh shepherded the two girls into the house, casting a last anxious glance over her shoulder before shutting the door.

Rosco moved towards Renfield, clenching and unclenching his fists as if preparing for a fight. Renfield found himself shuffling backwards, trying to maintain the distance between them.

'Hey, Rosco. Long time no see.'

'I don't call myself that now,' said Rosco sharply. 'What do you want?'

He must not have heard the news. If he had, there was no way he'd be asking that question.

'You've been out.'

'Aye, all day. Took the missus and weans out to the country.'

He was trying to talk like a hard man, accentuating the Glaswegian in his accent and dropping in words that weren't normally part of his vocabulary. And if there was one thing Rosco wasn't, it was a hard man.

'What's this all about, Renfield? And what's with the getup? That your work outfit? You look like a total bam.'

Renfield was used to the snide comments about his line of work that invariably came whenever he ran into former associates from school. Most of them had been born to succeed and given every opportunity to do so. But he was always destined to be big, slow Ted Renfield, held back two whole years and only at Willow Bank because Dr George Renfield was determined no son of his would be sent to a school for halfwits. It wasn't that he was stupid. His brain just tended to work more slowly than everyone else's. Given enough time, he was more than capable of figuring things out. He just wasn't so good at the sums and the reading and writing.

'Foley's dead, Rosco.'

For a brief moment, Rosco stared at Renfield in profound shock. Then, the look in his eyes became one of fury. Grabbing Renfield by the upper arm, he marched him down to the street.

'What the hell are you doing mentioning that prick's name for?' he hissed. 'We agreed to have nothing to do with that bastard as long as either of us drew breath.'

Renfield looked past Rosco. He saw Shonagh watching from the living room window, toying anxiously with the choker around her neck. He gave her less than a minute before she called the cops.

He turned back to Rosco with renewed urgency. 'Don't you get it? Someone killed Foley. Stabbed him to death in Kelvingrove Park, man. I know you lot all think I'm a numpty, but even I can work out what that means.'

At the mention of the park, Rosco flinched reflexively. Renfield saw him glance over his shoulder, towards the warmth and safety of his nice house. Towards his nice wife and daughters.

'You see? It's *her*, man.' Renfield's voice dropped to a whisper. 'She's coming for us.'

'Don't talk such utter shite!'

But Renfield was in full flow now, the fear that had been growing inside him manifesting itself in the panicked, barely coherent stream that now poured from his mouth.

'She's coming for us – and you know what? After what we did, I wouldnae fucking blame her.'

Rosco looked back to the house again, then grabbed hold of Renfield and dragged him a few yards up the pavement, placing a tall hedge between them and Shonagh.

'Now you listen to me.' He jabbed a finger in Renfield's face. 'What's done is done. It isnae me now.'

'Rosc—'

'Shut up. I told you, I'm not Rosco anymore. I'm Ross Garvey. I've got a wife and kids and a bloody mortgage. I've moved on. Made a life for myself. A *good* life. And I don't need you or Foley or any of they other cunts fucking it up for me.'

'But Foley—'

'Foley,' said Rosco, 'was always sticking his prick where it wasnae welcome. So maybe he finally bit off more'n he could chew and someone decided to teach him a lesson? Big deal! That's none of my business, and if you've any sense at all, you won't make it yours either.'

Renfield stared at him in silence. He wanted to grab him by the lapels. Give him a good shaking. Knock some sense into him. But it was abundantly clear that, rather than heed the warning,

Rosco was going to stick his head in the sand and pretend it had nothing to do with him.

Well, he'd tried. He'd given it his best shot. And if Rosco wasn't prepared to listen, chances were the others wouldn't either.

Without another word, Renfield turned and headed off into the night. As he tramped up the street, soles crunching on the frosty ground, he heard Rosco's voice behind him.

'You leave me and my family alone, Renfield. Don't come here again.'

Renfield didn't look back. He just kept on walking.

14

The Idealist

'Keep going. I'm right behind you.'

Anna gulped down a lungful of air and wondered for the umpteenth time what the hell had possessed her. Mark's invitation to experience 'the best view in Glasgow' had sounded mighty tempting at the time, but she now realised that if she'd had any sense, she'd have backed out as soon as she discovered what it entailed. And now here she was, halfway up a spiral staircase that seemed to be growing steeper with every step, making her way up the narrow turret leading to the summit of the university's bell-tower.

'I'm friends with the key-holder,' Mark had explained offhandedly as he unlocked the small side door on the upper floor of the main building. 'Got him to fix me up with a copy.'

As they continued their ascent, he told her the university used to organise tours of the tower during freshers' week, until health and safety concerns put a stop to them – a revelation which did nothing to reassure Anna. As she passed a narrow slit window, she caught a brief glimpse of the snow-covered West Quadrangle far below. She shut her eyes and forced herself to put one foot in front of the other.

At the top of the stairs, she stepped through the opening and found herself on the observation platform at the top of the tower. The wind whistled around her. She was completely exposed, the cold air slicing through her coat and piercing her skin. Her heart was hammering nineteen to the dozen. Her vision began to blur. She shut her eyes, certain she was going to be sick.

She felt Mark drawing alongside her. 'And breathe.' He laid a hand on her arm. 'I should apologise. A lot of people don't realise how high up it really is.'

Anna opened her eyes and managed a tight smile. 'Bring a lot of people up here, do you?'

'Only the ones who've had papers published in Italian journals.' He headed over to the handrail at the tower's southern edge. 'Sometimes I come up if I need to think. You'd be amazed how much perspective you gain from putting two hundred and eighty feet between yourself and civilisation.'

'R–really?' Anna did her best not to sound like she was about to spew.

'You probably don't want to hear this, but the view really is something else.' He turned, holding out his hand. 'Come on. I promise you won't fall.'

She wanted to refuse, but she'd made it this far. To back out now would be like admitting defeat. She swallowed heavily and headed over to join him.

As soon as she reached the edge, she felt a fresh rush of panic. The handrail barely reached up to her waist, and beyond it was nothing but a long, sheer drop to the ground below. Her fingers and toes began to tingle, that way they always did when she looked down from more than a couple of storeys up. Her knees shook, and for a brief, irrational moment, it occurred to her that it would be the easiest thing in the world for Mark to place his hand in the small of her back and give her a push.

Then she felt his hand on her shoulder, gentle enough not to spook her but firm enough to reassure her he wasn't going to let her fall.

'It's alright. I've got you.'

For a while, it was all she could do to remember to breathe. Her fluttering heart gradually returned to its normal rhythm. Her vision came back into focus. Spread out before her was a miniature replica of the city, or so it seemed. She could make out the arc of the River Kelvin, snaking through the parkland south of the university. Beyond it, the Kelvingrove Art Gallery was lit up in red and gold. Further south, beyond the dense network of tenements, the Armadillo and the Science Centre, on opposite banks of the

Clyde, shimmered in cool blues. The whole city was alive with colour.

Mark had been right – the view was stunning. It would have taken her breath away, if she'd had any left.

'Glad you came now?'

This time, Anna didn't have to force herself to smile.

***

Afterwards, they headed to the Common Room, a small bar down on Ashton Lane, about a five-minute walk from the university. Leaving Mark to book a table, Anna hung back in the foyer and rang Zoe.

'Bloody hell!' Zoe exclaimed, after Anna explained why she wasn't home yet. 'You don't waste any time. Two blokes in one day? Even I couldnae swing that.'

'Jeezo, woman! Get your mind out of the gutter. It's just someone from the university. We'll be talking shop mostly.'

'That what they're callin' it these days? Listen, it's nae skin aff my nose. I'm just headin' out to talk a bit of shop myself. You're no the only one wi' the busy social calendar.'

'Oh, *I* see. And what particular carnal delights are you planning on indulging in, dare I ask?'

'Oh, you know – bit of this, bit of that. See what takes ma fancy.'

'And who's the lucky guy?'

'A lady has her secrets.'

'Since when were you ever a lady?'

Zoe laughed uproariously. 'Aye, touché! Well – later, gator. These wild oats aren't gonnae sow theirselves.'

***

Later, Anna remembered little of the food itself. Her visit to the tower had, it turned out, done her a world of good. The high altitude had cleared her head, and she was now feeling sharper and more focused than at any point since she'd arrived back in Glasgow. Much of the conversation circled around general matters concerning her and Mark's respective fields and areas of overlap. As they were finishing up over coffee, however, they finally broached the subject of his lecture. As is typical when like-minded academics get together, they spent a great deal of time picking over the minutiae of research methodology and interpretation of data. Mark, however, seemed determined to get Anna's thoughts on the piece as a whole and refused to let the matter drop, urging her not to pull any punches.

'If you want my honest opinion,' she said, already knowing this could only end in tears, 'as a piece of theatre, it was faultless. You got the audience's attention and you held it. You made them question their assumptions about society and about themselves.'

'I'm sensing a "but" in there.'

'*But*, in all honesty, I thought it was irresponsible.'

Mark frowned. 'How so?'

'It's pure shock jock tactics. You make people *ooh* and *ah*, get them shaking their heads and saying to themselves, "oh dear, isn't it terrible?" But at the end of the day, you're not actually effecting any real change other than to turn the whole debate into a circus.'

'Now hang on.' Mark's tone, while still impeccably civil, nonetheless carried an underlying warning: *bite me and I'll bite back*. 'I was speaking to an audience largely consisting of laypeople. I needed to grab their attention and shake them out of their complacency – and, by your own admission, I succeeded. I'm here to challenge the status quo. And in that respect, I'm not too concerned if a few people think I'm being uncouth or dumbing down the debate. Because, when it comes down to it, my goal is to change minds and improve outcome for victims. And part of that is about removing the barriers to women reporting their ordeals.'

'In which case, you've holed yourself below the line with that "three per cent" business. Have you thought about the message you're sending? You're saying all rape trials collapse anyway, so what's no point even trying? You blame societal attitudes for the low rate of reportage, but I don't see how screaming, "You're all doomed!" from the rooftops is supposed to advance your aims.'

'Because I'm trying to draw attention to the iniquity of it all! I want people to wake up to how messed up things are. I want us to evolve to the point where victims of rape can feel confident that, when the time comes for their day in court, they'll get a fair hearing and the system will work in their favour.'

'And, in the process, shaming those women who choose not to come forward?'

Mark simply threw up a hand in exasperation.

'Did it ever occur to you that not all women who've been raped *want* "their day in court"? Some of them just want to put it behind them and move on with their lives as best they can.'

'Sure, but I want us to get to a place where they don't have to feel that that's their only recourse.'

'What if that's the recourse they want? This fetishising of the judicial system as some sort of be-all and end-all is…well, it's obscene.'

Mark shrugged weakly. 'It's the only way we have of getting justice.'

'Justice? You think what these courts dispense is *justice*?' She was talking louder now, jabbing her finger at him as if that somehow lent credence to her argument. 'What, a few years behind bars and time off for good behaviour? Are you honestly telling me you call that justice?'

'Well, alright. I'll not use the word "justice", if you object to it so strongly. Let's say it's about allowing these women the chance to tell their stories. To have their voices heard.'

'And what about the ones who choose to remain silent? Who *want* to remain silent? They don't need you brow-beating them, telling them reliving everything in front of an audience is somehow in their interests – or worse still, something they should feel obliged to do. You think there's this one-size-fits-all solution you can just force onto every case, but life isn't like that.'

Mark sat, brows furrowed in contemplation, saying nothing.

'I mean, I get it. You're an idealist. And maybe you can afford to be, locked away in your ivory tower, coming out every now and then to put on a show for a captive audience. But I do real work with real victims and their real attackers, and I can tell you, you're on a hiding to nothing if you think you're going to affect some widespread change.'

'Well, I can try,' said Mark quietly.

She knew she'd gone at him too hard, but it was too late for regrets now. She suddenly realised how much the entire thrust of his lecture had angered her, beyond just the intellectual laziness of whipping his audience up into a frenzy of indignant outrage by parading a sympathetic, photogenic 'victim' before them. Buried beneath all that lamenting about societal attitudes was the inference that all that was really needed to make the system fit for purpose was a tweak here, a spot of re-education there.

She forced herself to adopt a more conciliatory tone. 'In that case, you've got an insurmountable problem in the way the judicial system is set up. The onus is on the prosecution to prove the accused did it, but the accused can't be compelled to give evidence. Ergo, the victim becomes the *de facto* defendant – the one in the dock, the one whose character and integrity end up being torn to pieces. Like your Ms Smith. Face it – the system is fundamentally broken, and if you try to reform it, all that happens is the whole thing gets dragged through endless committees and consultations, any radical ideas get watered down, and you end up with a bunch of minor tweaks that do absolutely nothing to get to the heart of the problem. If you really want to change things, you should be looking to do away with the system altogether.'

'But the system is what stands between order and anarchy. Without it, you'd end up with mob rule. With vigilante justice. Is that what you want?'

A sudden image of Andrew Foley lying face-down in the snow entered Anna's head unbidden. Jesus, where did *that* come from? She swallowed heavily and wrenched her mind away from it.

'I can see why some people would consider it an attractive option. People who've exhausted every other avenue.'

Mark's smile faded.

'Look, I understand your position. I can even respect it. You think the system can be made to work. That's great. It's laudable. But it's pure fantasy – I'm sorry. The average person – by your own admission, I might add – is so conditioned by ingrained prejudices that you're never going to get a fair trial from a jury plucked at random from society. You don't change centuries-old attitudes just like that.'

'So it's going to take some time. I never said it'd be easy. Look, I get that you're tired of fighting the system, of seeing no light at the end of the tunnel. But maybe, just maybe–'

'No, you *don't* get it!'

An uneasy silence descended. This time, she was aware that several of her fellow diners had stopped eating and that she was now the centre of attention. But it was too late. She had to say this.

'You don't change people by wagging a finger at them and telling them they're wrong. People aren't receptive to that sort of re-education. They just become more stubborn. Decide it's political correctness gone mad or what have you.'

Mark laughed grimly. 'So, basically, the whole of civilisation is a write-off?'

'Parts of it are.'

Mark gave a frustrated sigh and fell silent. They'd reached an impasse. Their waiter, judging now to be an opportune moment, scuttled over and began to clear the table.

Anna sank lower into her seat. She hated that the evening, which had started with such promise, had ended in such bitterness. It hadn't been her intention to be so confrontational. She might not share Mark's idealism, but there had been no need to burst his bubble so cruelly – to tear his work to shreds and dump the remains unceremoniously in his lap.

Mark tapped the waiter's arm. 'Can we have the bill, please?'

Anna reached for her purse. 'Let me.' She felt it was the least she could do to salvage something from the situation.

Ever gracious in the face of defeat, Mark smiled and dismissed his offer with a wave. 'Please. I insist.'

15

People Don't Change

In the end, they split the bill, accepting that it was as close to a truce as they were going to reach that night. Afterwards, on hearing Anna proposing to walk back to Zoe's, Mark insisted on accompanying her, saying he couldn't countenance her making the journey unaccompanied. The real reason, she suspected, was that he didn't want to let the evening end on such a sour note. In a way, she was glad – neither did she.

As they tramped north through Kelvindale, they avoided the subject over which they'd crossed swords at dinner, instead trading notes on their respective childhoods. His turned out to have been far more interesting, not to mention varied, than hers. He'd been born in Vermont but, thanks to his father's role as head of overseas operations for a large shipping firm, had lived on every continent and been conversant in half a dozen languages by the age of eighteen. *Hence the unplaceable accent.*

'A veritable citizen of the world, huh? So why Glasgow?' She couldn't help but struggle with the notion that someone who'd been to the most exotic, far-flung corners of the globe would choose to settle in the very place she'd been so desperate to see the back of.

'Is this the moment where I make the obligatory crack about the weather?'

'Tell me about it. I just flew in from Rome. Nothing like sub-zero temperatures and ankle-deep snow to remind you what you haven't been missing. Seriously, though.'

Mark thought about it. 'In truth, I'd have to say it's the people. They're a bit like the city itself – rough and ready on the outside, warm and welcoming on the inside. What about you? Why Rome?

I mean, with your name, I'm guessing there's some sort of family connection.'

She smiled. 'Most observant of you, Doctor. I suppose it just sort of made sense. I spoke the language already, I liked the architecture, the food, the whole ambience…but honestly? When I was applying to universities, "anywhere but Glasgow" was pretty much my official mantra.'

'I take it you're not given to suffering from homesickness, then?'

'Absolutely not,' said Anna, with a level of conviction that surprised even herself. 'I'd lived here all my life. Couldn't wait to see the back of it.'

Mark laughed quietly, as if enjoying a private joke.

'What's so funny?'

'Well, we're quite the pair, aren't we? Here's me with no real roots to speak of, and here's you going out of your way to reject yours.'

'You make it sound like it's a conscious effort. I'm not *trying* to reject anything. I just think it's way too easy to fetishise stuff like who your parents are or where you come from. At the end of the day, I decide what sort of person I am.'

Mark frowned. 'That's a bit naïve, surely.'

'How so?'

'Well, you can't exactly disentangle yourself from your roots just like that. We're all shaped by the particulars of our upbringing, whether they're cultural, religious or even something as fundamental as the city we're from. No matter how much we might want to deny those things, they're still a part of who we are. Without them, we'd just be grey, faceless machines.'

Anna pursed her lips and said nothing.

Mark glanced across at her, giving a knowing smirk. 'I know what your problem is.'

'What's that, then?'

'You just don't like the idea of being defined by something you have no control over.'

'And is that such a crime? Wanting to be judged on my own merits?'

Mark held up his hands in a peace gesture. 'Hey, I hear you. But deep down, I reckon everyone wants to belong to somewhere… and for somewhere to belong to them.'

Anna didn't answer. She sensed this was another matter on which they weren't going to see eye to eye. Which was fine. Though to an outside observer their conversation might seem heated, even combative, she liked the fact that Mark didn't simply accept everything she said, and she hoped he felt the same. She viewed this sort of exchange as far healthier than one where two people with opposing viewpoints danced around the big issues for fear of offending the other. There was a famous rule about not discussing football, religion or politics with people you didn't know, but Anna didn't hold with that. Well, maybe the football bit, which held about as much interest for her as reading a manual on watching paint dry, but generally speaking, she thought people who avoided controversial matters for fear of discovering a difference of opinion generally weren't worth talking to.

They turned onto Astley Street. Anna could see light streaming out of the Callahan house through a crack in the living room curtains. Someone must be home. They halted at the foot of the garden path and turned to face one another.

'Well,' she said, with a light-hearted shrug, 'this is my stop.' She hesitated, reluctant to part company without having done something to address the unspoken rift between them. 'Sorry about…you know, earlier. I might've been a little more forthright than was strictly necessary.'

'Nonsense,' said Mark amiably. 'It's always good to have your beliefs challenged.'

'And were they?'

He grinned. 'No, I still reckon you're barking.'

She shook her head, smiling mirthfully. 'Well, in any event, thanks for walking me back. Whatever our differences of opinion, it's good to know civilisation isn't a *complete* write-off.'

Mark bowed and made a theatrical flourish with his hand. '*Non è che un pensiero.* It was a pleasure to meet you, Anna Scavolini, and an even greater pleasure to argue with you.'

Anna raised an eyebrow, impressed by his command of the language and amused by the flamboyance of the gesture. He extended his hand. She accepted it, allowing her fingers to linger just a smidgen longer than necessary on the coarse hairs on his knuckles. For a brief instant, their eyes met, as if they'd both sensed something passing between them.

At the same moment, out of the corner of her eye, she saw the curtains in the living room move slightly. They were being watched.

The moment passed. She let go of Mark's hand, and with a smile and tip of his head, he turned and began to head back the way they'd come.

'Mark!'

He stopped and turned expectantly towards her.

'People don't change. Not the way you want to change them.'

'You're wrong. Watch me.'

He flashed her a wink and headed off into the night.

***

Stepping into the hallway, Anna heard the chatter of the television – a late evening news bulletin, by the sounds of it – emanating from the living room. She kicked off her shoes and headed through.

Inside, she found Victor lounging on the settee, doing a passable job of pretending he hadn't been curtain-twitching less than a minute ago. Hearing the creak of the door, he dialled down the volume and turned to her.

'Oh, hey. I didn't hear you come in.'

Anna forced a smile while inwardly gritting her teeth. It wasn't that Victor was unpleasant or went out of his way to make things difficult. She just never knew what to say to him, and he, it seemed, suffered from the same affliction. In spades. It was as if his air of perpetual discomfort was contagious.

She gestured towards the screen. 'What're you watching?' The answer was self-evident, but it seemed as good a conversation starter as any.

'Oh!' he exclaimed, as if she'd walked in on him masturbating. 'I'll turn it off if you–'

'No, it's fine.'

She headed over to the settee and sat next to him. The springs squeaked as he shifted uncomfortably in response to her proximity.

'How's you?'

'Okay, I guess.' He sounded more than a little defensive.

'Zoe not back yet?'

'Nuh.'

Christ, Victor. Give me something *to work with here.*

'She tell you where she was going?'

Victor scoffed. 'Never tells me anythin'.'

Anna chanced a glance at him. 'Well, between you and me,' she said conspiratorially, 'she's off with her mystery man.'

She was fishing, hoping Victor might be party to some nugget of information she wasn't, but he simply looked at her blankly. 'Who?'

'Didn't you know? She's got some secret toy-boy on the go. Won't tell me who he is. Not even a name.'

Victor gave her an odd look that she couldn't make sense of. It might've been incredulity, or indeed something vaguely akin to scorn – or something else entirely. She had a sneaking suspicion he knew more than he was letting on.

A still image of Andrew Foley appeared on the TV. Next to it, the newsreader was putting on that grave expression presenters always reserve for matters of life and death. The volume was too low for Anna to make out what he was saying, but she could guess the gist of it. *Senseless attack…hard-working family man…relatives distraught…police are appealing…*

She glanced across at Victor and found that he, too, was glued to the screen.

'The cops haven't been here again, have they?'

He shook his head, eyes not moving from the TV.

'This morning, when they were here – did they, um, ask you anything?'

'Nothin' much.'

She thought he might be ducking the question, but she couldn't be sure. With Victor, the line between evasiveness and a chronic lack of social skills was an exceptionally fine one. Anyway, she didn't see much point in pressing him. He'd probably just clam up entirely.

'Well, if they do show their faces again, you can tell them from me I want my passport back.'

'They questioned Zoe.'

'I know. Last night at the station. They interviewed her before me. Kept me waiting ages 'til–'

'As if she had anything to do with it!' he snapped. 'As if she'd hurt anyone!'

Loath though she was to defend the police after how they'd behaved with her, she couldn't help but feel the need to offer up at least some sort of explanation on their behalf, if only to stop Victor working himself up into a tizz.

'They're just covering their bases. You know, dotting the I's and crossing the T's. It doesn't mean they think she–'

Victor's head snapped round to face her, eyes burning with indignation. 'Dunno why you're sticking up for they bastards. They treated you like crap too. They've got no right to...' He stopped, mid-rant, suddenly self-conscious. 'Sorry,' he muttered, lowering his head.

Anna said nothing. She'd been caught off guard by the utter vehemence of his outburst. Still, that was brothers and sisters for you. As an only child herself, she had nothing to compare it to, but she'd always recognised the bond between the Callahan siblings as a formidable one. Zoe had made no secret of the fact that she considered Victor to be the most infuriating boy on the planet and thought nothing of dissing him and mercilessly poking fun at him, both behind his back and to his face, but she'd always made it abundantly clear she was the only one permitted to invoke that privilege. Anna could vividly remember her as a gallus fourteen-year-old, marching up to a group of bullies in the year above who'd been tormenting Victor and telling them, under no uncertain terms, that the next one to so much as look at her brother funny would be picking their teeth up off the floor. The bullies had no trouble believing her and left Victor alone after that. Anna had no trouble believing her either, and though she couldn't quite imagine Victor punching someone's lights out, she had no doubt his loyalty to his sister was every bit as intense.

She supposed it had to be, for them to still be living together after all this time.

The news bulletin was over. In its place, a perky blonde meteorologist, wearing something more akin to a meringue than a dress, was gesticulating enthusiastically in front of a map showing snowfall the length and breadth of the country, from John O'Groats to Gretna.

'That, uh, that guy outside,' Victor said.

Anna glanced across at him. 'Mark?'

'The two of youse seemed awfy…'

'Awfully what?' said Anna, bristling. He *had* been watching them.

'Nothin'. Sorry.' He lowered his eyes. 'I just…wouldnae want you gettin' took advantage of.'

'He offered to walk me back, and I accepted. That's all there is to it.'

'That's never all there is to it.'

She didn't have to guess what this was about. Back in the old days, Victor had, in a moment of weakness, confessed to Zoe that he fancied Anna something rotten. Of course, Zoe, who suffered from a pathological inability to keep a secret, immediately went running to Anna and blabbed to her. For Anna, who couldn't think of a single person she was *less* attracted to than Victor, the whole situation was incredibly awkward – though her embarrassment was as nothing compared to Victor's once he realised she knew. After that, encounters between them became even more strained, if that was even possible. It was as plain as day he still carried a torch for her.

In the uncomfortable silence that followed, the sudden ringing of the doorbell registered as deafeningly loud. Seizing the initiative, Anna lurched to her feet in a single, abrupt movement. 'I'll get it,' she announced, and strode from the room.

She headed to the front door and squinted at the frosted glass, but could see nothing behind it but the darkness outside. Making sure the door was on its chain, she unlocked it, turned the handle and opened it a crack.

'Hello?'

No answer.

She reached into her pocket and took out her key-ring. Positioning the longest key between her clenched knuckles, she took the door off the chain, opened it all the way and peered out. There was nobody there.

Cautiously, ready to bolt back inside at the first sign of trouble, she stepped out onto the porch. She looked around. Sniffed the chill air.

'Hello?'

Again, she was met by the overpowering sound of silence.

Probably just kids arsing about. She turned to go back inside.

As she did so, she heard footsteps racing up behind her. Before she could react, a hand closed around her shirt collar, yanking her backwards. She missed her footing and went down hard, the back of her skull connecting with the paving stones. As she stared up at the night sky, head swimming, a shape swung into view – a man, or so it seemed to her, wearing a balaclava that obscured his face completely, barring a small horizontal slit for the eyes. They were piercing, angry, blue, burning into hers with such intensity that she found herself incapable of shutting them or looking away.

With a gloved hand, he held up a small portable tape recorder and pressed a button. The wheels of the cassette began to turn. A voice, clearly that of an automatic text recognition program, cut into her like a knife.

'IF YOU VALUE YOUR PRETTY HEAD, ANNA SCAVOLINI, BACK OFF. GO BACK WHERE YOU CAME FROM.'

The figure pressed the button again. The wheels came to a standstill.

Neither of them moved. Their eyes remained locked in wordless communication, the intensity of her attacker's leaving Anna in no doubt that the threat behind those words was deadly sincere.

'Anna!'

The figure looked up at the sound of Victor's voice. Lurching upright, he disappeared from view. From the ground, Anna heard the sound of pounding footsteps. She felt Victor hurtling past her, the slap of his trainers continuing up the path into the street. She listened to them fade into the distance.

Move, Anna. Get up. You can't just lie here all night.

She eased herself into a sitting position. The back of her head throbbed, and when she gingerly touched it, her fingers came away with blood on them. Her keys lay on the ground next to her. Fat lot of good they'd been.

She'd just managed to get herself onto her feet when she heard footsteps padding up the pavement towards her. She whirled around, keys at the ready, but it was only Victor, flushed and out of breath. He came to a halt and stared at her, a look of gormless confusion on his face.

'He got away,' he said, between gasps. 'He was fast. I didn't see which way…'

Anna nodded, but she wasn't really listening. Her legs had turned to jelly. An all-too-familiar tremor gripped her hands. In fact, she was shaking all over, her teeth chattering uncontrollably as she struggled to catch her breath.

'I–'

But that was as far as she got. Next thing she knew, her knees had buckled and she was on the paving stones once again. Her vision clouded. She heard the roar of wind in her ears, even though the night was perfectly still. The last thing she saw before everything went black was Victor bending over her, still wearing that same vacant, confused expression.

16

Absolution

The girl looked young, but Renfield told himself they all looked like that. It wasn't exploitation. It was a consensual transaction – an exchange of money in return for the receipt of a service. She knew what she was doing, and if she didn't like it – well, she could always do something else. Anyway, it had got her off the street. Out of the icy cold. Really, if you thought about it, he was doing her a favour.

Or so he told himself as they traipsed up the graffiti-scarred stairwell, the tang of stale urine heavy in the air. They were in a particularly barren part of the East End known unofficially as Glasgow's second red light district. After dark, those found wandering that long, narrow stretch of road could, broadly speaking, be divided into two groups: the girls who offered their services and the men who purchased them.

He followed her into a cramped bedsit on the top floor. The wallpaper was peeling and browning, the corners of the ceiling mottled by condensation. A bed with crumpled sheets and a tired, grubby mattress took up most of the room. A small sink and the cracked mirror above it were the only other amenities.

The girl slipped off her jacket and turned to him, all chapped lips and panda eyes.

'What's it to be?'

'What?'

'Ten for a handjob, fifteen for a blowjob. Twenty for the whole shebang. Kissing's extra.'

He wondered whether her parents knew what she did for a living. Wondered if she had any.

'Twenty it is, then.'

She snatched the money from his hand and pocketed it.

'How old are you?' he said, as she began to unbutton her top.

She turned impatiently. 'How old d'ye want me to be?'

He thought about it. 'Seventeen.' *Same age* she *was.*

'Okay. I'm seventeen.'

It probably wasn't far from the truth.

She continued to strip, giving the process all the allure of a patient disrobing for a doctor's exam. Realising he should do likewise, he perched on the end of the mattress and slipped off his trainers. As she brushed past him, he caught a glimpse of the livid bruises on her lily-white thighs. The razor burns on her pubis. She slipped into bed and sat, arms folded, waiting for him.

He scrambled out of the rest of his clothes and joined her beneath the covers. She reached over to the cabinet, produced a condom from a tobacco tin and offered it to him.

'Bareback's thirty.'

As he tore open the wrapper, he felt not the slightest inkling of any stirrings down there. He willed himself to get hard, tried to picture the girl from the pool with the belly button ring and quivering breasts, but it was useless. There was nothing remotely arousing about any of this – not the girl, not his surroundings, and definitely not the situation.

She frowned. 'You waitin' for somethin'?'

'It's fine. I just need a minute.'

He lowered himself on top of her, hoping the sensation of skin against skin would stimulate some sort of response in him.

Nothing.

She sighed impatiently, grabbed hold of his cock and began to move her hand up and down the shaft with bored, practised efficiency.

He shut his eyes, once again trying to form a mental image of the belly-ring girl. But it was no use. All he could see when he opened his eyes again was the greasy-haired, pasty-faced girl lying beneath him, her small tits like pancakes, staring past him up to the ceiling with half-vacant eyes, the beginnings of a cold sore on her lower lip.

He climbed off and sat on the edge of the bed with his back to her.

'Sorry.'

'Makes nae difference tae me, pal. Either way, ye're still payin'.'

He said nothing.

'Look, it's nae use beatin' yersel up over it. Ye're no the first punter who couldnae get it up.'

He laughed drily. He was ashamed, alright, but it wasn't over not being able to get hard for a girl who probably wasn't much more than half his age. Or, to be more accurate, it wasn't the 'not getting hard' part. It was the other bit. The 'girl half his age' bit. He wondered how she'd ended up selling herself to sad, desperate men like him, what wrong choices she'd made. He found himself wanting to know her as a person, not just some random whore whose body he'd purchased for less than the cost of a month's gym membership.

'What's your name?'

'What d'ye want it tae be?'

Renfield turned to face her. She'd assumed the same arms-folded, time-is-money pose as before, a bored look on her face. He felt an intense urge to grab her, to shake her, to slap her, to make her take this seriously. But he didn't. He kept it together, just as he'd managed to keep it together every day for the last ten years.

'I want to know your real name.'

She rolled her eyes. 'Call me Mandy if ye like.'

He had no idea whether that was indeed her name or simply something she told nosy clients to shut them up, but he figured it was the best he was going to get.

'And what do you think of me, Mandy?'

She scoffed. 'I don't know ye.'

He said nothing. Just sat there, head craned over his shoulder, looking at her expectantly.

She sighed. It was a sigh that said, *Oh, so you're going to be one of* those *ones*. 'I think ye've got a nice body and a nice dick. I think ye don't need to be payin' lassies like me tae fuck ye.'

'No, I mean…I mean, as a person. Like, do I seem like a nice guy to you?'

Mandy thought about it. 'I s'pose, aye. Maist punters who couldnae get hard would've battered me by now.'

He wondered what sort of a world she must inhabit where not getting battered was considered an unexpected perk.

'Well, that's where you're wrong. I'm not a nice guy.'

'Aye ye are,' she said, without meaning it.

'I did something once.' He was leaning forward, chin tucked against his chest, hands clasped. 'To a girl like you. Well, like you but not like you – you know what I mean?'

'Yeah,' she lied.

'What I mean is…if I asked you to forgive me, would you?'

He had no idea where that came from. And neither had she, judging by the look of incredulity on her face when he turned to look at her.

'Forgive ye for what?'

For using you. For making you listen to all this. For simply being the latest in a long line of men who see a malnourished girl shivering on a street corner and decide the most fitting course of action is not to buy her a bowl of hot soup but to pay her for sex.

For what we did to her.

'Just…forgive me.'

She shrugged. 'Aye, alright. You're forgiven. I absolve you of your sins.' She made the sign of absolution, then burst out laughing. It was a hoarse, guttural, ugly laugh – one that belonged to a much older woman.

Renfield began to dress. By the time he'd finished, she was already lighting a cigarette. As far as she was concerned, the transaction was concluded.

He slipped a hand into his pocket and pulled out a crumpled £10 note – the only money he had left on him. 'Here. Get yourself a square meal.'

She blew a defiant cloud of smoke. 'Charity, is it? How d'ye know I'm no just gonnae blow it on smack or whatever?'

'Suit yourself.' He pocketed the money and turned to go.

He made it halfway out of the door before she called to him. 'Hey.'

He turned to find her up on her haunches, her scrawny little body exposed for anyone passing in the hallway to see.

'Never said I wouldnae take it.'

A wave of revulsion coursed through Renfield. In that instant, as he gazed back at her from the door, he thought she was repulsive, ugly, shameless. And it was men like him who'd made her that way, and there wasn't a thing he could do about it. Taking out the £10 note again, he placed it under a chipped mug on the shelf above the sink, then let himself out.

As he made his way down the corridor, he heard her hurrying to retrieve the money before he could change his mind.

***

Stepping into the street, he tilted his head back, gazing up. It was a clear night, the sky a great black canvas flecked with stars. He let his breath out, a cloud of condensation wafting up towards them.

A chill ran up his spine. The hairs on the back of his neck prickled. Someone was there, lurking in the shadows. Just waiting for the opportunity to pounce.

He whirled around to face his would-be attacker. But there was no one there. The street was deserted, abandoned to the bleak midwinter night by anyone with an ounce of sense.

Renfield felt the anger rising up inside him again. He clenched and unclenched his fists, his rage bubbling over into a wild, ragged outburst.

'WELL? COME ON, YOU FUCK! WHAT ARE YOU WAITING FOR? I'M RIGHT HERE!'

But there was no reply. The street was empty, and Renfield was alone.

17

The Man

Ross Garvey blinked himself into consciousness, wondering what had disturbed his sleep. He listened intently, but could hear nothing apart from the steady breathing of Shonagh lying next to him.

He closed his eyes once more.

'Daddy.'

This time, he sat bolt upright. In the gloom, he could make out the shape of Ailsa, his youngest, standing at the foot of the bed clutching the threadbare teddy she always took to bed with her.

'What's wrong?'

Ailsa said nothing. She remained rooted to the spot, staring back at him.

He glanced at the digital alarm clock on the bedside table. 02:15.

He groaned and rubbed his face, forcing himself to wake up properly, then eased himself out from under the enveloping warmth of the electric blanket. Nocturnal disturbances like these had become a regular occurrence in the Garvey household of late. One of the boys at Ailsa's nursery had told her an invisible monster lived under her bed, one that ate little girls, and it was now rare for them to get through more than a few nights without some sort of upset.

He padded over to Ailsa and knelt facing her. 'What's the matter, sweet-pea? Need the loo?'

She shook her head.

He checked. She wasn't wet. Another small mercy.

'Can't you sleep?'

She shook her head again.

'How come?'

'The man.'

He frowned. 'What man?'

Ailsa stared back at him, her wide eyes two giant saucers in the dark. 'The man in our garden.'

Ross's stomach twisted into a sudden knot. Scooping Ailsa up off the ground, he slipped out of the bedroom and crept down the hallway. The room she and her sister shared was on the north side of the house, facing the back garden. With Ailsa still in his arms, he sidled over to the window and drew back the curtain.

Standing in the garden, next to the swing set, was a figure in a black hoodie. His head was bowed, obscuring his face. He didn't move. He just stood there, still, like a statue.

***

Five minutes later, with Ailsa tucked up in bed once more, pacified by the promise that *Daddy will see to it*, Ross opened the back door and stepped outside, clutching a golf club he'd picked up on the way. The figure, still standing there, remained completely still.

'Who are you?' His voice sounded shrill in the quiet of the enclosed garden. 'What d'you think you're doing?'

The figure didn't respond. Didn't move at all. He stood there, head low, hands in pockets.

'Well? Answer me!'

Nothing.

'Renfield, if that's you again…'

But he knew, even as he said it, that this wasn't Renfield. The physique was all wrong. Anyway, he couldn't imagine Renfield remaining this inert for so long.

A wave of fury coursed through him. This was his property. How dare someone come here in the middle of the night? Frighten his daughter? Try to intimidate him? How *fucking* dare they? Club in hand, he began to advance, the hard snow crunching under his slippers. He reached out with his free hand, grabbing the intruder's shoulder.

'I asked you a fucking ques—'

The figure's arm went up. Something cold and hard pressed against Ross's neck. He moved to bat it away, but before he could raise his hand, he heard a loud pop, followed by what felt like a punch to the jugular.

The pain that followed was indescribable. It began as a cramping of the muscles – every muscle, from top to toe, growing tighter and tighter, as if he was being squeezed in a vice. He tried to move, but his limbs refused to respond. With every moment that passed, each of which felt like a thousand lifetimes, the pain grew in intensity, until he was convinced his body was going to spontaneously rend itself into pieces.

Then, as suddenly as it had started, the pain subsided. For a moment, he felt a strange sense of weightlessness, as if he was floating in mid-air. Then he was falling, falling through space. He landed face-first, hitting the ground hard.

As he lay there writhing, heart racing, limbs twitching involuntarily, he was aware of his attacker circling around him, crouching down beside him. The figure remained perched on his haunches, studying him silently. Then, in a sudden, swift movement, he whipped out and snapped open a switchblade.

For a brief moment, Ross caught sight of the face beneath the hood. His eyes contracted in surprise.

'You,' he said.

His attacker smiled, then drove the knife home.

18

Elegy

Saturday, 19 December

In the early hours of the morning, Anna heard the bedroom door opening and someone slipping in. She recognised the movements as Zoe's and listened as she crossed the room, kicked off her heels and got undressed. The duvet rustled, and Anna felt the mattress sag on the other side.

'Hey, pal.' Zoe sounded half-asleep herself. 'You have a nice night?'

'Not bad.'

'That's good.' She shifted closer to Anna, nestling against her and sighing contentedly. 'Mm, you're all warm and snuggly.'

Zoe herself was quite the opposite. Her bare legs, entwined with Anna's, were like slabs of ice. Her breath smelled of booze, and the reek of cigarette smoke clung to her hair. Wherever she and her mystery paramour had been, it must've been quite the party.

Lying there in the dark, Zoe snoring softly in her ear, a dead weight against her, Anna replayed the night's events in her head. She'd ended up in A&E at Victor's insistence, having her head examined first by a young junior doctor who looked as sleep-deprived as she was, then by a CT scanner. After cooling her heels in a cubicle for the better part of an hour, she'd been given the all clear and sent packing. She'd made Victor promise not to breathe a word to Zoe about what had happened. The last thing she wanted was for the whole situation to turn into a massive drama. At least she could rely on Victor not to run his mouth off. Her attack was unlikely to become the talk of the town provided he remained her sole confidant.

In times of intense crisis, our survival instincts are more acutely honed than usual, resulting in what behavioural psychologists call the fight or flight response. Throughout her life, when faced with the choice of doubling down or retreating, Anna had invariably done the latter. This time, however, something was stopping her. Her enquiries the previous day had clearly gotten someone's attention, and if that someone had been sufficiently unnerved to turn up at the house and threaten her, then that suggested she was onto something – even if she herself didn't yet know what that something was.

'IF YOU VALUE YOUR PRETTY HEAD, ANNA SCAVOLINI, BACK OFF. GO BACK WHERE YOU CAME FROM.'

Go back where you came from… These words had awakened something in her. A sense of outrage, of indignation. *This* was where she came from. Glasgow. Her birthplace. Her city. And she was damned if she was going to be driven from it by anyone. Fuck that for a game of soldiers. She would not be threatened or bullied. She resolved then and there that, when the time came for her to leave, it would be on her terms and no one else's.

Perhaps Mark was right. Perhaps where she came from mattered more to her than she'd realised.

***

She was up long before sunrise. She'd dozed in fits and starts, and she could tell from the ache in her muscles and the itching in her eyes that her lack of sleep was catching up with her. Her jaw ached too – a sure-fire sign she'd been grinding her teeth again.

In the bathroom, she opened her pillbox, shook out two pills, then thought better of it and put them back. She'd missed last night's dose, her debate over dinner with Mark having pushed it from her mind completely. But no big deal. She'd missed the odd dose here and there before, and indeed on occasions had deliberately come off them for a couple of days at a time – usually if she had an important deadline looming and needed to keep her mind sharp. They tended to sap her energy at the best of times and, after a couple of nights in a row of severely interrupted sleep, were liable to render her virtually catatonic. She'd get back on the wagon tomorrow, she told herself, after a proper night's kip.

Stepping into the shower, she turned the water up as hot as she could bear it and stood breathing in the steam, trying to clear her head. It did little in that respect, but as least it battered some of the lethargy out of her, and by the time she emerged, she was feeling, if not exactly perky, then at least alert enough to plan her next moves.

Step number one, she'd already determined, was to go to Andrew Foley's memorial service. Despite the emptiness of her promise to Juliet, she realised she wanted to be there, not to see who else turned up. The popular image of the killer as an obsessive compelled to return to the scene of the crime and haunt his victims' funerals might be something of a TV trope, but it was a possibility she wasn't willing to discount completely. And if there was even the slightest chance of him turning up to admire his handiwork, she wanted to be there to witness it.

Juliet had said ten o'clock at St Lucian's, a Roman Catholic church five miles north of Ruchill on the road to Kirkintilloch. Anna set about rousing Zoe, whom she figured could do the talking if they ran into anyone they knew. Despite clearly being less than thrilled at having the covers stripped off her at such an uncivilised hour, Zoe gamely hauled herself out of bed, and they rucked up at the gates at a quarter to ten.

The church itself was a modest affair shielded from the road by a belt of well-tended evergreens, among which was nestled a life-sized marble statue of a crucified Jesus, which Anna found both unsettling and vaguely gratuitous. Deciding she didn't fancy being in such close proximity to this grim monument to death, she relocated to a bench on a small hillock overlooking the churchyard, where she and Zoe watched the crowd assembling in dribs and drabs outside the chapel. The mourners congregated in little clusters, the majority men in their late twenties or early thirties – a swathe of dark suits and hunched shoulders.

'Look,' said Zoe, pointing. 'There's Adam Sinclair. And Richie Deans too. See the one over there scratchin' his schnoz? God, I'd totally forgot he even existed.'

Anna could see why. The man in question, chatting with two others near the chapel's entrance, looked about as memorable as a beige wall. But then, the same could be said for most of them. They were, to a man, bland and interchangeable in their matching outfits – a testament to Willow Bank's ability to churn out high-achieving identikit drones destined for sensible, boring, well-paying jobs.

One of the men standing with Richie, who had his back to Anna and Zoe, turned his head slightly to one side. Anna recognised the nose and had the same reaction as the previous day, thinking for a brief moment that Andrew had risen from the dead, before realising it was actually Gavin. He looked nervy and distracted, clearly only half-listening to the conversation. Watching as he shifted his weight from one foot to the other, she wondered whether she was merely witnessing the discomfiture of a man trying to make sense of his cousin's death, or that of one with something to hide. How tall was he? Six-foot, six-foot-one? How did that compare to the man who'd attacked her last night? She couldn't be sure. All she'd really seen of him had been his eyes. In fact, just as with the figure she and Zoe had crossed paths with on the Kelvin Way, she couldn't truly be certain it *had* been a man.

Feeling increasingly dubious about the whole venture, she was about to suggest to Zoe that they call it quits when she caught a movement out of the corner of her eye. She turned towards the graveyard over at the other side of the chapel. There, among the crumbling, moss-encrusted tombstones, stood a well-built man in jeans and a leather jacket. Like them, he was watching from afar, making no move to join the gathering. She had a feeling she knew him from somewhere.

She nodded in his direction. 'Who's that?'

Zoe followed her gaze, frowning as she tried to place him. 'Think that's Ted Renfield. Aye, I'm sure it is. Fuck me, he got *buff*.'

'Was he in our year?'

'Naw. Well, sorta.' She gave Anna a sly smile. 'When we started, he was a year ahead of us, then he was the same year as us, and by the time we left, he was a year behind us. Ya get me?'

Anna nodded. She had a vague recollection of Renfield, a rather slow-witted, academically-challenged boy who, rumour had it, had failed Willow Bank's entry exam and only got in because his father sat on the board of trustees, or had bribed someone who sat on the board of trustees. Predictably, he'd served as the butt of a lot of people's jokes, but had managed to avoid total ostracism by excelling on the rugby pitch. His peers still laughed at him behind his back, of course, but were pragmatic enough to concede that a halfwit who was good at sport, while still a halfwit, nonetheless had his uses. Anna remembered feeling rather sorry for him, though she had to admit she'd never intervened against any of this barely-veiled bullying.

Zoe nudged her. 'Looks like it's showtime.'

Anna turned as a black BMW pulled into the grounds and crawled up the path towards the chapel. The mourners turned expectantly towards it, their conversations ceasing. It came to a stop and a short balding man in his late sixties, presumably Andrew's father, emerged from the back seat. As Anna watched, he turned and helped a woman in a tight black dress out of the car. It was Juliet, her chosen attire accentuating her pregnant belly more than ever. As the man let go of her arm and turned to shut the door, she stood swaying like a reed in the wind. Ten o'clock and she was already half-cut.

The man took Juliet's arm, and together, they headed towards the chapel. The crowd parted to let them through, then began to file in behind them.

Anna beckoned to Zoe. 'That's our cue.'

They headed downhill, joining the back of the procession. At the entrance, Anna paused for a moment and glanced back towards the graveyard, but Renfield was gone.

***

The service was a bland and dour affair, devoid of any meaningful details about Andrew's life beyond the usual platitudes already repeated by the media ad nauseam. The man who'd arrived with Juliet was, as Anna had suspected, Andrew's father. He spoke briefly about his son's short life and apologised on behalf of Andrew's mother, who was too distressed to attend. The priest, a ruddy-faced young man who looked as if he was being slowly strangled by his dog collar, took it upon himself to represent Juliet's side of the family, adding that they 'sent their condolences' – which, given what Juliet had said yesterday, Anna suspected was an unholy lie.

As a rule, she had no time for religious ceremonies, and Christian even more than the rest, due in no small part to their ubiquitous nature. More than that, though, they'd always served to highlight her own lack of belonging. Sitting in the back row on a cold hard pew, listening to the priest reading from the Good Book in a monotone, she was more acutely aware than ever of being an outsider, an interloper. Very rarely did she actively *feel* Jewish, but this assuredly was one of those occasions.

Zoe leaned over, lips close to her ear. 'D'you suppose it helps, believin' in all this shite?'

'Beats the hell out of me.'

But she was glad Zoe was there, on hand to whisper inappropriate blasphemies and, in doing so, remind her that she wasn't the only one who found the whole charade both alienating and faintly ridiculous.

***

Once the service concluded, the mourners lined up to run the gauntlet at the door – Andrew's cousins, aunts, uncles, his younger brother, and finally Juliet and her father-in-law. Anna and Zoe attached themselves to the end of the queue and dutifully waited to shake hands with a bunch of people they didn't know.

When they came to Juliet, she stared at Anna, bloodshot eyes blinking in surprise. 'I didn't expect you to actually *come*.'

Faced with this ingratitude, Anna felt half-inclined to remind her of just how desperate she'd looked and sounded yesterday, but bit her tongue.

Outside, she found Gavin lingering on the path, alone. She'd expected him to be part of the line-up at the door and had been surprised to find him absent. *Second* cousin, she reminded herself. Barely even family at all, if you thought about it.

She turned to Zoe. 'Go on. I'll catch you up.'

'*Oh* aye?' grinned Zoe, somewhat predictably. She winked and wandered off, whistling an innocent ditty, leaving Anna to head over and join Gavin.

He stared at her in surprise. 'You look awful.'

Nothing like a spot of honesty to make a girl feel self-conscious.

'Thanks. You've seen better days yourself.'

'No, I didn't mean…It's just, you look like you could do with a couple extra hours' shut-eye.' He ran a hand through his curls, decidedly awkward now. 'Sorry. I shouldn't have said…I mean, I know how you ladies are about your looks.' He gave a lopsided smile, and a glimmer of the old Price wit shone through.

So says a man who trims his nasal hair, thought Anna. When you were shorter than everyone around you, you tended to notice these things.

'Marky-boy keep you up all night, did he? I gather you and he decamped for a little *tête-à-tête*. You should have seen the look on the head of department's face when he realised he'd been stood up.'

'Actually, we wrapped things up at a very civilised hour. He escorted me home, if you can actually believe it.'

'Yes, old Westmore always was one for that sort of thing. I believe it's something they call "chivalry".'

At that moment, Anna heard the approaching clip-clop of heels on gravel. They turned as a tall and exceptionally attractive brunette wearing fishnet tights and a bum-hugging pencil skirt made her way over. She looped her arm through Gavin's and glanced at Anna with a look of undisguised suspicion.

'You about ready to go, Gav?'

'In a minute. Some people I have to shake hands with first.' He turned to Anna. 'This is Charlotte,' he explained. 'Anna, Charlotte. Charlotte, Anna.' Leaning towards Anna, he dropped his voice to a whisper. 'Keep her occupied for me, will you?'

He turned to Charlotte and kissed her so chastely she might have been his sister, then extracted himself from her grasp and headed over to a gathering of men a little way off.

Anna stood facing Charlotte awkwardly. She was distractingly beautiful, but there was something of the porcelain doll about her. She had massive round eyes, the brows trimmed to thin crescents, and was wearing enough makeup to stock a beauty shop counter. She stared back at Anna blankly, clearly waiting for her to break the ice.

'So you're here with Gavin?'

'Oh – yeah.' Charlotte smiled enthusiastically, not noticing the redundancy of the question.

'How long have the two of you been...?'

'Oh, about six months.' She had a soft, melodic voice, so quiet that Anna found herself having to lean in to make her out.

'So, what do you do?'

'Oh, I work at Mingozzi's. I'm an assistant greeter.'

Mingozzi's was an upmarket restaurant in the Merchant City, and she said its name like she expected Anna to drop to her knees in awe. Anna considered telling her she was a lecturer at the Sapienza, but thought better of it. She was rapidly forming the opinion that Charlotte was relying on her looks to compensate for a chronic lack of personality, while the fact she began every sentence with 'Oh' suggested it was a source of constant surprise to her that anyone wanted to hear her thoughts. She wondered what Gavin saw in her – aside from the obvious.

'How do you know Gav?'

It was the first time Charlotte had initiated a line of conversation, and Anna thought she detected a hint of suspicion once again. *Probably thinks I'm an old girlfriend.*

'We were at school together. Don't worry, we weren't an item or anything.'

Charlotte gave a slight smile. 'Oh, I'm not worried about *that*.'

Anna was taken aback. The assistant greeter was looking down her nose at *her*. She wondered just how strung-out she actually looked. She took a certain pride in her appearance, at least to the extent of making sure she was neat and tidy, and the thought that two people in a row had passed comment on how she looked left her feeling decidedly self-conscious about it.

She decided to change the subject. 'So, did you ever meet Andrew?'

'Oh, no,' said Charlotte. 'I just…'

Anna nodded understandingly. 'You wanted to be here to support Gavin. That's nice.'

Charlotte smiled, pleased with the thought that she'd done a noble deed.

Anna was saved from having to make any further attempts at conversation by the sound of approaching footsteps. She turned to see Gavin making his way back over.

'Are we done now?' said Charlotte, a petulant whine in her voice.

'Just about. Why don't you wait for me in the car?'

Gavin handed his keys to Charlotte. She hesitated for a moment, shot one last distrustful glance in Anna's direction, then headed off down the path.

Anna turned to Gavin. 'She seems nice.'

'Yes,' said Gavin, in a tone suggesting he'd never considered this before. 'She's working over Christmas, poor lamb. The restaurant twisted her arm. It's double-time, but still – no one wants to be at their work on Christmas Day, right?'

'Guess not.'

In truth, Anna had always assumed Gavin was gay. She couldn't remember him ever having a girlfriend when they were at school, or indeed showing any particular interest in the opposite sex. And, while it was unwise to stereotype, there was a certain flamboyancy about both his manner and mode of dress that would certainly fit the profile. And Charlotte…there was something a bit too perfect about her, as if he'd chosen her out of a catalogue of similar models, based on his perception of what constituted the ideal girlfriend. She certainly hadn't detected anything approaching a romantic spark in their interactions.

She studied him, asking herself whether he could be the one who'd attacked her. It seemed unlikely on the face of it. Yes, he'd known where she was staying, but then so had Mark. So, for that matter, had the police. And any one of them could have mentioned her whereabouts in passing to anyone else. The pool of suspects was far wider than just the people she'd directly interacted with.

'What are you thinking about?'

She stirred, realising she must have been staring at him for some time. 'Oh, sorry. Just sort of zoned out. Lack of sleep, y'know.'

'Tell me about it.' He gave a small, humourless laugh. 'Heh, it's funny.'

'What is?'

'Just this conversation I remember us having, back when we were teenagers – me and Andrew and some of the other boys. We were talking about how we'd go about offing ourselves if we felt the need.'

'Sounds like a cheery exchange.'

Gavin pulled a rueful face. 'Well, you know the sort of morbid banter teenage boys are wont to indulge in. Anyway, we ran through all the possibilities – everything from overdosing to shooting yourself in the face. Most of it was highly impractical. But Andrew had actually thought it through. According to him, the biggest problem was that most of the methods available took way too long, meaning there was plenty time to change your mind. He said, if he ever wanted to kill himself, he'd take himself to the top of the tallest building he could find and chuck himself off. No room for second thoughts once you'd started.'

Anna stared at him. 'Jesus.'

'I don't mean he actually had suicidal thoughts,' Gavin added hastily. 'We were all just trying to show each other how tough we were – how we weren't scared of death or whatever. Only now I'm here saying goodbye to him, and all I can think is how bloody naïve we all were back then.'

Anna said nothing. Under the circumstances, she suspected any platitudes would only sound redundant.

Around them, people were beginning to make tracks. Gavin stirred. 'You coming back to the house?'

'Sorry?'

'Jules is throwing a *soirée chez Foley* in honour of the departed. Alcohol is bound to be involved. I have to run Charlotte into work, but I'm heading there straight after. If you don't mind taking the scenic route, we could go together.'

Anna would have preferred to walk over hot coals than endure another visit to that place. 'I, uh, I've already made plans.'

'Okay.' He sounded genuinely disappointed. 'Well, I'll save you a seat just in case.'

They said their goodbyes, and Gavin set off down the path. Anna gave him a couple of minutes, then headed that way herself.

'IF YOU VALUE YOUR PRETTY HEAD, ANNA SCAVOLINI…'

Those didn't sound like words Gavin would use. Come to that, they didn't sound like words anyone she knew would use.

And yet whoever had spoken them clearly knew *her*.

Her thoughts turned to Renfield. She wondered whether he'd had any dealings with Andrew. They must've rubbed shoulders at one point or another. Had Andrew ever picked on him – enough to prompt him to seek revenge? And he'd seemed awfully shifty, lurking among the tombstones and slinking away before things got underway. But she could hardly talk – gate-crashing a private service on the off-chance the killer might somehow reveal himself to her.

Up ahead, she saw Zoe waiting at the gates. Anna could tell from her expression all was not well. A few steps later, she saw why. Just beyond the gates, next to his grey Volvo, stood Norton.

'He wants to talk to you,' Zoe muttered as Anna came to a halt next to her.

'What about?'

'Havenae a Scoobie.'

'Just a few moments of your time, Dr Scavolini,' said Norton, making his way over to them.

Anna suspected this was a rather generous estimate. Without acknowledging Norton directly, she turned to Zoe. 'You'd best head. No sense you waiting about for me. We can hook up once I'm done here.'

'You sure?'

'I'm sure.'

Zoe eyed Norton distrustfully, evidently unconvinced. 'Fair do's. Got some Christmas shoppin' to be doin' anyway. Time's it?'

Anna checked her watch. 'Just gone ten-thirty.'

'Pulse opens at twelve. I'll catch ye there, 'kay?' She turned to look at Norton, arms folded, giving him devil eyes. 'Don't let him gie you any o' his shite.'

She turned and set off down the road. Anna waited until she'd disappeared from view, then faced Norton with an expectant look.

'I suppose it's too much to hope you've come to give me back my passport.'

'I'm a little surprised to see you here,' he said, ignoring her question. 'That is, given that you barely knew the victim.'

'You didn't know him at all, and yet *you're* here.'

It was a stupid comment, and they both knew it was beneath her. As like as not, Norton's reasons for being here were the same as hers.

'Sleep well last night?'

'Not really,' she said guardedly. 'But I managed to get some shut-eye.'

'No nocturnal excursions?'

She glanced at him warily. 'What exactly did you have in mind?'

Norton's expression didn't change from the troubled frown he'd been wearing since she'd got there, but she now sensed an edge of warning behind it – a *don't test my patience* sort of vibe.

'I gather you paid a visit to the Western Infirmary's A&E department last night.'

Before she was able to stop herself, Anna responded with a sharp, angry intake of breath. 'You accessed my medical records? That's not even legal.'

'No, but one of our officers was there on other business and happened to recognise your name on the board.' He folded his arms, leaning towards her in a manner that she found more than a little intimidating. 'What took you to A&E last night, Dr Scavolini?'

'I slipped on some ice and bumped my head. I wanted to get checked out. Make sure I was okay. That's all.'

'And *are* you okay?'

'I'd be a lot more okay if you lot stopped harassing me.'

She had no intention of telling him the truth – not if there was any risk of it impinging on her freedom of movement. The last thing she wanted was to be told that, for her own safety, she was to be assigned a police guard at all times – something she didn't put past Norton.

For a moment, he held her gaze, doing that thing again of studying her intently, looking for some crack in her armour. 'Come on,' he said eventually, gesturing towards the Volvo. 'I want to show you something.'

'Where are we going?' She made no move to follow him.

Norton shrugged airily. 'Oh, just for a little drive.'

She still didn't move. 'Do I have to?'

Norton paused to consider this. 'No, but something tells me you're the inquisitive sort.'

19

Jenny

Inquisitive or not, she didn't ask where they were going. She saw little point. Norton was clearly determined to take her on a magical mystery tour, and no amount of cajoling on her part was going to tempt him to shed any light on their ultimate destination.

As they drove south, cruising through the genteel suburbs to the north of the city, Anna opened her bag and took out the essays she'd brought with her to Glasgow, fully intending to mark them over the festive period. However, what her wide-eyed first-years had to say about contemporary responses to non-violent crime in post-millennial Western Europe now seemed singularly unimportant in the grand scheme of things, and she soon gave up trying to concentrate on the words, contenting herself instead with watching the road ahead as they passed through Anniesland and Knightswood, following the motorway towards the river.

They entered the Clyde Tunnel, and as darkness enveloped them, she thought back to her childhood – to the countless occasions on which she'd made this very trip, sitting in the back seat of her parents' car, trying to hold her breath for the tunnel's duration. Even now, she found herself doing it instinctively. Then they were out in the light once more, and she breathed again. They'd crossed the river and were now on the Southside, roaring up the dual carriageway as it wound its way uphill.

Anna sat in perplexed silence as they followed the road to the roundabout at the edge of Elder Park, circled around it, then doubled back along the Govan Road for a quarter-mile or so, before taking a left turn and pulled into the grounds of the

Southern General Hospital. She waited, mystified, as Norton pulled into an empty parking space before finally speaking.

'You planning on telling me what we're doing here any time soon?'

Rather than answering, Norton simply turned the key in the ignition, silencing the engine, and opened his door. He got out, turned and peered in at Anna expectantly, as if to say, *Coming?*

Growing more irritated by these cloak-and-dagger antics by the second, she got out and followed him.

The hospital itself seemed to have been designed to actively discourage people from seeking medical attention, its austere architecture betraying its origins as a Victorian mental asylum. They were planning on tearing it down, she'd heard, and replacing it with an all-singing, all-dancing modern complex – and not before time. Equally discouraging to Anna were the two police officers cooling their heels outside the main entrance, one with a sidearm holstered in his belt. Norton flashed his ID at them as he strode on by. Anna followed quickly, averting her eyes from the threatening instrument.

They headed through the sprawling complex, following the signs to the intensive care unit. At the entrance, they were met by another armed guard who waved them through on the strength of Norton's ID.

The door clicked shut behind them. They were in a hospital ward much like any other, with half a dozen individual rooms on either side of the central walkway. Norton led Anna past the open plan nurses' station to the room furthest from the entrance, the drawn blinds behind its full height viewing window obscuring its interior. He came to a halt and faced her, gazing at her with his tired, watery eyes.

'Why are we here?' she said wearily, a part of her wondering whether there was any point asking.

Norton took a deep, unhappy breath before speaking.

'Another man was attacked last night.'

'When? Where?' The questions came tumbling out before she could engage her brain. 'I mean, I don't see why that has anything to do with me.'

'In the early hours of the morning in Bellahouston. And I'm sorry to say it has plenty to do with you.'

'Why?'

'Two reasons. One: the victim is another former Willow Bank pupil.'

'Who?'

Norton tapped the window. The blinds were opened from inside by a middle-aged nurse, her hair twisted into a severe bob. She regarded Anna through the glass with a look of curiosity laced with suspicion, and it took Anna a moment to shift focus from her to the occupant of the bed behind her.

He was in his late twenties, she reckoned, with heavyset, jowly features and heavy-lidded eyes. He was deathly pale, but his breathing seemed steady and unlaboured. At first, she thought he was wearing a polo-neck, until closer inspection revealed it to be a bandage. Her eyes strayed southwards. The bedclothes appeared to be raised a good thirty centimetres or so above his body by some sort of wireframe apparatus.

'Recognise him?' Norton's voice cut through her thoughts.

Her eyes returned to the patient's face, studying it. She remembered him now, though he'd put on a fair bit of weight. He'd been in the year below her, but they'd had some dealings with one another in their capacity as representatives of the school's anti-bullying committee – a half-hearted endeavour designed to show that the school took bullying seriously, but which, predictably, was avoided like the plague by those who truly needed it. A nice, diligent lad, at least as far as she could remember.

'Yes. That's Ross Garvey. I…we didn't really know each other that well.'

'I had a feeling you were going to say that.'

Was he suggesting she was lying? She let it slide. 'Is he…?'

Norton made a vague gesture in Garvey's direction. 'Well, as you can see, he's holding on for now, but they're keeping him under heavy sedation.'

'So he hasn't been in a position to identify his attacker.'

She took his silence as confirmation.

'You said there were two reasons why this involved me. What was the other?'

Norton shifted his weight uneasily. 'The, er, modus operandi is identical to that of the attack on Andrew Foley.'

'You mean he was stabbed? That's not exactly remarkable.' *Not in the knife-crime capital of Western Europe.*

Norton said nothing. There was something he wasn't telling her, but she could see she wasn't going to get anything more from him – at least, not for the time being. She returned her attention to Garvey, his chest rising and falling with each breath. The nurse resumed her seat behind an easel desk strewn with charts.

Footsteps came down the corridor towards them. It was the officer from the door, phone in hand.

'Sir, DCSI for you.'

Norton took the phone from him and dismissed him with a nod. He'd no sooner put it to his ear, however, than a man in nurses' scrubs came striding over. 'You can't use that here,' he informed the DI curtly. 'They interfere with the equipment.'

Norton glowered at the man in exasperation, then turned to Anna with a sigh. 'D'you mind?'

Anna shook her head. Norton gave her a grateful nod, shot the nurse another dark look, then turned and headed for the exit. Satisfied that proper order was restored, the nurse returned to his seat at the nurses' station.

Anna watched Norton go, still none the wiser as to what this was all about. Why had he brought her here? To frighten her? To see how she'd react? She wondered whether this visit was sanctioned. She doubted it. For purposes of corroboration, a unique characteristic of Scots Law, police officers always operated in pairs, and yet here was Norton, acting as an independent agent.

Still, if it meant not having to suffer another encounter with DS Murray…

As she stood there, looking through the window at Garvey, an idea came to her. It was potentially risky, and she'd no idea how much time she had before Norton got back, but she was determined for this trip not to be a total waste of her time. She took stock of what she was wearing: plain shirt, coat, trousers, court shoes. Add to that the strung-out appearance both Gavin and Charlotte had remarked on, and she supposed she might just about pass for a sleep-deprived DC accompanying her boss on a fact-finding mission. She inhaled a lungful of air, steeling herself, and opened the door to Garvey's room.

The nurse glanced up briefly from her desk as she stepped in, but quickly deemed her presence unremarkable and turned her attention back to her charts. *So far so good.* Anna advanced towards the hydraulic bed, surrounded by monitors showing a dizzying array of numbers and waveforms, including one emitting beeps at a slow, steady rhythm. Dwarfed by all this paraphernalia, Ross Garvey seemed very small indeed.

'Terrible what happened to him, in't it?'

Anna turned to find the nurse looking at her over the top of the desk.

'You and that other detective work the gether, aye?'

'We drove over together, yeah,' said Anna, deliberately responding to a different question from the one asked.

'Been doin' this long?'

'Uh, no. No, I just arrived in Glasgow two days ago.'

The nurse's face crinkled into a sympathetic wince. 'Well, I'll tell you somethin'. I've been doin' this job fifteen year, and I never seen anythin' like this before.'

Anna's eyes returned to Garvey, 'His neck…'

'Aye, they done a number on that too. Tried tae cut his throat. As if the rest wasnae bad enough. They reckon it's a toss-up whether he'll be able to speak again.' She made her way over to Anna. 'I tell ye, this part of the job fair gets you down. My relief was supposed to be in at eleven, but she's a no-show. And God forgive me, but I'm absolutely gaggin' for a fag. Dreadful affliction, I know. But ye know what they say – whatever gets ye through it.'

'I could watch him for you,' Anna blurted out, before her mind even had a chance to process what her tongue was saying. 'Uh, I mean, just for a few minutes. Give you a chance to stretch your legs?'

The nurse looked at Anna uncertainly. 'S'no exactly procedure.'

To put it mildly, thought Anna. She shrugged, as if to say it was six and half a dozen to her.

The nurse thought about it for a long, agonising moment. 'Aye, alright. Just mind, anythin' happens, you hit that big red button on the wall and half the hospital'll come runnin'.'

She flashed a grateful smile and headed for the door. Anna followed, shutting it behind her. As the nurse's footsteps receded, she turned back to Garvey. He hadn't stirred, but from the steady rise and fall of his chest, she surmised he was asleep rather than unconscious. Tiptoeing so as not to disturb the strange serenity that enveloped the room, she approached the bed.

'Ross,' she whispered.

No response. She shook him gently by the shoulder.

'Ross.'

This time, his eyelids flickered. He blinked several times and peered up at her through puckered lids. He opened and closed his mouth, trying and failing to form words.

'It's okay, Ross. Don't try to speak.'

He frowned and blinked sluggishly. His head lolled to one side, and his eyelids drooped. Whatever they had him on was heavy-duty stuff.

Anna shook him again, more vigorously. 'Ross, listen to me. You're in hospital. Do you remember what happened to you?'

His eyes opened. He gazed up at her blearily. It was anyone's guess whether he'd understood her. She racked her brains, wondering how to communicate with a semi-conscious man who couldn't speak.

'Ross, I want you to blink once for yes and twice for no. Understand?'

An eternity seemed to pass, then Ross slowly, forcefully closed his eyes and opened them again.

Anna smiled, nodding encouragingly. 'That's good. Well done.'

She glanced up at the clock above the bed. The nurse, or Norton, could be back any minute. She'd have to cut to the chase.

'Ross, this is really important. The person who did this to you – do you know who it was? Did you recognise them?'

Another eternal wait, then another slow, deliberate blink.

Anna's heart began to pound. 'Was it a man?'

Blink.

'Was it someone you were at school with?'

Blink.

'Was it Ted Renfield?'

Two blinks, and a very definite shake of the head.

She hesitated. Bit her lip. Then asked tentatively, 'Was it Gavin Price?'

Two blinks...or at least they *seemed* to be two blinks. The movement of his lids was so sluggish she couldn't be sure.

'Was that a yes or a no, Ross?'

Two blinks. Three blinks. Four blinks. She was no longer convinced these were meaningful signals, just involuntarily responses. Even if she could get him to understand her, what was she going to do? Go through the entire alphabet with him until he spelled out the name of his assailant?

She became aware of a soft tapping sound. Looking down, she saw his left hand was rising and falling, patting the mattress.

'What is it? What're you trying to tell me?'

The patting continued.

'I'm sorry – I don't understand. You'll have to–'

His fingers curled into a claw shape. Unclenched. Clenched again.

Now she understood. 'You want to write something?'

Blink.

The next few seconds passed in a blur. She fished her pen out of her pocket. Pressed it into Ross's hand. Wrapped his fingers around it. Grabbed her folder full of essays from her bag. Slid it under the pen. Then time seemed to slow to a crawl. She held her breath. The seconds ticked agonisingly by as Ross dragged pen across paper in stiff, jerky movements. At first, there seemed no rhyme or reason to the shapes he was carving – just random, jagged lines and curves. Her heart began to sink.

But then, as she continued to stare at the scrawled shapes, they began, as if by some dark arts, to transform before her eyes into actual letters.

A 'J'.

An 'E'.

An 'N'.

Another 'N'.

Garvey's stamina was flagging now. His trembling hand etched one last shape, then went limp, the final stroke of the pen extending to the bottom of the page in a trailing line.

The tail of a 'Y'.

Jenny.

Anna mouthed the word silently to herself. Where else had she heard that name recently? She suddenly remembered Kelly-Marie's words to her outside the Foleys' residence.

When we were…y'know, doing it…he liked to call me 'Jenny'.

Her head jerked up sharply. 'Who's Jenny?'

But Ross didn't seem to hear her. Exhausted by the effort, his eyelids fluttered, then closed completely. His breathing grew steadier, more regular. He was asleep once more.

Anna stood up, clutching the folder to her chest. There was no point trying to wake him up again. It was a miracle she'd managed to get even this out of him. Time now to make good her escape while she still could. She slid the folder into her bag and slipped out.

She found Norton in the corridor outside the ICU, wrapping up his call. The officer who'd summoned him was waiting by his side.

Norton turned at the sound of her approach.

'We finished here?' she said briskly.

Norton handed the phone back to the officer and gave a weary nod. 'We're done.'

***

Back inside the Volvo, Norton put the key in the ignition and fiddled with the heating. They sat there wordlessly, each staring ahead as they waited for the car to warm up.

Anna broke the silence. 'Why did you bring me here? Why did you want me to see…that?'

Norton exhaled unhappily. He gazed up at the ceiling as if seeking divine intervention.

'They weren't just stabbed,' he said eventually. 'They were castrated.'

It took a moment to sink in. At first, Anna wondered if she'd misheard. It seemed so far-fetched. So horrific. In her mind's eye, she returned to the night in Kelvingrove Park, to Andrew Foley stumbling towards her, to the vast quantities of blood that covered everything from his lower abdomen to his trouser legs. She'd assumed it all originated from a single wound. Now, however, she homed in on his unbuckled belt and her initial assumption, before she'd noticed the blood, that he'd been partaking in the services of a rent-boy. She recalled, too, the wireframe apparatus keeping the bedclothes away from Garvey's body.

'Oh, Jesus.'

Her hand flew to her mouth. She wanted to get out of the car, get as far away from all of this as possible – but when she reached for the door handle, she found it locked. And now she wanted to grab Norton, shake him, yell at him to let her out this instant. But it was all she could do to keep taking long, deep breaths, forcing herself to remain calm.

'We've managed to keep that detail out of the press. For that reason, we can be fairly sure it's not a copycat.'

Slowly, Anna turned to face him. A slick of sweat trickled down her back. She could taste bile at the back of her throat.

'I wanted you to see Ross Garvey because I want you to be in no doubt as to the sort of animal we're dealing with. Given your status as our star witness and the…unusual brutality of both attacks, we're understandably concerned for your own safety. I've discussed the matter with my superiors, and we believe the best course of action is to take you into protective custody.

'It's not as drastic as it sounds,' he added hastily, seeing her alarmed expression. 'Think of it as a free holiday, if you like. We put you up in a rather nice flat in an undisclosed location at our expense, lay on all the mod cons – cable TV, your pick of takeaways, et cetera. It keeps you out of harm's way, and–'

'And lets you keep an eye on me.'

'*Should* we be keeping an eye on you?'

She didn't trust herself to answer that.

'Is there anything else you want to tell me, Dr Scavolini? Here, now, in confidence? I promise you, whatever you say, it won't leave this car.'

She said nothing. Not only did she not trust herself – she didn't trust *him*. She didn't think Norton could read minds, but was rapidly coming to the conclusion that he delighted in giving people just enough rope to hang themselves.

His shoulders sagged. 'Fair enough. Just so we're clear, you're refusing our offer of protective custody?'

She nodded.

'It's your decision, and you're free to change your mind at any time. But let me impress on you once more that one man is dead, and another is fighting for his life. If the person responsible should set his sights on you…'

She met his eyes without blinking. 'I've been taking care of myself since I was eighteen years old. I hear what you're saying, and I appreciate the offer, but I have to do this my own way.'

Norton gazed back at her for a long, hard moment. 'You're a stubborn woman, Dr Scavolini. I just hope it doesn't end up costing you dearly.' He turned the key in the ignition. The Volvo came to life with a shudder and a splutter. 'Can I drop you somewhere?'

'Nearest station's fine.'

She sensed him watching her, looking for some tell, some crack in her armour. She continued to stare straight ahead, convinced that if she met his eye, he'd see straight away that she was holding something back. Then, with a disgruntled harrumph, he put his foot to the pedal and pulled out of the parking bay.

20

Bastard

Once Norton had dropped her at Queen Street, Anna headed straight for the taxi rank and commandeered a cab to Kirriemuir Road. Doing her best to tune out the din from the radio, she took stock of her priorities – namely obtaining answers to the two questions that burned in her mind: who was 'Jenny', and what was her connection to Andrew Foley and Ross Garvey? Whoever she was, it was clear Garvey associated her in some way with what had been done to him, though Anna had to concede that he had been delirious, his responses to her yes/no questions inconclusive at best. Regardless, it seemed not unreasonable to surmise that, as the missing link between the two victims, finding the elusive Jenny was the logical next step towards finding the killer.

A killer whose methods could scarcely be described as devoid of symbolism.

She wondered what precisely she was getting herself into. At some point between now and the events of the previous day, she'd stopped being a bystander, giving up any pretence that her actions were merely those of a concerned acquaintance anxious to pay her respects. She'd made up her mind to say nothing to the police until she'd made doubly sure she wasn't chasing a false lead. The last thing she wanted was to admit she'd duped her way into interrogating an attempted murder victim behind their backs if it all turned out to be for nothing.

Several cars lined the Foleys' driveway. Inside, she found the hallway packed to overflowing with guests, their mood singularly upbeat. A collective decision had evidently been reached that Andrew's memory was better served by celebrating his life than by mourning his death. She looked around, hoping to catch sight of Juliet, but the lady of the manor was nowhere to be seen.

Pushing through the crowd, she headed for the living room, where she found every available seat and a good deal of the floorspace occupied. As she scanned the room, she spotted Gavin laying claim to an armchair. She really would have preferred to avoid yet another strained encounter, but before she could make herself scarce, he caught sight of her and got to his feet with a wave.

'I know I promised I'd save you a seat,' he said, once he'd joined her by the door, 'but it turns out space is at a premium. So many of us turned up, she had to open up the second conservatory.'

'Where *is* "she"?'

If Gavin was put out by her brusqueness, he hid it well. 'Kitchen.' He nodded towards the door. 'Careful. I saw her disappearing in there ten minutes ago looking mightily shifty.'

Anna crossed the hallway to the kitchen. She knocked lightly on the door, but when no response came from within, she pushed it open. Juliet stood by the breakfast bar, a bottle of red wine to her lips, in the midst of taking a hefty swig. She turned to face Anna, clutching the incriminating bottle.

'You can call off the search party,' she sneered. 'I was just coming out.'

'I don't think anyone's looking for you,' said Anna – truthfully. It was abundantly clear Juliet was surplus to requirements. Everyone seemed to be getting on just fine without her.

Juliet thought about this, then relaxed a little. She plonked the bottle down and eyed Anna disdainfully. 'Can't seem to get rid of you, can I? Perhaps I need to come up with a hilarious nickname for you.'

Anna didn't dignify that with a response. She'd expected obstreperousness from Juliet, and knew that getting answers to the questions she intended to ask would be like pulling impacted wisdom teeth, but she was determined not to leave empty-handed this time.

Juliet eyed her guardedly. 'What did you make of the service, then? I couldn't tell whether it was his nibs being eulogised or Jesus Christ himself. Still, not much to be risked by playing to the gallery, eh?'

These didn't exactly seem like comments typical a woman who'd just lost her husband – even one who was a serial philanderer. Anna's eyes strayed to the half-empty bottle. She considered asking Juliet whether she'd drunk it all herself, then decided against it.

Juliet caught her looking and scowled. 'I'm not an alcoholic, you know.'

'Right.'

'I mean it. I don't usually…I just needed something to get through the day.'

There was an element of the plaintive child in her self-justification, and Anna couldn't help wondering whether this petulance had something to do with the fact that someone other than herself was the centre of attention today. She watched as Juliet traced the head of the bottle with a finger, almost as if she was testing herself, proving she was capable of not giving into temptation.

Anna cleared her throat. 'I wanted to ask you something.'

'I thought we already played that game yesterday.'

Anna said nothing.

Juliet rolled her eyes. 'Oh, go on, then. It's not as if I've got a houseful of guests to entertain or anything.'

'Does the name "Jenny" mean anything to you?'

'Who's she? One of his whores?'

The word set Anna's teeth on edge, but she couldn't afford to let herself be offended by Juliet's choice of language. She considered telling her how it was she'd first come to hear that name, but decided against it. Better to leave poor Kelly-Marie out of it.

'I think she's someone your husband knew.'

Juliet laughed dryly. 'I'll bet. Her and everything else north of the Clyde with tits and a pulse. Permit me to ask the obvious: what does any of this have to do with you?'

It was a question Anna didn't feel particularly inclined to answer, not least because she wasn't entirely sure she could.

Juliet sighed and dismissed the matter with a wave of her hand. 'Oh, what does it matter? If you want to play at Nancy Drew, knock yourself out. You can hardly do a worse job than the Keystone Cops. No, as it happens, I don't recall him having a dalliance with anyone called Jenny – but then, I didn't exactly keep records.'

'What about–'

Just then, a burst of raucous laughter went up in the living room – harsh, men's laughter of the sort that always made Anna feel instinctively unsafe. Juliet flinched, knocking the bottle off the table in the process. It landed on the floor, shattering into fragments. Cabernet Sauvignon spread outward across the laminate tiling.

Juliet's reaction was curious. Anna would have expected someone as house-proud as she clearly was to immediately set about clearing up the mess – or, more likely, summon the hired help to do it for her. Instead, she drew in her breath sharply and looked around fearfully, her entire body tensing for a blow that never came.

Anna knew that look all too well.

Juliet attempted to cover with a laugh of her own, but it came out as a strained cough. As another burst of merriment rang out, she nodded towards the door. 'Hark at that lot. Wouldn't be half as quick to sing his praises if they knew what he was really like.'

Anna shut the door, silencing the noise. 'Juliet, what *was* he really like?'

Juliet hesitated, tugging distractedly at her collar. She glanced past Anna towards the door, then grabbed her abruptly by the forearm, holding her in that same vice-like grip she'd used yesterday.

'I don't know how much more of this I can take,' she hissed, eyes wide and plaintive. 'All morning I've been listening to people telling me what a great soul he was – so kind, so considerate, so gentle. If I have to hear one more anecdote about the wonderful things he did for them, I'm going to…I'm going to…' She trailed off, unable to articulate precisely what she planned on doing. 'They all talk like they knew him, but they didn't. Not like I knew him.'

She released Anna's arm and turned away, suddenly self-conscious. She stood facing the window, arms wrapped tightly around herself. Anna watched as her bony shoulders rose and fell. This was about more than just her husband being unfaithful.

'Juliet. Tell me what he did.'

Juliet turned to face her. She looked frightened. Trapped, with nowhere to run. The careful façade of respectability she'd built for consumption by the outside world lay in ruins.

'Alright,' she said. 'But not here.'

***

Anna followed her upstairs, through the master bedroom and into the adjoining en-suite. Juliet shut and locked the door behind them. Then, before Anna knew how to react or where to look, she unzipped her funeral dress and let it fall to the floor. She wore a silk négligée underneath, stretched taut by her belly.

'Come closer. I won't bite.'

Mystified, Anna did as she was told. Juliet waited until there was barely an arm's length between them, then gestured to her jutting right clavicle. A thin white line ran along the skin just beneath it – an old surgical scar.

'March sixteenth. Fell down some stairs. Broken collarbone.'

She unhooked the left strap of her négligée and lowered it to expose a small, sagging breast. Several tiny circular burn-marks were visible on the pallid flesh, like multiple supernumerary nipples. Anna didn't need to ask what had made them.

'July eighth. Stubbed a ciggy out on myself. Repeatedly.'

She covered herself again, much to Anna's relief, then leaned forward, parting her hair to reveal another scar, this one red and noticeably more recent than the first, extending horizontally along the crown by about five centimetres.

'September fourth. Walked into a plate glass mirror.' She smiled thinly at Anna. 'I was always doing clumsy things, you see. Injuring myself. Not in places anyone would see, you understand – which is all for the better, when one has appearances to maintain.'

Anna's instinctual response was one of revulsion. Revulsion at this catalogue of violence and the man who had perpetrated it, yes, but also revulsion at Juliet's shamelessness, exposing her rent flesh like this. Forcing her to confront, in graphic detail, these artefacts of domestic abuse.

Her eyes fell once again on Juliet's stomach.

'You shouldn't drink. It's not its fault who its father was.'

She wasn't sure why she said it. It was a point that deserved to be made, but now was hardly the time.

Juliet looked at her, brows furrowed and lips pursed as if trying to process this. Then, quite unexpectedly, she burst out laughing. 'Oh, darling, you've got the wrong end of the stick. It's not his.'

'It's not?' Anna blinked in surprise.

'He's not the only one who had *friends*.' Juliet leaned towards Anna, adopting a theatrical whisper. 'Just between us girls, he couldn't get it up. Not reliably, anyway. Not unless coercion was involved.'

Anna did her best to ignore the churning in the pit of her stomach. 'He didn't…he didn't by any chance hang onto his school yearbooks, did he?'

Juliet looked at Anna with the patient weariness of one used to dealing with those whose needs are considerably less sophisticated than her own. 'You're beginning to annoy me now.'

'Just humour me, and then I'll be out of your hair.'

Juliet scoffed softly, then shrugged, as if to say it was no skin off her nose. She led the way back to the bedroom, Anna trying not to look at the marital bed as they passed it. Juliet approached the dresser by the window and manoeuvred herself awkwardly onto her knees. She opened the lowermost drawer and, after a spell of rooting around, produced an A4-sized book. Hauling herself upright, she handed it to Anna, then perched on the bed, eyes turned towards the ceiling to communicate her boredom.

Anna held the heavy tome in both hands. It was bound in bonded leather and bore the Willow Bank crest, emblazoned in gold on the front cover. Below it, also in gold, was '1997–1998'. Andrew would have been in his final year.

At the end of every school year, Willow Bank produced a book which served both to trumpet the achievements of the past twelve months and as a rogues' gallery for the so-called senior school – the fourth, fifth and sixth years. Anna skipped past the pages focused on sporting medals won and embarrassing photos taken on class trips to far-flung corners of the globe before coming to the student biographies, arranged alphabetically by surname: *Adams; Aitchison; Barnes; Bashar; Callahan, Victor; Callahan, Zoe...*

She wondered what had become of her own yearbooks. Her mum might have hung onto them, but they could just as easily have ended up in the bin, so little sentimental value had they held for Anna herself. And yet, as she leafed through page after page devoted to former classmates, a plethora of emotions kindled within her. Confronted by this array of long-forgotten faces, she found herself experiencing feelings of...well, not quite nostalgia, but certainly an acute awareness of just how much time had passed. How many people she'd completely lost track of.

She turned another page and found herself confronted by Foley's mugshot. There he was, just as she'd remembered him, grinning cockily, his eyes flirting with some female, real or imagined, just out of view. Her own eyes strayed to the block of text below.

'Both the life and soul of the party and a diligent student,' she read aloud, 'Andrew has his sights set on a career in accountancy. If–'

'If he shows as much dedication to the pursuit of his career as he does the opposite sex, he shall have a long, boring, prosperous future ahead of him,' Juliet finished, reciting from memory with her eyes closed.

Anna turned, surprised.

Juliet offered a sad smile. 'He wasn't always a bastard, you know. There were two sides to him. He'd beat me, but then he'd cry and say he was sorry and beg for my forgiveness. Sometimes, he'd cry as he was doing it. It becomes a part of one's life, you know? The jibes, the putdowns, even the physical stuff. You end up missing it once it's not there. Like an itch that needs scratching – know what I mean?'

Anna didn't, but thought better of saying as much. She turned to the next page, then the next – and then, quite suddenly, she stopped.

The girl she found herself looking at was beautiful, no doubt about it, but not in the way that normally turns men's heads. Hers was a clean, wholesome sort of beauty, untouched by either makeup or affectation. Her blonde hair fell in waves onto her shoulders. Her eyes, half-hidden behind a low fringe, gazed down into her lap, avoiding the camera. A small half-smile played at the corner of her lips, as if she and only she was party to some precious secret. Even before she read the name below the picture, Anna felt her breathing quickening in anticipation. Somehow, she knew instinctively that this was who she was looking for.

Jennifer Guilfoyle.

Her heart accelerating, she continued to read.

Fourth-year Jenny is a bit of an enigma – so much so that she failed to submit a profile to the committee. A sensitive soul with a strong moral compass (having a policeman for a dad will do that to you), the blonde belle is a butterfly just waiting to unfurl her wings and fly.

'That the one?' Anna turned to find Juliet leaning over her shoulder, her interest seemingly piqued. 'Hmm. Less obvious than his usual type, but she fits the bill. Blonde, blue eyes, the perfect storm of looks and low self-esteem. He'd have been ploughing her for sure. Know her?'

Anna didn't, but it occurred to her that, if Jenny had been in fourth year when Foley was in sixth, she'd have been a contemporary of Victor's. In any event, she had what she was looking for: a full name and a face to go with it.

Behind them, there was a tentative knock. They turned to see Kelly-Marie hovering uncertainly in the doorway. 'Is everything alright, Mrs Foley? Only you'd been gone a while, and I thought—'

Juliet rolled her eyes. 'Oh, do piss off, you glorified dishwasher. If I want you, you'll know because I'll snap my fingers.'

Kelly-Marie said nothing. She didn't even look hurt. She just turned and left without another word.

'I'm going to have to get rid of that one,' Juliet said. 'It's not as if I'll be able to afford to keep staff for much longer anyway.'

Anna said nothing, but her look told Juliet exactly what she was thinking.

Juliet sighed wearily, as if she was fed up having to justify herself. 'I don't hate her because she spread her legs for him, you know. I hate her because she's a doormat who just takes whatever I dish out. I wouldn't expect you to understand.'

'I understand perfectly,' said Anna. 'He made you into a victim, and you take it out on her because it makes you feel better about yourself, knowing there's at least one other person lower down the pecking order than you.'

Juliet gazed back at her, patently unmoved. 'How frightfully philosophical of you.'

Anna opened her mouth to respond, then stopped. There was nothing to be achieved by attempting to redeem Juliet. She gestured curtly to the yearbook. 'Mind if I borrow that? I'll bring it back as soon as—'

But Juliet was way ahead of her. She flexed the book's spine, loosening it, then tore the page out and handed it to Anna with the sort of smile an adult gives a particularly simple child.

'On the house,' she said, clearly viewing it as an act of great benevolence.

Anna stared back at Juliet, trying to work out how she felt about her. There was disgust, yes, but also pity. And, perhaps most unexpectedly of all, grudging respect. However damaged Juliet was, she'd emerged from years of abuse unbroken, and if her high-handed arrogance was her way of coping with what she'd had to endure, then fair play to her. *Better to be a hard-nosed bitch than a pushover.* While there was much about her behaviour Anna couldn't bring herself to condone in a million years, she couldn't help but think that if anyone had earned the right to bellow insults and help herself to a crafty swig of wine to get through the day, it was her.

So she left it at that.

***

On her way down the stairs, she ran into Gavin.

'How is she?' He nodded towards the upstairs landing.

'She's fine. She's…you know, dealing with it her own way.'

'We both know what *that* means.'

Anna experienced a brief flash of something approaching indignation on Juliet's behalf, but she bit her tongue.

Gavin nodded to the folded page in her hand. 'Whatcha got there?'

'It's nothing.' She pocketed it self-consciously.

Gavin looked doubtful for a moment, then gave an easy shrug. 'Come on. I'll set you up with something stiff. That's not an innuendo, by the way.'

Anna smiled dutifully, but shook her head. 'I need to get into town. I promised Zoe I'd meet her.'

'Ah, come on. Stay and reminisce about the good old days. There's a whole crowd down there of fellow Willow Bank survivors dying to be reacquainted with you – including quite a few eligible bachelors.' He did a suggestive eyebrow wiggle.

Anna sighed and shook her head. This reminded her all too much of family gatherings, during which her mother was wont to view all men of eligible age in terms of their suitability as marriage material for her daughter – a tendency which hadn't diminished as either of them had gotten older. At the last one, the inveterate Mrs Scavolini, clearly worried Anna was going to spend the rest of her life a spinster and thus fail to provide her with any grandchildren, had tried, with characteristic lack of subtlety, to pair her off with a variety of suitors, growing increasingly exasperated as Anna rebuffed them one by one. 'What's the matter with you?' she'd demanded. 'You could have any of the men in this room.' To which Anna had replied, 'I don't *want* any of the men in this room.' Her mother, who hadn't considered what Anna might or might not want, had said very little for the remainder of the event.

Anna tried to move past Gavin, but he anticipated her and blocked her path. 'You know,' he said, a sardonic smile playing on his lips, 'I can't help but think we've been in this spot before – you getting what you want, then doing a runner.'

Anna said nothing. She knew it was true, and how much of a heel it made her seem, but right now, she wasn't particularly concerned about whose sensibilities she offended.

Gavin's shoulders sagged in defeat. 'Well, if I can't change your mind, at least let me give you that lift I promised.'

***

In the end, Anna accepted his offer, for the sake of expediency if nothing else. As he gunned his Honda towards the city centre, she called Zoe to say she was on her way and to ask her to arrange for Victor to meet them as well. Zoe sounded dubious as to the likelihood of Victor doing anything she told him to, but agreed to see what she could wrangle.

When they pulled up outside Pulse a little after one, Anna didn't get out right away. She didn't want to part company with Gavin without knowing the answer to a question that had been fermenting at the back of her mind throughout the journey. In the space of forty-eight hours, Andrew Foley had gone from being a boy she used to fancy to a serial adulterer to, finally, a violent abuser. Were signs there all along and she'd simply been too infatuated to pick up on them? And how much had Gavin, who'd been far closer to him than she ever was, known? She was loath to even broach the subject, lest it shatter any remaining illusions, but she had to know.

'Gavin.'

He stirred and glanced across at her. 'Yeah?'

'What would you say if I told you I'd heard some things about Andrew? About him and women.'

'I don't follow.'

'I mean about the way he treated them.'

As euphemisms went, it was a pretty feeble one, downplaying Foley's behaviour something rotten. And yet, she couldn't help but feel compelled to shield Gavin as much as possible from the full extent of his cousin's behaviour.

'You mean he was a user?'

'No. Well, yes, but not just that. I mean…' *Go on, Anna. Just say it.* 'I mean he was violent.' It came out in a breathless staccato, as if getting it out quickly would somehow make the truth less painful.

Gavin's eyes narrowed. 'And what would make you think that?' Realisation dawned, and he sighed, sinking back in his seat. 'You've been talking to Juliet, haven't you? I told you what she's like. She's poison, Anna. Pure poison. She lies habitually.'

'She's not the only one I've been talking to.'

'Oh? Who else, then?'

'That's immaterial. Anyway, hard as it might be to fathom, I believe Juliet. I've seen the marks on her.' Her voice became an angry whisper. 'She had cigarette burns on her tit, for Christ's sake.'

Gavin was visibly shaken by this. 'And are you sure she didn't do that to herself? 'Cause knowing Juliet, I wouldn't put anything past her.'

'Are you even listening to yourself? Yeah, of course she did – and I suppose every woman in Glasgow who ends up in A&E with a black eye and a split lip after the football just happened to walk into a door.'

'Point taken. I just…well, I mean, come on, Anna. We're talking about my cousin here.'

'Your second cousin, who I seem to remember you claiming not to have been particularly close to.'

Gavin remained very still. He sat, arm resting on the window frame, staring out into the grey afternoon. Anna was about to give up and abandon him to his thoughts when he finally spoke.

'I didn't know anything. Not for definite, anyway.'

'But you had your suspicions?'

Gavin nodded reluctantly. 'I always knew he had somewhat…I guess you could say, *old-fashioned* views on women. Thought there were boy jobs and girl jobs and so on. Not outrageously offensive stuff, not really, but you could tell he thought things would be a lot better if society was still like it was in the fifties. And I knew he was possessive. Like, any time he was going with a girl, he'd always be super-paranoid about other boys paying her any attention. Would accuse them of having designs on her and suchlike, or her of making eyes at them. Not that he was ever particularly scrupulous himself when it came to other people's girlfriends. But no, by and large, he never said anything that made me worry. Apart from this one time…'

'What happened?'

Gavin looked at Anna uneasily, as if trying to gauge whether she was ready to hear this. 'A bunch of us were talking about girls. The usual stuff – who's hot and who's not, and so on. We got onto talking about what was and wasn't acceptable in a relationship. I said whatever rules you set had to be adhered to by both parties. Like if you were going to be unfaithful, you'd have to be okay with them doing the same. But Andrew wasn't having it. He kept banging on about how men and women had different biological urges. How it was fine for men to play the field because that's what they were programmed to do. And then he said – and I'll never forget this – he said, "If I found out any girl of mine was screwing behind my back, I'd rape the bitch 'til she bled." And then he just shrugged and took a swig of beer – you know, as if it was a perfectly normal thing to say.'

Anna had no idea how to respond to this. Pretty much anything would have sounded utterly superfluous.

'And what did *you* say?' she finally asked.

'I don't remember,' said Gavin, a little too quickly. 'I mean, you know what kids are like. They say and do some pretty stupid things. I guess I always tried to tell myself he'd grown out of these views. But if what you're saying is true…'

Anna was silent. She knew, of course, that he'd said nothing – just as the rest of his friends had no doubt done the same. She knew well enough that displays of insensitivity were a potent form of currency among teenage boys, vying to outdo each other by professing the most callous and misogynistic views imaginable. This particular example was extreme, but not even the worst she'd heard. If it had been anyone other than Foley, she'd have shuddered inwardly and dismissed it as ignorant banter. But given what she now knew…

'You know he once took the rap for me when I crashed my folks' car?' Gavin said.

'I didn't,' said Anna, wondering what that had to do with anything.

'It was the first thing I thought of when I heard the news. I'd not long passed my test, and I got absolutely bladdered and ran it into the neighbours' wall. Andrew was riding shotgun and made me swap places with him. It's thanks to him I'm still allowed to drive and have a career worth mentioning.' He hesitated. 'I guess what I mean is, it's difficult for me. You know, to hears those things about him. To reconcile the Andrew I thought I knew with…' He trailed off, then gave Anna a sidelong glance. 'I should've said something, shouldn't I? Should've challenged him. *All it takes for evil to triumph* and all that.'

'Would it've made a difference?'

'I don't know. But that's not the point, is it? The point is I should've called him out on it, and I didn't.'

'You were young. He was your big cousin. You looked up to him. And it's not as if you thought he actually meant it.'

She knew she was making excuses for him, desperately trying to convince herself he hadn't been at fault. Gavin glanced over at her, and she saw from his expression that he wasn't buying it any more than her.

'Does it make me a bad person?'

'I don't know,' said Anna truthfully. 'I suppose it doesn't make you any worse than all the other people who close their eyes and ears every day to things they'd rather not confront.'

'Not sure that makes me feel any better.'

'Put it this way – d'you think it would've made a difference if you'd spoken up? D'you think he valued your opinion so highly it would've completely changed his life's trajectory?'

'I suppose not.'

'There you go, then. Andrew was the abuser, not you. Alright, so maybe, if you'd said something back then, you'd feel better about yourself now, but it wouldn't've changed things a jot otherwise.' She reached across and laid a hand on his arm – a gesture that felt stiff and unnatural, but which she felt compelled to make. 'You're not responsible for his actions, so don't beat yourself up over it. Hey.' She flashed him an encouraging smile, trying to lighten the mood. 'Quit making it all about you, ya big prima donna.'

That made him smile, however apathetically.

Anna undid her seatbelt. 'I'd better be going. Thanks for the lift.'

Gavin winked half-heartedly. 'Any time, any place.'

Anna shouldered her bag and stepped out into the street.

'Anna.'

She turned. Gavin had rolled down the passenger window and was leaning across towards her.

'Did you make a decision?'

'About what?'

'About sticking around. Yesterday, you were waiting to see how things panned out. I just wondered if you'd had any more thoughts about going back to Rome.'

'What do you think I should do?'

Gavin's jaw clenched agitatedly. 'Personally, if I were you, I'd be getting on the next flight out of here. Whoever killed Andrew… well, they didn't mess about, did they? I'd hate to think of you in their crosshairs.'

She studied his face. If there was any malice lurking behind those soft eyes of his, he was hiding it exceptionally well.

'We'll see. For the time being, I'm sticking around.'

21

Rumours

As she descended into the pit, Anna found that, devoid of perspiring bodies and pulsating lights, Pulse seemed like a different place entirely. More serene, more…civilised. The basement was empty and deathly quiet, the people who normally frequented the place on a Saturday afternoon no doubt using the last weekend before Christmas to get their shopping done.

Anna crossed the empty dancefloor, peering into the various nooks and crannies, hoping to catch sight of…

'Looking for Zoe? She's not here yet.'

Anna turned in the direction of the voice. The blonde bartender who'd served her the other night was behind the counter, polishing a shot glass.

'Oh? Has she called?'

'Rang a few minutes ago. Bus ran into a snowdrift or something.' She gestured to the row of stools facing the bar. 'Make yourself at home. What's your poison?'

Anna ordered sparkling water, which the bartender refused to let her pay for, insisting that 'any friend of Zoe's, yadda yadda yadda'. As she headed over to the fridge and opened a bottle of Highland Spring, Anna fished her essays out of her bag, determined once again to make an effort to get on with the job she was actually paid to do. As she laid the folder on the counter, however, her eyes couldn't help but linger on Ross Garvey's limp scrawl.

Can't escape you, Jenny, can I?

'Here you go.' The bartender slid her glass across to her. She nodded to the page Anna was reading. 'What's this?'

'Student essay. This one's arguing that all thieves should be pardoned as victims of capitalist oppression.'

The bartender laughed. 'Oh, that sounds right up my alley.'

'Property,' said Anna solemnly, 'is no longer a theft.'

The bartender produced a pack of cigarettes from her jeans pocket. 'You don't mind, do you? We're not supposed to, but when the cat's away…'

'…the mice will play. It's fine. Inhale away.'

The woman grinned. She lit up, took an appreciative drag and leaned against the bar, tilting her head back and exhaling smoke through her nostrils. Anna returned to the essay.

'So what did you make of last night?'

Anna lifted her head. 'Sorry?'

'The "Three Per Cent" lecture, up at the uni? You came in late, stood at the back. If I'd known you were coming, I'd've saved you a seat.'

'Oh – I didn't realise you were there.'

The bartender's lip curled in amusement. 'Clearly I'm not gonna be winning any awards for Best Actor, then.'

Anna's eyes widened. 'That was *you*?'

The bartender – Carol, as Anna now realised she was – grinned. 'Ha! I'd like to claim I totally disappeared into the role, but truth is, I just forgot to put my contacts in. Hence the big old speccies.'

Anna grimaced. 'Sorry. I'm rubbish with faces. Yeah, you were really good. You had *me* convinced, anyway.'

It all sounded rather hollow to Anna's ears, but Carol seemed pleased. 'Thanks. Sorry I couldn't stick around to say hi. I was already running late for my shift. Doing am dram for Mark Westmore doesn't pay the bills, more's the pity.'

'You a part-time postgrad, then?'

Carol shook her head, smiling. 'Flattery'll get you everywhere. Nah, just a concerned citizen. Anything to do with women's rights, I'm there. Went to my first Take Back the Night at sixteen. Lost a coupla teeth for my trouble. Been a champion of the oppressed ever since.'

She opened her mouth wide enough for Anna to see that she was indeed missing two lower molars.

'Fucking pigs, eh? Funny how it's always young women, students and people of colour on the wrong end of a truncheon and never the types that actually deserve a good hiding.'

Anna couldn't help but wonder just who she had in mind. 'You never thought to get those fixed?'

'Scars of battle.' There was a note of pride in Carol's voice. 'Every time I feel the gaps, it reminds me we haven't won yet. 'Sides, my girlfriend tells me they add character.'

'Can't argue with that.'

Silence descended once more. Carol resumed smoking, while Anna attempted to focus on her essay. It was easier said than done. Try as she might, the words on the page merged into a blur, and her thoughts kept drifting back to her conversation with Gavin. She figured, in light of Carol's declared interests, she'd be as good a sounding board as any.

'Mind if I ask you a question?'

Carol tipped ash into the tumbler she was using as an ashtray. 'Shoot.'

'Say there was a man who knew a friend of his held unsavoury attitudes about women but decided to keep quiet about it.' She kept her tone casual, hoping to make this sound like mere academic speculation. 'And say that friend went on to commit acts of violence against women. Would he then be responsible for his friend's actions?'

'Definitely.' Not so much as a hint of hesitation on Carol's part. 'The ones that say nothing are as guilty as the ones doing it. End of.'

Anna was a little taken aback by her vehemence. 'Wasn't expecting *quite* such a black and white interpretation.'

'You mean there's shades of grey to femicide? News to me.'

'No, but people often say things they don't…' She trailed off, aware of how feeble it sounded.

'So,' said Carol, 'we talking hypotheticals here, or did you have someone specific in mind?'

And so Anna gave her the gist of Gavin's confession – albeit a heavily depersonalised version which named no names.

Carol listened intently, her only interjection an audible *Fuck!* when Anna recounted Foley's words about what he'd do to an unfaithful girlfriend.

'You didn't tell me you were talking about teenagers,' said Carol, when Anna had finished. 'That's a bit different, I'll grant you. They can be right stupid little pricks. But it just goes to show the schools should be teaching respect and women's rights in sex ed instead of just banging on about how to put condoms on bananas.'

'Hey, no argument there.' It occurred to Anna that this conversation was developing in a not dissimilar fashion to her debate with Mark the previous night, only this time with her as the moderating voice. 'Thing is, I get where you're coming from – but peer pressure's a big factor. Folk don't always find it so easy to speak out.'

Carol pursed her lips and thought about it. 'There's this quote I'm fond of. People credit it to Alasdair Gray, but he didn't come up with it. *Work as if you live in the early days of a better nation.* I think we should be doing that. If I can't live in a world where these things don't happen, then I hope at least to one day live in one where no one remains silent. Not the bystanders…and not the victims.'

As she said this, she fixed Anna with her eye. It seemed to Anna that the look that passed between them was one of mutual understanding – a recognition that they were kindred spirits bonded together by unspoken, shared experience. It wasn't a feeling Anna particularly liked. She was left with the distinct impression Carol had seen some part of her that shouldn't have been visible.

The spell was broken by the sound of footsteps on the stairs. They turned to see Zoe stepping into view, weighed down by half a dozen laden shopping bags. Victor followed in her wake, trailing reluctantly behind her and looking distinctly bleary-eyed. Zoe came to a stop at the foot of the stairs and stood beaming at them.

'Aw, in't that nice? My two favourite peeps gettin' on like a house on fire. So what's the goss?'

***

Once they were all settled round a table in the corner and lunch and the inevitable round of drinks had been distributed, Anna got the others up to speed regarding her discoveries. She hadn't planned to involve Carol, but the bartender showed no sign of going anywhere, and Anna didn't want to waste any time. In any event, she and Zoe seemed to be on good terms, and Zoe was usually a pretty solid judge of character. So Anna told them everything she knew, as succinctly as possible. As the *pièce de résistance*, she produced Jenny Guilfoyle's yearbook profile.

Zoe examined the photo. 'Aye, I 'member her. Shy girl, kind of a wallflower. Sang in the school choir. She was ages with you, wasn't she, Vic?'

Anna turned to Victor. 'D'you remember her at all?'

Victor heaved his shoulders noncommittally.

Zoe nudged him in the ribs playfully. 'Aye ye do. Come on, ye cannae pull the wool over yer big sister's eyes. What's wrong? Didnae fancy her, did ye?'

'Course I didn't,' muttered Victor, avoiding her eye.

'How come you're blushin', then? Hey, I wouldnae blame you if ye did. She's well pretty.'

'Fuck off,' snapped Victor, his cheeks glowing. 'She look like she'd've given me the time of day?'

'Alright, leave him alone,' said Anna. She turned to face Victor, trying to draw him into the conversation. 'D'you remember anything about her, Victor – anything at all?'

Victor shrugged and tugged distractedly at his sleeve. 'She was…I dunno, quiet, I guess? Just kinda done her own thing. Our paths didnae really cross that much.' He hesitated, then added awkwardly, 'Some of the guys used to take the piss – y'know, ask her for blowjobs and what have you. I mean, I get it. She was kinda nice-lookin', I s'pose, but, well…I mean, she wasnae my type.'

'Right.' Zoe was sporting a lascivious grin. 'And, uh, just what *is* your type, little brother?'

Victor lowered his eyes and muttered something inaudible. Zoe shot Anna a mischievous look. They both knew exactly what – or rather *who* – Victor's type was. Her smile faded when she clocked Anna's stony expression.

'Jeez,' she muttered. 'Sorry I spoke.'

Anna folded her arms. 'Okay, then, seeing as you're such a font of knowledge, what do *you* remember about her?'

Zoe pursed her lips and thought. 'I remember the rumours. About what happened to her.'

Anna was on the alert at once. 'What happened to her?'

Zoe bit her lower lip. She looked very much like she regretted saying anything. 'Okay, look – this was after my time and yours, so it might only be Chinese whispers. It was Paul Docherty from her year told me, and he heard it off someone else too, so…Anyway, supposedly it happened at one of they parties.'

'Parties?'

'You must've known about 'em. Heard the stories, anyway. I dunno who it was started 'em, but by the time we were senior school, they were pretty much the top social event of the week. Wild, wild parties – we're talkin' the best grass, more booze'n you knew what to do with…Sex too, if that was your thing. They got held at all different places, but it was the same crowd goin' tae all of them. You know the ones – those guys who always thought they were the bee's knees, acted like they were older'n they actually were. The ones whose folks were *connected*.'

Like Andrew Foley.

'Anyway, it was a pretty big deal if you got yersel invited. And there was certain…expectations.'

'What sort of expectations?'

'I mean, there was a lot of pressure for lassies to give it up. Actually, way I heard it, it was pretty much a condition of entry. You accepted the invite, you were basically acceptin' that you were gonnae be asked to put out.'

'Jesus,' Carol muttered.

'I mean, I was never took tae do wi' any of it,' said Zoe hastily and, to Anna's ears, rather defensively. 'Face didnae fit. But I knew lassies that *were*, and from what they said, there wasnae much that was off limits.'

'But how does Jenny fit into all of this?' said Anna. 'She doesn't seem like she'd be the type to get involved in that sort of thing.'

'I know, right? That's why I'm thinkin' mibby this story's all bollocks. But hey, dinnae shoot the messenger. Anyway, what I heard is she ended up at one o' these parties, and whatever happened to her, it fucked her up royally. Word was some of the boys had made her do things she wasnae comfortable doin', but I didnae ask for chapter 'n' verse. Thing is, she must've known what she was gettin' intae. *Everyone* knew what they parties were about. If she wasnae happy about it, she shouldnae have gone.'

The look on Carol's face was one of utter derision. 'So, in your book, if a girl accepts an invite to a party, she's actively consenting to be fucked three ways from Sunday?'

'I never said I *agreed* wi' it,' Zoe replied defensively. 'I was just sayin'...' She trailed off. 'Sorry. God, I didnae mean...I just, well...sorry.' She offered a sheepish shrug and fell silent.

'It's alright,' said Anna softly. She knew there was no malice in Zoe's comments – just a hefty dose of naïveté. 'So what became of Jenny afterwards?'

'Ended up droppin' out of school not long after, and naeb'dy ever heard fae her again.'

Anna turned to Victor. 'Is that right?'

Victor gave another evasive shrug. 'I heard she left, yeah, durin' sixth year. But naeb'dy ever said what that was about. One day, she just wasnae there anymore. I figured she just moved away. I mean, she didnae exactly have many friends, so I don't think anyone really missed her.'

Anna was silent. She'd been aware that these events took place and had had a general idea of what they were about – wild, hedonistic affairs arranged by boys whose parents went away on business a lot and left them plenty money to spend. And she'd known there was sex involved. There usually was when alcohol and teenage libidos entered the equation. She'd always assumed it was all above-the-board consensual stuff. But to hear Zoe talk, it sounded as if these boys had basically been running a grooming ring, taking advantage of girls who weren't in a position to say no.

She pointed to the yearbook profile. 'This mentions her dad – says he's a policeman. Know anything about him?'

Zoe perked up. 'Aye, big beefy guy, wild hair. Bit of a scary mofo, actually. He was a pretty big noise round these parts – high heid yin in the CID or some such. Might still be – I dunno. But I reckon he was the reason Jenny was such a recluse. Like, he kept her on a short leash, wouldnae let her have any fun. There was a rumour he'd beat up a boy who got fresh with her. Mibby that's how she went to the party? Like, stickin' it to the man?'

Anna remembered the burly man she'd seen during her run the previous morning, watching the crime scene techs from near the top of the hill – the one whose presence had made her feel so inexplicably uneasy.

'They didn't by any chance live up on Woodlands Hill, did they?'

'Aye.' Zoe sounded surprised. 'Lynedoch Place. How'd you know?'

'Call it a hunch.'

'A hunch, is it? So whatcha thinkin', Miss Marple? What's your next move?'

Anna chewed her lip pensively. 'I think I'm going to start by heading up there and paying him a visit. See if he can put me in touch with his daughter.'

Zoe frowned. 'Sure that's a good idea? Ye don't think she could be waitin' for ye with a butcher's cleaver?'

Carol scoffed. 'What, you think she's running around knocking men off like this is *Sudden Impact* or something? She's not the one doing this, and you can quote me on that.'

'How not?' Zoe rolled her eyes. 'Lemme guess – 'cause she's a lassie.'

'That'd do for a start.'

'She's right,' said Anna, as Zoe gave a snort of derision. 'Statistically speaking, female killers are a rarity in and of themselves. And the tiny minority who do kill are more likely to poison or shoot their victims. Mutilations like these are virtually non-existent.'

'Sure,' said Zoe. 'Disnae meant they don't happen, though.'

Anna shook her head. 'Castration *says* something. It's symbolic. A message. A specific punishment for a specific crime. And I hope I'm not overgeneralising here, but I don't think women place that much symbolic importance on that particular piece of anatomy. Seems more like something a man would *think* a woman would do.'

'And what about equal opportunities? I'm more than capable of loppin' someone's balls off.'

'Oh, for fuck's sake,' said Carol.

'Say that a bit louder, why don't ye?' said Victor. 'Course, that's if you actually *want* to be hauled in for another round of questionin'.'

Zoe folded her arms like a petulant child. 'It was just a joke! Lighten up, the lot of yese. Whatever happened to *'Tis the season to be jolly*?'

An uneasy silence fell. Victor, for want of something to do, began to pick unenthusiastically at his lunch. Anna stared down at her own plate, her food barely touched. She couldn't face it.

It was Carol who broke the silence. 'Okay, I'm gonna say it if no one else is. Have I entered some parallel universe here? Why're we even talking about going looking for this Jenny, *or* her dad? Shouldn't this be the sort of information we take to the police?'

'She's got a point,' said Victor, and went back to mopping up gravy with a chip.

'Aw, c'mon, where's the harm?' said Zoe. 'We're only gonnae ask if we can see her. I was kiddin' about the butcher's cleaver, FYI,' she added in a stage whisper.

'It's probably a waste of time,' said Anna, aware that her reasoning had a somewhat hollow ring to it. 'Odds are I'm barking up the wrong tree entirely, and I'd rather find that out myself rather than go to the cops with some half-arsed story and end up making a tit of myself.' She was already on her feet, forestalling any further debate.

Zoe pushed back her chair. 'Well, hold up. I'll come with. We can make tits of ourselves the gether.'

'I'll handle it myself.'

Zoe stopped short, looking hurt. Anna winced. She hadn't meant it to come out sounding so harsh.

'Look, I'm just going to head up there, knock the door and ask the dad if he knows where I can find Jenny. I'd rather not freak him out with a whole posse showing up on his doorstep.'

'Fair point,' said Zoe, somewhat dubiously.

'I still don't like it,' said Carol.

'Good thing it's not your decision,' said Anna, before she could help herself.

'Aye, alright!' exclaimed Zoe. 'There's nae need for that. Just time out, all o' yese.'

No one spoke. Carol scraped back her chair and began to clear the table, deliberately ignoring Anna, who stood facing them, feeling like a first-class heel. The mood had turned decidedly sour, the warm feelings of camaraderie and of pooling and sharing their respective points of view having evaporated like water in the desert.

'I'll see you back at the house, yeah?' she said to Zoe.

'Aye,' said Zoe, her tone uncharacteristically cool. 'Well, you know how tae get in touch.'

Anna turned to go. She'd got as far as the stairs when she heard Zoe's voice behind her.

'It's the house with the green door. And watch out. If there's any truth in that story about him duffin' up some kid, he must be a right nutjob.'

Sound advice, thought Anna as she climbed the stairs.

22

Void

Anna stood at the top of Woodlands Hill and gazed out across Kelvingrove Park, its snow-topped slopes unfolding in the shadow of the mounted statue of the Field Marshal of Kandahar. Further afield still, the university and its bell-tower rose up behind a dense mass of trees. There was a more pronounced nip in the air now. Either it was the effect of the higher altitude, or the temperature had dropped significantly.

It took her five minutes to find Lynedoch Place, a gently sloping side street on the other side of the hill. Narrow, closely-packed sandstone townhouses were the name of the game here, and she found the one she was looking for about halfway down the slope. She was glad Zoe had mentioned the green door, otherwise she'd have had to resort to random knocking.

She climbed the wide stone steps and rang the bell. She waited a full minute, but no one answered. After ringing again, to no avail, she headed down to street level and gazed up at the large bay windows. The ground floor curtains were closed. The blinds on the upper floors had been lowered. It looked for all the world like the owners had shut up shop. Perhaps they'd gone on holiday? It wasn't an unreasonable proposition given the time of year.

Then she noticed the snow – or lack thereof. Someone had cleared a path from door to pavement and left the shovel propped against the fence for good measure. It had last snowed on the evening of the seventeenth, a mere two days ago – meaning whoever had cleared the path had done so since then.

She headed down to the foot of the slope and followed the pavement as it curved right. A little way down the road, a narrow cobblestoned lane ran behind the houses, most of which had rear gardens accessible via gates or doors. Counting her way along, she found the one corresponding to the Guilfoyle house. It opened onto a neat, well-tended garden dominated by an ancient oak tree listing wearily to one side. A swing hung forlornly from its largest branch. Footprints in the otherwise unblemished snow led away from it towards the house.

In for a penny, in for a pound. She'd already inveigled her way into an ICU bay by posing as a detective; breaking into a house seemed comparatively small fry.

The door was unlocked. Stepping over the threshold, she found herself in a large, low-ceilinged kitchen. Like the garden, it was neat and orderly. A couple of plates and two sets of knives and forks lay on the draining board. On the long wooden table in the middle of the room, a local tabloid lay open, a crossword half-finished. Anna checked the date. It was today's edition.

'Is anyone there?'

Her voice boomed in her own ears. Once again, she was met with silence.

She headed out into the hallway. To her left, a flight of stairs led up to the first floor. To her right, a panelled door opened onto the living room, which lay in semi-darkness. From the doorway, she could make out the shapes of furniture inside – a sofa, an armchair, a low table.

Using the torch on her phone to light the way, she stepped inside, moving cautiously to avoid bumping into anything. She stopped at the window and peeled back the curtain slightly. The street outside was quiet and still.

As she let the curtain fall shut, a sudden noise above her caused her to start and drop her phone, plunging her into near-total darkness. Dropping to her knees, she fumbled for it, heart hammering in her ribcage. A moment later, she heard it again – the creak of floorboards overhead.

Abandoning any thought of retrieving her phone, she scrambled to her feet and fled towards the door. Along the way, her shin collided with the table. She gave a yelp and limped on, tumbling out into the hallway. There, she hesitated, fighting her natural instinct to flee.

With the light of the outside world on her face once again, her courage began to return. She took the door off the latch and opened it a crack, ensuring she'd have a means of making a hasty getaway should it prove necessary. Then, gulping her fear back down into her stomach, she climbed the stairs.

At the top, she found herself on a narrow landing with a door to her left, one to her right and another straight ahead, all closed. She stopped and listened, but heard nothing.

'Hello? Is there someone there? I just want to ask some questions.'

She felt in her pocket for her keys, readying them as a weapon. Telling herself she wasn't going to freeze this time if the need arose, she chose the door on the left and pushed it open cautiously.

It appeared to be the master bedroom. Above the neatly-made double bed was a framed black and white picture, which upon closer inspection turned out to be a police graduation photograph. Three rows of severe-looking men stared back at her, straight-backed and dressed in neatly-pressed uniforms, their hairstyles dating the image to the early seventies or thereabouts. Looking at their stern faces, she doubted a single smile had ever been cracked between them.

Behind her, a floorboard creaked. She spun around, but there was nobody there.

It was then that she noticed the door on the other side of the landing was now slightly ajar.

Got you.

She crossed the landing in a few quick strides and opened the door, keys at the ready. Her eyes swept the room, taking in the décor. This was clearly a teenage girl's abode. Like Zoe's, it seemed to have been frozen at some point in the late nineties, though this one was far more stereotypically girly. The wallpaper, duvet and carpet were a variety of shades of pink; a couple of oversized teddy bears took pride of place on the bed; the walls were adorned with tasteful landscapes and Rennie Mackintosh prints.

It wasn't until her third sweep that she noticed the pair of feet poking out from under the row of clothes hanging in the open wardrobe. Small feet, women's feet, wearing plain grey socks and no shoes.

Moving on tiptoe, Anna crossed over to the wardrobe and knelt down. She heard an intake of breath behind the wall of jumpers and blouses. Slowly, she parted the clothes, revealing the person behind them.

She was a woman, about Anna's age or perhaps a little younger, though it was hard to be sure, given the ageless, shapeless corduroy trousers and pullover she was wearing, and the unkempt mop of blonde hair that obscured much of her face. She sat on the floor of the wardrobe, knees drawn up to her chin, watching Anna guardedly from behind her low fringe. She was completely still, apart from her rapidly blinking eyes and the rise and fall of her chest as she took quick, shallow breaths.

'It's okay,' said Anna. 'I'm not going to hurt you.'

The woman stared back at her, blue eyes vacant, mouth hanging slightly open.

Anna had seen that look before. Back in the early nineties, on the drive back from a day trip to Loch Lomond, her father had hit a deer that had wandered out into the road. He'd stopped and got out to look, warning Anna to stay in the car, but curiosity had got the better of her, and after a moment, she followed him. She found him kneeling on the road next to the creature. It was young, little more than a fawn, lying on its side, stomach heaving as it struggled to breathe. As she approached, it stared up at her, unable to move, the solitary eye facing her a great dark void. She'd found herself transfixed by that eye, gazing into the nothingness that lay behind it.

Now, in this woman's eyes, she saw that same fear. That same lack of comprehension. With mounting horror, she realised she was looking at the adult Jenny Guilfoyle.

'Sweet Jesus,' she heard herself murmuring, 'what did they do to you?'

Jenny stared back at her, like a feral beast cornered and trapped.

'I won't hurt you,' Anna said again, though by this stage, she realised she'd no hope of making herself understood. 'You're safe.'

Jenny continued to gaze at her with that same haunted expression. It was childlike…No, pre-childhood. She remembered seeing a documentary about people with an extreme form of catatonic schizophrenia, locked inside their own bodies, unaware of their surroundings and unable to move or speak. Some of them had had faces like Jenny's.

On the floor below, the front door slammed. Anna stiffened. Footsteps in the hallway.

'Jenny?'

A man's voice, deep and loaded with suspicion.

Anna watched Jenny, waiting to see if she would reply. She gave no sign of having heard at all.

She heard heavy boots slowly ascending the stairs. She looked around desperately for either a means of escape or a place to hide. She found neither, and climbing into the wardrobe alongside Jenny wasn't much of an option. There was no time to make a run for it – and no point either, for she'd only encounter the man, who was surely Jenny's notorious father, on the stairs. There was no option but to stay where she was. She got to her feet and stood facing the door, doing her damnedest not to tremble.

The footsteps reached the landing and stopped. For a moment, there was silence, broken only by the blood pounding in Anna's ears. Then they began again, quicker than before, striding towards her. The door flew open to reveal the burly, wild-haired man she'd seen in Kelvingrove Park the previous day. His bulky frame filled the doorway, scuppering any hope of ducking past him and making good her escape. His eyes darted from Anna to Jenny, still in her cubby-hole, then back to Anna again.

'Who are you? Who let you in?'

'I…the door was open. I heard a noise and–'

'Shut up.' He frowned, tilting his head as he studied her. 'I've seen you before. Yesterday, in the park. Who are you? What do you want with us? Answer me!'

She began to speak, tripping over the words as they tumbled from her mouth. 'My name's Anna Scavolini. I was at school with your daughter. I came to ask her what she knows about the murder in Kelvingrove Park two nights ago and the attack in Bellahouston this morning. I–'

'Jenny, wait for me downstairs.' Guilfoyle's eyes didn't leave Anna's face as he spoke.

Again, Jenny gave no response.

Guilfoyle's shoulders sagged. Wearily, he stepped past Anna, went over to his daughter and, with surprising gentleness, took her hands in his. She lifted her head, meeting his eyes. He began to speak, his voice low, the words inaudible. His tone was soothing, and as Anna continued to watch, she sensed a change in Jenny's demeanour. The fear seemed to leave her, and she became docile. Pliant.

Still holding her hands in his, Guilfoyle lifted her to her feet and helped her out of the wardrobe. 'Go on now.'

Jenny held her father's gaze, still with the same blank, open-mouthed expression, then turned from him and headed towards the door. Anna stepped aside to let her through. Jenny seemed not even to register her presence as she passed her and headed downstairs, her soft footsteps slowly receding.

Anna turned towards Guilfoyle. He stood facing the wardrobe, his back to her. It occurred to her that now would probably be a good time to leave. But before she could move, his shoulders straightened, and he turned to face her, fists balled. Neither spoke. It was like the warm-up to a boxing match – one in which the combatants were grossly mismatched, and only one had any desire to fight.

His attack came before she even had a chance to register what was happening. With surprising agility, he bounded across the room, grabbed her by the collar of her coat and shoved her up against the door. She felt her feet leaving the ground as he hoisted her up, holding her aloft in a vicelike grip. She kicked wildly, hands scrabbling at her throat, the very breath being squeezed out of her. His beady, vicious little eyes bored into her.

'Listen carefully, because I'll say this only the once. Whoever you are, whatever it is you're after, you don't trouble me or my daughter again. Just because I'm not a cop anymore doesn't mean I don't still have plenty of friends on the force who'd be more than willing to help out an old colleague. Folk like Bill Norton at Yorkhill. All I have to do is pick up the phone, and believe me when I say I can make sure life becomes very, *very* unpleasant for you. Are we clear?'

Anna nodded frantically, unable to speak.

For a moment, she remained suspended in the air. Then, as suddenly as he'd grabbed her, Guilfoyle let go. She hit the floor, landing on her hands and knees, choking and spluttering. As soon as she was able, she struggled to her feet and fled. She reached the ground floor, wrenched open the door and burst out into the open air. She ran and she ran, eventually coming to a halt at the mouth of Park Gate, gasping for breath, eyes watering in the stinging cold. She was shaking uncontrollably. The blood was rushing to her head. Pins and needles danced on the tips of her fingers. A host of long-suppressed memories flooded her conscious: the taste of Carlsberg in her throat, the bitter scent of aftershave in her nostrils, the feel of rucked-up sheets against her back, a mocking voice saying, *You're not a child, are you?*

This had all been a massive mistake. She should never have come back. She should have listened to the voice at the back of her mind warning her everything she'd spent the last ten years avoiding would be waiting for her the moment she set foot in this accursed city again.

She just hadn't counted on those memories manifesting themselves quite so literally.

23

Misunderstanding

Anna stumbled down the steps to the Kelvingrove subway station. She bought a ticket from the machine, feeding in the coinage with trembling hands, and jumped aboard an outer circle train just before it pulled away from the platform. It didn't matter where she was headed. She just needed to feel she was on the move.

As the train with its jam-packed carriages rattled through the narrow tunnel beneath the city, the immediacy of her encounter with Guilfoyle receded, and her thoughts turned to Jenny. She realised now that Juliet had got off comparatively lightly – if it was even possible to think in such terms. Whatever Foley had done to Jenny to reduce her to such a piteous state must've been beyond horrific. Attempting to banish all thought of it from her mind, she closed her eyes and concentrated on taking deep, measured breaths.

When she next stirred, they were coming into Hillhead, meaning the train had almost completed a full circuit. Glasgow's subway system wasn't exactly elaborate – a ten-kilometre oval loop encompassing fifteen stops. However, it still meant that she must have been out for a good half-hour. Her lack of sleep – or was it her lack of medication? – was beginning to take its toll.

She joined the mass exodus from the carriage. They were now in the middle of the late afternoon rush hour, and she made slow progress up the stairs, crushed amid a heaving mass of bodies, breathing in a cocktail of stale sweat and deodorant. By the time she stepped out onto the West End's central artery of Byres Road, she was positively grateful to feel the cold air on her face. Head low, she headed up the pavement, pushing – or so it seemed – against the general tide of movement.

She hadn't gone more than a few paces, however, when she began to sense that someone was following her. It began as a tingling at the base of her neck, followed by a prickling of the hair on her back and arms. She tried quickening her pace, but this was easier said than done on the tightly packed pavement. At the first opportunity, she turned off onto Ashton Lane, hurrying up the narrow cobbled alley, breath rising to a panicked rasp. She felt a hand on her shoulder. Her heart leapt into her throat. She swung around, convinced she was going to find herself face-to-face with Jenny's father, but instead found herself taking in the bemused smile of Mark Westmore.

'I thought it was you,' he said. 'I called after you, but you kept walking. Didn't you hear me?'

Anna shook her head. She was out of breath, and her tongue seemed to have no intention of doing her brain's bidding.

Mark's brows furrowed in concern. 'Anna, what's wrong?'

***

At Mark's suggestion, they headed to the café on the first floor of the Grosvenor Cinema and requisitioned a table by the window. There, Anna told him everything that had happened. She censored nothing from her tale, and, as she spoke, realised she was giving him a fuller account than she'd given even to Zoe. In the warmth of the café, surrounded by the gentle hubbub of conversation and the smell of freshly-ground coffee, the events of the last two days seemed a distant memory, and it all began to sound increasingly far-fetched as she put it into words. Even her encounter with Guilfoyle, so terrifying at the time, now scarcely seemed real, like something out of a bad dream.

Mark made no attempt to discredit her account, to tell her she was making connections where none existed or that she was blowing this out of all proportion. He listened carefully, only interjecting now and then to clarify the odd detail. When she'd finished, he still said nothing but sat deep in thought, running his fingers over the stubble on his chin.

'What are you thinking?' she asked, when the silence became too much to bear.

'I think,' he said slowly, 'that you should be telling all this to the police, rather than to me.'

'You think they'd listen to me? I know how it all sounds. They'll think I'm a complete wackjob.'

'Perhaps. But you don't strike me as someone who's given to flights of fancy, or who jumps to conclusions without properly assessing all the facts at your disposal. I doubt you'd be telling me any of this if you didn't have good grounds to believe it. So yes, maybe you're wrong. Maybe you've got the wrong end of the stick entirely and there's no connection between this woman and the two attacks. But if there's even a sliver of a chance you're on the right track, then I reckon it's far too much to handle yourself. It needs to be dealt with through the proper channels.'

'I appreciate your candour.'

It was more or less what Carol had said earlier, and she found herself bristling anew at the insinuation she was out of her depth. Given the way the police had treated her thus far, they weren't exactly top of her list of people to turn to. And then there was the fact Guilfoyle had specifically named Norton in his threat to make things difficult for her. If those two were old comrades-in-arms, how could she possibly expect a fair hearing?

Still, Mark had a point. She was just one woman going up against a killer whose stock-in-trade was genital mutilation. And loath though she was to admit it, she knew the police were the only ones in a position to actually do anything with her information.

She gave a nod of resignation. 'Okay. I'll talk to them.'

'Wise decision.' Mark pushed back his chair and stood up. 'Come on, then.'

'What, *now*?' The afternoon was getting on. It would soon be dark. She'd been planning on leaving it till the following morning.

But Mark was already offering her her coat. 'Why not? No time like the present.'

***

They walked the mile or so to Yorkhill Police Station in silence. Mark, clearly picking up that Anna wasn't in the mood for talking, made no attempt to strike up a conversation, and she was grateful for that. She'd been planning on telling him to leave her at the door, but when they got there a little after five, he bounded up the steps with her and accompanied her in uninvited. In a way, she was glad. She now realised she appreciated the company, not to mention the show of solidarity. Somehow, she fancied her story would seem less like the rantings of a crazy person if someone else in the room was seen to believe her.

They presented themselves at reception, Anna asking to speak to Norton. The desk sergeant said he was out attending to another matter, but that DS Murray was in the building, and would he do? Anna couldn't think of anyone she wanted to see less, but she sensed that it was either talk to Murray or leave empty-handed. And in any event, perhaps it was better this way, given Norton's apparent links to Guilfoyle. So she gritted her teeth and said that yes, DS Murray would do nicely, and she and Mark were directed to the waiting area.

Murray arrived ten minutes later, all polished brogues, neatly-ironed trousers and bored contempt. 'Shall we get on with this?'

He ushered them into a poky little office at the back of the building. Seated behind his desk with the pair of them facing him, perched on small classroom chairs like schoolchildren called to the headmaster's office, he listened as Anna went through her account for what was now the third time that day.

This proved to be the least complete iteration of her story, skipping over her interrogation of Ross Garvey in its entirety. She explained that Norton had told her about the specific nature of the attacks – a detail which seemed to incense Murray, though he passed no comment – and that this had got her thinking. She told the truth about Jenny as far as was possible, though she left out the whole 'breaking and entering' bit. And of course, she said nothing about Foley's abuse of Juliet. To do so would have been a betrayal of trust too great to contemplate. With so many holes in the narrative, her account sounded even more far-fetched and plagued by circumstantial evidence than the version she'd given Mark, and it was abundantly clear she'd already lost Murray before she'd even begun. Nonetheless, she pressed on gamely, concluding with her encounter with Jenny and her father.

When she finally fell silent, Murray made a big show of stroking his chin sagely as he contemplated what he'd heard. 'Hmm, well, yes, this is a very...*elaborate* story, Ms Scavolini. You certainly get about, don't you?'

'You need to bring Guilfoyle in for questioning,' she said, ignoring the implicit innuendo. 'If I'm right, he's got more than adequate motivation. Find out where he was both nights – for elimination purposes, if nothing else.'

Murray's expression was one of calm disinterest. After a moment, he reached for his desk phone and dialled an extension. Eyes not leaving Anna, he spoke into the receiver.

'Denise, can we send a car round to the Guilfoyle house on Lynedoch Place...?'

***

They returned to the reception area to await further instruction and whiled away the next half-hour sitting side by side on hard plastic chairs as late afternoon gave way to early evening. Mark didn't complain. He just sat there, arms folded, one leg crossed under the other, as if it was perfectly normal to be spending Saturday night sitting in a dingy police station twiddling his thumbs.

Anna glanced across at him, watching him out of the corner of her eye. He was wearing an old, threadbare pullover with an open neck shirt underneath. A tantalising tuft of dark hair protruded from its collar. In her mind's eye, she found herself following its trail beneath his clothes as it ran down to his stomach...and beyond.

She wondered what it might be like to go to bed with him. She wasn't someone who was predisposed to hopping into the sack with the first man she found passably attractive, but nor did she believe sex was something you only did with someone you felt a deep connection to or with whom you planned on spending the rest of your life. And with Mark, there was clearly a connection of some sort. Perhaps not a romantic one per se, but they had an undeniable rapport, and however much their thoughts on the way forward for society might differ, she sensed that, in the broadest sense, they were nonetheless on the same page. 'Chemistry' was a silly word to use to describe what happened when two people hit it off, but there was unquestionably *something* there.

She'd had perhaps eight lovers in the space of the last ten years, the majority of them older than her – not outrageously so, but she'd always found herself drawn to men who had at least a couple of years on her. *With increased age comes increased maturity* and all that. She'd been with the most recent for almost a year and had even genuinely entertained the possibility that he might be marriage material – until, as with all her other relationships, it had floundered on the rocks of self-sabotage six months ago. And she knew, if she entered into anything with Mark, it would just end in the same manner as all the others – suddenly and destructively.

Still, there was no harm in looking, and in wondering.

The clock had just turned six when the doors opened behind them, letting in a gust of cold air. Anna turned to see Guilfoyle stepping over the threshold, flanked by a couple of uniformed officers. She instinctively shrank lower into her chair, but they passed without paying her the slightest attention, their footsteps echoing on the linoleum as they headed deeper into the building.

'That him?' said Mark.

Anna nodded.

'He looks–'

'I know.'

'No, I mean, he looks like a poor old soul.'

'That's not how it felt to me when he had his hand round my throat.'

Mark winced apologetically. 'Sorry. I'm sure it must have been horrible for you. What I mean is, he's playing the part awful well.'

And what part would that be? Anna wondered.

***

It had been fully dark outside for some time when Anna finally heard footsteps approaching once again. She turned to see Murray and Guilfoyle coming towards the waiting room. They halted in the doorway to exchange a few words. Then, as Anna watched, Murray extended his hand. Guilfoyle took it, shaking it in a manner that could only be interpreted as convivial – or perhaps even vaguely Masonic. As he did so, he turned, looking straight at Anna. He hesitated, then gave Murray an amiable pat on the shoulder and headed towards her. She sat rigid in her chair, her breath in her throat, as he came to a halt before her. He towered over her, his eyes sharp and intense beneath their bushy brows.

And then he smiled. 'I'm sorry about our little misunderstanding earlier,' he said, in a tone far gentler than the one with which he'd addressed her before. 'I imagine I must've given you quite a fright. Well, the feeling was entirely mutual, believe you me. It's not every day you come home to find your front door lying open and a complete stranger in your house. Still – no hard feelings, eh?'

He extended a meaty paw towards her. Alarmed and bewildered in equal measure, she stared up at him, making no move to accept it. As the situation grew increasingly awkward, Guilfoyle retracted his hand. He shook his head, let out a small, mirthful harrumph, then turned and tramped off, making for the exit.

Murray waited till the door had swung shut behind him before turning to Anna and Mark. His eyes burned cold.

'My office. Now.'

They followed him back to the office and took their seats, Anna feeling more than ever now like a wayward pupil summoned to account for herself. Murray settled in his own chair, folded his hands on the desk and sucked in his teeth. Anna braced herself for the coming storm.

'I've spoken with former Detective Superintendent Guilfoyle at some length. I'm satisfied with the account he's given of his whereabouts on the dates and times in question, and doubly satisfied he has no knowledge of or any role whatsoever in either the murder of Andrew Foley or the attack on Ross Garvey.

'In fact, he's extremely aggrieved about this whole affair, not least at us for dragging him here for no good reason. He alleges you broke into his home and spooked his daughter, who as you've no doubt gathered has a severe mental impairment. She requires constant care, which he has been unable to provide while he's been here having his time wasted.'

'His daughter,' said Anna, 'was raped.'

'His daughter was nothing of the sort!' Murray exclaimed, his voice rising above hers. 'She suffered a skiing accident at the age of seventeen which resulted in a serious head injury.'

Anna shook her head adamantly. She didn't believe it, not one word of it.

Murray sat, neck wound into his collar, seething, his normally exemplary posture abandoned. 'You've a very high opinion of yourself, *Ms* Scavolini. You think we've been twiddling our thumbs while you've been out playing cops and robbers? We've been conducting our own enquiries. Unlike yours, however, ours are sanctioned by law.'

Anna wondered if he'd been mentally rehearsing that little speech. If so, no doubt it'd sounded more impressive in his head.

'I've told you what I know. What you choose to do with that information is your business.'

'What you *know*?' Murray's tone dripped sarcasm. 'All you've given me is a mixture of guesswork and half-baked fantasy. I'd have thought, as a learned woman, you'd understand the need to have solid facts to back up your assertions. But then, maybe you're used to having your wisdom accepted without question, *Ms* Scavolini.'

'Now just a minute–' Mark began.

Anna laid a warning hand on his arm, cutting him off.

Murray tilted his head to one side, as if looking at her from a different angle would help make sense of her. 'Why does this matter so much to you? Where exactly do you get off on poking your nose into something that has hee-haw to do with you? Less than forty-eight hours ago, you were trying to make us believe you barely even knew Andrew Foley.'

Anna fixed him with steely eyes, determined not to let him belittle her or force her into backing down. 'Because I want the truth. I want to know what he and Ross Garvey did to Jenny.'

'What makes you so utterly convinced they did *anything* to her?'

'If you saw her yourself, you wouldn't be asking me that.'

Murray's lip curled into a parody of a smile. 'Oh, I doubt that. I'm afraid I don't have your particular brand of woman's intuition.'

'And just what do you mean by that?'

Murray smirked to himself, as if he'd just thought of something incredibly funny. 'You're the feminist criminologist. You tell me.'

He leaned back, folding his arms. He was clearly delighted with himself, thinking he'd scored a major point. Of course, she knew exactly what he was implying. *The uptight, humourless man-hater who sees rape everywhere.* She'd heard it all a hundred times before. She looked at Murray sitting there, lording it over her, and realised she wanted to punch him right in his smirking face. In him, she saw every ignorant misogynist she'd ever encountered, every member of the old boy network who'd ever looked down his nose at her on account of her gender. She imagined leaning over the desk, grabbing him by the collar and smashing his head off its hardwood surface.

'Tell me,' she said, her tone impressively cool, 'is this attitude shared by the whole of Strathkelvin Police Force, or are you just an especially potent example of the Neanderthal tendency in law enforcement?'

She was glad she wasn't able to see Mark's face.

The smirk left Murray's lips. He sat up straight and fixed her with a look that suggested he'd like to do to her many of the same things she'd just fantasised about doing to him.

'You're to leave the Guilfoyles alone,' he said sourly. 'That's not a request.'

'Or what? You'll make life very, *very* unpleasant for me?'

'Just stay away from them,' Murray snapped. 'The only reason that man's not pressing charges against you is because I persuaded him this whole mess could be sorted amicably. A word of advice, *Ms* Scavolini: under the circumstances, you ought to consider it profoundly unwise to–'

'IT'S *DOCTOR*!'

Normally, the use of 'Ms' instead of her actual title wouldn't have rankled half as much as it did now. At least it wasn't the presumptive 'Miss' or the infinitely worse – by her reckoning – 'Mrs'. However, the already charged atmosphere in the room, combined with the fact Murray *kept* doing it, had created a perfect storm. Fuck the niceties. Fuck worrying about coming off as a stuck-up arsehole. This was about basic respect.

She was on her feet now, eyes fixed on Murray, hands clenched by her sides, voice trembling as she tried to maintain her composure. 'I have a PhD in criminology from one of the top academic institutes in Europe. Your colleague the Detective Inspector manages to remember my proper title. I've made the effort to remember yours. I'd appreciate it if you extended me the same courtesy.'

Her eyes didn't leave his face. He was smiling again, but this time, it was the thin, triumphant smile of someone who knew he'd won. He'd succeeded in pushing her over the edge. And she'd played right into his hands.

But right now, she didn't care.

'You're a fucking cunt,' she said. 'I hope you meet this killer, and he cuts *your* balls off. Then the rest of us would really have something to laugh about.'

Murray said nothing, but his jaw tightened. The look on his face was one of pure, undisguised hatred, and Anna knew that, with that single statement, she'd made a serious enemy.

Her nerve, and her composure, abandoned her. She felt angry tears pricking at her eyes. Determined not to let him see them, she wheeled and stormed out.

***

She stood outside the entrance, shaking with rage. And that rage, in no small part, was directed at herself. She knew she should have kept a lid on it. Knew she'd allowed her buttons to be all too easily pressed. Knew all she'd succeeded in doing was make herself seem unstable, irrational and aggressive – none of which did her case any favours. However objectionable Murray and his views might be, she'd always prided herself on her ability to disarm her opponents with reasoned logic instead of resorting to cheap slurs and foul language.

The fire within her gradually subsided, and she became conscious of just how cold it was. It must be a good few degrees below zero now, and the night air stung her cheeks. She wondered where Mark was. Inside, apologising to Murray on her behalf, probably. She couldn't decide whether the thought made her angry or glad. She supposed she should, by rights, be grateful. She'd put him in a tremendously awkward position, and if he was prepared to smooth things over on her behalf, so much the better. At least it meant she wouldn't have to go on bended knee and deliver an insincere apology in person.

She heard the door opening behind her. She turned as Mark emerged from the building. He looked at her. She looked back at him. She didn't trust herself to say anything. Her tongue had got her into more than enough trouble for one day.

'Come on,' he said. 'Let's get out of here.'

***

They walked once more in silence, heading back up towards the West End. The streets were quieter now, though still busier than usual for the time of day, the sounds of buoyant conversation carrying far in the still air. Outside a florist's on Byres Road, spruce trees lay propped up at the kerbside. Fairy-lights twinkled in the windows of the flats above the delis and coffee shops. Somewhere nearby, a busker was playing 'Tidings of Comfort and Joy' on a violin.

At the bus stop, Anna stopped and checked the timetable. The number 90, due in fifteen minutes, would take her more or less back to Astley Street.

She turned to Mark. 'Well, this is me.'

Mark gave a slight smile. 'This is getting to be a habit.'

'You don't have to wait,' she snapped, automatically defensive.

He laughed. 'There's gratitude for you!'

'Sorry. I didn't mean…' She trailed off, feeling useless and ungrateful and inarticulate and about a dozen other things, none of them good. 'Heh. I seem to have developed a real knack for putting people's noses out of joint today.'

'Don't worry. My nose remains in its rightful place.'

She looked at him, eyeing up his profile. 'It's a good nose.'

'Thank you. I happen to think it's one of my better attributes.'

He caught her eye and smiled again. She laughed, feeling unaccountably capricious, and sat down on the bench inside the bus shelter, shaking her head ruefully.

'Been quite a day.'

'It has.'

He sat down next to her, hands folded between his knees. For a while, they sat listening to the comings and goings in the street outside. The busker had moved onto 'Hark! The Herald Angels Sing'.

'This woman,' said Mark eventually. 'Jenny Guilfoyle. She obviously got under your skin.'

'You could say that.'

'I hope you don't mind my asking, but *why*? I mean why her specifically, over all the others? What is it about her?'

For a long while, Anna was silent. She wanted desperately to make some excuse, or to change the subject entirely and talk instead about something flighty and trivial. But it was no use. She saw now that, though the encounter with Murray had brought things to a head, in reality, she'd been building towards this conversation all day, working herself up to telling someone what was really going on. And now here she was, facing the moment of truth.

It was always going to be Mark, she realised. There was nobody else she'd have felt comfortable sharing this with. She took a deep breath, filling her lungs with icy air, preparing herself for what was to follow.

24

Not a Child

Wednesday, 8 April 1998

'So there's this thing at the Colquhouns' place the night,' says Zoe. 'We're both on the invite list.'

Anna looks up from her textbook. 'The Colquhouns? I don't think I know them.'

She's sitting on the bathroom floor with her back up against the tub, swotting for her upcoming sociology exam. Zoe lies soaking behind her, red locks cascading over the side.

'You wouldnae. Youngest one's in third year, I think. His brother went off to uni last year. Anyways, they're throwin' a massive shindig at their folks' place. *Which*, by the way, reminds me, take your nose outta that thing, sad sack! You're meant to be on your holidays.'

She reaches over the side of the tub and grabs the textbook out of Anna's hands. Anna gives a shriek and snatches it back. The corner where Zoe seized it is damp and sudsy.

'Now look what you've done!' She wags a finger in Zoe's direction. 'See if I don't pass this with flying colours? I'm coming for you.'

Zoe grins. 'Dem's fightin' words.' She pauses for no longer than a heartbeat. 'So I said we'd show our faces.'

'You did what? Oh, *Zoe!* You didn't think maybe you should've checked with me first?'

Zoe thinks about this, then shrugs. 'Nuh.'

'It's a *school* night, Zo.'

Zoe rolls her eyes. 'It's not a school night. It's the Easter holidays. You don't have school nights when there's no school.'

'You know what I mean. I've got a lot riding on this exam. *Some* of us have high hopes of getting into university next year.'

Zoe sticks out her tongue. Anna sticks hers out back.

'Ach, c'mon. All work and no play makes Anna dull as a dingleberry. Y'know what they're sayin' about you?'

'I couldn't care less what they're saying about me.'

They're both silent for several moments – Zoe, though Anna can't see her, no doubt smirking away to herself, biding her time until...

'So, uh, who's "they"?'

No reply. Anna turns and glares at Zoe expectantly, but Zoe just smiles impishly and mimes zipping her mouth shut.

'Come on. I want names.'

Zoe nonchalantly sticks a sudsy leg up in the air and flexes it. 'Well,' she says, 'Andrew Foley for one.'

Anna feels herself sitting up just a little straighter. 'And he'll be there?' She tries to make it sound like an innocent enquiry – like she couldn't care less either way. She doesn't make a very good job of it.

'You betcharooney.'

Anna doesn't respond immediately. Mentally, she's going through the study schedule she painstakingly drew up before they broke for the holidays. All those neat little rows and columns designated to different subjects, all thrown askew by an unexpected turn of events. It's all incredibly inconvenient.

Still, Andrew Foley...

She makes a decision. 'No pot. No drinking games. No leaving me holding your glass while you cop off with some random. Home by midnight.'

'Deal.'

Zoe extends a dripping hand over the side of the tub, and they shake on it.

They fall silent for a couple of minutes, Anna continuing to read up on structure versus action, Zoe continuing to prune slowly. Then, apropos of nothing...

'So d'ye reckon I should shave my pubes?'

Anna turns to Zoe, on the cusp of laughter – then sees the expectant look on her face and realises this is a serious question that carries with it the expectation of a serious answer.

'Zoe,' she says firmly, 'that's a decision for you and you alone.'

***

And so, a little after eight, Anna finds herself making her way up the slate path to the big house at the end of Copeland Drive. Zoe's up front, all made up and dressed to the nines in a miniskirt that barely covers her bum. Anna fights a rear-guard action – taking short, slow steps, stretching out the journey for as long as possible.

Inside, the party's in full swing, the guests congregating in the hallway, in the living room, in every spare nook and cranny. As she follows Zoe through the throng, Anna recognises a few faces from school. Most of them, though, she's never seen before. They look older. University students, she reckons. Some of them are dancing to the music being pumped out of a high-end sound system. Others stand around, chatting, necking from open bottles. The boys act cocky, the girls flutter their lashes and run bashful hands through silky hair. Everyone seems to be in the process of pairing off.

At first, she sticks close to Zoe, determined not to let her out of her sight. But, as time presses on and Zoe continues to network and flirt and laugh at punchlines Anna can't make out over the din, she feels increasingly like a third wheel, a killjoy. After a while, she peels off and leaves Zoe to her own devices. She wanders through the house, clutching an open bottle of Carlsberg and only ever pretending to drink from it.

She's standing in a corner of the dining room, trying to tune out the conversation around her as she runs through the arguments for and against Weberian theory, when she sees him making his way through the crowd – Andrew Foley, all six-foot-two of him, with those perfectly sculpted features and that high-bridged nose. She realises he's making a beeline for her, and her heart does a little flutter.

'So you made it,' he says.

'Seems so,' she manages to reply.

'Manage to give the cramming a rest for the night, eh?'

He says it jokingly, with no apparent malice, but it makes her feel even more self-conscious than she did already. With most people, she wouldn't give a stuff if they thought she was a swot or a party-pooper – but Andrew Foley isn't most people.

'Oh, I don't know. I might have the odd textbook squirrelled away on my person somewhere.' She curls one leg around the other, attempting to flirt with him – an act that doesn't come at all naturally to her.

Andrew looks as if he's on the verge of enquiring as to which particular part of her person she might be alluding, but at that moment, another boy, taller than him and no less good-looking, swaggers over and claps an arm around his shoulders.

'There you are! Have you tried the punch? McVeigh's mum made it, but he's slipped in a little extra something...' He stops, noticing Anna for the first time. 'And who's this? Well, well – Andrew Foley, you dark horse!'

'She's just a girl from fifth year,' says Andrew, and a little bit of Anna dies inside. She watches as the pair of them exchange a few more words, but she doesn't hear anything they say. Her world is far too busy caving in around her. And then Andrew's off – to check out the hallowed punch, no doubt – leaving Anna with this older boy, whose name she's been too busy feeling sorry for herself to catch.

'And what is it you do, Anna?' she hears him say.

'Me?' She tries for an easy shrug. 'I just, y'know, go to school.'

She's acutely conscious of him being older than her, more travelled, more worldly-wise. In his eyes, she must seem like a daft wee kiddie.

He smiles. 'The gateway drug to university, I'm told.' He glances over his shoulder, as if making sure Andrew's definitely gone, then turns back to Anna. 'Though I have to say–' his eyes travel up and down her curves appreciatively '–fifth year or not, Andrew Foley doesn't know what he's missing.'

She shifts awkwardly, wondering if he means what she thinks he means. 'So, uh, I don't think we've met before…?'

'Oh no,' he says, his eyes continuing to explore the contours of her body, 'I'm pretty sure I'd remember.'

She takes a gulp of Carlsberg – an actual gulp this time, not a pretend one. Normally, this sort of attention would make her want to run for the hills. But right now, she's still smarting from Andrew's dismissal of her. *Just a girl from fifth year.* At least now she knows which way her bread is buttered.

'So tell me,' he says, raising a suggestive eyebrow, 'what do fifth years do to get their kicks these days?'

'Oh no.' She wags a chiding finger. 'I don't give up trade secrets so easily. At least not 'til I'm considerably drunker than I am now.'

'Well, then, we'd better do something about that.'

***

They retire to a sofa in a reasonably quiet corner of the living room. As the evening unfolds, they cover a variety of topics, albeit mostly of the academic variety. He tells her all about his time at Durham University – the lectures, the tutorials, the debating societies, the student life. To Anna it sounds positively utopian – to inhabit such an intellectual environment, surrounded by like-minded people, all imbued with a thirst for knowledge to match her own. He quizzes her about her own aspirations, showing genuine interest in her intent to pursue a degree in sociology. She finds herself relaxing in his company, enjoying the back-and-forth between them. In spite of the gap in age and experience, she never gets the sense he's looking down his nose at her. Rather, he seems to regard her as an equal, and his interest in her views seems nothing less than sincere.

The room begins to fill up. It's getting harder and harder to make themselves heard over the din, and she senses his frustration. 'Let's see if we can find somewhere more civilised,' he says, and they get up and go.

By now, she's on her fourth or fifth bottle of Carlsberg, and the little voice at the back of her head is telling her, as she tails him up the stairs, that she's already had more than is good for her. But she ignores it and follows him along the velvet-floored landing and into what turns out to be the master bedroom.

In the years to come, she'll ask herself over and over what on earth she was thinking – why she didn't sense that there was something off about this. But in the here and now, it seems eminently sensible to carry on the discussion in here, perched on the bed, facing one another, knees almost touching. And even when the conversation stops and the kissing starts, it feels like a natural progression of what came before. It's not until he's undone the top buttons of her blouse and slipped a couple of fingers between them that she decides it's time to call a halt to the proceedings.

She takes hold of his hand, withdrawing his fingers from her skin. 'I don't think we should…'

'Why?' He looks surprised. 'I thought you were into this.'

'I am,' she insists, eager to save face. 'I just think we should go back downstairs, is all.'

He looks towards the door, and she now notices it's closed. He turns back to her with a look that borders on irritation. 'No one's come looking for us. I bet you anything they haven't even noticed we're gone. Now relax.'

He pushes her back onto the bed and sets to work on her trousers. She lies there, staring up at the ceiling, thinking, *I don't want this. Not here. Not now. Not with him.*

'I…I've never done this,' she blurts.

It's actually a lie – she lost her virginity over a year ago in an ill-advised fumble with James Scott from her English Lit class – but she figures the thought of having to deal with the potential complications will put him off.

But he is unperturbed. 'Don't worry. I won't ask you to do the heavy lifting. Come on. You're not a *child*, are you?' The question is soaked with contempt.

She doesn't want him to think that. That's positively the *last* thing she wants him to think – not after he's spent all evening treating her like an equal. Like an adult. And this is what adults do, isn't it? Adults sleep with one another and don't get squeamish about it. It's natural. It's healthy.

And it's going to happen anyway, whether you like it or not.

He slips off her trousers and underwear and tosses them aside, then gets up to remove his own clothes. Her eyes drift towards the nightstand. The LED display of an alarm clock blinks 11:13.

She looks back to find him standing at the foot of the bed, naked now. His body is hard and muscular. His penis, unsheathed and erect, protrudes from between his legs, listing slightly to one side. The sight of it sends a panicky shiver coursing through her. She had no idea they could get so…*big*. She clenches her thighs together defensively, shockingly pale in the near-darkness.

He kneels on the bed. Looks her in the eye.

'Don't worry,' he says, 'you'll enjoy it.'

He forces her legs apart.

She shuts her eyes.

***

Silence now envelops the room. The grinding and the thrusting have stopped, and she can no longer hear his muffled groans or smell his aftershave. She feels him clambering off her, the mattress shifting under her as it adjusts to its reduced load. As he gets off the bed, she feels his hand on her thigh – more of a slap than a pat or stroke. She remains still, mannequin-like, listening as he moves around the room, retrieving his clothes and getting dressed. He halts at the foot of the bed. For several seconds, she senses him standing there, gazing down at her nakedness, at her vulnerability, at his handiwork. Then, he withdraws. The door creaks. His footsteps retreat down the corridor.

She gives it a full minute before opening her eyes. The door lies slightly ajar, a thin sliver of yellow light falling on her bare leg.

She looks over at the alarm clock. It is 11:18.

She gets up stiffly and begins to search for her clothes. She finds them piece-by-piece and dresses slowly, meticulously, determined not to have so much as a hair out of place. The sounds of the party carry on unabated below, distant and muffled by the insulation.

She trips down the stairs, feeling clumsy and ungainly. Mercifully, nobody pays her the blindest bit of attention. Guests have been coming and going all evening, and one silly little girl who's drunk more than is good for her doesn't merit more than a couple of disinterested glances.

She lets herself out and vanishes into the night.

25

Cuckoo

Saturday, 19 December 2009

In all the years since it had taken place, this was the closest she'd come to telling anyone the full story. She still left certain parts out – small, embarrassing details like her failure to find her underwear and her suspicion he had kept it – but otherwise gave Mark a full and frank account. As before, Mark listened patiently and in silence throughout, giving her the time and space needed to tell it in her own manner and pace.

'There was only another week or so left of the school holidays. Then it was straight into the exam period, and I didn't have time for anything else. I just pushed it to the back of my mind. And then, when I finally did start to think about it, I spent the longest time trying to convince myself nothing had happened – or, if it had happened, that I'd wanted it. It just seemed easier that way. I mean, if I didn't want to go through with it, I should've made my objections clearer, right? Or I should've done more to resist. It took me years to face up to what happened. To what it was. I kept telling myself these things didn't happen to people like me – whatever that even means. Funny how you can know all about the myths but still fall prey to them yourself.'

Mark said nothing. He looked shocked, and she couldn't help but suspect this was at least in part because she'd chosen him as her confidant.

'It all caught up with me a few years later, in the final year of my undergraduate degree. I'd been having these extreme ups and downs for a while, which I'd been putting down to stress. I never went completely cuckoo or anything, but for a while, it felt like I stopped being me. A colleague recommended I see a therapist, and she finally gave me an official diagnosis: type one bipolar disorder, with a side order of emotional dysregulation.' She gave a small, self-deprecating smile. 'That was a bolt out of the blue, let me tell you. But in retrospect, it made sense of a lot of things. I'm not saying what happened at the Colquhouns' *caused* it, but I think it's safe to say it exacerbated something that was there already. I'm on the level now,' she added hastily, catching the look on Mark's face. 'Lithium keeps it in check. I mean, it's always with me, but at least now *I* control *it*, not the other way round.'

Mark opened his mouth to say something, then seemed to think better of it. 'You've got a support system in place, right?' he said, after a moment. 'Friends, family, co-workers…?'

She gave him an indulgent look. 'You must've figured out by now I'm not one for broadcasting my problems to the world. My condition is "need to know" only, and that's how I like it. As for the other stuff, for the longest time, the only ones who knew were me and *him* – that's if he even understands what he did. But I let Zoe know when we first got back in touch a few months back. Well, dropped a few well-placed hints. She doesn't know any details – the whens and the wheres. But she knows it happened. And you know what she said?'

'What?'

'"What you need is a holiday."' Anna laughed softly. 'Good old Zo. Always did have a practical solution to everything.' She breathed out a sigh. It turned to vapour in front of her.

'And is it…' Mark began tentatively, 'is it why you left Glasgow?'

Anna shook her head. 'No. I always planned on getting out. But it's certainly one of the reasons I stayed out. Thing is, I really did think, after all those years, that it might just be possible to come back to a clean slate. I actually let myself believe that. But the truth is, it never leaves you. It gets right under your skin and stays there. It changes the way you see the world. Changes the way you see *people*.'

Mark sat next to her, eyes on the ground, still digesting what she'd told him. 'If you could go back,' he said at last, 'would you have done anything differently?'

'You mean like not get raped? Yeah, in a heartbeat.'

Mark looked pained. 'No – I mean, would you have told anyone?'

She knew what 'anyone' meant. 'Think I'd have been one of your three per cent, do you?'

He looked like he'd been slapped, and she wished she hadn't said it.

'Believe me, I've played the "what if?" game. What if I hadn't gone to the party? What if I'd stuck closer to Zoe? What if I'd laid off the Carlsberg? What if I hadn't gone upstairs with him? What if I'd shouted for help? And yeah, "what if I'd gone to the police?" is definitely on that list. But I'm way past that stage. Life's not a Choose Your Own Adventure. You don't get to go back and pick a different option because you don't like how things turned out. So – and I mean this in the nicest possible way – you asking me if I'd have done anything differently is about as helpful as offering to read me my horoscope.'

Mark lowered his eyes, chastened. 'Fair point.'

'It's a farce, Mark. It always has been. And deep down, you know it. There's no such thing as justice. Not really. We just pretend.'

The barb clearly stung. It was ever thus – decent-minded folk like him were invariably the hardest hit when confronted by the ugly reality that the world wasn't a fair and just place.

She touched his arm lightly, going for the conciliatory approach. 'Thanks for everything today. I really appreciate it. I'll be okay now.'

She was telling him she wanted to be alone, and he seemed to get it. He got to his feet and stood gazing down at her, his eyes deep with impotent sadness – this man who wanted to make the world a better place but was powerless to do anything for the person right in front of him. She reached for his hand and squeezed it lightly, knowing that any notion she'd ever entertained of anything happening between them was now well and truly dead in the water. Ironically, in opening up to him, in exposing herself so fully, she'd ensured that any prospect of future intimacy was impossible to contemplate.

A number 90 bus came into view. She got to her feet and indicated for it to pull over, then turned to Mark.

'I want you to promise me something. Not a word about any of this to Gavin.'

'Of course.' He seemed affronted by the very notion.

'I didn't mean about…about what happened to me. I mean about what I told you this afternoon. Jenny, Foley, the killer coming after me – all of it. He already blames himself for Foley turning out to be a wife-beater. I'd rather not up the burden on his conscience, if I can help it.'

'I understand. Not a word.'

The bus came to a juddering halt at the kerb. They made their chaste goodbyes, and Anna clambered aboard. She went up to the top deck and sat near the back, as far away from the other passengers as possible. As they pulled away, she peered down at the departing street, hoping to catch sight of Mark. He was already off, heading in the opposite direction, head tucked into his collar, hands jammed into his pockets.

She was certain she would never see him again. And, as she watched him continue to recede into the distance, she realised this was precisely why she'd felt able to tell him all that she had.

***

The house was in darkness when she got in. A small and decidedly weedy-looking Christmas tree now was now crammed into the living room next to the TV. The remains of a Chinese takeaway littered the coffee table, and there was a distinct whiff of cannabis in the air. Zoe and Victor had had quite the party in her absence, it seemed. She felt a surge of jealousy at how straightforward and angst-free their lives were compared to her own. They might at least have waited for her. Mind you, maybe this was payback for being such an obstreperous cow earlier. If so, she supposed she probably deserved it.

She suddenly realised just how drained she felt. Two unsettled nights and an absolute emotional rollercoaster of a day will do that to you, she supposed. There didn't seem much point forcing herself to stay up – not when the alternative was sitting alone in an empty house watching bad TV and picking over someone else's leftovers. So she took herself upstairs and went straight to bed, where she lay listening to the creaks and groans of the old house as it, too, settled down for the night.

26

Night Shift

Renfield had got back to his flat shortly before the sun came up, his clothes literally frozen to his skin. As he huddled by the radiator, waiting for the circulation to return to his fingers and toes, he noticed the red LED on the answerphone blinking. It was an old classmate, Richie Deans, saying that Foley's family had organised a memorial service for ten that morning and did he want to come? He didn't, but curiosity got the better of him, and so, without time for breakfast or even a shower and a shave, he pulled on some fresh clothes and set off.

A sizeable crowd had already gathered outside St Lucian's by the time he reached the gates, including an array of faces he recognised from the old days. It dawned on him just how much he hated them – *all* of them. They weren't his people, weren't his friends, and he had no desire to reacquaint himself with them just so they could look down their noses at him all over again. They'd all be merchant bankers and CEOs now. He was still just Ted Renfield, the only pupil in the history of Willow Bank Academy to have spent eight years in the place, the perennial butt of every 'retard' joke. He watched from the cover of the cemetery until the mourners filed into the chapel, then slipped away.

He spent the rest of the morning wandering aimlessly and without direction through town. All around him were reminders that Christmas was coming. Shoppers hurried past him, laden with bulging bags; notices in windows implored people to hurry up and part with their money or face enduring disappointment; and on Buchanan Street in the city centre, young and old alike queued to get their picture taken inside a giant snowdome.

He thought about just clearing out. He could pack his bags, leave Glasgow and Foley and the rest far behind him. But where would he go? He hadn't the means, either financial or otherwise, to jet off to some far-flung corner of the globe. And he certainly wasn't going to his family in Perth. He couldn't face their lingering looks of disapproval and disappointment any more than the self-satisfied mockery of his former classmates. And deep down, he knew it didn't matter where he went or how far. What was coming after him would catch up with him sooner or later.

He was over four hours late by the time he showed up for work, breathless and dishevelled, to be subjected to the mother of all take-downs by his boss. Mr Macdonald threatened to fire his sorry, worthless ass then and there, only relenting when Renfield promised he'd not only work late to make up for the hours he owed but would stay for the entire night.

And so Renfield found himself working the graveyard shift with Beggsy, a callow youth whose only interests were weed, girls – or 'chicks' as he called them, and of whom he had little apparent experience – and maximising one's chances of winning the lottery, a subject to which he devoted most of his limited mental faculties. Just after midnight, Renfield, who'd long since grown tired of his endless babbling about how ball 23 had been drawn more times than any other in the last decade, suggested that Beggsy might like to slip off early. The gym had been deserted all evening, the last customer having left over an hour ago. Beggsy was only too glad to oblige.

With the place to himself, Renfield locked the doors, put up a makeshift 'back soon' sign, tuned the radio to an all-night music station, turned up the volume as loud as it would go and set about filling the nagging void in his mind by making use of the gym's facilities. He started with bench presses, then moved onto the treadmill, then finished off by laying into a punching-bag, pounding it until his knuckles bled.

Afterwards, he stood in the shower, his brain in neutral, conscious of nothing but the distant thumping of the music and the water cascading down on him. His eyelids grew heavy. He hadn't slept for almost two days, and the warm water soothed his tired limbs, like gentle fingers massaging him, assuring him that it was alright, that he could let his eyes close, just for a moment…

He snapped his eyes open. He didn't know how much time had passed or what had caused him to stir. He turned off the water and drew back the curtain. A haze of steam greeted him, the geography of the room only faintly visible behind it.

'Someone there?'

He could hear nothing – just water dripping from the showerhead and the curtain, and the distant strains of 'Merry Xmas Everybody' on the radio.

Stepping out of the shower, he crossed the floor and peered into the adjoining changing room. He found nobody there, or in the adjacent corridor. He called out again, but heard only his own voice echoing in the empty passageway. He headed back to the shower room, still shrouded in steam.

And then he saw it. A shape – dark, almost imperceptible. A figure, standing statuesque on the far side of the room.

Renfield stopped dead. 'Hello?'

No reply.

'Beggsy? Not funny, man.'

Still not a word. The figure didn't move.

The blood in Renfield's veins turned to ice. She'd come for him at last.

Any thought he'd entertained, when the time came, of standing his ground and waiting for the inevitable promptly vanished. He turned tail and ran, his bare feet slapping on the damp tiles. As he fled through the changing room, he slipped on a puddle – the result, if he'd only had the presence of mind to realise it, of his decision not to dry off minutes earlier – and went flying backwards. The base of his skull took the full force of impact as he hit the hard floor.

As he lay there, blinking heavily to clear the fug from his eyes, *she* stepped into his field of vision and gazed down at him wordlessly, her features hidden under a dark hood. A blade gleamed in her hand. This was it. After all this time, it really was the end.

And, at least in some small way, it came as a relief.

***

At 2346, a code red call was put out from Bay 6 in the Intensive Care Unit at the Southern General Hospital. The patient, a Mr Ross Anthony Garvey, 27, had gone into cardiac arrest. Adrenaline and atropine were given, and continuous CPR was performed for thirty minutes. However, despite the best efforts of the Crash Team, all measures proved unsuccessful and resuscitation was abandoned at 0019 on Sunday 20 December.

Mr Garvey's wife was contacted at home shortly after her husband's arrest, but adverse weather conditions prevented her from arriving prior to the time of death.

27

Kiss and Tell

Sunday, 20 December

Anna came to at first light, feeling decidedly unrested. She reached for her watch. Eight forty-five. She let her head flop back onto the pillow. This was ridiculous. It was like being jet-lagged, except she'd only gone back an hour. Zoe's side of the bed lay empty; there was no evidence of her having slept there.

She dragged herself over to the window. On drawing the curtains, she saw that it had snowed again overnight, though it was holding off for the time being. A dense carpet of white covered the roofs of the houses visible beyond the fence at the foot of the back garden. She hoped Zoe had been savvy enough to stay put last night, wherever she was, and hadn't attempted to make her way home in it. At least, if she was in someone else's bed, she'd be warm and safe.

Mechanically, Anna pulled on her jogging gear and set off on her morning run, determined to clear her head. With the snow several inches thick on the ground, it was heavy-going. There was little to no traffic on the roads – the rest of the world, it seemed, had considerably more sense than her. Following the same route she'd taken on Friday, she headed south towards Kelvingrove Park, entering via the north gate and setting off along a footpath that followed the contours of the river. The ground sloped steadily downward and the trees grew denser. The branches overhead had caught the bulk of the snowfall, creating a tunnel which blotted out the pale sun and muffled the sound of her feet on the tarmac.

As she rounded a corner, a figure came into view up ahead – a man, tall and lean, heading along the narrow path towards her. She couldn't put her finger on what it was about him, but the sight of him caused her heart to ratchet up a gear. It was something about his manner, about his gait, about the way he strode up the path like he owned it, seemingly with no intention of making way for her. As the gap between them steadily shrunk, he lifted his head and their eyes met. He seemed to leer at her, his eyes tracing the curves of her body beneath her running gear, and for a brief instant, it occurred to her just how much he resembled Foley. Or Gavin. Or both of them. She couldn't be sure anymore.

She darted sideways, skirting around him and continuing on past him. A moment later, she risked a glance over her shoulder. The man walked on without a backward glance. Any relief, however, was tempered by a burning anger at the casualness of his sexism. The sheer and utter mundanity of it. The notion that it was somehow okay for him to look at her like that, as if he was eyeing up some goods in a shop window.

She put on another burst of speed and ran on.

***

By the time she got back to the house, she was as groggy as ever and had a painful stitch into the bargain. There was no sign of Zoe, and Victor hadn't materialised either. His bedroom door was closed, and when she put her ear to it, she was able to make out the slow, steady rhythm of his breathing. She took a piping hot shower, closing her eyes and shutting off her brain as the water cascaded over her tired body. Afterwards, she sat in the kitchen wrapped in a towel, feeling very much like she was experiencing all the negative effects and none of the benefits of a heavy night on the tiles. She was glad now that she'd come off the lithium. She shuddered to think how she'd be feeling if she was having to contend with its energy-sapping qualities as well.

With breakfast a decidedly unappetising option, she turned instead to the small matter of the murders. She still considered

Guilfoyle the most likely culprit. He had the motive and the wherewithal, and she found it all too easy to picture him doing… well, *it*. The lack of hard evidence was a problem, though, and there remained a nagging doubt at the back of her mind – a sense that something didn't quite fit. A day or two ago, she'd have had no trouble putting her finger on what that was. Now, however, her mind was so clouded that she was finding it increasingly difficult to keep track of all the variables in play – the suspects, the potential motives, the chronology of events.

She shut her eyes, returning to the incident on the front porch two nights ago, and for a brief instant, she saw those piercing blue eyes staring into hers all over again. *Blue eyes. Blue eyes.* She tried to remember who – if anyone – among the various people in whose company she'd spent time over the last few days had blue eyes. Gavin? She didn't think so. Mark? No, she was fairly sure his were brown. Guilfoyle? His beady little eyes had bored into her for long enough the previous day, though she'd spent the better part of that encounter trying to avoid looking at them.

She opened her own eyes, and she was once again back in the familiar comfort of the Callahans' kitchen. But she knew, better or worse, that this was going to consume her until it was resolved one way or another. Besides, no one – not a brute like Guilfoyle and especially not an unreconstructed chauvinist like Murray – was going to dictate to her what she could and couldn't do.

She knew that if her accusations against Guilfoyle were to have any legitimacy, she would need considerably more ammo against him. And before she even *considered* speaking to the police again, she needed to assuage her own doubt. Part of the problem was that she'd only heard the Jenny Guilfoyle story third-hand. Jenny wasn't in a position to answer her questions, that much was clear, and in any event, she knew her chances of getting access to her again were non-existent. She could get one step closer to the source, though.

She retrieved her laptop from upstairs and commandeered the phone line. It didn't take her long to find the information she was looking for. Paul Docherty, the boy who'd been the source of Zoe's information about Jenny, was now working at a legal aid firm in Summerhill, an area of Glasgow that boasted a life expectancy comparable to that of the Gaza Strip. That surprised her. Willow Bank prided itself on the fact that the vast majority of its pupils went on to have distinguished, well-paying careers. Advising low-income families – most likely on a pro bono basis – from one of the most deprived parts of the city didn't exactly fit the profile. And yet a minimum of cross-referencing confirmed that this was indeed the same Paul Docherty Zoe had spoken of. She called the centre and asked if Docherty was working that day. Yes, the receptionist informed her, he'd be in at midday and would she like to make an appointment? Concluding that this was as good a way of securing an audience with him as any, she took the earliest possible booking, then hoofed it over to Summerhill, taking a bus to the city centre and another on to her destination.

'Careful,' said the driver with a wink as she disembarked, 'it's bandit country out there.'

***

Bandit country was about right. The Summerhill Law Centre was on the ground floor of a concrete monstrosity on an industrial estate in the middle of nowhere, rendered all the more desolate in the grey morning. Near the entrance, an upturned trolley minus its wheels and the charred remains of a dog waste bin told Anna in no uncertain terms that she was a long way from Kelvindale. She headed into reception, presented herself at the desk and was directed to the waiting area. There she sat, biding her time, the portable heater in the corner doing absolutely nothing to combat the continual draught from the gap under the door.

At precisely two minutes to twelve, the door slammed open, and a tall, gangly young man in a parka and cheap polyester suit hurried in, shoulders hunched against the cold, a bacon roll clamped between his teeth. He nodded a greeting to the receptionist, removed the roll long enough to mutter something about it being *fuckin' freezin' oot there*, and promptly disappeared through to the back.

The receptionist smiled over at Anna. 'Mr D will be with you in a moment.'

Anna smiled back, thinking that if she really *was* here about a legal matter, this brief sight of Mr D wouldn't have instilled her with any great confidence.

He was still eating when, five minutes later, she was shown through to his office – a pokey affair with files piled high on every available surface. Docherty, seated behind his desk, gestured for her to come in. She perched on the plastic chair facing the desk and waited for him to finish eating. He had pale, almost translucent skin and a very pronounced Adam's apple. His dark, greasy hair was plastered to his forehead, partially obscuring his eyes. She wondered whether anyone had ever told him he'd missed his calling as a member of a nineties punk band.

He swallowed and fixed her with a pleasant but thoroughly artificial smile. 'Now then–' he checked his diary '–Anna, what can I do ye for?'

She decided to cut to the chase. 'I've got some questions for you. I don't know whether you'll want to answer them, but–'

Docherty laughed. 'That's no normally how it works, princess. Usually we start wi' *me* askin' *you* the questions.'

He was affecting a broad Glaswegian accent, but laying it on too thickly to be wholly convincing. Anna could tell right away this wasn't his natural mode of speech. He was either trying to blend in better with the locals, reinvent himself, or both.

'You and I were both at Willow Bank Academy in the nineties. I wanted to ask about someone who'd have been in the same year as you.'

The smile disappeared from Docherty's face instantly. 'Aye? There's no many fae that place'd gie me the time o' day. Fewer still that'd come lookin' fur me oot here.'

She could see this wasn't going to be straightforward. Still, there was nothing for it but to try. 'Jenny Guilfoyle. Remember her?'

'Nuh.' His eyes didn't leave hers. His poker face was impressive – she had to give him that.

'Really? That's not what I heard.'

'Aye? Well, I cannae help whit you've heard. And if'n ye're no here about a legal matter, then I cannae help ye, period.'

He slammed his diary shut and, getting to his feet, made for the door, clearly intent on turfing her out. As he passed her, she stood up herself. Blocking his path, she stood on tiptoe, bringing her eyes level with his.

'I've seen her, Paul. I know you know something about how she ended up like that.'

Docherty gazed back at her. He gave a smug, sneering smile, and she got the sense he was enjoying having something she wanted and therefore being in a position to call the shots. 'So what are ye, then? A reporter? If ye are, ye're about ten years too late. Naeb'dy gave a stuff at the time, though ye'd have thought "Posh Boys Gang-Bang Choirgirl" wid've had copies flyin' aff the shelves.'

'And is that what happened?'

Docherty slid a finger under his lank hair, picking at something behind his ear. 'See, problem is, I'm no sure I should be answerin' that. Might draw unwanted attention tae massel. I'd need some cast iron guarantees.'

'Such as?'

'That ye'd keep ma name out of it. Look.' He suddenly leant towards her, clamping a hand on her arm. He looked her dead in the eyes, showing the whites of his own. 'I don't know you from Adam. You say you were at Willow Bank, but I've only got your word for that. I don't want to open the papers next morning to find I've been part of some kiss-and-tell op.'

His mode of speech had changed. His accent had softened, the laboured Glaswegianisms giving way to a mode of Scottish Standard English not unlike her own.

She withdrew her arm. 'I'm not a reporter, and I *was* at Willow Bank. If you don't remember me, maybe you remember my friend Zoe – or what about her brother Victor?'

'Victor?' Docherty brightened somewhat. 'Old ginger-pubes hisself? Aye, I 'member him. Used to cadge the odd rolie off of him. So you're *not* a reporter, then?'

'No.'

'Oh. Right.'

He made his way back over to the desk. She couldn't tell whether he was relieved or disappointed. The prospect of being part of some elaborate sting had probably brightened up his day.

'Look, if it's a matter of money...'

Docherty shook his head and scoffed. 'It's no about money – though God knows we're no exactly minted here. I just don't see what's the point in rakin' up ancient history. What's past is past. Is it no better we all just move on?'

'And what about the ones who can't move on? What about Jenny? Come on.' She adopted a more conciliatory tone. 'You told Zoe about what happened to her. All I'm asking is that you do the same for me.'

Docherty chewed his bottom lip, his eyes flicking this way and that as he pondered his options. Eventually, he gave the smallest of nods and settled back into his chair. Anna did likewise, poised and ready.

'So how much d'ye know already?'

'I've heard two versions. One is that she was in a skiing accident and suffered a head injury.'

Docherty scoffed. 'That's bollocks.'

'The other's the one you told Zoe – that some boys interfered with her at a party.'

'Aye. That one's true.'

'And how do you know that?'

'Simple. I was there.'

A small frisson ran up Anna's spine. 'You were there? Then you know who was involved, and what...' *And what they did.*

Docherty shook his head. 'I left 'fore it got underway. But I heard the murmurings. I knew what was planned, more or less.'

'I think you'd better start from the beginning, don't you? When did this take place, where, who was involved and what happened?'

Docherty shifted in irritation, and for a moment, she was afraid she'd pushed it too far and he was going to clam up completely. But, after a moment, he shrugged.

'It was the last day of school 'fore the Christmas break. I was in fifth year, so that would've been, what, ninety-nine? You remember how, on the last day, they always let us away at midday? Well, word got round there was this get-together at Rosco Garvey's place – you mind, his folks had that big hoose up on Park Terrace?'

The outer circle on Woodlands Hill. Anna nodded.

He shot her a wary glance. 'You know about the parties? What went on at 'em, I mean.'

'I've got the gist.'

He seemed to relax somewhat. 'Aye, well, folk tended to exaggerate a bit, but only a bit. I mean, 'fore that day, I didnae have any direct experience. But you know how it is – you're seventeen, your hormones are racin', you still havenae popped your cherry, and you hear about these parties where everyone's gettin' their end away. A boy can't help but be curious, know what I mean?'

She did, but she had no great desire to hear the details. 'And how did you…I don't know, did you get invited to these things or did you just turn up?'

Docherty shrugged. 'It was pretty much an open door, far as I could tell. I mean, you sort of knew if you'd be welcome or not – like, you knew if your face didnae fit, and mine didnae. But it's no like they had bouncers to turn you away if you didnae know the secret handshake.' He tittered quietly to himself at the idea of it. 'But that day, I figured I'd just chance my arm. Time I got there, the place was so heavin', I was able to pretty much just keep ma heid doon and no draw any attention tae massel. There was a few fae my year there, and a bunch fae the year above. A few studenty types too. You know the sort – the ones who gatecrash high school parties lookin' for barely legal pussy.'

Anna's stomach roiled at his choice of words, but she said nothing.

'That bloke that was killed the other day was there.'

'You mean Andrew Foley?'

'Aye. I recognised his picture in the paper. Smug bastard. I didnae like him. Kept giein' it how he was this big student from Lunn-dunn and expectin' us all tae worship the ground he walked on. He was the ringleader. It was him and Rosco G and Ted Renfield, all mutterin' together about how they were gonna show the polisman's girl a good time.'

Anna recalled the figure she'd spied among the tombstones outside St Lucian's the previous day. 'Renfield was in on it as well?'

Docherty gave her a conspiratorial look. ''Tween you 'n' me, Renfield was thick as two planks. He wasnae really part of that gang. More of a hinger-onner. Just went along wi' whatever the others telt him to do. But the way they were talkin', sounded like the whole thing'd been planned in advance. Like, they knew she was gonnae be there and were just bidin' their time.'

'So she wasn't there when you arrived?'

'Nuh, but she showed up no long after. Just sort of appeared. I've nae idea who invited her or how they had such a pull over her. She was the type ye wouldnae see deid at a do like that – y'know, choirgirl, straight-A student, cop's daughter. I reckon some o' the lads must've thought her daddy'd sent her there to bust 'em. Ye've never seen contraband disappear so fast.'

'What happened then?'

Docherty lowered his eyes. 'I, well…I kinda bowed out at that point. I knew whit was gonnae happen. Didnae really wanna be around tae see it. So I left 'em to it.' He looked up at Anna sharply, responding to a rebuke she hadn't made. 'I'm no proud o' massel. But whit was I gonnae dae? Stand up tae Foley and that lot all on ma lonesome?'

That would have been a start, Anna thought. 'Go on.'

'After Christmas, she didnae come back tae school. Naeb'dy really said anythin', but folk must've wondered. Then, a coupla weeks later, this story started goin' about that she'd come aff her skis and cracked her heid. I called bullshit on that. Specially seein' as her da went on a rampage pretty soon after.'

Anna felt herself sitting up that little bit straighter. ''Scuse me?'

'I dunno the specifics, but he was goin' about tryin' tae get to the bottom a' what happened. S'posedly, a buncha the boys that used tae go tae they parties got picked up by him and his polis mates and had the screws turned on 'em. I dunno if it was just a night in the cells or if they roughed 'em up or what, but somethin' serious must've happened, 'cause the parties wound down pretty sharpish. And then, no long after New Year, he was let go.'

'Let go as in...'

'As in dishonourably discharged, aye. Course, he got a golden parachute, and they made out it was early retirement, but I heard there was CCTV footage of him knockin' seven shades outta some'dy in one o' the cells.'

'Somebody? One of the boys from the party?'

'I dunno, do I?' Docherty snapped. 'You asked me what happened and I've told ye what I know. All it is is rumours – could be bullshit fae top to tail. But see if it was *my* daughter and I thought someone might know who done it, you bet yer bottom dollar I'd be out there breakin' kneecaps.'

Anna was tempted to ask him if he was able to account for his whereabouts in the early hours of Friday and Saturday.

'I seen her again,' he said. ''Bout a year after.'

'Where?'

'Kelvingrove Park. I was cuttin' through it when I seen this bloke comin' along the path towards me, pushin' a wheelchair. They got closer, and I realised it was Jenny and her old man. I just kept on walkin', but I seen her face, and it was like...I dunno, it was like she was empty inside. Like there was nothin' left a' her. I'd never seen anythin' like that before. I thought...I hoped she might've, like, got better, but from what you're sayin'...' He shook his head unhappily and fell silent.

There was a knock on the door. The secretary leaned in.

'That's your twelve-fifteen here, Mr D.'

Docherty nodded. As the secretary withdrew, he got to his feet, all business. 'Well, that's me back tae the grindstone. Hope ye got somethin' fae our little chat.'

As he began to rifle through his papers, presumably in search of the notes for his next case, Anna got up to go. She'd made it as far as the door her spoke again.

'I lied earlier.'

Anna turned to face him. 'Sorry?'

Docherty was slumped low in his chair, eyes fixed on the desk. 'I didnae try and get her tae leave wi' me. I made that bit up. S'what I wish I done. What I *should've* done.'

It was the Gavin Price situation all over again, still beating himself up ten years later for having looked the other way. Only, in Docherty's case, the cause and effect of his dereliction of duty were far more explicit.

She assumed he was done. She was just about to turn to go when a harsh, adamant light suddenly kindled in his eyes. This time, he looked straight at her as he spoke.

'Whoever done Foley in, if ye ask me, they done the world a favour. They shouldnae be tryin' tae lock 'em up. They should be giein' 'em a bloody medal.'

***

Anna saw herself out. As she passed through the waiting room, she glanced briefly at the figure seated by the heater – a young woman with the sunken eyes and papery skin of chronic poor nutrition. She had a livid bruise on her cheek and a cut to her lip that was just beginning to scab. One leg jiggled constantly, an anxious tic of which she was either unaware or past caring about.

It occurred to Anna, as she stepped out into the cold, that this was probably a form of penance for Docherty – working here, doing his best to help those that 'decent' society had abandoned. She wondered if, like her, he, too, had played the *what if?* game and come to the same conclusions as to its futility.

28

Fugitive

Anna peered at her reflection in the dirt-encrusted mirror of a public lavatory. Her face was drained of colour. The skin around her baggy, bloodshot eyes was dark and translucent. Try as she might, she couldn't get her mind to focus.

She needed a fresh plan of action. Her conversation with Docherty had done nothing to disavow her of Guilfoyle's guilt. Quite the opposite, in fact. The question was, who to go to with her concerns? Certainly not his old colleagues at Yorkhill. She remembered Guilfoyle's grim reference to his 'friends on the force' all too well. How deep did that friendship run, she wondered? Did it extend, as per Docherty's insinuation, to going after people who'd been present at the party? Perhaps that was why Murray had been so dismissive of her when she'd implored him to look into Guilfoyle – or indeed why Norton had been so eager to put her into protective custody, out of harm's way. And why was a DI taking such a hands-on role in the investigation anyway, to the point of making house calls? What if this went to the very top?

She shook her head, dismissing the idea. It just wasn't plausible, this notion of the police turning a blind eye while a former colleague went around reaping bloody vengeance. And yet, this was nothing if not an unprecedented situation. With the bounds of credibility already stretched to breaking point, was adding in police collusion really such a massive leap? Surely, if ever there was a time for indulging in mad conspiracy theories, it was now.

She wished there was someone she could open up to about this – someone who could act as a sounding board and advise her on how to proceed. She couldn't burden Zoe with what she'd learned – it was bad enough already that her enquiries had brought the killer to her very door. And then there were the other potential confidants – Mark, Gavin, even Carol. She wasn't going to drag them into this. It wasn't their fight.

With a sinking feeling in her gut, she realised she was completely and utterly alone.

***

She jumped on a bus heading for the city centre. Progress was painfully slow, frequently grinding to a halt altogether. She sat pressed up against the window, with the decidedly corpulent man next to her taking up all of his own seat and a fair amount of hers too.

'Don't worry, hen,' he said, after she'd checked her watch for the umpteenth time. 'Might never happen.'

She considered telling him it already had, then decided against it and went back to window-gazing. He harrumphed at her unwillingness to entertain his banter, muttered something that sounded suspiciously like 'sour-faced bitch' and folded his arms, further reducing her already severely depleted personal space.

As the bus continued its achingly slow journey, a plan began to take shape. There was no way she was going anywhere near the Yorkhill mob again – not after her bust-up with Murray yesterday and certainly not given Guilfoyle's name-dropping of Norton. But that didn't mean bypassing the police altogether. There were other divisions in the city with whom Guilfoyle wouldn't have a relationship. Surely one of them would take her concerns seriously.

A little after two, she stepped into the foyer of Gallowgate Police Station and presented herself to the desk sergeant. She told him she had information pertaining to a serious crime – information she would only share with a senior officer. The sergeant gave her a sceptical look, but he disappeared into the back office and, fifteen minutes later, returned with a middle-aged, sandy-haired man in tow, who introduced himself as DCI Lauder. He took her through to a cheerily lit, comfortably furnished interview suite and invited her to tell him her concerns.

She gave Lauder as full an account as possible, laying out her suspicions regarding Guilfoyle. Lauder listened attentively throughout, giving *uh-huhs* and *I sees* at appropriate intervals. As she spoke, she was aware there was something she was forgetting. It was there at the back of her mind – a nebulous, indefinable shape, like a word on the tip of her tongue. But she was too on edge, too preoccupied, too bloody shattered to put her finger on what it was.

'You understand why I couldn't go to Yorkhill.'

'Yes, quite.' Lauder got up, nodding slowly as he chewed over the information. 'Well, I appreciate you bringing this to me, Dr Scavolini. Not to worry – we'll handle it from here. If I could ask you to stay put just a bit longer while I set things in motion.' He paused, hand on the door handle. 'How did you get here?'

'Bus.'

Lauder gave an exaggerated shudder. 'Taking your life in your hands there. Don't worry – we'll run you home.'

Once he'd left, Anna sank back into the folds of the settee and gazed up at the wall clock. It was after half three. Where had the time gone? The seconds ticked by, becoming minutes. Still Lauder didn't materialise. What was taking so long? Good *God*, she was tired. The effort of telling her story had sapped what little energy she'd had left. If he didn't hurry up, he'd come back to find her passed out on the couch.

She was on the verge of going to look for him when the door opened. Lauder stepped in, followed by a couple of uniformed officers.

'Sorry to keep you waiting so long. I've discussed the matter with my superiors and agreed a plan as to how to proceed from here.'

'And Guilfoyle?' She looked at him expectantly.

'We'll handle things from here on in,' Lauder said, his tone firm but considerate. 'In the meantime, if you'd be so kind as to follow these two gents. Go on. You look exhausted.'

It was all far from satisfactory, and yet under the circumstances she felt that there was nothing for it but to accept what he was saying. As she passed him in the doorway, she turned and fixed him with a steely look.

'You *will* deal this, won't you? You won't just brush it under the carpet?'

Lauder dipped his head. 'You have my word.'

Anna wasn't sure how much the word of a man she didn't know counted for, but it would have to do. And, to be honest, it was a relief to be able to finally hand the matter over to someone else – someone who, at the very least, hadn't treated her concerns with contempt. And now it was out of her hands. All she could do now was wait for Lauder's investigations to run their course.

'It's fifty-eight Astley Street,' she told her two minders as she clambered into the back of the waiting car.

'Don't worry,' said the driver. 'We know where we're going.'

She briefly wondered how that could be, as she couldn't remember having given the address to anyone at the station. By now, however, her brain was beyond making sense of anything more complicated than fastening her seatbelt. As they set off, she felt sleep encroaching, aided and abetted by the gentle hum of the engine and the damp warmth of the radiator. Without intending to, she sank into a pleasant and dreamless slumber.

***

She came to with a start. The car was stationary now, and cold – the engine and heating had both been turned off. The front seats were empty. The light was failing, and at first, she couldn't figure out where she was. They appeared to be parked on a slope, and the buildings outside were unfamiliar. This definitely wasn't Astley Street.

As the sleep lifted from her eyes and they adjusted to the gloom, she gazed up at the sandstone townhouses with mounting confusion. It wasn't until she noticed the green door of the nearest house, however, that realisation dawned and icy fear gripped her.

What the actual fuck…?

And now the door was opening, and two men were coming out. No – three men. Her two police minders first, hands tucked into the pockets of their stab vests. And then, behind them, Guilfoyle, ducking slightly to avoid the doorframe. He nodded and laughed in response to something one of the officers had said. All very pally.

If she'd been thinking clearly, if she'd been on her medication, if she hadn't just woken up, she probably would have acted more rationally. But now, instinct took over completely. She scrambled out of the car and ran.

Barely giving any thought to where she was going, she darted up a narrow side street, tripping over the cobblestones as she followed its westerly course. Behind her, she heard frantic shouts and hurrying footsteps, and she knew her escape had been noticed and pursuit wasn't far behind.

She continued along the path as it wound its way past an assortment of lockups, the raw air burning her lungs. It began to climb higher and curve left, and soon, she was back out in the open at the top of Woodlands Hill, standing at the mouth of Park Gate with Kelvingrove Park spreading out before her. She heard a roar of tyres behind her. She spun around to see the police car pulling into view. She hadn't a hope of outrunning it. Her only option was to go where it couldn't follow.

She sped across the road, through the park gates, past the mounted statue and hurtled down the slope, making for the same line of trees under which she'd crossed paths with the leering walker earlier that morning. Her chances of evading capture seemed to her to be higher there than out in the open. Digging deep into her energy reserves, she put on another burst of speed, leaning from the ankles like she'd been taught in her track running days. She reached the trees and dived under their cover.

Pressed against a thick trunk, she struggled to simultaneously catch her breath and take stock of her situation. She figured she'd got a decent enough head start on the two cops, taking into account the time needed to stop the car and get out to follow her on foot, but that wasn't going to do her much good. Though there was no snow on the ground beneath the trees, she'd left a handy trail of prints running downhill to her present location. She had to throw her pursuers off the scent – and fast.

The sound of running water reached her ears, and an idea came to her. One that every sane part of her was screaming at her not to heed. But it was her only chance.

She scrambled down the sheer slope leading to the edge of the river and stepped in. It reached up to her knees and was cold beyond anything she'd thought possible – the sort of cold that physically hurt. Like knives digging into her flesh. Into her bones. It was all she could do not to cry out. Clenching her teeth, she began to wade downstream, making for the stone bridge that straddled the river in the centre of the park. It would have been an ordeal even in the full heat of summer, but somehow, she kept going. She ducked under the arch, pressed herself against the inner wall and tried to slow her ragged breathing. There she waited, convinced that at any moment she'd hear voices and the rush of feet, and then the game would be up. But no sound reached her ears, save that of the river itself, bubbling and flowing as it continued its journey towards the Clyde.

Time passed, and her legs and feet began to go numb, but still, she didn't move.

***

It was fully dark when she finally risked a peek at the outside world. Slowly, agonisingly, she waded to the northern side of the bridge and peered out from under the arch. She saw no sign of life. The park was still and eerily silent. Even the Kelvin Way off to the west seemed unusually quiet. The heavy snowfall from the previous night must still be keeping traffic to a minimum.

There was nothing for it but to make a move. For all she knew, the police could be lying in wait for her, biding their time until she poked her head above the parapet. But she knew if she stayed in the water much longer she'd be risking hypothermia. Deciding to chance it, she waded over to the bank and crawled up the slope on her hands and knees. She rose up slowly, ready to throw herself flat at a moment's notice. But she saw and heard nothing. The park was empty.

Her trousers, plastered to her legs, were as stiff as stovepipes, and she could barely feel her toes, but none of them appeared to be in danger of dropping off just yet. Still, she knew she had to get herself to somewhere warm, and quickly. Zoe's was out of the question – it was the first place the police would look for her. And, having lost her phone yesterday, she couldn't even call her. She, a law-abiding citizen who'd never stolen so much as a packet of sweets as a child, was now a fugitive from the law.

Something landed on her cheek, an even colder spot on her already chilled skin. She looked up. It was snowing again. Big fluffy flakes fluttered down from the heavens, underscoring her pressing need to find shelter.

With nowhere else to go and nobody else to turn to, she mustered what remained of her energy and began the slow, painful trek to the university.

29

White Knight

'You're lucky my internet's on the fritz at home,' Gavin said cheerfully, 'otherwise we'd never have run into each other.'

Anna said nothing as he ushered her into his apartment and shut the door behind them. Gavin lived in the Merchant City, an area of the city centre favoured by wealthy young professionals, on the top floor of a six-storey building overlooking the Tolbooth Steeple. The apartment itself was a small but no doubt pricey affair, its centrepiece an open-plan living room/kitchen that looked to have been furnished exclusively from an Ikea catalogue.

'You can borrow some things of Charlotte's,' he said, when she raised the question of a change of clothes.

'You're sure she won't mind?'

'I won't tell if you don't.'

He showed her through to the bedroom, then went to the kitchen to 'rustle up a little something.' Feeling distinctly like an intruder, Anna explored the contents of the various closets and drawers. Charlotte's taste in clothing was, to put it mildly, more provocative than hers, with more short skirts and lacy thongs than any sane person could know what to do with. In the end, though, she found a pair of plain flannel slacks she wouldn't feel too embarrassed to be seen in, changed into them and headed out to the living room.

Gavin was behind the breakfast bar, putting the finishing touches to their food. 'Have a seat. I'll be through in a mo.'

Anna headed over to the leatherette sofa and sank into it. A flat screen TV faced her, a nature show running on mute. She picked up the remote and channel-cycled until she came to an evening news bulletin.

It didn't take long for her to realise things had taken a turn for the worse. Ross Garvey had died in hospital during the night, it was announced, and another murder had taken place – one Ted Renfield, killed at the sports centre where he worked. She tried her best to dredge up some sort of sympathy for these men, but there was nothing there but an empty numbness. On the screen, Norton was shown addressing a room full of microphones, gravely informing them that Strathkelvin Police Force was treating the situation with the utmost seriousness, that all leave had been cancelled with immediate effect, and that additional officers were being drafted in from other divisions to assist in what was now being treated as a hunt for a serial killer. She waited for the inevitable postscript to the tune that they were also urgently seeking a Dr Anna Scavolini 'to assist with their enquiries', but it never came. Far from allaying her fears, this only served to send her mind into a fresh fit of paranoid overdrive. Given that she'd fled police custody mere hours earlier, surely she ought by now to be the subject of a nationwide manhunt? It didn't make sense…unless, that is, it suited their interests for her to be made to quietly 'disappear'.

'Here.'

She looked up to find Gavin standing over her, offering her a glass of red. She took it wordlessly and shifted to make room for him on the sofa.

'I think we've had enough of that.' He reached for the remote and switched off the TV, then raised his glass to hers. 'Cheers.'

***

As the evening drew on, Anna touched none of Gavin's food, but she accepted every refill on offer. The wine coursed through her veins, warming her through and taking the edge off her anxiety, to the extent that she began to feel almost relaxed. Gavin prattled on about this and that, mostly relating to his plans for the festive period.

'I don't know about you,' he said, 'but the whole enterprise leaves me cold. All this spending inordinate amounts of money on presents nobody really wants, the endless family gatherings where you sit around trying to think of something to say to people you actively avoid the rest of the year…Frankly, I'd happily just crawl under a rock and hibernate 'til it's all over and done with.'

His tone was light, but even in her somewhat drowsy state, she got the sense there was something premeditated about this speech, laying the groundwork for whatever was to follow.

'My parents have a cabin at Pitlochry. I sometimes head out there if I need to escape from civilisation. And–' he paused to empty the remainder of the bottle into Anna's glass '–I know where they keep the spare key. I've half a mind to take advantage of their absentee landlordism, and – well, there's room enough for two.'

'I thought Charlotte was working over Christmas.'

Gavin turned to face her. 'I wasn't talking about Charlotte.'

Oh.

He got to his feet and stood over her, swaying slightly. 'You don't need to decide right away. But give it some thought.' He picked up the empty bottle and headed for the kitchen.

On the face of it, Anna thought, going off grid didn't sound like a bad idea at all. If nothing else, it would give her time to plan her next move. It was the unspoken strings accompanying the offer that gave her pause. Common sense, if not experience, told her that when a man invites a woman to join him at a secluded bolthole, he has only one thing in mind.

Gavin returned with a fresh bottle and proceeded to pour them each a generous measure. With a contented sigh, he settled down, flinging his arm over the back of the sofa in what Anna was dimly aware constituted a grave violation of her personal space. She'd long since lost track of how much she'd had to drink, which invariably meant it had been too much.

'So, any thoughts on my little proposal?'

'It's tempting,' she admitted.

'So give into temptation, Dr Scavolini!' He grinned at her and swallowed a mouthful of wine.

'You're drunk,' she said.

'So are you,' he said agreeably. He downed the contents of his glass, motioned to Anna's and, when she offered no objection, helped himself.

'It's a gorgeous place. Three bedrooms, two of them ensuite. And there's this big wide living room with an open fireplace. Just think – a bracing walk over the moors on Christmas morning, then home to lunch in front of a blazing log fire.'

As he spoke, his right hand – the one he hadn't placed behind Anna – had begun to snake towards her. He rested it on her thigh – a move that would normally have made her recoil immediately. Right now, though, the inappropriateness of the gesture barely registered, though the hairs on her leg stood to attention in response to his touch.

'I'm not trying to pressure you.' He caressed her with slow, concentric strokes. 'But I'm not naïve, Anna. I know there's... *something* between us. I always liked you, though you only ever seemed to have eyes for Andrew. But I'm not the boy I was back then, and you...well, I don't think my affection's an entirely one-way street, do you?'

She found herself shaking her head, saying, 'No' – though she wasn't sure whether she was saying, *No, it's not a one-way street* or *No, it definitely* is.

He continued to stroke her thigh, his hand moving ever closer to her waistband. 'And when two people like each other...well, I don't think it does either of them any good to engage in a self-denying ordinance, do you?'

'What about Charlotte?'

'I don't care about Charlotte.'

She wondered what it was that made a certain breed of men believe that line was one any woman wanted to hear.

'It's you I want,' he murmured.

And now he was leaning into her, his nose brushing against her cheek as his lips suckled her neck, and she was leaning back and shutting her eyes and surrendering herself to him.

The sudden ringing of a phone was deafening in her ears. They both froze, him leaning over her, one hand cupping the back of her neck, the other lingering between her legs. He lifted his head. Their eyes met, silently communicating their shared discomfort.

'I have to get it,' he said. 'Sorry.'

He scrambled over the back of the sofa and made for the kitchen alcove, where the trilling phone was mounted on the wall. He snatched it up. 'Price,' he said sharply. Then, more softly, 'Oh, hey, honey. What's up?' And then a gentle laugh. 'Really? Oh, no way. And what did you say to *him*…?'

And so it continued, his voice dipping to a low, affectionate murmur, Anna forgotten or at the very least pushed to some far corner of his mind. She listened to his voice rising and falling as he continued his back-and-forth.

In a sudden, unanticipated moment of clarity, she saw herself from the point of view of an outside observer: a vulnerable woman who'd gone home with a man she barely knew – a man who'd plied her with alcohol and had, until moments earlier, been in the process of trying to get into her pants. Would probably have succeeded too, had it not been for Charlotte's impeccable timing. She saw history repeating itself. She was sixteen years old and lying on the bed in the house on Copeland Drive, waiting for it to be over. She was Ms Smith, having her sexual history raked over and denigrated in the witness box, condemned by the jury for her failure to conform to their narrow model of propriety. She was every woman who'd ever fallen victim to the presumption of consent – to the myth that the lack of an explicit 'no' equated to an implicit 'yes'.

And Anna Scavolini was no one's victim.

She lurched to her feet and headed to the bathroom, where she'd left her socks and shoes drying on the radiator. They were still damp, and the combination of wet and warm actually felt worse than wet and cold, but it was either that or go barefoot. Either way, she was getting out of there.

When she returned to the living room, the sofa remained empty. She could hear but couldn't see Gavin, the linoleum creaking as he paced the kitchen area, continuing to murmur sweet nothings down the phone line to his moronic girlfriend.

She hesitated for the briefest of moments, then strode out into the hallway, unlocked the door and slipped out into the night.

***

She crashed out into the street, gasping as the cold air hit her. Her head was spinning. Her vision kept shifting in and out of focus. The Tolbooth Steeple rose up in front of her like some ancient, grim monument, dwarfing her and everything around her.

A flash of headlights. A roar of tyres deep in snow. A shout of *Watch where ye're fuckin' staundin'!* as someone shoved past her. The narrow pavement was awash with pedestrians hurrying in both directions. In her disoriented state, it seemed to her that the best course of action she could take was to get out of their way. And so, with nowhere else to go, she stepped into the road. Immediately, she was greeted by a cacophony of horns and angry yells. There wasn't much traffic, and what little there was moved at a snail's pace, but for the irate drivers who'd already spent considerably longer on the homeward crawl than they'd anticipated, the sight of some fool stepping into their path was like a red rag to a bull.

'Stupid bitch!'

'Get off the road!'

The car directly in front of her had its headlights set to full beam. The blare of its horn was near-deafening. Blinded, she shut her eyes and raised her hands in front of her face, expecting to feel the impact of the bonnet at any moment.

Suddenly, a hand on her shoulder.

'Anna?'

A voice she knew.

She lowered her arms to see Victor staring wide-eyed at her, his face inches from hers.

'What happened to ye?'

She stared back at him in numb silence. Seeming to sense that he wasn't going to get anything out of her, he took her arm and escorted her back to the safety of the pavement.

'Where's Zoe?' she managed to say.

'Out lookin' for you, same as me. We've been tryin' tae get in touch all day.' There was an accusatory note in his voice.

'I...I lost my phone,' she said helplessly. 'The police–'

'I know. They came tae the house. Don't worry, they're gone now.'

***

What followed was little more than a blur to Anna. She was aware of Victor hailing a taxi. Of him bundling her into the back and clambering in beside her. Of him telling the driver to take them to Astley Street and doing up her seatbelt for her. She offered no resistance. She had no strength left, either mental or physical, to object.

Lulled by the taxi's vibrations, her mind wandered back to what had happened in the flat. She kept replaying it over and over, and the more she thought about it, the angrier she became. She was supposed to be attuned to this sort of thing. She should have read the signs.

The house lay in darkness as they pulled up to the kerb. She insisted on getting out and walking up the path unaided, though her legs were like rubber. She climbed the stairs with Victor hovering behind her like a nervy mother hen. He followed her to Zoe's room and lingered in the doorway as she stumbled over to the bed. As she sat down, a fresh wave of nausea gripped her. She felt her surroundings beginning to seep away, like paint running on a canvas. She leaned forward, eyes clenched shut, convinced she was going to throw up.

'Anna? Are you okay?'

Of course I'm not okay, you colossal tool, she thought. But she nodded and dismissed his concern with a wave. 'It's fine. It'll pass.' She tried to concentrate on breathing slowly and steadily.

'I...I don't...what's wrong? Did he give ye somethin'?'

She shook her head. 'I'm fine, really. Just too much to drink and not enough to eat.'

'Um, maybe I should call a doctor?'

'No. I just want to be alone.'

'Are you sure? I reckon you oughta have someone wi'–'

She jerked her head upright, glared across the room at him. 'I said I'm fine. Would you just fuck off!'

For a moment, he didn't move. Just stood there gawping. Then, slowly, he backed out of the room, drawing the door to behind him.

Alone at last, she let her head drop between her shoulders. The dizziness was clearing, but everything still seemed strangely off-kilter, as if she was on a ship that was listing slightly to one side. She heard the creak of the floorboards in the room opposite. Victor was pacing back and forth, no doubt continuing to fret about her. *Bloody Victor.* Where Gavin had started, he'd picked up the slack. In his own impotent, aggravating way, he was just as bad, boxing her into the supplicant role society imposed on her gender.

And then, without having given conscious thought to what she was doing, she was on her feet, striding down the corridor towards Victor's room. She was spoiling for a fight, and it didn't much matter which of these various men was on the receiving end of her ire. They were all much of a muchness.

She thrust open the door. Victor spun around to face her with gormless surprise.

'Anna–'

'It's not alright, you know. What you do, it's not okay.'

'What I…what I do?'

'You – all of you. You're like gannets. The moment you get a whiff of vulnerability, you swoop in to see what pickings are on offer.' She was talking fast, the words pouring out in an uncensored stream of consciousness. 'You think you've got a right of access to our bodies, and you expect us to be grateful when you don't give in to your impulses. You expect us to be enthusiastic and submissive and glad of your attention at all times, even when we're tired or crabbit and just want to be left alone.'

'I–I don't–'

'Yes you do. You do it every minute of every day. And the ones like you – the goody-two-shoes who make out you're all enlightened and progressive – you're no better than the rest of them. You worm your way into the narrative, you make yourselves the gallant heroes, our protectors, our saviours, and us your helpless damsels in distress. Well, I've got news for you – I'm not your concubine, and I need a white knight like I need a fucking hole in the head.'

He just stood there staring at her. They were close together, almost touching. She could hear his shallow breathing, the hammering of his heart in his chest. Or was it her own?

And then she was lunging towards him, pressing herself up against him, her lips trying desperately to connect with his. He recoiled and backed off, hands raised defensively in front of him, eyes wide and disbelieving.

'What the fuck?'

'What's the matter, Victor? Isn't this what you want?' She put her hand to her breast, began rubbing it in a suggestive, circular motion through the fabric. 'Are you telling me this isn't what you've wanted since you were fourteen?'

Victor continued to back away, shaking his head, then nodding, then shaking it again. 'I don't…I mean, not like this.'

She advanced towards him, forcing him up against the wall. 'Not like what? Like this?' She rubbed her tit again, her eyes not leaving his. 'You sure you don't want this?'

He lowered his head, averting his eyes in shame. 'Don't.'

'Come on, Victor. Here I am. Yours for the taking.'

He lifted his head, his eyes brimming with painful embarrassment. She sensed him losing the battle against his impulses, his resistance gradually eroding…

And then their lips were interlocking, his tongue rough and eager in her mouth, his clammy hands pawing at her body through her clothes. She gripped the hem of his T-shirt with both hands. He raised his arms, and she lifted it over his head. The skin beneath was alabaster and smooth to the touch. She dropped to her knees.

Unclasped his belt. Relieved him of his jeans. She could see from the shape against the fabric of his boxers that he was already hard. She took them down, and his erection sprang free – undersized, unthreatening. She took him in her hand, her fingers travelling up the shaft to the livid head. He quivered to her touch and moaned softly, and she wondered if he was going to spurt right there and then. It wouldn't have come as a surprise if he did – she doubted he'd had much prior experience, if any. Sensing that time was of the essence, she backed onto the bed, drawing him down on top of her. His breathing intensified. His dick slapped against her thigh, leaving a trickle of pre-ejaculate on Charlotte's fancy trousers. They both fumbled with her stubbornly uncooperative belt buckle. 'Fuck,' he muttered. His fingers scrabbled with growing frustration. Somehow, one of them or the other managed to get it undone. She raised herself up on her elbows. He slipped off her trousers and underwear and tossed them aside. She lifted up her knees, parting her legs for him. For a moment, he stalled, and she wondered if she was going to have to show him what to do. Then, with a sudden, violent thrust that smashed the breath from her lungs, he entered her. He gripped the headboard as he ground into her, a seemingly desperate urgency underpinning each frantic thrust. 'Slowly,' she told him – but to no avail. A few seconds later and it was all over. With a groan, he discharged his load and went limp on top of her, burying his head in her shoulder.

***

For a while, neither of them moved or spoke. Anna lay on her back, sandwiched between Victor and the mattress. She felt him shrinking and softening inside her, but he made no move to withdraw. His breathing slowed. She began to wonder if he'd fallen asleep or passed out or something. She grew increasingly conscious of his weight bearing down on her, crushing her, threatening to suffocate her…

'I love you,' he murmured.

'I'm sorry,' she said.

He raised his head and stared at her in slack-jawed stupefaction. She turned away. A few excruciating seconds passed before he abruptly pulled out of her, lurched to his feet, snatched up his clothes and fled the room.

She drew the bedclothes over her exposed lower half and lay there in the dark, motionless. She knew what she should be feeling right now. Guilt. Shame. Pity. But try as she might, she couldn't muster anything other than total and utter apathy. His declaration had kindled nothing in her at all, not even revulsion.

Sex, in and of itself, didn't hold any great trauma for her, though she'd learned from experience that certain situations tended to act as triggers. She hated doing it with the lights out, for instance, and had a marked aversion to being undressed by another person. But it wasn't as if she was frigid or sexually dysfunctional or any of the other labels men used to describe women who didn't offer it up on tap. She had as healthy a libido as anyone else – or so she assumed. But what had just happened had had nothing to do with desire on her part. It had been about...actually, what *had* it been about? Proving a point? If so, what? That, when it came down to it, all men were driven by the same base urges? No, all she'd succeeded in proving was that she was the most psychologically dysfunctional person on the planet.

Time passed, but still she didn't move. She was aware of every little sound in and around the house. The *drip, drip, drip* of a leaking tap in the bathroom. A muffled thud as a clump of snow slid off the roof and hit the ground. A dog barking incessantly somewhere up the street.

She became aware of another sound – the gentle hum of some sort of vehicle. No, *two* vehicles, coming from different directions. One was coming from the south, up from Maryhill; the other approached from the east. As she listened, they both pulled onto Astley Street, drew up outside the house and stopped.

She slipped out of bed and crept to the window. Hugging the wall, she opened the curtain a crack and peered out.

Two police cars were parked on opposite sides of the road. As she watched, the doors of the nearest opened and two burly officers got out. One spoke into the walky-talky clipped to his lapel. They advanced up the path.

Anna withdrew into the shadows and crouched close to the floor, her breath caught in her throat. So this was it. They'd come for her.

Hurrying on tiptoe towards the bed, she snatched up her trousers and pulled them on. If nothing else, she wasn't going to be caught with her bits on display when they came for her.

She was easing her feet into her still moist shoes when the doorbell rang. She heard movement in the bathroom, followed by footsteps clumping down the stairs. As she listened, continuing to crouch low lest she be seen from the window, she heard the front door opening, then two voices – Victor's, and another she didn't recognise. She couldn't make out the words, but she heard the accusatory tenor of the stranger's voice and the defensiveness of Victor's responses.

Her only hope of escape lay in having the element of surprise. She had no idea how many officers there were in total, but it seemed safe to assume that two cars meant at least four. And, physically, any one of them would be more than a match for her. But, if she acted quickly and caught them off guard, she might just stand a chance.

It was now or never. She wrenched open the door and took off like a shot, pelting along the narrow corridor and down the stairs. She could see Victor at the bottom with his back to her, facing the two officers standing on the doorstep. One of them spotted her and gave a shout. She cleared the remaining stairs in a single leap, did a one-eighty-degree turn and sped towards the back of the house. She hurried through the kitchen, unlocked the back door and plunged out into the night.

The Callahans' back garden was small, boxed in on its left and right by houses, with a flimsy wooden fence at its far end. Beyond it was another row of houses, and beyond those lay Ruchill Park. If she made it that far, she stood a semi-decent chance of throwing her pursuers off her scent.

Too late, she glimpsed a shape emerging from the shadows to her right. She tried to veer in a different direction, but it lunged towards her, arms outstretched, heading her off. Her keys were in her hand before she was even aware of what she was doing. She lashed out blindly and was rewarded by a yelp of pain. The figure fell back, cursing. She ran on, no thought in her head now other than of reaching the fence. She was more than halfway there. Almost home free.

At that moment, she stepped on a patch of ice beneath the snow, and her foot skidded out from under her. She tried to right herself, but to no avail. Her hands clenched the air ineffectually as she went down, landing hard on her hip. Slowly, painfully, she rolled onto her back and lay there, too winded to move.

A figure loomed overhead. As her vision came back into focus, she found herself staring up at Murray, his hand pressed to the side of his bleeding neck.

The look on his face was anything but kind.

30

Hell

They took her and placed her in a dank, windowless room with only a wall-mounted security camera for company. After a while, a pair of unsmiling female officers came in wearing disposable gloves. They made her strip naked, bend over, spread her buttocks and all the other ignominies that accompany a full cavity search. Throughout it all, she was conscious of the red light of the wall-mounted camera winking at her as it captured every indignity, every act of ritual humiliation she was forced to undergo. She was sure Murray and his cronies were gathered round a monitor nearby, watching as her ordeal was beamed to them in glorious Technicolor.

Then they left her alone, without any clothes, without even a blanket to crawl under. The room was bitingly cold. She retreated to the one corner that wasn't covered by the camera's merciless gaze, sat on the floor, drew her knees up, buried her head in them and tried to switch off completely.

This was what Hell must look like, she thought, if such a place existed.

The minutes dragged by agonisingly, until eventually the door opened and one of the stone-faced officers returned – but only to toss in a colourless, shapeless jumpsuit. As the door clanged shut, she snatched it up and scrambled into it. It smelled decidedly dubious and was stained with God knows what, but she was in no position to be choosy.

The wait continued. For a while, she paced in circles round the tiny room to keep warm, but then it occurred to her that they were probably getting a kick out of that as well. So it was back to sitting in the corner, wondering just what they were planning on doing to her. She felt tears beginning to well behind her exhausted eyes.

Don't, she told herself. *Don't shout or scream or show any emotion at all. That's just what they want.*

***

After a veritable eternity, the door opened once more and a thin-faced young constable, as unsmiling as the pair who'd searched her, ordered her to come with him. She followed him without objection, reflecting on how quickly and completely they'd succeeded in demolishing her resolve and sense of self-worth. Who needed thumbscrews?

After a lengthy trek through the cavernous depths of the station, they came to an interview room – the same one where Norton and Murray had interrogated her on the night of Foley's murder. No lukewarm coffee for her this time. The officer just nodded to the desk and turned to go.

'When do I get my phone call?'

It was the first time she'd spoken since she'd been taken, other than to confirm her identity when she was being clerked in.

The officer just smirked and shut the door.

She sat down, despondent. Under Scots law, suspects could be detained and questioned for up to six hours without access to legal aid – a state of affairs she'd always suspected was open to the most heinous abuse. It was all very well telling yourself you were going to say nothing to incriminate yourself during those six hours, but she knew that, under sustained questioning, the temptation to say something, *anything*, quickly became unbearable.

She tried to think logically. If Murray and his associates were planning to 'disappear' her, they would hardly have taken her back to headquarters and booked her in, leaving a CCTV and paper trail for all to see. Far more likely, they'd have taken her to some desolate, Godforsaken location and put a plastic bag over her head or a bullet in the back of her neck or whatever it was people like them did when they wanted people like her to vanish without a trace. No – it didn't wash.

Why, then, had they so forcibly apprehended her, dragged her in here and treated her like a common criminal? It couldn't just be about teaching her a lesson, though there was little doubt in her mind that this was Murray's primary motivation. She'd never seriously entertained the notion of them suspecting her for the murders – but having said that, she hadn't exactly done herself any favours by inserting herself so forcibly into the investigation. At the very least, she expected she was going to be made to account thoroughly for her movements over the last few days.

She was racking her brains, trying to figure out whether she had an alibi for any of the murders, when the door slammed open behind her. She scrambled out of her seat and spun around as Norton stomped in.

'Inspector, thank God. I don't know what this is about, but there's been a huge–'

'Sit down and shut your mouth.'

His tone was so sharp she did as she was told without hesitation. She watched warily as he stood, fists clenched by his sides, glowering at her. He looked tired and unwell, and in place of his usual self-effacing manner there now burned a still, savage anger that sent a shiver running down to her tailbone. Until now, she'd regarded Murray as the bad cop to Norton's curmudgeonly-but-essentially-good cop. Now, however, she realised Norton was probably just as dangerous in his own way. Perhaps more so. *It's always the quiet ones…* Having a torch shone up her arsehole might well prove to be peanuts compared to what he had in mind for her.

'Why am I here?' she said eventually, when it became clear he wasn't going to speak first. 'Why…*this?*'

'I was hoping you would tell me,' said Norton quietly.

***

There seemed little point trying to keep anything back now. She was sure Norton would know if she did, and that any evasion on her part would only make things worse for her than they already were. And in any event, she was past caring. She found herself recounting it all as calmly and dispassionately as if it had happened to someone else. Throughout it all, Norton barely looked at her. For the most part, he stood leaning against the wall, pinching the bridge of his nose as if fighting a crippling headache – which perhaps he was. He certainly looked to be in seriously rough shape. Once she'd finished – with her capture, manhandling and humiliation at the hands of Murray's cronies – he ran a hand slowly over his craggy features.

'You're wide off the mark. So wide off the mark, you're not even in the right hemisphere. Tony Guilfoyle didn't kill these men. I can tell you that with absolute confidence.'

'Bullshit.'

Norton sighed, but didn't rise to the provocation. 'Whatever you think you know about him, know this – he's a dedicated, highly-decorated officer who served his community proudly and diligently for a great many years.'

'A highly-decorated officer who beat a boy to a pulp in one of these cells.'

Norton shook his head. 'He did no such thing.'

'And you know that for a fact, do you?'

'As it happens, I do.'

She sneered contemptuously. 'Oh, really? How?'

'I know because it's not his style. In all the years I worked under him, I never once saw him lay a finger on a suspect. Not even the dregs of humanity – the rapists and the child molesters. And believe me, there's plenty of others I couldn't say the same of.'

'Forgive me for not considering you a paragon of objectivity.'

Norton tilted his head to one side, regarding Anna with what seemed like disappointment. 'You don't like us very much, do you?'

'What could possibly have given you that impression? You've all been so hospitable.'

A pained look crossed his face. 'For what it's worth, I regret the way this has played out. The way you were treated tonight – that's not how things are done here. Not on my watch. The men responsible will be disciplined.' He lifted his head, his eyes flashing dangerously once again. 'But don't think for a moment you're without blame in all this. Housebreaking, withholding evidence, assaulting an officer of the law, interfering with a murder investigation at every level…I wonder what sort of a view your employers would take of a rap sheet like that?'

Anna's throat tightened. At no point had she ever considered the ramifications of her actions on her career. She could kiss goodbye to her lectureship for a start. And what university would be willing to employ someone with a criminal record of the sort being described? She closed her eyes in despair. She was fucked, and she only had herself to blame.

She heard a soft thud as something landed on the table. She opened her eyes to see her passport lying before her.

'Here's how it's going to work,' said Norton. 'I'm prepared not to pursue the charges against you on the condition that you allow me to deal with my sergeant myself.'

'Brush it under the carpet, you mean?'

'No, that's not what I mean. DS Murray will live to regret his actions. You have my word on that. But you must understand that if I instigate a formal investigation into his conduct, then I won't be in a position to keep your own actions out of the spotlight. Believe me, if Internal Affairs get involved, they'll leave no stone unturned.'

Anna stared down at her passport. The whole thing felt sordid beyond belief. Half of her wanted to just slip off quietly into the night and pretend the whole thing had never happened. She had form for doing that. But the other half wanted to see Murray humiliated every bit as much as he'd humiliated her; wanted him to feel the full force of the very law he'd been charged with upholding. That wouldn't happen if she accepted Norton's deal.

Under the circumstances, she could just about accept the need for them to strip-search her. They could have afforded her considerably more dignity, but given the injury she'd inflicted on Murray, she understood why they'd deemed it necessary to make sure she wasn't concealing anything else that could be used as a weapon. But the sneering contempt with which she'd been treated; the leaving her naked in that dingy little room; the sheer *pleasure* they'd clearly derived from debasing her like that…Tonight's violation was, in some ways, worse than the one that had occurred eleven years ago. At least that had happened behind closed doors and she hadn't been made into an exhibit.

And yet, when all said and done, what difference did it make? She knew how it worked. These people closed ranks and looked after their own. Any investigation would only be a whitewash. Just one more injustice on top of the immense catalogue of injustices that characterised this rotten, corrupt boys' club.

It wasn't worth it.

'Fine,' she said.

For a moment, Norton looked almost disappointed. Perhaps he hadn't expected her to fold quite so easily. Or perhaps he felt as debased by the grubby little deal as she did. Perhaps he'd been hoping she'd say, *No, take the bastards to the bloody cleaners and sod the consequences.* But she wasn't going to risk her reputation, her career, her liberty, on a point of principle. She wasn't brave enough to be a martyr.

At length, he dipped his head in acknowledgement. 'An officer will be along in a minute to show you to the desk.'

He turned to go. In the doorway, he hesitated, then turned once again to face her. 'I would suggest giving serious consideration to cutting your stay here short. I'm told Rome's quite mild this time of year.'

He remained where he was for a moment, then stepped out, closing the door behind him.

As soon as he'd gone, Anna grabbed her passport and clutched it with trembling hands. She intended to waste no time in putting it to use.

31

Feart

Monday, 21 December

The sun was beginning to rise as she emerged from the police station. Unable to summon a taxi for love nor money and with public transport seemingly having ground to a halt, she walked the two and a half miles back to Astley Street. It was a miserable trek, and her feet were once again sodden within minutes of setting out, but it seemed somehow appropriate that her journey reflected her current mood. At some point during her incarceration it had stopped snowing, but it still lay over a foot deep on the ground. The air was dead and still, as if the whole city was being smothered beneath a heavy, colourless blanket.

By the time she drew near the Callahan house, the order of events was clear in her mind – a shower and a bite to eat, then on to the airport with all haste. If there wasn't a direct flight to Rome, she'd take whatever was heading in that approximate direction. It was just approaching nine am. Both Callahans rarely got up much before midday, if they could help it. If fortune was on her side, she'd be able to get in and out of the house unnoticed.

No such luck. Even as she was reaching for the handle, the door flew open to reveal Zoe, looking bleary-eyed and exhausted. Angry too. Angrier than Anna had ever seen her.

'You cow,' she said. 'You absolute cow.'

Beyond the door, Anna caught a glimpse of Victor retreating into the living room and instantly understood the reason for Zoe's fury. She hesitated, paralysed by a pang of guilt, but she quickly overcame it and, pushing past Zoe, barged into the house and made for the stairs.

'What's the matter wi' you?' Zoe was hot on her heels, her voice rising in disbelief. 'How could ye dae somethin' like that? You're no the person I knew ten years ago. You're different. Cold.'

Anna laughed humourlessly. 'Really? You can't think of any possible reason why that might be?'

She reached the top of the stairs and continued along the corridor, Zoe pursuing her, her infuriatingly shrill, infuriatingly persistent, infuriatingly *Glaswegian* voice ringing in Anna's ears like a drill.

'You have to stop blamin' yersel, Anna. It's no your fault what happened. You didnae ask to be raped.'

Anna stopped dead. She turned to face Zoe, burning with white-hot rage. How dare she? How fucking *dare* she say it out loud? And what the fuck did she think she knew about it?

'I don't blame myself. I blame you.'

Zoe stared at her blankly, the look on her face reminding Anna of a big stupid dog who wants to know why its owner won't play with it.

'I never wanted to go to that party. You *knew* that, but you kept badgering me, nag-nag-nagging that way you always do, 'til I got sick of listening and gave in. So rest assured, Zoe, I don't need *you* to tell me it's not my fault.'

She could see the cogs of Zoe's mind whirring behind those wide, uncomprehending eyes as she slowly put two and two together. Anna left her to finish working it out and charged into the bedroom.

She was on her hands and knees, jamming clothes into her case with neither rhyme nor reason, when Zoe's footsteps came to a halt behind her.

'You should've told me.'

Anna stopped what she was doing and turned to face her. 'Really? You think so? And tell me, Zoe, what the fuck business would it have been of yours? What is it about you that's so special that makes you think you had a God-given right to know? It happened to me. To no one else. And if I decide not to share my private business with the whole world, then I'm under no fucking obligation to run that by you first.'

'So that's it, then? Off again wi'out so much as a by-your-leave?' Zoe was no longer dumbstruck. She was furious now, *really* furious, her own outrage more than a match for Anna's. 'Suppose I shouldnae be so surprised, really. I mean, that's you to a T, in't it? When the goin' gets tough, you bail out and leave the rest of us to get on wi' it. Reckon mibby ye'll stretch tae a postcard this time, or an email? 'Cause when all said and done, Anna, me 'n' you, it's aye been a bit of a one-way street, hasn't it?'

It was all coming out now – a decade and more of evasions and half-truths and unspoken resentment laid bare. Anna jammed the last item of clothing into her case and slammed the lid shut. She got to her feet and turned to go, only to find Zoe barring the way.

'You're a fuckin' coward, Anna. You think all this "me against the world" shite makes you look strong, but all you're doin' is showin' everyone how feart y'are.'

'Move.'

For a moment, Zoe remained where she was, a pained look in her eyes as she battled conflicting emotions. There was anger there, yes, but also sorrow, and Anna knew that this was breaking her. A part of her almost hoped Zoe would try to physically restrain her. Because she was spoiling for a fight, yes – but there was another reason as well. Deep down, a part of her wanted Zoe to stop her walking out, and thus salvage something of their friendship.

But it wasn't to be. Anger beat sorrow. Zoe shifted aside, and Anna strode out. She tramped down the stairs, hauling her case behind her, walked out the front door and didn't stop until she reached the street. Then, turning, she gazed back up at the familiar old house where she'd whiled away so much of her adolescence. This was it – her last, irreversible break with the past.

She turned her back on the house and set off, leaving it, and the last vestiges of her old life, behind her.

***

She made it to the city centre and headed straight for the bus terminal, from which a shuttle service departed every ten minutes for the airport. The waiting room was packed with shivering travellers, the overall mood vacillating between rage and despair. It quickly became clear there were no departures imminent, and an enquiry at the kiosk confirmed the reason: owing to the heavier-than-anticipated snowfall last night, all flights had been suspended for at least the remainder of the day.

With nowhere else to go, Anna headed into a nearby café for a bite to eat. The focaccia she ordered had the consistency and taste of cardboard, but she forced it down anyway. It was, she now realised, her first solid meal in nearly forty-eight hours, and she felt considerably better for it, though she could've done with several hours' kip and a fresh set of clothes too. She hadn't slept since the night before last and was still wearing the same sweat-encrusted blouse she'd had on since yesterday. Not to mention Charlotte's trousers, complete with their tell-tale cum stain as a reminder of last night's act of lunacy. She had to settle instead for a splash of water under her arms in the café toilet before putting on the least dubious-smelling of the tops she'd bundled into her case. Before heading out, she took a couple of lithium tablets, chasing them down with a handful of water. Every insane decision she'd made over the last forty-eight hours – from inveigling herself into Ross Garvey's hospital room to doing a runner from the police – could be traced back to her coming off them. If she hadn't, she'd never have behaved so foolishly yesterday – of that she was certain. The entire day read like a monumental catalogue of insanity. Now, more than anything, she wanted to leave this abhorrent city far behind her. Let others deal with its problems. They were nothing to do with her. She didn't belong here.

She tramped down to Queen Street Station, only to discover that it, too, was in lockdown. Only the subway was still running. There was nowhere on that ten-kilometre circuit she particularly wanted to visit, but it beat stomping around the city centre waiting for spring to come.

The train was virtually deserted – just her and a shaggy-haired young man who sat methodically picking his nose, examining what came out and wiping it onto the underside of the seat. She sat, head tucked deep into the collar of her coat, hoping he wouldn't try to start a conversation with her. He looked like the type who might. As a pre-emptive measure, she closed her eyes and pretended she was asleep.

***

She must have actually dozed off for a while, for the next time she looked up, the carriage was empty and the train was idling at a platform. She sat forward, straining to read the sign on the far wall. Kelvinbridge.

The intercom crackled to life. 'Attention passengers, please note that this train is terminating at this stop.'

It was like some kind of a sick joke, depositing her *here* of all places.

She disembarked, dragged her case up the steps to Gibson Street and stood on the bridge, gazing down at the water below her. She pictured herself wading downstream, knee-deep in the icy froth, and wondered for the umpteenth time what on earth had possessed her. Lifting her head, she looked out at the white expanse of Kelvingrove Park, the bare trees looking all the more forlorn in the cold light of morning. She knew she had nothing whatsoever to gain from returning to that hated place again.

And yet…

She shook her head. Reminded herself she'd sworn to have nothing more to do with it, with the murders, with *any* of it. She grabbed her case and turned to go.

And yet…

Something, be it curiosity, fate or a desire for self-flagellation, was compelling her to go in there one last time, to get one last look at where this whole nightmare had begun, before turning her back on it once and for all.

***

The site of Foley's death was even sadder and more forlorn than the last time she'd seen it. The police cordon fluttered in the gentle breeze. A shrine of flowers had been laid, the daffodils and lilies and others whose names she didn't know frozen solid. Further up the hill, a heavily-built figure in a greatcoat was making his way down the slope, hands outstretched for balance. He was the only other person in the park. He could have chosen a safer route, she thought. If he wasn't careful, he was going to do himself an injury.

Her eyes returned to the shrine. There was a lot of truth in the old adage that you only ever heard good things about the deceased. When a child was knocked down by a car, they were always a universally popular straight-A student, never a social outcast who'd been suspended for attacking another pupil with a pair of scissors. When someone was knifed in a mugging, he was always a devoted family man beloved by his wife and two-point-four children, never a serial bigamist who knocked the missus about. It was as if polite society couldn't cope with the notion that, just sometimes, bad things happened to bad people.

She looked up again. The man was nearer now, a few hundred yards away, kicking up great clumps of snow as he waded towards her. Something about that gait, about the bulk of his figure, caused her to stiffen. It wasn't…was it? It *was*.

Guilfoyle.

Fear gripped her. Grabbing her case, she turned tail and began to run.

'Ho! Stop!'

She ignored him and ploughed on, but it was heavy going, and she knew she was going nowhere in a hurry. To have any hope of outrunning him, she'd have to abandon her luggage.

She was on the verge of doing just that when she heard a dull thud behind her, followed by a painful groan. She turned to see Guilfoyle lying face-down in the snow, unmoving.

Her better nature overcame her. She couldn't just leave him lying there. It was anyone's guess how long it would be before someone else came this way. Shoulders hunched, ready to flee again at the slightest hint of trouble, she waded back the way she'd come and hauled him to his feet, nearly buckling under his weight.

'Are you hurt?'

Guilfoyle lifted his head and looked at her. His eyes were bloodshot and brimming. 'She's gone,' he said simply.

'Who's gone? What are you talking about?'

'My daughter. She's disappeared.'

32

Private

It took no small amount of time and effort to get Guilfoyle up the hill. He was staggeringly uncooperative – a dead weight in her arms, letting her do all the work. Several times, she considered abandoning him to his own devices, but she couldn't do it. The state he was in, he'd probably just lie down in the snow and wait for nature to take its course.

Somehow, they made it back to Lynedoch Place. She set him in the big armchair in the living room, cranked up the heating and stood marvelling at the transformation in him. Wrapped in an old rug, shaking all over, he was a pale shadow of the man who'd so thoroughly scared the shit out of her two days ago. It was hard to believe now that she'd ever perceived him as a threat.

As he sat there stewing, she noticed something small and black by the hearth –her phone, which had evidently lain there unnoticed since she'd dropped it two days earlier. She pocketed it and turned to face Guilfoyle. The shivers were beginning to subside. She'd given him as long as was reasonable.

'Mr Guilfoyle?'

He lifted his head and gazed up at her with hooded eyes.

'If Jenny's missing, you're going to need to tell someone. The police–'

He shook his head vehemently. 'No. No police.'

Not the reaction she'd been expecting.

'Why on earth not?'

Guilfoyle said nothing. He lowered his head, wilting under her gaze. Anna's eyes narrowed. She recognised that look.

'Are you *embarrassed* by her?'

'What do you expect?' he snapped, jerking his head upright. 'It's not the kind of thing you shout from the rooftops, is it? Your daughter being a…'

'A what? Being a what?'

'Well, you've seen her, haven't you? I don't know what the correct term for it is.' He shook his head. 'People don't understand. They don't know how to react. It's easier if they don't see her.'

'Easier for who, exactly?'

He didn't dignify that with a response. Just stared morosely at the fireplace. She opened her mouth, a rebuke on the tip of her tongue, then stopped herself. Now was not the time to pass judgement on his parenting skills.

'When did you first notice she was gone?'

Guilfoyle thought about it. 'At about quarter past ten. I'd gone to pick up the morning paper. Got back to find the door lying wide open.'

'Any sign of forced entry?'

He shook his head. 'I never thought to lock it. She…she never goes out.'

'Never?'

Guilfoyle's eyes flared angrily. She didn't pursue that particular line any further.

'Was anything else missing? Clothes, money, any of her belongings?'

'No, nothing. Just what she had on.'

'Which was…?'

'Trousers, jumper, slip-ons. Dear God, she'll catch her death.'

That thought had occurred to Anna too, which was partly why she was so determined to get things moving as quickly as possible.

'And is there anywhere she might have gone? Somewhere that holds particular significance for her?'

'No, of course not. Look–' Guilfoyle was clutching the arms of the chair now, attempting to rise to his feet. Realising he didn't have sufficient strength, he gave up and sank back down. 'She wouldn't have just gone off. I'm certain of it. Someone must have taken her.'

'And do you have any idea who?'

Guilfoyle eyed her under his bushy brows. 'At first, I thought perhaps you had something to do with it.'

'Me?'

'You were sniffing around here the other day. You seemed awfully interested in her. But then I saw you in the park back there, and I realised…'

Anna eyed him suspiciously. There was clearly a lot he still wasn't telling her, but her first priority was Jenny. And the longer they faffed around, the less chance they had of finding her safe and well.

'We're going to need pictures of her. We need to get her image circulated as quickly as possible.'

She saw him hesitate once again, and this time, impatience gave way to out and out disgust.

'Get over it,' she told him sharply. 'Your daughter's wellbeing matters a sight more than your pride.'

'I know that,' he snapped. 'I never implied…'

But he *had* implied it, in his actions past and present, and they both knew it.

'Come on,' she said, more conciliatory. 'They're going to need something recent.'

'I don't *have* anything recent. I've got nothing since before.'

She didn't have to ask him what 'before' meant.

'Before will have to do, then. But we'll need *something* to work with.'

Guilfoyle thought about it for a moment. Then, with a great effort, he raised himself out of the armchair and stood before her on shaky legs.

'Follow me.'

***

She followed him upstairs and stood in the doorway of Jenny's room, watching as he knelt gingerly by the bed. He reached beneath it and slid out a battered cardboard box, then eased himself back onto his feet and set it down on the duvet. As Anna stepped forward to inspect it, he sank into the wicker chair next to the dresser, worn out.

Inside was a collection of teenage girl trinkets – bracelets, a couple of signet rings, a tattered copy of *The Complete Poems of Christina Rossetti*. Also present was a small pink vibrator, the sight of which caused her to instinctively glance in Guilfoyle's direction, gripped by an inexplicable feeling that she was seeing something she ought not to. But his eyes were downcast, lost in his own world. He'd no doubt been through the box countless times.

Underneath this top layer, several photographs lay loose, in various sizes, many of them dog-eared and crumpled. She began to sort through them. Most were of no great interest – snaps of windy beaches and snowy hills, shots of ducks taking flight from a pond – but peppered among these humdrum images of the natural world were images of Jenny at various ages: at around eleven or twelve, standing in her Willow Bank uniform outside the school gate; in her mid-teens, posing against a brilliant blue ocean, wearing a pair of comically oversized shades; standing at the foot of a snow-clad slope, clutching a pair of skis, her features all but obscured by a woolly hat and a high-necked thermal top.

'Oh! She *did* ski.'

Guilfoyle stirred. 'Nearly every winter, I took her to the Alps, from age twelve until…' He trailed off. 'I thought, if I told people she'd been hurt skiing, it would at least sound halfway convincing.'

'But you knew what had really happened.'

'I had a fair idea.'

'So why lie?'

Guilfoyle gave an unhappy, irritable shrug and said nothing. Anna didn't press the matter any further, but she could guess some of his reasons, not least because they were the same ones that had led to her own silence. Embarrassment, self-denial, a belief that what happened was somehow down to you…They might not be rational, but they were certainly powerful.

'When did you know?'

Guilfoyle's head lifted. 'When? I knew something had happened as soon as she came home from school that day. She always used to have a hug and a kiss for her old man, but that day, she was hours late getting back, and when she came through the door, she disappeared up the stairs without so much as a word. I heard the bathroom door slamming and the shower starting to run, and it didn't stop running for the next three hours. In the morning, I found her clothes in the bin. Her school things and her…underwear. They had blood on them. That's when I knew for sure.'

He wasn't looking at Anna as he spoke – or, it seemed, anything else in the room. His eyes were distant, glazed, as if gazing back into the past.

'She didn't come out of her room. I waited as long as I could, then I went up and knocked. She didn't say anything, and the door was locked. For all I knew, she could be dead in there. So I forced it open, and I found her just sitting on the bed, staring straight ahead – expressionless, like. I got down on my hunkers, shook her, called her name, but there was nothing there. I didn't know what to do. I thought about calling the doctor, but…but it's not something you talk about, is it? Something like that, it's – well, it's private.' He shook his head and sighed. 'Stupid, stupid fool.'

'So you took her out of school, you holed her up in here – and then what?'

'And then?' Guilfoyle shrugged. 'I'd done my twenty-five years. I took retirement so I could be there for Jenny.'

Anna asked her next question with some trepidation. 'And have you ever…I mean, did you ever take steps to find the people responsible?'

'You mean apart from asking Jenny? I did – over and over, though I never got so much as a peep out of her. But if you're asking did I take the law into my own hands, then the answer's no. There's a lot of nonsense doing the rounds – about me going around roughing people up and suchlike. People have…fertile imaginations.'

'I can't believe you weren't tempted.'

Guilfoyle gave her a sharp look. 'You can believe what you like, but revenge was never at the forefront of my mind. In the beginning, it was enough of an ordeal just getting from one day to the next. And later, I thought…well, I thought I was better off *not* knowing.' He saw Anna's look of incredulity. 'If I'd found out who they were, I wouldn't have been responsible for my actions. And if got put away, where would that have left Jenny?'

She saw his point. And, more to the point, she saw that, over the last several years, he would have had plenty of time on his hands to reach this logical conclusion.

'And you did this all on your own? You never thought perhaps you needed some help? For both of you, I mean,' she added hastily, as Guilfoyle's eyes flared again.

'I thought we could manage. I'm sure we've all got things we'd do differently if we could go back. Hindsight's a bloody wonderful thing.'

His eyes were glassy. She couldn't tell whether he was actually crying or if that was just how they naturally looked.

Perching on the end of the bed, she continued examining the contents of the box. At the very bottom, underneath the photos and various other accoutrements, was a small, A5-sized picture frame, lying face-down. She lifted it out of the box and turned it over. Inside the frame was a photograph of a teenage girl and boy in the sort of pose that couldn't help but convey the awkward tenderness of young love. He had his arm around her. Her shoulders were drawn in, a small, self-conscious smile playing on her lips. The girl was Jenny. And the boy…

The boy.

She turned to Guilfoyle, holding up the frame. 'Who's that with her?'

Guilfoyle glanced briefly at the picture. 'Oh, him. He was her boyfriend for a brief while – the summer before. They thought I didn't know, but they couldn't have been more obvious.' A small, almost wistful laugh. 'I didn't approve, not at first, but the more

I got to know him, the more I began to think maybe, just maybe, he was just the right one to bring her out of her shell. He was a year older and…you know, sensible. Considerate too. Not like the boys she was ages with. In the end, I couldn't help but give them my blessing.'

Anna said nothing. Her heart was pounding.

Guilfoyle harrumphed brusquely and got to his feet, wiping his eyes with a mighty paw. 'There, uh, there might be some more pictures in the attic.' He headed out into the hallway and began to climb the stairs to the second floor, the steps creaking under his weight.

Anna didn't move. She continued to stare down at the picture, and the boy, her breath coming out in shallow gasps, her heart hammering a staccato rhythm. Wireframe glasses, blond curls, and, only barely visible in the pocket-sized picture, a small dark mole just above his upper lip. She'd know that face anywhere.

Jenny's boyfriend had been Gavin Price.

33

Tower

She was still staring at the photo when her phone began to vibrate in her pocket, a sensation so unexpected that she dropped the picture frame. Lurching to her feet, she fished the phone out and checked the caller ID.

'Mark?'

'Anna?' His voice came through crackly and slightly breathless. 'Are you okay?'

'Sorry?'

'I mean, did you get home safe last night?'

She bent down to pick up the picture. 'Last night? What are you talking about?'

'From Gav's. He called me after you left and…look, there's something funny going on.'

'Funny how?' She checked the photo frame for damage, only really half-concentrating on Mark's words.

'Alright, this may be nothing, but he said something to me last night, and I've been turning it over and over in my head ever since. He told me you'd been at his place most of the evening, that he'd gone to take a phone call and got back to find you'd left.'

Neatly glossing over the whole 'aborted seduction' part, then. 'Go on. I'm listening.'

'Well, he said he was worried about you – about your state of mind. He said you'd had a fair amount to drink and wasn't sure you were fit to take care of yourself, especially after you'd been attacked the other night.'

Anna could hear her own blood pounding in her ears as she digested those words.

'On Saturday, before I left you at the bus stop, you made me promise not to tell him about that.' A loaded pause. 'Anna, I didn't tell him. Did you?'

Anna stared down at the photo of Jenny and Gavin. At Gavin's wireframe glasses. *He used to wear glasses.* Meaning he probably wore contacts now. And you could get contacts that changed the colour of your irises. Changed them to blue, for example.

'IF YOU VALUE YOUR PRETTY HEAD, ANNA SCAVOLINI…'

She saw it now with utter clarity. The murders weren't the work of a vengeful father. They were the work of a vengeful lover.

Her phone let out a warning beep, indicating that the battery was almost drained.

'Mark, where are you now?'

'At work, and it was a wonder I got in at all, given–'

'Is Gavin there?'

'Not yet, but he should be in. The staff are all on 'til Wednesday–' Another warning beep cut off the rest of what he was saying. 'Hang on, I think I hear him at the door.'

'Mark, listen to me.' She was on her feet, moving towards the landing. 'I need you to hold on to him 'til I get there. Make sure he doesn't leave. I'll be with you as soon as I can. I'm serious – don't let him out of your sight, okay?'

'Alright.' Mark sounded deeply sceptical. 'But I'm not sure how–'

'Mark. Just do as I say. Please.' She was hurrying down the stairs now.

'Alright. I'll do my best.' A pause. 'Anna.'

'What?' She strode out into the street.

'What the hell is going on?'

'I–' she began. But at that moment, her phone emitted a last forlorn beep, then powered down. She hammered the buttons, but to no avail.

She glanced back over her shoulder towards the Guilfoyle house. She briefly contemplated heading back in and using the landline to call Mark back, but time wasn't on her side.

She made her way to the top of Lynedoch Place and turned west onto Park Gate. She could see the university bell-tower in the distance, rising behind the haggard trees that covered the park.

The park. Her most direct route.

She began to run.

***

She hurtled downhill at full speed, making for the bridge. *Shoulders down. Elbows bent. Breathe in through the nose and out through the mouth. Keep looking straight ahead, eyes on the prize.* At one point, she tripped on a tree root hidden beneath the snow, went flying and landed on her hands and knees, but she picked herself up without a pause and kept going. She crossed the river, scrambled up the slope and charged across the Kelvin Way, empty but for a solitary car abandoned by its owner beneath a mound of snow.

Five minutes later, she stumbled into the Department of Law and Social Sciences, making a beeline for the building directory at the foot of the stairs. Mark and Gavin's office was on the second floor. She tripped up the steps, strode along the corridor and thrust open the door labelled *Westmore / Price*.

The small, oak-panelled room was empty. As she stood in the doorway, drinking in her surroundings, all she could hear was her own raspy breathing as she struggled to fill her burning lungs. A packet of supermarket mince pies lay on one of the two desks, along with a couple of cloudy-looking glasses and a bottle of supermarket mulled wine. She knew instinctively that this desk, strewn with papers and stained with coffee rings, was Mark's. The other, tidy to the point of anal-retentiveness, had to be Gavin's.

Taking deep, deliberate breaths, she crossed over to Gavin's desk and eased herself into the chair, partly to take the weight off her aching legs and partly to give herself a chance to think. Had Gavin flown the coop? It was always possible. In which case, where was Mark?

She began to go through the desk drawers systematically, hoping to find some clue as to Gavin's whereabouts. Not that she had any concrete idea of what she hoped to find. Essay papers, books, stationery, a half-eaten stick of Rolos…none of it was any help to her. An eerie silence engulfed the room – the sort of silence where you feel compelled to make some sort of noise to check your ears are still working.

A sudden, dull thud made her jump to attention. She remained still, listening, trying to identify its origin. She looked around. There was no sign of anything having moved or fallen.

She heard the thud again, and this time, her eyes alighted on the cupboard door at the other side of the office. As she got to her feet and approached it, there was another thud, followed by another and another. A feeble sound, growing in tempo and urgency as someone behind it beat a desperate rhythm.

At the door, she hesitated, eyes on the key protruding from the lock. She shuddered to think what might be waiting for her behind it. Steeling herself, she unlocked it and turned the handle.

Mark Westmore tumbled out and collapsed at her feet.

He was bleeding, and bleeding badly, from a wound to his lower stomach. He'd long since given up trying to staunch the flow, though the fact his hands were covered in the stuff indicated that, initially at least, he'd made a decent fist of it. He stared up at Anna with wide, panic-stricken eyes. His face was marble-white. Fast, shallow breaths hissed through clenched teeth.

'A…Anna…' His mouth opened and closed like a landed fish.

Call an ambulance, the voice in her head screamed at her. *Call the police. Call SOMEONE.*

'I–I'll get help.'

She hurried across to the desk, snatched up the desk phone and dialled 999. She put the receiver to her ear and waited. Nothing happened. There was no dial tone, no busy signal, no *'Which service do you require?'* She looked down and saw why. The cable running to the wall had been sliced in two. Gavin had clearly intended for Mark to be beyond rescue.

She dropped the receiver and hurried back to him. His eyes were closed now. His breathing was faint and had slowed considerably. She knew, just as with Foley, that this could only end one way.

Dropping to her knees, she took his blood-soaked hand in hers and squeezed it. His eyelids flickered, then opened. He gazed up at her. He looked scared. Confused. Desperate. But there was no time for sentimentality on her part. The clock was ticking.

'Mark, where did he go?'

Mark's lips quivered as they tried to form words, but it was taking all his strength just to continue breathing. Eventually, he managed to emit a rasping, barely audible croak.

'What?'

He made the sound again, his mouth opening and closing ineffectually.

Anna lowered her head, bringing her ear close to his mouth. 'I'm sorry. I don't understand. What are you saying?'

For a moment, Mark didn't respond. Then, with a great effort, he took a deep breath, filling his lungs with as much air as they could sustain, then expelled it all in one final, desperate gasp.

'Tower.'

Anna lifted her head in time to see Mark's eyes glazing over. She felt his hand go limp in hers. She put two fingers to his neck, checking for the carotid pulse. She felt nothing.

She got to her feet slowly, averting her eyes. She felt tears beginning to brim and scrubbed at them angrily. She could cry later. In the meantime, all that mattered was apprehending Gavin and putting a stop to this, once and for all.

She turned towards the window. It faced east, looking out onto the West Quadrangle and the cloisters beyond, above which the bell-tower loomed up like a sentinel. And there, framed in one of the tall arched windows on its uppermost floor, just before it began to taper into a spire, stood a figure – tall, erect, statuesque, much like the tower itself.

Gavin.

As she stared up at him, their conversation outside St Lucian's three days earlier sprang to mind. A conversation about Foley, and his contention that the best way to kill yourself would be to throw yourself off the top of a tall building.

Oh, Jesus. He was going to jump.

***

She barrelled up the spiral staircase three or four steps at a time. Her aching legs were working mechanically now, propelling her upward, step by tortuous step. Once or twice she stopped to catch her breath or to quell the seasickness that threatened to engulf her, but she somehow managed to keep going, making it to the top floor of the tower in just over three minutes.

For the most part, the university bell-tower is a hollow structure, the majority of its ornate façade acting as an outer shell to a tall chamber designed to enrich the acoustic qualities of the bells. The exception is the upper floor – an attic of sorts above the bell-chamber itself, approximately twenty feet from floor to ceiling, accessible via a small door near the top of the stairs. It was this that Anna now stood facing, her trembling hand hovering in front of the handle. Regardless of what awaited her on the other side, there would be no turning back.

The tremor subsided. All around her was quiet. Nothing – not wind nor distant traffic nor even birdsong – disturbed the strange serenity that now enveloped her.

She turned the handle. With a laboured creak, the door swung open.

Gavin stood at the other side of the room, directly facing her. He had on the same pinstripe waistcoat and trousers as when they'd met for coffee on Friday – a lifetime ago. His arms were folded behind his back.

She opened her mouth to speak, then stopped. There was something not quite right about this scene. Some detail which didn't fit. It took her a moment to realise what it was.

The expression on Gavin's face.

She wasn't sure how a multiple murderer about to take his own life was supposed to look, but she was fairly certain his expression of frozen fear wasn't typical. To look at him, you would think *she* was the one who'd left the bodies of four men in her wake.

She advanced into the chamber towards him. As she did so, she sensed movement out of the corner of her eye. Before she had a chance to react, she heard the door shutting behind her. She froze, not daring to turn as footsteps crossed the wooden floor towards her and came to a halt just over her shoulder. She felt warm breath on the back of her neck.

'Hello, Anna,' said a voice directly behind her ear. 'We've been waiting for you.'

34

The Message

It came in a series of waves crashing over her in rapid succession, rising up to engulf her, building to an intense, glorious climax that caused every part of her to clench – her fingers, her toes, her buttocks, her clit. As they subsided, each one fainter than the last, like the calming of the sea after a storm, the spots dancing before her eyes cleared, and a mop of tousled blonde hair rose from between her parted legs.

Carol smiled. 'I'm guessing that went well.'

Zoe, flushed and panting, could manage nothing more coherent than an awkward, embarrassed, delighted laugh.

Carol crawled up the bed, flopped down next to her and nuzzled her shoulder. 'You okay?'

Zoe shook her head in disbelief. 'What *was* that?'

'You tell me.'

'That was...new.'

Carol's brows contorted into a frown. 'What, you've never–'

'Course I have. Loads of times. Just never like *that*.'

Carol laughed. She grabbed her cigarettes and lighter from the bedside cabinet, lit up and lay back, blowing a column of smoke towards the ceiling. As her breathing settled, Zoe glanced across at her, surreptitiously admiring her form. She smiled to herself. Sometimes she still had to pinch herself in disbelief at the turn her life had taken.

They were in Carol's one-bedroom flat above A Taste of India on Dumbarton Road. It was a cheap and cheerful affair that lacked the room to swing even an exceptionally small cat, but as a bolthole for spending a few hours getting up to various naughty activities in bed, it was ideal. And neither of them owned a cat anyway.

'What you thinking about?' Carol's voice cut into her thoughts. She shrugged nonchalantly. 'Nothing much.'

Carol's lip curled into a knowing smile. 'Liar.'

She took another drag on her ciggy. Then, setting it aside in the ashtray on the bedside cabinet, she patted Zoe's stomach, swung her legs over the side of the bed, got up and left the room.

Zoe listened as the bathroom door clicked shut and the shower began to run, then reached over and grabbed her phone. There was one missed call, from a number she didn't recognise. She rang it back and was put through to a call centre somewhere in India or Bangladesh, whereupon the operator immediately launched into a pre-written script, trying to sell her double glazing or a new boiler or something equally unwanted. She hung up and lay back, clutching the phone pensively. She had a lot to think about – though, right now, her most immediate concern was what she was going to do for Carol to repay her. It was a tough one. The most intense orgasm of your life wasn't an easy act to follow.

Gradually, her thoughts turned to Anna. She'd be airborne by now, probably – on her way back to her new life. She thought about the blazing row they'd had, about the home truths that had been spat out so bitterly, about the fact that they would, in all likelihood, never see one another again. It had been brewing for a while – ever since the moment on Thursday night when the taxi had pulled up to the kerb next to Wizard of Paws. She'd sensed the change in Anna immediately – a strained sort of remoteness, as if she'd become almost like a ghost. As if she was there and yet not there. Of the two of them, Anna had always been the more reserved, the more reluctant to lay bare her true feelings. But this had been different. Zoe had known deep down that they'd never be able to pick up again from where they'd left off. She'd tried to deny it, of course, overcompensating with her grandiose plans for trips to the Lighthouse and Silverburn. But the truth of the matter was, she'd known all along that the connection they'd had growing up was destined to remain parked in the previous century. She just hadn't expected things to crash and burn quite so spectacularly.

Her phone blinged its text alert. She flipped open the lid and examined the display. For a brief moment she thought – perhaps even hoped – it might be from Anna, telling her she hadn't been able to get a plane and was coming home.

But it wasn't from Anna. And as she read the lengthy and at times incoherent message, scrolling through the lines of text with repeated flicks of her thumb, a feeling of deep unease began to develop in the pit of her stomach. Her throat ran dry. The sweat clung cold to her skin. She wondered now whether, deep down, she'd known all along, or at the very least had a strong suspicion – ever since that moment four nights ago when she and Anna had run into the figure in the hoodie as they walked up the Kelvin Way.

She was still staring at the screen, re-reading the message for the umpteenth time when she heard movement in the doorway. She looked up to see Carol standing there, a towel wrapped round her, gazing at her with a look of profound unease.

'Zoe? What's wrong?'

35

What You Did

Victor slowly circled Anna, a black plastic stun gun clutched in his outstretched hand. Her eyes tracked him warily, but she didn't move a muscle. Her life, she sensed, depended on it.

'Anyone know you were comin' here?'

She thought quickly. 'The police.'

'Liar,' he said, the inklings of a smile playing at the corner of his mouth.

'Anna—' Gavin began.

But that was as far as he got. Victor spun around to face him, stun gun at the ready. 'Shut up, Beast. No one said you could speak.'

Gavin shut his mouth, cowed instantly. He stood there by the window, straight as an arrow, arms behind his back. He looked at Anna, eyes pleadingly wide.

Victor turned to face her again. 'On the floor. Sit down.'

Slowly, Anna lowered herself onto the floor and sat, one leg folded under the other, eyes not leaving him for a second.

'Here's how it's going to work,' said Victor. 'You're here to watch. That's all. You get in my way, you get fifty thousand volts in your neck. Understand?'

There was something different about him. Something new and altogether more commanding. This was not the same shy, awkward maladroit who'd pined after her during their teenage years, or who'd fled in shame last night after their disastrous sexual encounter. Right now, he held all the cards. And yet, at the same time, she could tell from the tension in his voice, from the tremor in his outstretched weapon arm, that it was taking all his willpower to keep his composure and to contain not just one prisoner but two.

And that, potentially, was an opportunity for her to exploit, if she bided her time and played her cards right.

'I said, "understand?"'

'I understand.'

He smiled, almost pleasantly. 'Good. Then we can begin.' He turned to Gavin. 'That's your cue, Beast.'

Gavin stared back at Victor, shoulders rising in the beginnings of a confused shrug.

Victor's eyes narrowed. 'It's dead simple. Every time I ask a question and you don't answer, you get a taste of this.' He waggled the stun gun in Gavin's direction. 'Not enough to fry your brain – not yet, anyway. Just enough to make you beg me to stop.'

'But what…what do I–?'

'Turn around.'

'Wh–what?'

'Turn around and get on your knees.' As Gavin's petrified eyes widened even more, Victor scoffed. 'I'm no gonnae push you, if that's what you're worried about. Think I'd make it that easy for you?' He flicked the gun. 'Do it now. I'm no gonnae ask a second time.'

Anna watched, heart hammering, as Gavin made an awkward hundred-and-eighty-degree turn and sank to his knees. She saw now that his hands were bound behind his back with cable ties. They were cruelly tight, digging into his wrists, the skin around them painfully swollen. He was perilously close to the edge. The tall arched windows were unglazed, leaving nothing between him and the nothingness of a long, steady drop to earth. One swift shove was all it would take.

Victor shot Anna a look, warning her not to try anything clever, then crossed the floor and stood directly behind Gavin.

'What do you see?' His tone was gentle, almost paternalistic.

'I…' Gavin began, then stopped, at a loss as to what was being asked of him.

'C'mon. Let's hear it. Describe what you see.'

'I…I see the East Quadrangle.'

'Further.'

'Um…the Kelvin Way. The park.'

'Tell me about the park.'

'I see…I see snow. Trees. Um…the River Kelvin. I–'

'TELL ME!' Victor roared, jamming the gun into the nape of Gavin's neck.

Gavin let out a frightened yelp. 'I DON'T KNOW WHAT YOU WANT ME TO SAY!'

Victor continued to press the gun into Gavin's flesh. 'December the twenty-second, 1999. Ten years ago, almost to the day. Tell me what you did.' He withdrew the gun, leaving twin pressure marks where the electrode prongs had dug into the skin. 'Tell me,' he repeated. He glanced over his shoulder. 'Tell Anna.'

Anna said nothing. Though her stomach was knotted with fear, she realised she wanted very much to hear what Gavin had to say.

'Tell me,' said Victor.

Gavin let out a strangled sob, causing his entire body to convulse. His head sank low. For a moment, he said nothing, and Anna mentally prepared herself for the worst.

Then, at last, he began to speak. At first, he was almost inaudible, and Anna had to strain to make out what he was saying. But gradually, as she inched herself closer and as he gained in self-assurance, the threat of violence deferred, his words became clearer.

'It started the weekend before Christmas, just after the universities broke up…'

36

The Debt

Saturday, 18 December 1999

He'd barely slept a wink the night before, too wound up to let his mind switch off. School wasn't due to finish until Wednesday, but in many respects, today felt like the true start of the holiday season, and the date had been etched in his mind for weeks. It was the reason he now stood on a windswept platform at Queen Street Station, waiting for the 1306 from King's Cross, buzzing with a mixture of nervous anticipation and just plain nerves.

Today was the day Andrew came home.

People referred to them as cousins, though in reality, it was something of a lazy shorthand. Same great-grandparents, different grandparents. But blood relatives nonetheless and, in spite of the two-year age difference between them, probably as close as actual cousins, if not brothers. Or at least, they had been at one point. Of late, they'd drifted apart somewhat as their interests and beliefs diverged. Now, as the train pulled up to the platform, Gavin found himself reflecting that life was indeed more straightforward when Andrew wasn't around. He could be his own man, not constantly being judged in comparison to his older, more academically gifted, more worldly-wise cousin. With Andrew around, he felt he was always destined to be the sidekick.

And then there were the other things – the things about Andrew that made him decidedly uncomfortable, if not quite brave enough to actually challenge, and of which he'd become increasingly aware as his own worldview solidified. He found himself wondering why he'd agreed to Andrew's suggestion – more of a summons, really – to meet for celebratory drinks. He should've cried off, said he had something on that he couldn't get out of. But he sensed that Andrew would have immediately seen through that ruse, and knew from experience that trying to bullshit him simply led to more trouble in the long run.

Still, as the doors slid open to reveal Andrew's grinning face, for a brief moment, he forgot his anxieties and matched it with a smile of his own.

'Alright, ya big bufter? See you've still got a face only a mother could love.'

'Oh yeah? That's not what yours was saying last night before I kicked her out of bed.'

Then followed the traditional displays of macho affection – the manly hug, the hearty thumps on the back. And then it was off to the pub for drinks and catch-up. Gavin had enjoyed something of a growth spurt over the last year, and the novelty of being able to go up to the bar and order a pint without being asked for ID still hadn't worn off. In fact, the ordering was almost more pleasurable than the drinking itself. *See me,* it said. *I am a man, not a boy.*

At first, the mood was buoyant as they traded notes on their respective academic years. Andrew was now halfway through his three-year degree and had already received offers from various accounting firms – thanks in no small part to his father's greasing of the wheels behind the scenes. He, in turn, pumped Gavin for information about events back in Glasgow, and they spent a good while laughing about the various outrages committed by mutual acquaintances. So far, so good. It wasn't until they were on their third pint that the conversation began to stray into territory that made Gavin less than comfortable.

'So then, cuz–' Andrew traced the outline of his beermat with a lazy finger '–been getting any action of late?'

The mouthful Gavin had just attempted to swallow caught in his throat. He choked it down, shook his head. 'All quiet on the Western Front.'

'Oh? You and the lovely Jennifer no longer an ongoing concern?' A knowing smile. 'Been hanging you out to dry, has she?'

For the umpteenth time, Gavin cursed the day Andrew had got wind about him and Jenny. Some friend of a friend – he'd never found out who – had clearly spilled the beans to him, and since then he'd been insatiable, haranguing Gavin unceasingly for details about their relationship, demanding to know when he was going to meet this special lady. Now, Gavin sensed, things were coming to a head.

'You know,' Andrew said, with studied severity, 'it's really not on – her holding out on you like that. And more fool you, letting her get away with it. Where's your bloody self-esteem, man?'

With as much patience as he could muster, Gavin tried to explain that it had been a mutual decision, that it simply wasn't something either of them was interested in pursuing at the moment. But he knew he was fighting a losing battle, as Andrew's expression shifted from incredulity to outright contempt.

'Got you wrapped round her little finger, hasn't she? Even got you believing your own spiel. What's the matter, cuz? Something wrong with your prick, or d'you just not know what to do with it? Maybe you need someone to show you how it's done.'

Gavin knew where this was headed, and he didn't like the destination one bit.

'You ought to set me up for a confab with her. See if I can't loosen her up for you. You never know – a session with a slightly more mature member of the family might just make her a little more open-minded.' Andrew was clearly warming to the idea. 'A little birdie tells me Rosco Garvey's having a *soirée* at his place on Wednesday to celebrate the end of term. Why don't you bring her along and we'll see if we can't get her to unlock the old chastity belt?'

Gavin managed a nervous laugh. 'Won't be necessary. Me and Jen, we're doing just fine.'

'Oh no, dear cousin. I insist.'

Andrew slid a hand across the table and gripped Gavin's arm, just tightly enough to leave no doubt that he meant business. Until now, he'd been smiling – a sly, sardonic smile, but a smile nonetheless. Now, however, it faded from his lips, to be replaced by a look that was cold, hard and all business.

'I seem to remember a little incident over the summer during which I did you a rather large favour. Saved your bacon, as I recall. And I can't help but feel there's been a bit too much "take" and not enough "give" when it comes to our relationship of late.'

Gavin said nothing. He knew how Andrew's mind worked so well, he could practically write the script himself. He was referring, of course, to that disastrous July night when, severely over the limit and running high on the elation of having just passed his driving test, Gavin had got behind the wheel of his parents' car and promptly rammed it into the garden wall at the foot of the road. Pointing out that the penalty would be less severe for someone who was stone-cold sober and had passed his test more than two years earlier, Andrew insisted on taking the blame. And in that instant, something fundamental changed between them. Gavin had always been aware that his life was lived in his older cousin's shadow. From that point on, however, he knew he was irrevocably in Andrew's debt, and that it was only a matter of time before that debt would have to be settled. And now, as they sat in a quiet corner of Waxy O'Connor's, they both knew they were inching their way towards that moment.

'Be a shame if word got out about what we did. Probably wouldn't damage my career prospects too much, and in any event, I can always rely on old *pater familias* to smooth things over. But someone planning on pursuing a law degree?' He shook his head and tutted. 'Fancy finding out how that would go down?'

He fell silent, letting it sink in. Gavin gazed morosely into the dregs of his glass.

'So we're agreed, then? Wednesday at one, Rosco's place. You'll both be there?'

Gavin nodded unhappily. The beer was fermenting in his stomach like acid.

***

And thus it was that, four days later and a little before one pm, he found himself walking hand-in-hand with Jenny up the hill towards Park Terrace.

It had taken no small amount of effort on his part to persuade her to come. 'What sort of party?' she'd said, eyeing him uncertainly. Then, in a hushed whisper, 'There won't be *alcohol*, will there?' But bit by bit, he'd succeeded in chipping away at her resolve until, that same morning, she'd finally said yes, but only because Gavin would be there.

Music and varied sounds of merriment spilled from the house as they climbed the steps to the door. The party was evidently in full swing already. Gavin rang the bell and stood back, shoulders hunched and jaw set. Jenny shot him a worried look, and he forced a smile, dismissing her concern with a wave of his hand.

The door swung open, and there stood Rosco, clutching an open beer bottle by the neck and grinning broadly.

'Wahey! It's the lovebirds! Come on in.'

They stepped over the threshold, Jenny taking off her coat and handing it to Rosco like the innocent, trusting thing she was. As Rosco disappeared to hang it up, Gavin was suddenly overwhelmed by an intense desire to be anywhere but here. Whatever was about to go down, he didn't want to be around to witness it.

'I just remembered,' he blurted out. 'There's something I forgot. I'll be back soon.'

'Gav?' Jenny turned from hanging up her coat and gave him an anxious look.

'I'll not be long.' He was already backing towards the door.

'Well...I'll come with you.'

'No, Jenny.' He took her firmly by the arms, looked into her wide eyes. 'You need to stay. Hey–' a light-hearted smile, belying his nausea '–I'll be back before you know it.'

She said nothing. Just stared back at him, confused, hurt and ill at ease. Unable to bear her gaze any longer, he turned and hurried out. With the sounds of the party ringing hollow in his ears, he jammed his hands into his pockets and tramped down the steps towards the street.

***

He stayed away for as long as he could, whiling away the hours as the pale winter sun rode down towards the horizon, bathing the West End sandstone in its golden haze. He spent much of his time in the little café in the grounds of Kelvingrove Park near the southern gate, choking back cup after cup of Fairtrade coffee. And, when he couldn't sit still any longer, he resorted to pacing the surrounding streets, working his way through an entire pack of Marlboros, though he'd never smoked before or since.

As dusk drew in, he stood under the eaves of the café finishing his last cigarette, watching as pupils in Willow Bank uniforms passed through the park in dribs and drabs, all coming from the direction of Woodlands Hill. He waited until he spotted a trio of boys he didn't recognise and approached them.

'Hey.'

They stopped and turned to face him, fanning out slightly as if in anticipation of a fight. They were a good couple of years younger than him and stared back with wide-eyed apprehension.

'You come from Rosco's?'

They looked at one another, silently conferring. Then one of them, their appointed spokesperson, nodded. 'Yeah.'

'Party still on?'

Another silent conference, then a head-shake. 'There was only a few people still there when we left.'

'Did anything—?' he began, then thought better of it. He gave them a gruff nod. 'Okay, thanks.'

As the boys hurried on, casting wary glances over their shoulders, he turned and looked up in the direction of Park Terrace, the windows of the outer circle glinting in the half-light.

He'd left it long enough. Whatever had happened up there, it was time to go and face it. He took a final drag on his cigarette, tossed it aside and set off.

***

As he approached the house, he saw that it was in darkness, barring a solitary light in the living room window. The front door was unlocked. He entered without knocking and headed towards the light. The door swung open to his touch to reveal a sight as horrifying as it was incongruous.

Jenny lay face-down on the floor, seemingly unconscious and naked from the waist down. Andrew stood over her, one hand on his belt buckle, frozen into inaction by Gavin's arrival. Three other boys stood watching, their faces betraying varying degrees of surprise, guilt and apprehension. Rosco was there, of course, and Ted Renfield. The third was the lanky, sullen-faced ginger kid from Jenny's year. Gavin couldn't remember his name, or anything much about him at all, other than that he was Zoe Callahan's brother and that there was probably a picture of him in the dictionary under the word 'loser'.

Andrew's lip curled into a smile. 'So you've decided to show up at last, cuz. Just in time for the main event.'

Gavin couldn't take his eyes off Jenny's lifeless form. 'What… what happened?'

'Oh, that?' Andrew gave her a brief, nonchalant glance. 'Small difference of opinion. She didn't much fancy what we had in mind. Decided she wasn't going to stick around. But we caught up with her and…persuaded her to come back with us.'

'Is she…is she alive?'

Andrew laughed – a harsh, guttural rasp. 'Course she's alive, you clod. You think I'm going to dip my wick in a dead thing?'

Dead thing. Dead THING.

'I was going to go first,' Andrew went on, stepping over Jenny and making his way towards Gavin, 'but I'm more than happy to stand aside now you're here.'

Gavin, beyond words, simply stared at him, rooted to the spot.

Andrew shrugged. 'Fair enough. I never was much of a fan of sloppy seconds anyway.'

***

It took place in near-total silence. The only audible sounds were Andrew's grunts and Gavin's pounding heart. Four pairs of eyes remained glued to the gruesome spectacle – Gavin, Renfield, Rosco, Callahan, all watching, all doing nothing. In the middle of it, she came round and began to struggle, but she soon gave up, evidently realising it was futile.

And then it was the turn of the others. One by one, they all took a shot, all with varying degrees of enthusiasm. Renfield first, then Rosco, then last of all Callahan. He took the longest to persuade, though in the end, even he got on with it, and when he'd finished, he gazed up at the others with such wide-eyed servility, cravenly seeking their approval, that Gavin half-expected Andrew to pat him on the head and tell him, *Well done. Today, you are a man.* Throughout it all, she just lay there, eyes open but empty, as if she'd already taken herself to somewhere far, far away.

'And what about you?' said Andrew, turning to Gavin, once everyone else had had a go. 'After all, she's *your* girlfriend.'

Gavin didn't reply, and Andrew didn't ask him again.

For a while, Jenny continued to lie there, motionless. Eventually, she got unsteadily to her feet, collected her skirt and underwear from the corner of the floor where they'd been tossed and slowly, gingerly, got dressed. The others paid her no attention. Gavin couldn't bring himself to look at her. He stared at the floor, waiting until she'd limped past him before lifting his head. They listened to the front door opening and shutting, to her making her way down the stone steps, to her shuffling footsteps as she set off down the pavement.

At length, Andrew got to his feet. 'About time we made a move.' He nodded to their host. 'Cheers again, Rosco. Most hospitable as always.'

The other two made similar noises. As they began to gather their things, Andrew crossed to Gavin and clapped him on the shoulder. 'You as well, little cousin. Your folks'll be thinking you've got lost.'

Rosco saw them to the door. It was after six and pitch black outside. Callahan peeled off almost immediately, vanishing into the night without a word of explanation. On Gibson Street, Gavin and Andrew left Renfield at the bus stop and continued on up to Kelvinbridge.

At the foot of the steps up to Great Western Road, they came to a halt. For several moments, they stood there in a kind of numb silence, each occupied by their own thoughts.

'Listen,' said Andrew, breaking the spell, 'if you want to meet up over the holidays for coffee or whatever, or just to chill, you know where to find me.'

'Yeah, maybe I'll do that,' said Gavin. He turned towards the steps.

'Hey.'

He stopped in his tracks and turned.

Andrew gave him a long, hard, appraising look. At length, he gave a curt, approving nod. 'Now we're even,' he said, then turned and walked off.

37

Justice

Monday, 21 December 2009

It didn't come out as succinctly as that, of course, or half as coherently. There was a lot of obfuscation from Gavin, a lot of snivelling and prevarication, and on several occasions, details had to be coaxed out of him by Victor, either with the threat of the stun gun or a sharp cuff to the back of the head. Bit by bit, though, it was all laid bare.

When his account finished, Gavin lowered his head and fell silent. He was still kneeling at the precipice, his hands – white from lack of circulation – hanging limp behind his back.

Victor turned to Anna. 'Well, what do you think? Quite a story to tell the grandweans, in't it?'

Anna said nothing. In all the time Gavin had been speaking, she'd remained seated on the floor. However, by shuffling forward, inch-by-inch, she'd managed to close some of the distance between them without Victor noticing. She judged that there were now no more than five metres separating them – close enough that, with the element of surprise, she could potentially clear the gap before Victor had a chance to react.

And what then, Anna? And to what end?

Suppose she managed to get the stun gun out of his hand? Did she really fancy her chances in a one-on-one fight with someone who'd managed to overpower and kill four other men? Did she really think she could stop him?

And did she even *want* to?

'I wanted you to be here.' Victor again, his voice invading her thoughts. 'I think, deep down, I always hoped you'd figure it out.

When I saw you comin' through the park, a part of me was kinda glad.'

He's going to make me watch, isn't he?

After all she'd heard, a very significant part of her was inclined to let him get on with it. And yet the thought of being there, trapped in the same room, listening to the screams…

'Come on – say something.'

Anna swallowed heavily, forcing down the bile that had risen in her throat. 'You…you're a monster,' she managed to whisper.

She wasn't sure whether she was addressing Victor or Gavin, or whether she was referring to the rape, or to the murders, or indeed both. All the barriers of distinction had broken down. Killer, rapist, she no longer cared who had done what. They were both as bad as each other. All she wanted was to get out of there and leave them to it.

Victor gazed at her sadly. 'I know what I am,' he said softly.

For a moment, he stood still and silent, gone to some distant place in his mind. Then a renewed determination came into his eyes. He turned to Gavin.

'Of course, you were the worst. The worst out of all of us. That's why I've kept you 'til last. She was your girlfriend – your fuckin' *girlfriend* – and you just stood by and let us do that to her.'

Jenny. Her disappearance, forgotten amid all the revelations of the last half-hour, or however long it had been, loomed large in Anna's consciousness once more.

'Where is she?' she demanded, turning her guns on Victor. 'What have you done with her?'

He looked at her blankly. 'I dunno what you're talkin' about.'

'Yes you do. She went missing this morning. If you didn't take her, then who did?'

But even as she spoke, doubt crept into her mind. He had no reason to lie to her – not anymore. And if he hadn't taken Jenny, that meant she was still out there somewhere.

'Anna,' said Victor, his tone insistent, 'I swear to you, I have no idea what you're on about.' He turned to Gavin, glowering at him accusingly.

'Don't…don't look at me!' Gavin protested, tensing in anticipation of another blow. 'I spent half the morning just getting here. Please – if she's gone, I had nothing to do with it.'

'No.' Victor's expression turned more contemplative. 'No, I don't suppose you've given her much thought at all.'

He ran a hand across his jaw distractedly. Plainly, the news of Jenny's disappearance had knocked him off his stride. He was wrong-footed, struggling with the knowledge that there was a part of these events over which he had no control. Which, depending on how he reacted, could either be a good thing or a bad thing. It might cause him to let his guard down, to make mistakes – but on the other hand, it also had the potential to make him more volatile. Anna knew she was going to have to tread carefully.

And again, all that was based on the assumption that she actually wanted to stop him.

A high-pitched trilling – deafeningly loud compared to the silence that preceded it – suddenly rang out. Victor snapped out of whatever spell he'd been under. Still angling the stun gun in Gavin's direction, he fished in his pocket with his free hand and whipped out his phone. He held it up to examine the screen, fumbling clumsily with the buttons. A moment later, he pocketed it again, now a good deal more rattled.

'Who was that?' said Anna.

'Zoe.'

A dreadful thought occurred to Anna. 'She…she's not in on this as well…?'

Victor's lip curled contemptuously. 'Of course not. Don't be bloody stupid.'

She believed him. The idea that Zoe – so big-hearted, so straightforward, so *moral* – could be involved in any way was patently absurd.

And now Victor was pacing, muttering to himself, his free hand behind his ear, scratching feverishly. Of course – she was his Achilles' heel.

'Well, what do you think she's going to say when she finds out about this?'

'Shut…shut up.' Victor jabbed the stun gun in her direction. 'I need to think.'

'She's going to tear strips off you, that's what she's going to do. Can you even imagine how disappointed in you she's going to be?'

'I said shut up!'

He paced some more. She didn't take her eyes off him. In his current state, she couldn't be sure what he'd do if she pushed him in the wrong direction.

'I'm goin' out,' he announced abruptly. 'I need…need to…'

He swept past her, still muttering. Before she had time to get to her feet, he'd unlocked the door, slipped out and slammed it behind him. She heard the key turn in the lock, then his footsteps receding down the stairs.

The moment his steps became inaudible, Gavin turned to Anna with frantic urgency. His skin was pale and clammy, his eyes wide with terror. Beads of sweat formed on his upper lip. 'You've got to help me,' he hissed. 'You've got to get me out of here. He…he's crazy.'

'Is he?'

She felt strangely detached from it all. With the immediate threat of Victor gone, at least for now, she could afford to take a step back – to weigh up her options before deciding how to proceed. To decide whether she had any intention at all of trying to intervene.

Gavin hesitated for a moment, then piped up again. 'Is…is Mark…?'

'Mark's dead.'

'Oh Jesus…' He lowered his head in silent remorse, chin resting on his chest. When he spoke again, the panicked urgency from before had given away to a resigned melancholia. 'You should've got out of here, Anna. Should've gone back to Rome when you had the chance. I did everything I could to persuade you…'

An image flashed into her mind of her staring up from the ground as a balaclava-clad stranger glared down at her, his threat rendered all the more chilling in its artificial, electronic form.

'IF YOU VALUE YOUR PRETTY HEAD, ANNA SCAVOLINI, BACK OFF. GO BACK WHERE YOU CAME FROM.'

She understood now.

'It was you. Outside the house on Friday night. You attacked me.'

Gavin nodded sadly. 'Juliet rang me that evening, just before Mark's lecture. Wanted to know if I'd sent you. Said you'd been asking all sorts of questions about Andrew. I knew you were like a dog with a bone. I had to do something to stop you prying. I… well, I thought I might be able to spook you into leaving. And when that didn't work, I hoped I could persuade you another way.'

The cabin at Pitlochry. 'Then why in God's name didn't *you* leave? When the others started to turn up dead, you must have had some idea what was coming your way.'

'Charlotte,' he said, simply and unhappily. 'We couldn't go anywhere, not with her working over Christmas. And if I just took off on my own…' He paused, licked dry lips. 'But…I don't know. Maybe, if you'd agreed to come with me…'

'What? You'd have just cast Charlotte by the wayside and made do with me?'

Somehow, even after all that had been revealed, this final detail still managed to sicken her. The thought of how close she'd come to taking him up on his offer made her shudder.

'I can only imagine what you must think of me,' he said. 'Christ knows I prob'ly deserve it. And believe me, I wish to God it hadn't happened. But it's not as if I had any choice in the matter. It was four against one.'

The look she gave him told him exactly what she thought of this excuse.

'You think they'd have listened to me? You think someone like Andrew would've thrown up his hands and said, "You're right, it's wrong – we'll stop"? You have no idea the hold he had over me.'

She wondered if he'd thought about Jenny at all in recent years, spending every day less than a fifteen-minute walk from her house. No, he probably hadn't. He, like his co-conspirators, had moved on with his life, consigning Jenny to the ash heap of history.

'At least I wasn't a part of it.' His tone was verging on petulant. 'At least I didn't *do* anything.'

'My thoughts exactly.'

'What was it you said to me the other day? "You're not responsible for his actions. Do you really think he valued your opinion so highly it would have changed his life's trajectory?"'

'The ones that say nothing are as guilty as the ones doing it,' replied Anna. 'End of.'

As deserved as it was, she was taken aback by the venom in her own voice. Gavin clearly was as well, judging by his expression. Or perhaps he was seeing his inaction, his dereliction of basic human decency, for what it really was for the first time. He lowered his head and said nothing more.

***

She heard footsteps beyond the door, coming up the stairs at considerable speed. She tensed immediately, but any thought of using the element of surprise to ambush and overpower Victor quickly went out of the window as the door opened and he stormed in, all business. Perhaps he'd been out there psyching himself up to do what he'd come here to do and had decided to get it over with before his nerve deserted him. At any rate, it was clearly time. He strode past Anna and made for Gavin, who, panic-stricken, did a reverse shuffle until his back was against the wall behind him. She saw the gleam of a knife in Victor's left hand. With his right, he levelled the stun gun in Gavin's direction.

'Victor, Victor, please, don't do this.' Gavin stared up at his captor with beseeching eyes. 'I'll do anything. Anything at all. Whatever you want. I'll go to the police. I'll tell them everything. I can say it was my idea. Say I orchestrated it all. Say you were never there, if that's what you want.'

'You think that's what I want?' Victor's voice dripped derision. 'You seriously think that's what this is about?'

Gavin blinked stupidly at Victor, his expression vacant.

Victor sucked on his teeth contemptuously. He muttered something that sounded to Anna like 'Pathetic.' She watched as he shifted from one foot to the other. He had a serious case of the jitters, his sweat-soaked hands struggling to retain a firm grip on his two weapons. And yet still, she didn't move.

Then, without warning, he sprang into action. He advanced on Gavin, knife at the ready. Gavin gave a yelp and prostrated himself at Victor's feet, completing the image of the penitent grovelling before his priest.

'Whatever you want!' he screamed, pressing his face into the floor. 'Please! I'm sorry!'

'You're sorry?' Victor's voice strained in disbelief. 'Oh, I'll bet you are. Sorry you got CAUGHT.'

With that, he jammed the stun gun into Gavin's neck. Anna saw him spasm and go down like a sack of fertiliser. She let out an involuntary shriek, her hand flying to her mouth.

Victor loomed over Gavin's twitching form. He sniffed in disgust. 'And that's what it comes down to, in't it? No decency. No responsibility.'

Anna doubled over and vomited, spewing the contents of her stomach onto the floorboards. She was still dry heaving, eyes and nose running, when she sensed Victor squatting down by her side. She felt his tentative hand on her back and recoiled, backing up against the far wall, arms raised defensively.

Victor gazed at her unhappily. He'd dropped the stun gun now, but not the knife. 'I deserve it, you know,' he said softly. 'Your revulsion. That's the difference between him and me. Men like him, they make excuses, say she was askin' for it or it wasn't *rape* rape or whatever. But not me. I know what I did. I had a choice. I deserve to die just as much as he does.' He was silent for a moment, then added, in a lower voice, as if speaking to himself, 'And I will. Soon as this is done.'

Anna slowly shifted her gaze over to Gavin. He lay motionless on the floor a few metres away, curled up in foetal position. He'd wet himself. A dark, wet patch was spreading from his groin. A part of her hoped he was dead – that Victor had somehow miscalculated and zapped him with too much electricity. But she knew these devices didn't work like that.

Victor sucked in a deep breath. 'I'd hoped you'd at least be able to understand how come I'm doin' this. You were sort of my inspiration.'

'Your *inspiration*?'

'The night you came home. Zoe's birthday party. I changed my mind. I decided I'd come after all. And as I was comin' down the stairs, I saw you and him. Foley. You were sittin' there on one of they sofas, blabbin' away, and I couldnae stand the thought of him gettin' his hands on you, and I knew I had to do somethin'. I knew I couldnae let him just walk away.

'So I followed him. I trailed him fae this pub to that. Watched him drink hisself halfway into a coma before he finally got turfed out of the Apollo. Then, when he went into Kelvingrove Park, I could hardly believe my luck. It was pitch black, there wasn't another soul about, and it…it just sort of happened. And the others…well, it was just a matter of findin' out where they lived. Where they worked. Only Renfield was under the radar, and even he wasnae that hard to sniff out. Some of 'em had websites and everythin'. And I just kept thinkin' to myself, *Why is it they get to have these perfect fuckin' lives and she – she's stuck in this nothin'?* I know you've seen her. I know you know what I'm talkin' about.'

Anna nodded softly. It wasn't really about Jenny, she thought. It was about these men, these boys, and the power they coveted. Jenny was merely a means for them to assert that power. If they'd been younger, it would have been comic books or Pogs they'd have been fighting over instead. And Victor – well, whatever he might claim to the contrary, she saw precious little evidence that what he was doing would benefit Jenny in any way. It wouldn't give her back her lost years; it wouldn't allow her to move on. In their own way, the murders were simply an articulation of the same one-upmanship that had led these boys to think nothing of luring a girl to a party with the express purpose of raping her.

And, just as before, innocents had been caught in the crossfire. She thought of Mark lying dead on the floor of his office. Poor, well-meaning Mark, who'd never hurt anyone, who'd just had the misfortune of being in the wrong place at the wrong time. And she thought of Juliet, and of the mourners at Foley's memorial service, and of the families of Ted Renfield and Ross Garvey – people she'd never met but who would now have to face this Christmas and every Christmas thereafter without their loved ones. The cost of Victor's actions was more than just four dead rapists. Like raindrops creating ever-expanding ripples on a surface of water, his spree had devastated the lives of countless others.

She heard groaning nearby. Gavin was in the process of coming to.

Victor followed her gaze. 'You know why people like him do the things they do?'

'Why?'

''Cause they don't understand the meanin' of the word "no". Over-privileged, self-entitled arsewipes who think they're untouchable. For them, you're status symbols. Property to be traded. And it disnae come fae nowhere, that attitude,' he added, as Gavin once again began to groan and flex his shoulders. 'It's nurtured in them. The families they come fae, the schools they go to…They're all brought up to believe they can and should get whatever they want.'

Anna looked at him long and hard. 'Do you actually believe that? Or is this just about you getting your own back because, ten years ago, you gave in to peer pressure?'

For a moment, Victor held her gaze, lips clenched shut, nostrils flaring with each breath. Then, without a word, he lurched to his feet and strode towards Gavin.

'Victor, stop.'

She was on her feet before she'd even given conscious thought to what she was doing. She stood there, feeling light-headed but oddly calm as he looked back at her over his shoulder, stooped with a fistful of Gavin's curls in one hand and the knife in the other.

'If you kill him, then that's it. Finished. No one will ever know what he did. Remember those tributes to Foley on the news? It'll be the same for him. They'll make him into a saint, and you into the monster who killed him.'

Gavin's head hit the floor with a thud. Slowly, Victor straightened up and turned to face Anna. He was like a coiled spring, tense and sweating, gnawing on his bottom lip. But, for now at least, he was listening.

'And Jenny – nobody's even going to remember she exists. It'll be all about you. And it shouldn't be about you. It should be about her. About what she's suffered. If you really are doing this for her, prove it.'

'How?'

'Go to the police.'

Victor's eyes widened. 'What?'

'Go to the police.' She said it again, more forcefully, with more conviction. 'Let them deal with him. Let it all come out in the courts. Let all that respectability be stripped away so everyone knows what he did. What he is.'

Victor shook his head. 'He'll never answer for it. They never do. You know that.'

Three per cent. A miserable three per cent.

Even now, Mark's words haunted her, and she knew in her heart of hearts what she was attempting to sell was a fantasy. The chances of Gavin ever seeing the inside of a courtroom were so slim as to be laughable.

And yet, a chance was still a chance. And however slim a chance it was, it was still better than more bloodshed.

'I know the system's awful.' Her voice cracked under the strain of what she was forcing herself to say. 'But it's all we've got. We have to put our trust in it. Otherwise, what hope is there?'

Victor looked at her incredulously. 'And you actually believe that? Seriously?'

No. A thousand times no.

'Yes.'

'And that's what you'd call justice, is it? There's no punishment enough for what he did. For what *we* did.' He shook his head vehemently. 'None.'

'It's not about punishment,' she said, and this time she almost allowed herself to believe she meant it. 'It's about the victim. It's about Jenny, and all the others like her. It's about *their* stories being told.'

The corner of Victor's mouth twitched. He licked his lips. Rubbed the underside of his nose with a knuckle. His fingers, clasping the hilt of the blade, tightened, then loosened, then tightened again. A distant look came into his eyes. Was he imagining a different future, the possibility of which neither of them had previously dared to entertain? One in which the system worked, where justice was meted out to the bad guys, and where the good guys got to live happily ever after?

The moment passed. He gave a thin smile, and she knew he'd seen through her bluff. He seemed almost pleased. It was as if, his assumptions about how the world worked now confirmed, he was on surer footing. There was no hope, no justice, no redemption to be found, and somehow that was easier to live with than the alternative.

'Anna,' he said, 'you always were a crap liar.'

He turned, grabbed Gavin by the collar and raised the knife above him. Anna lurched forward with a cry.

At the same instant, she heard a loud pop behind her, and Victor stopped in his tracks, seemingly frozen to the spot. She stared at him wide-eyed as he slowly straightened up, his hand reaching to his cheek, where a small circular hole had suddenly and inexplicably appeared. A tiny rivulet of blood ran down from it, like a solitary crimson tear.

There was another pop. This time, Victor recoiled violently, like a puppet whose strings had been given a sudden, sharp tug.

Something had ripped a hole in his jacket at the shoulder. The frayed edges of the fabric, singed and smoking, flittered in the gentle wind that sighed through the arches. He looked at Anna in confusion. She stared back at him, her breath caught in her throat.

He took a few tottering steps backwards, missed his footing and plunged off the edge of the tower. A few seconds later, she heard a dull thud as his body hit the ground two hundred and fifty feet below.

38

Afterwards

By the time Zoe had made her way up to the West Quadrangle and shoved her way through the throng of police officers, the paramedics had already given up trying to resuscitate Victor. He lay in the snow, eyes staring up unblinkingly at the bruised sky, a trickle of blood leaking from his ear. Multiple pairs of hands held her back, but she shook them off, broke through and fell to her knees, shrieking, weeping in torrents. She heard herself screaming, *Bastards! You fuckin' bastards! You fuckin' killed him!* But they all averted their eyes and pretended they hadn't heard her.

Arms encircled her from behind, and then Carol was holding her, saying, *It's okay, it's okay* over and over. She remained on her knees, her own hands reaching up to clutch Carol's enveloping arms, as someone stepped forward and draped a hi-viz jacket over Victor's body.

***

Six officers, armed with HK417 rifles, advanced up the spiral stairs in single file. About halfway up, they came upon a woman – five-foot-two, medium build, raven-black hair – making her way down to meet them. She confirmed that yes, she was Dr Anna Scavolini. When pressed as to the whereabouts of Gavin Price, she merely pointed up the stairs behind her.

Two officers escorted her down to ground level while the remaining four continued to the upper chamber. There, they found Price alone, sitting on the floor with his head bowed. Upon hearing their approach, he lifted his head and gazed up at them expressionlessly, then wordlessly offered up his hands for cuffing.

***

Anna stepped out into the university grounds, flanked on either side by her two minders. Beyond the gates up ahead, more officers were struggling to hold back a cartel of reporters, press photographers and television crews, plus a gaggle of slack-jawed rubberneckers. Someone caught sight of her, a flashbulb went off, and the inevitable frenzy of questions began.

She saw a familiar figure approaching – heavyset, balding, weather-beaten careworn face. Norton came to a halt in front of her and offered her a sad, empathetic smile and shrug of his shoulders. She hadn't the strength left to return either.

Out of the corner of her eye, she caught a flash of red. Turning, she saw a police car parked several feet away. Zoe sat in the back, head bowed, weeping silently. Next to her, Carol stroked her back, her lips moving as she whispered inaudible words of comfort. As Anna continued to watch, Carol leaned in, placed her lips on the top of Zoe's head and held them there. And with that gesture, she finally understood. Safe in the knowledge that Zoe would be cared for, she allowed Norton to lead her away to a separate car.

***

A little before four pm, when the darkness was beginning to descend, a woman walked into the reception area of Yorkhill Police Station. She was blonde, approximately five foot five, wearing plain corduroy trousers and a knitted pullover, and appeared to be in her mid-to-late twenties. Her appearance was described by the desk sergeant in his report as *unkempt*. She was shivering and showed signs of mild hypothermia, and when asked her name and why she was there, she initially failed to respond. It was only after several minutes had passed and multiple members of staff had attempted to engage with her that she finally spoke in a low, husky voice, so quiet that they had to strain to hear her.

'My name is Jennifer Guilfoyle. I'm here to report a crime.'

39

Sehnsucht

One Year Later

Anna stepped onto the platform at Queen Street Station. The sky was overcast and the air bitingly cold, and a flurry of overnight snow had delayed her train by over an hour. But she'd planned for such eventualities and still had some time to spare before she was due at the university.

Her interview took place in the conference room of the Department of Law and Social Sciences. There was an unspoken discomfort both on her part and, she sensed, that of her three interrogators. It could hardly have escaped anyone's notice that, should her application prove successful, she'd be stepping into a dead man's shoes. The department had limped on for the better part of a year without Mark, but could no longer continue to put off the inevitable. And the interview went well, at least as far as she was able to judge. They seemed impressed by her résumé and her spotless record, she answered all their questions satisfactorily, and though nothing was made explicit, the signals they gave off seemed promising.

***

Afterwards, she made her way to Lynedoch Place. The Guilfoyle house was much as she remembered it – a tall, blood-red sandstone building imparting the faded grandeur of a bygone period in history. At the door, she hesitated. She didn't overly relish a fresh encounter with Guilfoyle, and she fancied he wouldn't be overjoyed to see her again either, but she had to satisfy her curiosity. She rang the bell.

Upon opening the door, Guilfoyle looked confused, then surprised. 'It's you,' he said.

She agreed that it was.

'Will you be for coming in?' he asked – with, she sensed, some reluctance.

'I'm not stopping. I just wanted to make sure you were both okay.'

On impulse, Guilfoyle glanced over his shoulder, then turned back to Anna. 'Maybe you should see for yourself.'

He led her through the house to the back garden. There, standing side by side, they watched as Jenny, bundled up in hat, coat and gloves, slowly rocked herself back and forth on the swing hanging from the old oak tree that dominated the garden. She gave no indication of having any awareness that she had an audience, but it seemed to Anna that there was something different about her.

'She seems…'

'Yes,' Guilfoyle agreed. For a moment, he fell silent, then added, 'She hasn't spoken again – not since last Christmas. But she has moments where she's more lucid. Every now and then, she'll look at me and I'm sure there's a spark of something there. I know it doesn't sound like much, but it's something.' He sucked in a breath and expelled it through his nostrils. 'Some days are good days.'

Anna nodded. Jenny seemed at ease in her surroundings as opposed to being absent from them entirely. Anna got the impression she was content with her lot, in as much as that was possible.

'I'm hoping…' Guilfoyle began. 'Well, I'd like to think, when the time comes, she'll be able to testify.'

Anna gave a tight smile but said nothing. As far as she understood the situation, Gavin's contract with the university had been annulled, and he was now living at an undisclosed location while the Procurator Fiscal attempted to build a case against him. She wasn't sure which was more unlikely – that Jenny would ever be in a fit state to enter a witness box or that there would ever be a trial in the first place. However, she kept her doubts to herself. For now, it seemed enough that Guilfoyle had some hope to cling to, however forlorn it might be.

'Well,' she said, shifting, 'I should probably…'

'Yes, yes, of course.' Guilfoyle was evidently relieved. He hesitated, then awkwardly extended his hand towards her. 'Thank you.'

She wasn't sure what exactly his gratitude related to, but she accepted it, and his handshake.

***

She walked down to Kelvingrove Park, following the path to the old stone bridge. From there, she gazed out at the choppy waters of the River Kelvin and the ugly, pretty buildings that lay beyond it, their lights going on one-by-one as dusk began to creep in.

Glasgow. The city held many emotions for her – some good, some decidedly less so. There were still a lot of painful memories attached to the place, but while she hadn't exactly made peace with them, she'd at least come to accept that they existed in tandem with the more positive ones. She still lived with them day in, day out, but that was always going to be true, whether she was here or in Rome or on the other side of the world. Over the last twelve months, she'd found herself missing the place in a way she'd never thought possible and knew she could never adequately explain. Naturally, the panel had asked her why she wanted the job – why she wanted to uproot herself from the life she'd made for herself in Rome. She'd told them she believed in the work Mark had been doing and wanted to carry on fighting the good fight, no matter how uphill the struggle – and perhaps, one day, affecting some material change. *The early days of a better nation.*

But there was more to it than that – more even than the prospect of a promotion and a semi-decent pay rise. It had taken a decade-long absence, a return under circumstances not of her choosing and indeed a five-day nightmare for her to realise it, but she loved the place, for all its faults. The Germans had a word for what she was experiencing: *Sehnsucht*, a deep yearning for a thing that is distant and difficult to define. She could put it no more plainly than that she belonged here, for better or worse.

She sensed a presence behind her and turned to see a familiar figure standing at the edge of the bridge, her red hair a striking flash of colour against her monochromatic surroundings.

Anna lifted a forlorn hand in greeting.

Zoe raised hers in return.

She'd emailed Zoe about the interview, letting her know the date and time. It was the first time she'd attempted any communication since the events of the previous Christmas, and she hadn't been too surprised when it went unanswered. She'd doubted Zoe was in any great hurry to see her again.

They met halfway across the bridge and stood at a respectful distance, each searching for the right thing to say.

'Christmas again,' said Anna, for lack of a better opening gambit.

'Aye.'

Zoe's eyes were fixed steadfastly on the ground. Her subdued manner was entirely understandable, but Anna was still taken aback by how much she'd changed. Even her hair seemed to have lost some of its vibrancy, though that might just have been a trick of the fading light. She was left with an overwhelming sense that Zoe had, finally, grown up.

Zoe lifted her head and shrugged, hands in pockets. 'So what's new?'

'Nothing much.'

'Interview go okay?'

'Think so.'

'That's good.'

'Yeah.'

'So—' another expectant shrug '—this you home? As in *home* home?'

'Depends.'

'What on?'

'Well, I've not got the job yet, for a start.'

Zoe batted a hand dismissively. 'Ach, you'll ace it. You always were a right spod.'

Anna smiled. 'Thanks, I think.'

Another uncomfortable silence followed. Zoe traced a line in the snow with her foot. 'I've missed us this year. I know we hadnae seen each other the last ten year, but this year 'specially, I've really missed us.'

'Yeah,' said Anna. She knew exactly what Zoe meant, and it wasn't just because this year would have been particularly hard for her without Victor. Sometimes, you didn't realise how much something really meant to you until you had the opportunity to reach out and touch it.

'We shouldnae've left it like we did. I was hopin' mibby you'd stick around for a bit, but you skedaddled the moment the cops were done wi' you.'

Anna felt a flush of shame. 'I figured you wouldn't want to see me. Not after the things we said to one another.'

Zoe shook her head. 'That was just words. I never...' She trailed off, then started again on a different tack. 'You're, like, I dunno. You make me laugh. You stop me doin' things that are too mental. You're the only other person I know who gets what's so great about *Takeshi's Castle*. You...' She shrugged, frustrated by her inability to more eloquently express her feelings. 'I don't want us not to be friends,' she concluded simply.

Anna swallowed heavily. She had a lump in her throat, and her eyes were beginning to go moist. She scrubbed at them with the back of her hand. Bloody cold air, irritating them, making them water...Ach, who was she trying to kid? In front of her, she could see Zoe's bottom lip wobbling.

'Aw, Christ, Zo, I'm sorry. Sorry for everything.'

'I know, pal, I know. Me too.'

And then came the hugging and the uncontrollable sobbing from both of them as they clutched one another, faces nestled against each other's hair. They remained like that for a long time, their contented silence saying more than a thousand well-articulated words. They knew, of course, that it would never be quite the same between them as it had once been. The things they'd both said to one another, not to mention everything else that had happened, made it impossible for them to go back to the way things had been before. The old wounds might have closed over, but the scars remained. That said, this reconciliation, this cessation of hostilities, was – if nothing else – a start.

Like the man had said, some days were good days.

Gradually, the tears subsided, and after a while, they drew apart.

'So,' said Zoe, 'what now?'

'Dunno. Fancy a walk?'

'When d'you need to be at the station?'

'I've got time yet.'

And so they set off, following the main path as it led deeper into the park. They walked in silence, without the need for words. The night continued to draw in, and more and more lamps began to gleam in windows, illuminating the outer circle of Woodlands Hill in an arc of light.

Zoe looked at her watch, then turned to Anna. 'Gonnae miss yer train if you're no careful.'

Anna checked her own watch. She thought about it.

'Yeah,' she said. 'I suppose I might.'

THE END

Acknowledgements

I n pursuit of dramatic licence, I've taken the liberty of playing hard and loose with my portrayal of Glasgow, its institutions and their practices. There is no Strathkelvin Police Force, and to the best of my knowledge, the University of Glasgow has never employed anyone resembling either Gavin Price or Mark Westmore. The internal structure of the bell-tower is not precisely as described within these pages; however, dramatic expediency precluded a slavish devotion to reality. Many of the locations are real. Others are figments of my fevered imagination.

I'd like to express my heartfelt thanks Betsy Reavley and her team at Bloodhound Books for taking a chance on this project, and Ben Adam for his considered, insightful editing. This book wouldn't be where it is today without your guidance.

And, finally, thanks to the following for their invaluable advice: Jacqui Baird, Mark Cunliffe, Johan Fundin, Lee Howard, Sarah Kelley, Ashley Lane, Jackie McGregor, Daniel Sardella, Catriona Simon and Caroline Whitson. As the lady with the red hair would say, you're all pure amazeballs.

About the Author

M. R. Mackenzie was born and lives in Glasgow, Scotland. He studied at Glasgow University and has a PhD in Film Studies. In 2016, he contributed a chapter on the Italian *giallo* film to *Cult Cinema: An Arrow Video Companion*.

In addition to writing, he works as an independent Blu-ray/DVD producer and has overseen releases of films by a number of acclaimed directors, among them Dario Argento, Joe Dante and Seijun Suzuki.

When he's not doing any of the above, he works in a library, which tests his sanity and keeps him in touch with the great unwashed.

In the Silence is his first novel.

Lightning Source UK Ltd.
Milton Keynes UK
UKHW041022280619
345208UK00001B/6/P